THE
SINNER

By J. R. Ward

THE BLACK DAGGER BROTHERHOOD SERIES

Dark Lover
Lover Eternal
Lover Awakened
Lover Revealed
Lover Unbound
Lover Enshrined
The Black Dagger Brotherhood:
An Insider's Guide
Lover Avenged
Lover Mine

Lover Unleashed
Lover Reborn
Lover at Last
The King
The Shadows
The Beast
The Chosen
The Thief
The Savior
The Sinner

THE BLACK DAGGER LEGACY SERIES

Blood Kiss
Blood Vow

Blood Fury
Blood Truth

THE BLACK DAGGER BROTHERHOOD WORLD

Dearest Ivie   *Prisoner of Night*   *Where Winter Finds You*

FIREFIGHTERS SERIES

Consumed

NOVELS OF THE FALLEN ANGELS

Covet
Crave
Envy

Rapture
Possession
Immortal

THE BOURBON KINGS SERIES

The Bourbon Kings
The Angels' Share
Devil's Cut

J.R. WARD

THE SINNER

• THE BLACK DAGGER •
BROTHERHOOD SERIES

GALLERY BOOKS
New York   London   Toronto   Sydney   New Delhi

Gallery Books
An Imprint of Simon & Schuster, Inc.
1230 Avenue of the Americas
New York, NY 10020

First Gallery Books hardcover edition March 2020

GALLERY BOOKS and colophon are registered trademarks of Simon & Schuster, Inc.

For information about special discounts for bulk purchases, please contact Simon & Schuster Special Sales at 1-866-506-1949 or business@simonandschuster.com.

The Simon & Schuster Speakers Bureau can bring authors to your live event. For more information or to book an event, contact the Simon & Schuster Speakers Bureau at 1-866-248-3049 or visit our website at www.simonspeakers.com.

Interior design by Davina Mock-Maniscalco

Manufactured in the United States of America

10 9 8 7 6 5 4 3 2 1

Library of Congress Cataloging-in-Publication Data has been applied for.

ISBN 978-1-5011-9509-9
ISBN 978-1-5011-9511-2 (ebook)

To *you*.
You are so worthy of all the good things . . .
take care of your female. I have faith in you.

GLOSSARY OF TERMS AND PROPER NOUNS

abstrux nohtrum (n.) Private guard with license to kill who is granted his or her position by the King.

ahvenge (v.) Act of mortal retribution, carried out typically by a male loved one.

Black Dagger Brotherhood (pr. n.) Highly trained vampire warriors who protect their species against the Lessening Society. As a result of selective breeding within the race, Brothers possess immense physical and mental strength, as well as rapid healing capabilities. They are not siblings for the most part, and are inducted into the Brotherhood upon nomination by the Brothers. Aggressive, self-reliant, and secretive by nature, they are the subjects of legend and objects of reverence within the vampire world. They may be killed only by the most serious of wounds, e.g., a gunshot or stab to the heart, etc.

blood slave (n.) Male or female vampire who has been subjugated to serve the blood needs of another. The practice of keeping blood slaves has been outlawed.

the Chosen (pr. n.) Female vampires who had been bred to serve the Scribe Virgin. In the past, they were spiritually rather than temporally focused, but that changed with the ascendance of the final Primale, who freed them from the Sanctuary. With the Scribe Virgin removing herself from her role, they are completely autonomous and learning to live on earth. They do continue to meet the blood needs of unmated members of the Brotherhood, as well as Brothers who cannot feed from their *shellans* or injured fighters.

chrih (n.) Symbol of honorable death in the Old Language.

cohntehst (n.) Conflict between two males competing for the right to be a female's mate.

Dhunhd (pr. n.) Hell.

doggen (n.) Member of the servant class within the vampire world. *Doggen* have old, conservative traditions about service to their superiors, following a formal code of dress and behavior. They are able to go out during the day, but they age relatively quickly. Life expectancy is approximately five hundred years.

ehros (n.) A Chosen trained in the matter of sexual arts.

exhile dhoble (n.) The evil or cursed twin, the one born second.

the Fade (pr. n.) Nontemporal realm where the dead reunite with their loved ones and pass eternity.

First Family (pr. n.) The King and Queen of the vampires, and any children they may have.

ghardian (n.) Custodian of an individual. There are varying degrees of *ghardians*, with the most powerful being that of a *sehcluded* female.

glymera (n.) The social core of the aristocracy, roughly equivalent to Regency England's *ton*.

hellren (n.) Male vampire who has been mated to a female. Males may take more than one female as mate.

hyslop (n. or v.) Term referring to a lapse in judgment, typically resulting in the compromise of the mechanical operations of a vehicle or otherwise motorized conveyance of some kind. For example, leaving one's keys in one's car as it is parked outside the family home overnight, whereupon said vehicle is stolen.

leahdyre (n.) A person of power and influence.

leelan (adj. or n.) A term of endearment loosely translated as "dearest one."

Lessening Society (pr. n.) Order of slayers convened by the Omega for the purpose of eradicating the vampire species.

lesser (n.) De-souled human who targets vampires for extermination as a member of the Lessening Society. *Lessers* must be stabbed through the chest in order to be killed; otherwise they are ageless. They do not eat or drink and are impotent. Over time, their hair, skin, and irises lose pigmentation until they are blond, blushless, and pale eyed. They smell like baby powder. Inducted into the society by the Omega, they retain a ceramic jar thereafter into which their heart was placed after it was removed.

lewlhen (n.) Gift.

lheage (n.) A term of respect used by a sexual submissive to refer to their dominant.

Lhenihan (pr. n.) A mythic beast renowned for its sexual prowess. In modern slang, refers to a male of preternatural size and sexual stamina.

lys (n.) Torture tool used to remove the eyes.

mahmen (n.) Mother. Used both as an identifier and a term of affection.

mhis (n.) The masking of a given physical environment; the creation of a field of illusion.

nalla (n., f.) or *nallum* (n., m.) Beloved.

needing period (n.) Female vampire's time of fertility, generally lasting for two days and accompanied by intense sexual cravings. Occurs approximately five years after a female's transition and then once a decade thereafter. All males respond to some degree if they are around a female in her need. It can be a dangerous time, with conflicts and fights breaking out between competing males, particularly if the female is not mated.

newling (n.) A virgin.

the Omega (pr. n.) Malevolent, mystical figure who has targeted the vampires for extinction out of resentment directed toward the Scribe

Virgin. Exists in a nontemporal realm and has extensive powers, though not the power of creation.

phearsom (adj.) Term referring to the potency of a male's sexual organs. Literal translation something close to "worthy of entering a female."

Princeps (pr. n.) Highest level of the vampire aristocracy, second only to members of the First Family or the Scribe Virgin's Chosen. Must be born to the title; it may not be conferred.

pyrocant (n.) Refers to a critical weakness in an individual. The weakness can be internal, such as an addiction, or external, such as a lover.

rahlman (n.) Savior.

rythe (n.) Ritual manner of asserting honor granted by one who has offended another. If accepted, the offended chooses a weapon and strikes the offender, who presents him—or herself—without defenses.

the Scribe Virgin (pr. n.) Mystical force who previously was counselor to the King as well as the keeper of vampire archives and the dispenser of privileges. Existed in a nontemporal realm and had extensive powers, but has recently stepped down and given her station to another. Capable of a single act of creation, which she expended to bring the vampires into existence.

sehclusion (n.) Status conferred by the King upon a female of the aristocracy as a result of a petition by the female's family. Places the female under the sole direction of her *ghardian*, typically the eldest male in her household. Her *ghardian* then has the legal right to determine all manner of her life, restricting at will any and all interactions she has with the world.

shellan (n.) Female vampire who has been mated to a male. Females generally do not take more than one mate due to the highly territorial nature of bonded males.

symphath (n.) Subspecies within the vampire race characterized by the ability and desire to manipulate emotions in others (for the purposes of an energy exchange), among other traits. Historically, they have been discriminated against and, during certain eras, hunted by vampires. They are near extinction.

talhman (n.) The evil side of an individual. A dark stain on the soul that requires expression if it is not properly expunged.

the Tomb (pr. n.) Sacred vault of the Black Dagger Brotherhood. Used as a ceremonial site as well as a storage facility for the jars of *lessers*. Ceremonies performed there include inductions, funerals, and disciplinary actions against Brothers. No one may enter except for members of the Brotherhood, the Scribe Virgin, or candidates for induction.

trahyner (n.) Word used between males of mutual respect and affection. Translated loosely as "beloved friend."

transition (n.) Critical moment in a vampire's life when he or she transforms into an adult. Thereafter, he or she must drink the blood of the opposite sex to survive and is unable to withstand sunlight. Occurs generally in the mid-twenties. Some vampires do not survive their transitions, males in particular. Prior to their transitions, vampires are physically weak, sexually unaware and unresponsive, and unable to dematerialize.

vampire (n.) Member of a species separate from that of Homo sapiens. Vampires must drink the blood of the opposite sex to survive. Human blood will keep them alive, though the strength does not last long. Following their transitions, which occur in their mid-twenties, they are unable to go out into sunlight and must feed from the vein regularly. Vampires cannot "convert" humans through a bite or transfer of blood, though they are in rare cases able to breed with the other species. Vampires can dematerialize at will, though they must be able to calm themselves and concentrate to do so and may not carry anything heavy with them. They are able to strip the memories of humans, provided such memories are short-term. Some vampires are able to read minds. Life expectancy is upward of a thousand years, or in some cases, even longer.

wahlker (n.) An individual who has died and returned to the living from the Fade. They are accorded great respect and are revered for their travails.

whard (n.) Equivalent of a godfather or godmother to an individual.

CHAPTER ONE

Route 149
Caldwell, New York

Behind the wheel of her ten-year-old car, Jo Early bit into the Slim Jim and chewed like it was her last meal. She hated the fake-smoke taste and the boat-rope texture, and when she swallowed the last piece, she got another one out of her bag. Ripping the wrapper with her teeth, she peeled the taxidermied tube free and littered into the wheel well of her passenger side. There were so many spent casings like it down there, you couldn't see the floor mat.

Up ahead, her anemic headlights swung around a curve, illuminating pine trees that had been limbed up three-quarters of the way, the puffy tops making toothpicks out of the trunks. She hit a pothole and bad-swallowed, and she was coughing as she reached her destination.

The abandoned Adirondack Outlets was yet another commentary on the pervasiveness of Amazon Prime. The one-story strip mall was a horseshoe without a hoof, the storefronts along the two long sides bearing the remnants of their brands, faded laminations and off-kilter signs with names like Van Heusen/Izod, and Nike, and Dansk the ghosts of commerce past. Behind dusty glass, there was no merchandise available for purchase anymore, and no one had been on the property with a charge card for at least a year, only hardscrabble weeds in the cracks of the promenade and barn swallows in the eaves inhabiting the site. Likewise, the food court that united the eastern and western arms was no longer offering soft serve or Starbucks or lunch.

As a hot flash cranked her internal temperature up, she cracked the window. And then put the thing all the way down. March in Caldwell, New York, was like winter in a lot of places still considered northerly in latitude, and thank God for it. Breathing in the cold, damp air, she told herself this was not a bad idea.

Nah, not at all. Here she was, alone at midnight, chasing down the lead on a story she wasn't writing for her employer, the *Caldwell Courier Journal*. Without anyone at her new apartment waiting up for her. Without anyone on the planet who would claim her mangled corpse when it was found from the smell in a ditch a week from now.

Letting the car roll to a stop, she killed the headlights and stayed where she was. No moon out tonight so she'd dressed right. All black. But without any illumination from the heavens, her eyes strained at the darkness, and not because she was greedy to see the details on the decaying structure.

Nope. At the moment, she was worried she was about to provide fodder for True Crime Garage. As unease tickled her nape, like someone was trying to get her attention by running the point of a carving knife over her skin—

Her stomach let out a howl and she jumped. Without any debate, she went diving into her purse again. Passing by the three Slim Jims she had left, she went straight-up Hershey this time, and the efficiency with which she stripped that mass-produced chocolate of its clothing was a sad commentary on her diet. When she was finished, she was still hungry and not because there wasn't food in her belly. As always, the only two things she could eat failed to satisfy her gnawing craving, to say nothing of her nutritional needs.

Putting up her window, she took her backpack and got out. The crackling sound of the treads of her running shoes on the shoulder of the road seemed loud as a concert, and she wished she wasn't getting over a cold. Like her sense of smell could be helpful, though? And when was the last time she'd considered that possibility outside of a milk carton check.

She really needed to give these wild-goose chases up.

Two-strapping her backpack, she locked the car and pulled the hood of her windbreaker up over her red hair. No heel toeing. She left-right-left'd it, keeping the soles of her Brooks flat to quiet her footfalls. As her eyes adjusted, all she saw were the shadows around her, the hidey-holes in corners and nooks formed by the mall's doorways and the benches pockets of gotcha with which mashers could play a grown-up's game of keep away until they were ready to attack.

When she got to a heavy chain that was strung across the entry to the promenade, she looked around. There was nobody in the parking lots that ran down the outside of the flanks. No one in the center area formed by the open-ended rectangle. Not a soul on the road that she had taken up to this rise above Rt. 149.

Jo told herself that this was good. It meant no one was going to jump her.

Her adrenal glands, on the other hand, informed her that this actually meant no one was around to hear her scream for help.

Refocusing on the chain, she had some thought that if she swung her leg over it and proceeded on the other side, she would not come back the same.

"Stop it," she said, kicking her foot up.

She chose the right side of the stores, and as rain started to fall, she was glad the architect had thought to cover the walkways overhead. What had been not so smart was anyone thinking a shopping center with no interior corridors could survive in a zip code this close to Canada. Saving ten bucks on a pair of candlesticks or a bathing suit was not going to keep anybody warm enough to shop outside October to April, and that was true even before you factored in the current era of free next-day shipping.

Down at the far end, she stopped at what had to have been the ice cream place because there was a faded stencil of a cow holding a triple decker cone by its hoof on the window. She got out her phone.

Her call was answered on the first ring.

"Are you okay?" Bill said.

"Where am I going?" she whispered. "I don't see anything."

"It's in the back. I told you that you have to go around back, remember?"

"Damn it." Maybe the nitrates had fried her brain. "Hold on, I think I found a staircase."

"I should come out there."

Jo started walking again and shook her head even though he couldn't see her. "I'm fine—yup, I've got the cut through to the rear. I'll call you if I need you—"

"You shouldn't be doing this alone!"

Ending the connection, she jogged down the concrete steps, her pack bouncing like it was doing push-ups on her back. As she bottomed out on the lower level, she scanned the empty parking lot—

The stench that stabbed into her nose was the kind of thing that triggered her gag reflex. Roadkill . . . and baby powder?

She looked to the source. The maintenance building by the tree line had a corrugated metal roof and metal walls that would not survive long in tornado alley. Half the size of a football field, with garage doors locked to the ground, she imagined it could have housed paving equipment as well as blowers, mowers, and snowplows.

The sole person-sized door was loose, and as a stiff gust from the rainstorm caught it, the creak was straight out of a George Romero movie—and then the panel immediately slammed shut with a clap, as if Mother Nature didn't like the stink any more than Jo did.

Taking out her phone, she texted Bill: *This smell is nasty.*

Aware that her heart rate just tripled, she walked across the asphalt, the rain hitting the hood of her windbreaker in a disorganized staccato. Ducking her hand under the loose nylon of the jacket, she felt for her holstered gun and kept her hand on the butt.

The door creaked open and slammed shut again, another puff of that smell releasing out of the pitch-black interior. Swallowing through throat spasms, she had to fight to keep going and not because there was wind in her face.

When she stopped in front of the door, the opening and closing ceased, as if now that she was on the verge of entering, it didn't need to catch her attention and draw her in.

So help her God, if Pennywise was on the other side . . .

Glancing around to check there were no red balloons lolling in the area, she reached out for the door.

I just have to know, she thought as she opened the way in. *I need to . . . know.*

Leaning around the jamb, she saw absolutely nothing, and yet was frozen by all that she confronted. Pure evil, the kind of thing that abducted and murdered children, that slaughtered the innocent, that enjoyed the suffering of the just and merciful, pushed at her body and then penetrated it, radiation that was toxic passing through to her bones.

Coughing, she stepped back and covered her mouth and nose with the crook of her elbow. After a couple of deep breaths into her sleeve, she fumbled with her phone.

Before Bill could say anything over the whirring in his background, she bit out, "You need to come—"

"I'm already halfway to you."

"Good."

"What's going on—"

Jo ended the call again and got out her flashlight, triggering the beam. Stepping forward again, she shouldered the door open and trained the spear of illumination into the space.

The light was consumed.

Sure as if she were shining it into a bolt of thick fabric, the fragile glowing shaft was no match for what she was about to enter.

The threshold she stepped over was nothing more than weather stripping, but the inch-high lip was a barrier that felt like an obstacle course she could barely surmount—and then there was the stickiness on the floor. Pointing the flashlight to the ground, she picked up one of her feet. Something like old motor oil dripped off her running shoe, the sound of it finding home echoing in the empty space.

As Jo walked forward, she found the first of the buckets on the left. Home Depot. With an orange-and-white logo smudged by a rusty, translucent substance that turned her stomach.

The beam wobbled as she looked into the cylinder, her hand shaking. Inside there was a gallon of glossy, gleaming . . . red . . . liquid. And in the back of her throat, she tasted copper—

Jo wheeled around with the flashlight.

Through the doorway, the two men who had come up behind her without a sound loomed as if they had risen out of the pavement itself, wraiths conjured from her nightmares, fed by the cold spring rain, clothed in the night. One of them had a goatee and tattoos at one of his temples, a cigarette between his lips and a downright nasty expression on his hard face. The other wore a Boston Red Sox hat and a long camel-colored coat, the tails of which blew in slow motion even though the wind was choppy. Both had long black blades holstered handles down on their chest, and she knew there were more weapons where she couldn't see them.

They had come to kill her. Tracked her as she'd moved away from her car. Seen her as she had not seen them.

Jo stumbled back and tried to get out her gun, but her sweaty palms had her dropping her phone and struggling to keep the flashlight—

And then she couldn't move.

Even as her brain ordered her feet to run, her legs to run, her body to run, nothing obeyed the panic-commands, her muscles twitching under the lockdown of some invisible force of will, her bones aching, her breath turning into a pant. Pain firework'd her brain, a headache sizzling through her mind.

Opening her mouth, she screamed—

CHAPTER TWO

S yn re-formed in the midst of the cold drizzle, his shitkickers sinking into the mud, his leather-covered body readily accepting the weight of his muscles and the pump of his black heart, his dark function resumed from a scatter of light molecules. Up ahead, the lineup of expensive foreign sedans and SUVs made no fucking sense in the cement company's parking lot. Next to the stacks of concrete blocks, the heavy moving equipment, and the mixer trucks, they were a bunch of floozies standing among sumo wrestlers.

Walking forward, his tongue teased the tip of one of his fangs, the cut he deliberately made bleeding into his mouth. As he nursed at the taste, his hands cranked into fists and the sense that his brain was a fuse about to be lit was something he ignored.

Predators required prey.

So sometimes, you needed to eat even when your stomach was full.

As he approached a shallow overhang, the stout human man sitting beside the door on a plastic chair looked up from his *Daily Racing Form*. The bald lightbulb hanging from a live wire above his head made shadows of his eye sockets and his nostrils and his jaw, and Syn pictured the skull that would remain after death sloughed the mortal padding from the skeleton.

The man frowned. And by way of greeting, he moved a gun into view, placing it on top of his magazine.

"I'm here to see someone," Syn said as he stopped.

"Ain't no one here."

When Syn didn't leave, the man sat forward. "You hear what I said. Ain't nobody here for you—"

Syn materialized onto the human, picking him up by the throat and punching him into the building, the plastic chair flipping out of the way as if it had no intention of getting involved in problems that were not its own.

As he disarmed his victim, the human's meaty hands dug into the grip around its throat, and its legs flailed, banging the heels of its shoes against the building. The mouth, no longer slack with superiority, gaped in failed efforts to bring air down into lungs which were clearly starting to burn already.

Then again, fear had a way of demanding a dance from hypoxia, no matter how much of a wallflower oxygen deprivation was in the normal course of things.

"I am here to see somebody," Syn said softly. "And if you are lucky, it is not you."

Lowering the man such that those feet found purchase, Syn released pressure enough to allow for verbalization. But it was not because he wanted words. No, a response of that nature was a flimsy meal.

He wanted a proper scream to ring in his ears.

Syn unsheathed one of his steel daggers. As he brought the silver blade up, the man transferred his clawing grip from what was locked on his neck to the wrist and forearm controlling the weapon. The accompanying protest was like that of a child, of less consequence and constriction than the sleeve of Syn's leather jacket.

The tip of the dagger went into the man's left ear, and as the fist nick cut into the skin of the canal, Syn breathed deep.

Blood. Fear. Sweat.

He pressed his lower body into the man's. Syn's erection was not about sex, although given the way those watery, dark brown eyes flared, the man misinterpreted the response.

Closing his lids, Syn felt a surge of power in his body, the dominance, the aggression, the need to kill using pain taking him over. In the back of his mind, he warned himself that he should stop now. This was not the plan, but more than that, this would be over too soon and then cleanup would be inconvenient—and he was not referring to the blood that would spill and splash, speckle and soak.

"Fight me," he whispered. "Do it. Fight me—give me an excuse to drain your fucking brain out of the hole I drill into your skull."

"I got kids," the man stammered. "I got kids—"

Syn eased back a little. "You do?"

The man nodded like his life depended on the number of dependents he had. "Yeah, I got a boy and a girl, and—"

"Did you drive to work tonight?"

The man blinked like he couldn't understand Syn's thick, Old World accent. "Ah, yeah."

"So you've got your driver's license with you, right. Because you're such a law-abiding criminal."

"I—I, ah, yeah, I got my wallet. Take the money—"

"Good." Syn leaned down again, placing his right eye directly in front of his victim's right eye, getting so close that every time the man blinked, his lashes stroked Syn's own. "After I'm done with you, I am going to break into your house and kill them in their beds. And then your wife? You'll hear her scream from your grave."

Pure terror came out of every pore of the man, the sharp, tangy smell of it like cocaine to Syn's system. Racing heart, racing breath, racing blood—

A hidden door swung wide.

The fat, older man who pushed it open had a bulbous nose and acne scars that made his face look like the surface of the moon. His eyes were anything but pudgy and slow.

"Jesus Christ, guess you are the man I want. Come in—and don't kill him, will ya? He's my wife's cousin's husband and it'll make Easter a fuckin' nightmare."

For a split second, Syn's body did not listen to the release command—and not the one the human issued. His own brain was doing the ordering around, yet his hands refused to let go. Ah, but if he delayed gratification, he could kill another that would offer better sport. This was not the end. This was the beginning.

Like a tiger distracted off one carcass by the appearance of fresher meat, his fingers retracted, claws called home, and he stepped back. The almost-victim began coughing in earnest, slumping forward as if he intended to sweep the stoop with his face.

"Come through here," the older man said. "Better that nobody sees you."

Syn nearly bent in half to fit through the camouflaged doorway, and the narrow hall brushed the muscles of his shoulders and the older man's padding as they went along. Through the wall on the left, he heard men talking and shouting over cards, and he smelled the cigar smoke, the weed, the cigarettes. The alcohol. The cologne.

At the end of the corridor, there was another door, and on the far side of the flimsy panel, there was a cramped office. A desk littered with papers. An ashtray with a smoldering cigar nub. A worn swivel chair with raw patches for both ass cheeks. There was also a small black-and-white monitor showing the image of the man with the magazine righting his plastic throne and sitting back down outside.

"Have a seat," the old man said, indicating the hard chair on the far side of the desk. "This won't take long."

Syn noted the way the corridor's panel re-shut itself, disappearing into the wall. Across from him, there was another door with conventional hinges and a knob, and he angled his back to the corner next to it so he could visualize the old man, the hidden passageway's entrance, and the regular way into the office.

"So you come highly recommended," the old man grunted as he lowered his weight on knees that were clearly wearing out early. "I usually handle these things myself, but not in this case."

There was a pause. And then the human took out a laptop and put it on the paperwork. Turning the thing on, his cataract'd eyes flashed upward. "This filth needs to be taken off the streets."

The man turned the screen around. The photograph was black-and-white. Grainy. Like it was a camera phone shot of a newspaper article.

"Johnny Pappalardo. He's violated some rules that cannot be violated in my territory."

When Syn didn't acknowledge the picture, the old man frowned. "We got a problem?"

His pudgy hand dipped beneath the desk, and Syn moved faster than a human could track. Without changing the position of his eyes, he palmed a twin set of Glocks with suppressors and pointed one at the old man and the other at the door with the hinges and the knob.

Just as some kind of bodyguard lunged into the office.

As the humans froze, Syn said in a low voice, "Don't do that again. We've got no problem, you and me. Keep it that way."

The old man got to his feet and leaned over the desk. "Son, you ain't from here, are you. Didn't your friend tell you who I was—"

Syn pulled the triggers on both guns. Bullets landed into the walls to the side of both heads, causing the men to jump.

"I only care about the job," he said. "Don't make me care about you."

There was a tense period of silence. Then the old man lowered himself back into his chair with that grunt.

"Leave us." When the other guy didn't move, the old man snapped, "Jesus, Junior, you deaf?"

"Junior" looked at Syn and Syn spared him a glance. Same coloring as the old man. Same facial structure. Same way of narrowing the eyes. The only thing that differentiated the two was twenty-five years and seventy-five pounds.

"Shut the door behind yourself, Junior," Syn growled. "It'll offer you some cover when I pull this trigger again."

Junior checked in with his father one last time and then backed out.

The old man laughed. "You have no fear, do you." As he went to duck his hand into his cardigan, he said dryly, "You want to lower those guns?"

When Syn didn't reply, the old man shook his head with a grin. "You young boys. Too much gas in the tank. If you want to get paid, I'm going to have to take your money out of my pocket—"

"I don't want the money. Just the job."

The old man narrowed his eyes again. "What the fuck."

Syn moved over to the hidden door. As he willed the panel to slide back, the old man recoiled, but he recovered fast, no doubt assuming it hadn't shut right.

"You don't want the money?" he said. "Who the hell does a job without getting paid?"

Syn lowered his chin and stared out from under his lids. As his eyes flashed with all the menace of his *talhman*, the old man abruptly sat back in his chair as if he didn't like being in an enclosed space with the very weapon he had sought to purchase and was putting to use.

"Someone who likes to kill," Syn said in an evil growl.

CHAPTER THREE

As Butch O'Neal stood inside an abandoned mall's grounds-keeping building, he stared at a woman's vacant, frozen fear and had a wicked odd thought. For some reason, he recalled that his given name was Brian. Why this was relevant in any way was unknown, and he chalked up the cognitive drive-by to the fact that she kind of reminded him of his first cousin on his mother's side. That connection wasn't particularly significant, either, however, because in Southie, where he had been born and raised in Boston, there were only about a thousand red-haired women.

Well, and then there was the fact that he hadn't seen any member of his family, extended or otherwise, for what, over three years now? He'd lost count, although not because he didn't care.

Actually, that was a lie. He did not care.

And besides, the fact that this woman seemed to be a half-breed on the verge of going through the change was probably more to the point. Not exactly his experience, but close enough.

He'd been where she currently was.

"Am I scenting this right?" He looked over at his roommate. His best friend. His true brother, in comparison to the biological ones he'd left in the human world. "Or am I nuts."

"Nah." Vishous, son of the Bloodletter, son of the Blessed Virgin Scribe, exhaled a cloud of Turkish smoke, his hard features and goatee briefly obscured by the haze. "You ain't nuts, cop. And I am getting really sick and tired of scrubbing this woman, true? Her hormones need to shit or get off the pot."

"To be fair, you get sick and tired if you have to do most things once."

"Don't be a hater." V waved at the woman. "Buh-bye—"

"Hold on, she dropped her phone."

Butch went farther into the induction area and gagged. Fucking *lessers*. He'd rather have sweat socks shoved up his nose. Fortunately, the phone had landed faceup in the oily mess, and he took a handkerchief out and wiped it off as best he could. Placing the unit in the woman's pocket, he stepped back.

"I'm sure I'll see her again," V said dryly.

As she walked out into the rain, Butch watched her cross the asphalt and disappear up the cement stairs. "So she's the one you've been monitoring?"

"She just won't leave us the fuck alone."

"The one with the website about vampires."

"Damn Stoker. Real original. Remind me to ask her when I need help with puns."

Butch looked back at his roommate. "She's searching for herself. You can't turn that kind of thing off."

"Well, I got better shit to do than check on her hormones like I'm waiting for a goddamn egg to hard-boil."

"You have such a way with languages."

"Seventeen, now that I've added 'vampire conspiracist.'" V dropped the butt of his hand-rolled and ground it with his shitkicker. "You should read some of the crap they post. There's a whole community of the crackpots."

Butch held up his forefinger. "'Scuse me, Professor Xavier, given that we do actually exist, how can you call them crazy? And if she's a crackpot, how did she find this induction site at the same time we did?"

"You mind if I clean this mess of the Omega's up, or do you just want to stand here arguing the obvious while our sinuses melt and the rain sinks into all that cashmere you're wearing."

Muttering under his breath, Butch brushed at the shoulders of his Tom Ford. "It is so unfair that you know my triggers."

"You could have just worn leathers."

"Style is important."

"And I could have handled this by myself. You know I come with my own special brand of backup."

V lifted his lead-lined glove to his mouth and snagged the tip of the middle finger with his sharp, white teeth. Tugging the protective shield off what was underneath, he revealed a glowing hand that was marked on both sides with tattooed warnings in the Old Language.

Holding his curse out, the interior of the storage building was lit bright as noontime, the blood on the floor black, the blood in the six buckets red. As Butch walked around, his footsteps left patterns in the oily stink that were eaten up quick, that which covered the concrete consuming the prints, reclaiming dominance.

Lowering down onto his haunches, Butch dragged his fingers through the shit and then rubbed the viscous substance. "Nope."

V's icy eyes shifted over. "What?"

"This is wrong." Butch hit his handkerchief for cleanup. "It's too thin. It's not like it was."

"Do you think . . ." V, who never lost track of a thought, lost track of his thought. "Is it happening? Do you think?"

Butch straightened and went over to one of the buckets. Drywall bucket. Still had the brand name on it. Inside, the blood that had been drained from the veins of a human was a congealed soup. And for once, it had some meat in it.

"I think the heart's in here," he said.

"Not possible."

For centuries, inductees of the Lessening Society had always taken that particular organ home with them in a jar. Oddly, if they lost their heart after it was removed by their new master, they got into trouble with the Omega—which was why, after a kill, the Brotherhood had a tradition of claiming those jars whenever they could.

Slayers could lose their humanity. Their soul. Their free agency. But not that cardiac muscle they didn't need any more to exist.

"No, it is the heart," Butch said as he headed to the next bucket. "This one has it, too."

"Guess the Omega's getting sloppy. Or wearing out."

As Butch turned back to his roommate, he did not like the expression on the brother's face. "Don't look at me like that."

"Like what."

"Like I'm the solution to it all."

There was a long moment. "But you are, cop. And you know it."

Butch walked over and stood chest to chest with the male. "What if we're wrong?"

"The Prophecy is not ours. It is the property of history. As it was foretold, so it shall be. First as the future, then as the present when the time is nigh. And after that, with recording, it shall be the sacred past, the saving of the species, the end of the war."

Butch thought of his dreams, the ones that had been waking him up during the day. The ones that he refused to talk to his Marissa about. "What if I don't believe any of that."

What if I can't believe it, he amended.

"You assume destiny requires your permission to exist."

Unease scurried through his veins like rats in a sewer, finding all kinds of familiar paths. And meanwhile, as freely as the anxiety roamed, he became trapped. "What if I'm not enough?"

"You are. You have to be."

"I can't do any of it without you."

Familiar eyes, diamond with navy-blue rims, softened, proving that even the hardest substance on earth could yield if it chose to. "You have me, forever. And if you require it, you can take my faith in you, for as long as you need it."

"I didn't ask for this."

"We never do," V said roughly. "And it doesn't matter even if we did."

The brother shook his head, as if he were remembering parts and parcels of his own life, routes taken by force or coercion, dubious gifts pressed into his unwilling hands, mantles tossed over his shoulders, heavy with the manipulations and desires of others. Given that Butch knew his roommate's past as well as he knew his own, he wondered about the nature of the so-called destiny theory Vishous spoke of.

Maybe the intellectual construct of fate, of destiny, was just a way to frame all the shitty fucking things that happened to people. Maybe all the proverbial bad luck that rained down on the heads of essentially good folks, all that Murphy's Law, was actually not luck at all, just the impersonal nature of chaos at work. Maybe all the disappointment and injury, the loss and alienation, the chips off the soul and the heart that were inevitable during any mortal's tenure upon the ashes and the dust to which they were doomed to return, were not preordained or personal in the slightest.

Maybe there was no meaning to the universe, and nothing after death, and no one driving the metaphorical bus from up above.

Butch fished through damp cashmere to grip the heavy gold cross hanging from his neck. His Catholic faith told him otherwise, but what the fuck did he know.

And on a night like tonight, he wasn't sure what was worse. The idea that he was responsible for ending the war.

Or the possibility that he wasn't.

Putting his hand on V's shoulder, Butch moved down the heavily muscled arm until he clasped the thick wrist above the glowing curse. Then he stepped in beside his brother and lifted that deadly palm, the leather of V's jacket sleeve creaking.

"Time for cleanup," Butch said hoarsely.

"Yes," V agreed. "It is."

As Butch held up the arm, energy unleashed from the palm in a great burst of light, the illumination blinding him, his eyes stinging, though he refused to look away from the power, the terrible grace, the universe's mystery of origin that was inexplicably housed within the otherwise unremarkable flesh of his best friend.

Under the onslaught, all traces of the Omega's evil work disappeared, the structure of the maintenance building, its comparably fragile walls and floor and rafters of the roof, remaining untouched by the fearsome glory that reclaimed the humble space that been horribly used for as evil a purpose as ever there was.

What if the Prophecy itself is not enough, Butch thought to himself.

After all, mortals weren't the only things that had a shelf life. History likewise decayed and was lost, over time. Lessons forgotten . . . rules mislaid . . . heroes dead and gone . . .

Prophecies dismissed when another future comes along to claim the present as its victim, proving that that which had been taken as an absolute was in fact only a partial truth.

Everyone was talking about the end of the war, but was there ever really an end to evil? Even if he succeeded, even if he was, in fact, the *Dhestroyer*, what then. Sweetness and light forever?

No, he thought with a conviction that made his spine tingle with warning. There would be another.

And it would be the same as what had been defeated.

Only worse.

CHAPTER FOUR

The woman—she liked to call herself that, needed to, really, her true identity aside—stood in the crowd of bodies, the scents of those around her a once-tantalizing blend of humanity's sweat and blood and mortality. Music united them all through their ears, the beat stringing them one by one onto an audio-gasm garland that draped around the dance floor, the links swinging as hips rolled, backs arched, and arms swung in slow, sensual motion.

She was unmoving and unmoved as she sipped her fruit and alcohol alchemy through a metal straw, tasting none of the sweetness, feeling none of the buzz.

Closing her eyes, she yearned to find the metronome of the music, the penetration of the bass, the tickle of the treble. She wanted a body against her own, hands that palm'd down her waist to her hips, fingers that gripped her ass, a cock pressing against her skintight skirt. She wanted a mouth at the hollow of her throat. A tongue to lick into her between her legs. She wanted the beast with two backs, the down-and-dirty, the hard pound.

She wanted . . .

The woman was unaware of giving up again. But as she bent down and set her half-finished drink on the floor, she realized she was leaving. Again. With grace, she walked forth, turning to one side and another and then back again as she navigated between the men and the women who breathed and schemed, lived and died, chose and denied. She envied them the chaos of their free will, all those repercussions that would find them, good and bad, all the illusive goals never to be scored, all the distant horizons that would e'er be out in front, precious for the never-captured nature of their sunsets.

As much as she knew about damnation—and that was a lot—it turned out that a land of unwanted plenty was a fresh kind of hell, and she had a feeling the dogged, low-level malaise she suffered from was all about accessibility. If everything was within reach, nothing mattered, for the obtainable was a meal already gorged upon, the appetite ever-slaked creating a bloated, sickly feeling that disinclined one to ever dine again.

While the woman passed through all the shoulders and torsos, many eyes stared at her, double-taking, or never looking away in the first place. Lids popped wide, and jaws lowered ever so slightly, the impact of her presence jumping the wait line of so many chemically altered senses, barging its way into those brains ahead of other kinds of feedback.

When she had first returned here, to Caldwell, she had looked back at them, all of them, not just the ones in this club, but those striding on the sidewalks of the city, and stuck in traffic jams in their cars, and filing in and out of shops and offices and homes. With fervent expectation, she had searched for a response within herself to any of the unspoken invitations, a yes, a harmonizing drive to complete the chord, a brick to add to a collective wall, a penny of her own to make the dollar whole.

It had not come.

Lately, she stayed out a shorter time each night. And now, she did not venture out in the day at all.

The club's rear exit was tattooed with a warning in red letters that it was to be used In Case of Emergency Only. The woman pushed the bar and stepped out. As the alarm started going off, she walked away down the alley, lifting her face to the spring rain that fell from storm clouds above.

Is it cold? she wondered. It had to be cold after she had been in that oven of body heat.

Her stilettos clipped over the dirty pavement, and kicked up puddles, and, on occasion, failed to find suitable purchase on the uneven ground. And when she lowered her head, wind swept her hair back, as if the night wanted to see her properly, as if it wanted to regard her sadness as a kind friend would, with pity, with concern.

The shouting bass of the club faded in her wake, replaced by softer conversations created by rain dripping off fire escapes, and windowsills, and the fenders of abandoned cars. A stray cat howled and received no reply for its throaty efforts. A cop car sped by, in pursuit of a felon or perhaps, in a rush to save somebody from one.

The woman walked with no destination, although an empty berth of sorts found her when she sensed someone following her. Looking over her shoulder, she thought she might have been mistaken. But then . . . yes. There it was. A figure with long legs and broad shoulders, the man emerging from the shadows into the disinterested peach glow of the city's illumination halo.

The woman didn't vary her pace, but not because she wanted to be caught.

The capture soon occurred, however, the man closing the distance to come beside her, the erection in his pants and the testosterone surging in his veins making some kind of intersection between their bodies a foregone conclusion in his mind.

She stopped and looked up to the storm again. The rain tiptoed on her cheeks and forehead, a thoughtful guest that did not want to overly disturb its host.

"Where you at, girl," the man said.

Righting her head, she cranked a stare in his direction.

He had an almost-attractive face, something about the slightly-too-short distance between those dark eyes and the pinch of his too-thin lips robbing him of true handsomeness. And maybe the latter was why he'd gotten that tattoo on his neck, and why he greased his black hair back. He wanted to refute the priggish tint to his features. Probably also explained the way he stuck that blunt straight-out from between his uneven teeth, like it was an extension of his arousal.

"Now why you gotta be like that." He took the blunt away. Spit on the wet ground. Put the thing back. "What's your problem."

Neither were a question, so she did not answer that which he was not actually asking. She just stared into his greedy, gleaming black eyes, sensing his heartbeats even if they were something he did not notice.

Taking an inhale on the weed, he blew the smoke right in her face. And as she coughed a little, he looked down her body like she was an object to be taken off a shelf. As if he had a right to her, but hoped she fought him. As if he intended to hurt her and was looking forward to the pain he was going to cause.

"I'm giving you one chance," she said in a low voice. "Go. Now."

"Nah, don't think so." He flicked the blunt away, the lit tip flashing orange as it end-over-end'd into a run-off stream flowing to God only knew where. "I'm a nice guy. You gonna like me—"

She knew exactly when he was going to move and in what direction. He went for her long brunette hair, grabbing ahold of it like a rope and yanking her off balance, something that was easily done given the height of her heels. As her back twisted, and one of her ankles bent wrong, she resented the inelegant manner in which she fell.

And that was all on him.

Given the easy way he caught her, with a strong arm around her breasts, and a knife to her throat, she had the sense that he had perfected this over many attempts and successes, his best practices and training leading him to drag her out of what little light there was to the dense darkness of the alley's flanks.

Yanking her back against his body, he said, "You scream, I cut you. You give me what I want, I let you go. Nod, bitch."

She shook her head. "You really want to release me—"

The knife bit into the side of her throat, cutting her. "*Nod, bitch*—"

Devina took control of the situation by freezing the human where he stood, with that arm of his around her, that knife up to her jugular, that weight tilted back on his tailbone. Then she disappeared from his grip, and re-formed in front of him. Without her body where it had been, he looked like he was dancing with himself. Or about to slit his own throat.

Gathering her hair, which had been dislodged by his rough handling, the woman smoothed the gorgeous brunette lengths as if she were calming a skittish horse, and then she pulled the waves over one shoulder, where they were promptly content to rest in a profusion of beauty. With a steady hand, she put her fingers up to the wound he had made and collected the blood that welled from where the blade had dug into her neck. Looking down, she regarded the red gloss sadly.

Only an illusion. Part of the "clothes" she covered her true essence with when she wanted to pass. She wished it was real—

A strangled moan brought her eyes back up. The man was having a lot of trouble understanding the current turnabout, his mouth gaping, the shock and dismay on his face making him seem like a teenage boy who'd lost his bluster in the principal's office.

"I told you," she said softly. "You should have left me alone."

Leaning forward, she marked his lax lips with her blood, giving him a nice splash of lipstick to go with those beady eyes and that prissy little mouth.

"Wh-what-what—"

She slapped him with her open hand, hard enough to stun him. And then she slapped him again, drawing his own blood as he bit the inside of his cheek.

Putting her face in his, she whispered, "I'm going to make you pay for all the things you've taken that were not yours."

Then she kissed him, putting her mouth to his, sucking his lower lip in between her teeth—at which point, she bit through and pulled back, ripping a chunk off him. As he started to scream, she spit the flesh out into her hand and then rubbed the chunk in his face, smearing him with his own blood.

"You don't like this?" she gritted as he tried to move out of the way of his lower lip. "You don't like being forced to kiss when you don't want to?"

After she threw the piece of his mouth at him, she flicked her hand and sent him flying back through the air, slamming him into the damp, soot-stained bricks of the building he had intended on raping her against. Splaying out his arms and legs by force of her will, he reminded her of a turkey about to be trussed for Thanksgiving.

Even as his blood flowed down those make-me-tough neck tattoos, leaking out of his mouth that, courtesy of her remodeling, was now plenty big enough for his face, he was too shocked to scream. But he got over that when she put her palm out and sent the energy into him.

Sure as shit he made a noise then, the high-pitched call that of an animal impaled.

But she wasn't stabbing him. That sound was annoying, however.

With her opposite palm, she threw a spell at him, a transparent bubble forming around his head and containing the scream, sparing her ears the inevitable ringing that would persist long after he no longer did.

Devina split his skin down the center of him and tore it away, every-thing peeling off the muscle and bone underneath, his flesh falling from him as his now-useless clothes did, in two piles on either side of his feet.

Splayed wide, glistening in the rain, the man was still breathing and now there was very little blood, only lymph fluid oozing off the tendons of the toes. Things were twitching, though, hands and feet, mostly, but also the pec muscles. And then he lost control of his bowels.

Incontinence was so unseemly.

Disgusted, she called the bubble back to her palm and let him drop into a disjointed pile of joints. As she walked away, she went LeBron on the silencing spell, dribbling it at her side, the smacking on the alley's pavement echoing around, a beat of her own creation in which she had no more interest than those created by others piped in through speakers at the club.

When she got to the alley's dead end, some blocks to the north, she heard a commotion back where she had been and imagined the human had been found by someone. Sure enough, sirens began to sing in concert.

Although Caldwell at night spawned them like a replicator spell gone haywire, so perhaps it was another kind of emergency.

The woman stopped dribbling, capturing the bubble and standing it up on her fingertips.

The rain was falling even more tentatively, as if it couldn't decide whether to recline into a state of fog or not—or perhaps she had scared it? Nevertheless, as the infinitesimally small drops hit the bubble and slid off, they weaved a rainbow of color in their wake and made her think of the inside covers of old books with their swirls of watermarks. She further considered how long she had been on the earth and then of her relatively recent captivity, a problem she had solved with no small amount of ingenuity. However, she worried. When she had first escaped the Well of Souls through a resourceful seduction, she had expected the father of everything, the Creator, to chastise her and remand her back to the below, re-punishing her with an even greater sentence of isolation.

But the longer she was permitted to roam the streets of the city, the more that winter transitioned into spring, she was coming to realize her freedom was to be trusted. Yet the longer she was here, and the more she trusted her freedom, the more she realized that she was, autonomous ambulation aside, still in captivity. Still imprisoned. Still weighted by chains, though she could see them no better than she could visualize the bars that penned her in.

Surrounded by potential lovers and endless possibilities for consumption on all levels, she mourned the loss of her one true love and grieved the unprecedented separation that marked the end of their relationship. Jim Heron, the fallen angel, was in Heaven now, forever apart from her—and forever not alone. He was with that little, irrelevant girl, Sissy, who he stupidly gave a shit about, and his eternity with that mealy-mouthed pathetic made Devina want to destroy the earth itself. And then start on the rest of the galaxy.

So she was getting why the Creator did not care that she was out and about once again.

It was because her Father knew that she had no real free will, for her unrequited love was a dungeon within which she would e'er be set.

A surge of familiar pain made it hard to breathe and what blurred her vision presently was no longer the rain.

As she grew desperate for a release from her suffering, she pitched the bubble at the head of the alley. Upon impact with the slick bricks, the translucent containment broke apart, shattering as glass, releasing the very anguished sound her black soul had been making since the angel she loved had forsaken her for another . . .

Without love, even evil was unhappy.

It was strange to require the very thing that she existed to destroy, and to mourn its loss as if she were mortal and the cold, thieving hand of death had plucked a prized, irreplaceable apple from one's family tree.

This fucking sucked.

CHAPTER FIVE

To a vampire, the sunlight was what you feared, never the night. Darkness was freedom, shadows were safety, clouds over the loud, bright face of the moon a stroke of luck. The approach of the sunrise, in contrast, made flesh creep with warning, and the greater the peach glow to the east, the deeper the terror in the chest. No matter how strong the back, how powerful the dagger hand, how stout the will, those rays of gold were a scythe that was ever sharp, a flame that never extinguished, a pool in which there was only drowning, never rescue.

Syn stood upon great stone steps with his back to the Black Dagger Brotherhood's mansion, the humidity of the storm that had moved on lingering in the still air, like the scent of a female who'd departed a room. Before him, below him, there was a valley of pine and maple, the former fluffy with evergreen boughs, the latter studded with tentative buds that would become, in time and warmer weather, leaves that would unfurl, worthy blooms even though they sported no petals or perfume.

Disaster impended, however.

There. Behind the mountains. A faint blush, as if the cold, dark sky was embarrassed at the joy with which it greeted the coming sun.

If he stayed out here, if he cast his vampire eyes upon the deadly beauty, it would all be over. He would suffer briefly in an inferno of his own flesh, but after that, the long, chronic agony that had e'er been his life would be over.

"Cousin?"

Syn pivoted around. Silhouetted in the grand entrance, with the light from the vestibule framing his body as if he were holy, Balthazar, son of Hanst, was both a ghost and a living, breathing vampire. But that was the nature of thieves, wasn't it. They never made a sound and they were able to steal things without being caught—because no one knew that their hand had been in an unguarded pocket until it was too late.

"I'm coming," Syn muttered as he turned back to the horizon.

His eyes were starting to burn, and the skin across his shoulders was tightening, sure as if he were already being exposed to the heat that was to come.

As the grand door's heavy weight shut, he was grateful that his cousin knew and understood. Tonight, his *talhman* was close to the surface, that bad side prowling around, demanding to—

"You know, you're not going to look good with a tan that bleeds."

Syn jumped. "I thought you went back inside."

"No, you just want me to do that." Balthazar lit up a cigarette and exhaled as he clipped an old-fashioned lighter shut. "And before you tell me you're coming in again, I just want you to know I don't believe you."

"Don't you have someone to rob?"

"Nah." Balthazar made a pshaw with his hand. "I've given all that up."

Syn cracked a laugh. "Yeah. Right."

"You don't believe I can turn over a new leaf?"

"You were born without a conscience."

"That's a little harsh, don't you think."

"You don't even know when you're lying."

Balthazar held up his cigarette. "Oh, but you are so wrong on that.

And it's because I'm a master liar that I know when other people are fibbing."

As the male stared at Syn, Syn was of a mind to pick him up and throw him off the fucking mountain. "Isn't it getting hot out here for you?"

"If you're good, I'm good."

"Have you never wanted to have a moment alone?"

"At least I won't need to light my next cigarette." The bastard flexed his thumb. "You know, tendonitis is no joke."

Syn turned and faced his cousin. "You are insane. You realize that?"

"I'm not the one volunteering to be barbecued."

"What exactly do you call somebody who stands out here just because I am?"

"Ah, but that is not volunteering." Balthazar narrowed his eyes. "You're forcing me to kill myself."

Syn clapped slowly. "Good performance. Now get the fuck back inside before you get hurt for no good reason."

When Balthazar just stood there, smoking and blinking fast even though he was facing away from the sunrise, Syn crossed his arms over his chest.

"I'm not going inside—"

"Fine, we'll be torches together—"

Someone opened up the door, and cursed. "What the fuck are you two doing out here?"

Both of them whipped their heads around. Zypher, the outrageously beautiful bastard, was pulling a schoolmarm, his one working eye frowning with disapproval. The other one, which had been lost about two months ago in a stabbing with a *lesser*, was currently replaced by a falsie with a Captain America shield for an iris.

"This is none of your business," Syn snapped.

Balthazar motioned. "Come on out. I told him I wasn't going inside until he did."

Zypher jacked up his leathers and paraded out onto the steps, even though his face immediately flushed and he had to hold up an arm like someone was about to take out his good peeper with a poker.

"You know, I haven't seen the sun since before my transition—"

Syn resisted the urge to stamp his shitkicker. "That's the way it's supposed to work!"

"Then why are you out here?" Zypher put his palm out. "Balz, k'I have one of those?"

Balthazar offered his pack. "You don't smoke."

"But this is what they do in front of a firing squad." Zypher elbowed Syn. "Get it. Fire squad. Har, har, har."

Syn looked back and forth between the two of them as Balthazar lit the cigarette and Zypher—

Choked and coughed like someone had given him a mask hooked up to a tank full of diesel fumes.

"You know," Balz said as he pounded on the guy's back, "you're really not a smoker."

"Christ, how do you do this?" Zypher sputtered as he put the thing out on the tread of his boot. When he straightened, he reared back and hissed. "Hot, oh, hot—"

"Hey! What the hell are you guys doing out here! And why didn't I get invited to the party?"

All three of them turned around, which was kind of nice as the burn left Syn's face—although now his back felt like he could fry an egg on it. Syphon, the other of Syn's cousins, had stepped out of the vestibule, a look of confusion almost noticeable on his face. Not that you could see much of his puss given that both his arms were up and he was tilting back like someone had popped the lid off some plutonium in front of him.

"Come on out," Balthazar said. "We're killing ourselves because Syn won't come in."

"Oh, okay. Will do."

As the stupid motherfucker stepped blindly off the entrance's platform and tripped on the stairs, Syn let out a cursing streak that was almost as heated as the glowing orb of death WHICH REALLY DIDN'T HAVE TO BE A PROBLEM FOR ANY OF THEM BUT HIM.

"What is wrong with you people!" He wiped his sleeve over his watering, irritated eyes. "Get back in the house!"

Great, now his nose was running, too—like he'd just sucked back seventeen trillion Scoville units with a blowtorch chaser.

"Don't you get it," Balthazar said as he sneezed and teared up from the glare. "We've been with you for centuries."

"We don't leave a bastard behind," someone—Syphon?—said . . . who the fuck knew, his hearing was going now.

Zypher seemed to be nodding. Or else he was going into a seizure. "If you die, we all die—"

The voice that exploded out of the house was the kind of thing that made James Earl Jones sound like a soprano and turned Gordon Ramsay into a grief counselor.

"In the house *now!*"

Xcor, leader of the Band of Bastards, did not blink in the sun. Nor did he bow against the heat of the encroaching rays or shelter his face in any way. Harelipped, heavily muscled, and a vicious stallion of war, he, by his presence alone, made silly the stunt Syn was pulling.

One by one, they ducked their heads and filed by the great male who held the vestibule door wide. The relief was immediate. As soon as they stepped into the mansion, that system of impenetrable panels slamming shut behind them, the infernal rise in temperature relented, the spine of the onslaught broken.

Xcor didn't spare any of them a glance. Or, at least, Syn didn't think the male did. Hard to know, given that his eyes were still watering. No, that didn't cover it. It was more like he had a pair of golf sprinklers mounted on his face.

And to that end, he couldn't see anything of the splendor he'd entered. Not the marble columns, not the mosaic floor with its depiction of an apple tree in full bloom, not the gold-leafed balustrade up the blood-red stairs or the mural of warriors upon stallions three stories high on the ceiling.

Not the backs of the other bastards as they started to walk off toward the dining room, where Last Meal had been served for the community.

"Man, I'm hungry," Zypher said casually, like they hadn't all just been marshmallows on sticks. Or yelled at by the boss. "You know, I think I'm going to go keto."

"As opposed to what?" Syphon asked.

"Atkins."

"What's the difference?

"One you eat meat, and the other . . . you eat meat."

"Wow, look at you making the hard decisions."

"Don't make me take my eyeball out and throw it at you."

As they all went *groooosssss*, Syn caught Balz's arm and pulled him back. Staring the other bastard in the face, he spoke softly.

"Just so you know, I would have stayed out there. Until it was flames and nothing else."

"Just so you know . . ." Balthazar leaned in and spoke even more softly. "No, you wouldn't have."

"You're wrong."

His cousin shook his head. "I know you better than you do."

"Don't make a hero out of me. You'll only get hurt."

"Oh, I'm not making you a hero. No need to worry about that. But you would no more see the death of any of us than you would save yourself from a ring of fire."

"That makes no sense."

Balz just shook his head like he wasn't going to waste time with stupid and walked off. Syn wanted to go after him and force a fistfight, just to release his pent-up energy. But Wrath wouldn't have that in his house—and besides, there were young at the dining table. No reason to hasten their education into the dark arts of arguing with one's bloodline.

Turning away, Syn headed instead for the grand stairs that led up to the second floor. As he took the steps two at the time, he didn't know why he was rushing.

Bullshit. He knew exactly why.

When had he ever wanted to sit for a meal.

His room was located in the wing that he understood had been opened specially for the Band of Bastards' inclusion in the household. He thought the hospitality was wasted. For centuries in the Old Country, the bastards had lived on the fly, camping out in hovels and hiding places in the forests, sheltered from the sun on a wing and a prayer with weapons their blankets, aggression their food, and the blood of their enemies the libation that sustained them.

He had done much better with that, he decided as he opened his bedroom door. As opposed to these comforts of a home that would never be his own.

Stepping inside, his boots made hard impacts over the bare floor and there was no furniture to get in his way, no four-poster bed eating up half the square feet, no bureau in which to bunk his BVDs, no desk for correspondence he never received and answered, no chair to rest his bones even when he was so tired, he ached down to his marrow.

In his bathroom, which he had stripped of the cloud-like towels that had once rested on golden rods, flushing away them like birds from perches, he removed his clothes and weapons, each in proper sequence. First, the weapons, which he lined up on the marble counter in a neat, tidy little row of wrath. Two steel daggers. Four handguns, two with suppressors. Seven clips of extra ammunition, because he'd popped off one of his backups playing target practice with a *lesser*. And then a pair of throwing knives, a length of nylon rope, duct tape, a chisel, and a hammer.

Those last four on the list? No one else knew about them. They were for him. They were . . . private.

His clothes were next. The leather jacket first, which he folded over the edge of the claw-foot tub. The black T-shirt, which he folded and placed by the jacket on the heated marble floor. The boots which he lined up together by the shirt, the socks that he folded on top of the shirt, the leathers that he folded and draped on the jacket. When he was completely naked, he picked the shirt and the socks back up and put them down the laundry chute. He resented this. In the Old Country, he had worn his clothes until they had fallen off of him, replacing items only when necessary. At first, this conservation of resources had been out of necessity. Then it had been a matter of efficiency as he did not want to waste time on the inconsequential.

Now, he lived here. Where people didn't want to eat their roast beef next to someone who smelled of the street, of sweat, of *lesser* blood and gunpowder.

Of death, given and received.

This delicate sensibility had had to be explained to him and he resented the compliance that was required. But it was what it was. In the course of his life, he had had to yield to higher powers from time to time. Whether they were virtuous . . . or not.

Pivoting back to the display of the only things that mattered in his life—regardless of what Balz thought—he was drawn to the nylon rope.

And the chisel.

And the hammer.

His body moved forward, called by his private tools. On the approach, he saw different versions of them, flipping through memories of the many sharp edges and forced confinement aids he had used over the centuries as if they were photographs of people whose company he enjoyed and of happy events that had been shared amongst family and friends . . . parties, festivals, birthdays.

Without a conscious command from his mind, his hand reached out to the chisel, his fingertips traveling across the sharp end, the business end, the end that he had driven through many a soft tissue and into many a hard bone. Inside of him, his *talhman* roared, the horrible energy traveling from the center of his chest directly down his arm, to his dagger hand. A trembling ensued, shaky, shaky.

But not from weakness. From denied strength.

As he pictured using the chisel, the hammer . . . his saw and his axe . . . the other tools of his terrible trade . . . he saw the bodies of his victims lying on different kinds of floors. Wooden floors, finished and unfinished. Marble, stone, and ceramic tile. Carpets, rugs, linoleum. And then there were the outside scenes. The spongy mattresses of wet leaves. The cold gloss of iced-over ponds and drifts of snow. The grit of concrete, another set of knuckles to be leveraged. Then the ocean's yielding sand, the rocky shores of rivers, and the greedy splash of lake water.

Syn's breath quickened and sweat broke out across his chest, riding a wave up his throat, into his face.

In his mind, he pictured limbs bent wrong. Mouths cranked open in screams. Intestines blooming out of incisions he'd made in lower bellies.

Massaging the flat, steel face of the chisel with his forefinger, he warmed the cold metal with his body heat, stroking . . . stroking—

A tug on his cock made him look down at his stiffened sex in surprise.

It wasn't a tug. His erection had knocked into the handle of the drawer between the sinks.

Staring at his extended member, he regarded the flesh as if from a vast difference. And then he stroked the blade of the chisel.

The sensation translated immediately to his arousal, the thing kicking. Wanting more.

Picking the chisel up with his business hand, he held it in front of his face. So clean, so precise, its dimensions declared by sharp, unforgiving edges.

Down below, at his hips, he found his cock with his other palm. As he began to pump himself, he stared at the blade. Harder. Faster. Sharper. Cleaner. Until he couldn't tell where his thoughts about the chisel ended and the sexual instinct started. The two blended together, tendrils that started separate twisting up quick, forming a rope that tethered two things that should never have had anything to do with each other.

Sex and death.

Abruptly, there was a great surge within him, a rising heat and sense of urgency, and he opened himself to the twisted passion. Turning the chisel in his hand, he watched how the light from overhead played on the blade, winking, flashing . . . flirting, seducing. As he might have with a lover, his eyes went back and forth from the chisel to his cock, a momentum kindling, intensifying.

His *talhman* pulsed under his skin, the need to kill a second side of him that he suppressed as much as, and for as long as, he was able. Harder. Faster. Rasping breath, his. Pounding heart, his. Pressure in his veins, the cords of his neck popping, his head falling back as his lids squeezed shut. But it didn't matter that he couldn't see the chisel. He had a rich forest of images to wander through in his mind, a promenade of bloodied, torturing pleasure that was everything he couldn't feel down below.

Building . . . building . . . building—

Until . . .

Clicking. He became acutely aware of the clicking as his fist went back and forth along his shaft. And then he started to feel the burn of friction and not in a good way, in an abrasive fashion. Further below his stroking, his balls stung as they crawled up close to his body, like they were trying to discharge themselves in whole if they had to.

Stimulation turned to strangulation, as that which had been called forward was denied exit. Buildup became pent up. Culmination became frustration.

The alchemy he had created now turned against him, the abandonment with which he had released the hold on his head gone now, a gritted grimace righting things such that he saw himself in the mirror.

His reflection was ugly, the features that were harsh when composed now tormented by a sickening denial he was well familiar with. And then there was the chisel, right by his mouth, like a lover he had been kissing. And his hand pumping, the head of his cock purple from the squeezing and the dry rubbing.

Pain now. But like the pleasure that had come from thinking of killing, the origin of the agony was all mixed up. Was it the yanking on his
cock? Or something so much deeper . . . going back to very beginning
of him.

The very origin of him.

Giving up, Syn tossed down the chisel, disturbing the orderly lineup
of hammer and rope and duct tape. With a grunt, he fell forward and
gripped the edge of the countertop. His breath wheezed up and down
his throat and whistled through his teeth, while sweat dripped off his
chin, landing on the top of one of his bare feet.

There was nothing worse than chasing a release.

You never could catch.

CHAPTER SIX

The following morning in the *Caldwell Courier Journal*'s much diminished newsroom, Jo's knees went loose and her butt smacked
down into her office chair. As her hands started to tremble, she
made like she meant to put the glossy photographs on her desk instead
of having fumbled them into gravity's greedy clutch. The stack of images
fell in a fan, different angles on the gruesome face repeated until it was
like her vision was stuttering: The eyes open in terror. The features frozen in a scream. The exposed teeth like those of a wild animal.

No longer anything human.

"Sorry," Bill Eliott said. "Didn't mean to ruin your breakfast."

"Not at all." She cleared her throat and shifted the top image on the
pile to the bottom. "It's fine, I'm—"

Jo blinked. And saw the all-wrong body glistening under police lights on the backs of her lids. As her throat closed like a fist, she
thought about running out of the newsroom and throwing up by the
back door in the parking lot.

"You were saying?" She sat up taller in her crappy chair. "About
where the body was found?"

Bill crossed his arms over his chest and leaned back in his own chair across the aisle. At twenty-nine, and having been married for a year and a half, he straddled the divide between hipster and adult, his shaggy black hair and black-rimmed glass and skinny jeans more the former, the seriousness with which he took his job and his wife the latter.

"Seven blocks away from that techno club, Ten," he said.

"What the hell . . . happened to him." As Jo looked at the next picture in line, she willed her stomach contents to stay put. "I mean, his skin . . ."

"Gone. Taken off of him like someone had stripped a cow. A deer."

"This is . . . impossible." She looked up. "And this would have taken time—security cameras. There have to be—"

"CPD is on it. I have a contact. He's going to get back to us."

"Us?"

Bill rolled over on his chair and tapped the stack of horror. "I want us to write this together."

Jo looked around at the empty desks. "You and me?"

"I need help." He checked his watch. "Where the hell is Dick. He said he'd be here by now."

"Wait, you and me. Writing an article together. For publication in the real paper."

"Yes." Bill checked his phone and frowned. "It's not like we haven't been working with each other already on you-know-what."

She met his eyes. "You don't think this has anything to do with . . ."

"Not officially, I don't, and neither do you. We start talking about our little side project trying to find vampires and Dick's going to think we're crazy."

As a sharpshooter went through Jo's frontal lobe, she had the sense that she needed to ask Bill about something . . . something about the last night . . .

When nothing came to her, and the pain just got worse, she shook her head and looked back down at the photograph of the full body. The tangled, glistening mess was nothing but muscle and sinew over glimpses of shockingly white bone. Veins, like purple wires, added fine-line accents to the crumpled anatomy. And the bed upon which the corpse lay? Skin.

Well, to be fair, there seemed to be some clothes—

The familiar headache rippled through her skull, playing the piano keys of her pain receptors. As she winced, the newsroom's back door was thrown wide. Dick Peters, as editor-in-chief of the *CCJ*, walked in like he owned the place, his lumbering footfalls the advance of all that was arrogant and arbitrary, as only the truly below-average could be. Fifty years old, fifty pounds over Dad-bod weight, and retrenched in the sexism of the fifties, the fat folds padding his once-handsome fratboy face were a harbinger of the atherosclerosis that would claim him early.

But not soon enough. Not in the next fifteen feet.

"You wanted to see me," Dick announced to Bill. "Well, let's do this."

The boss man didn't slow down, and as he passed by like a semi on the highway, Bill got up and motioned for Jo to follow with the pictures.

Stuffing them back into their folder, she strode after the men. As subscriptions and advertisers fell off, everything had been downsized so it was only another twenty feet to the paper-thin door of Dick's fragile, declining temple of power.

But his authority was undiminished as he dumped his Columbo coat in a threadbare chair—and realized she was Bill's plus-one.

"What," he snapped at her as he took a suck on his Starbucks venti latte.

Bill shut the door. "We're here together."

Dick looked back and forth. Then focused on Bill. "Your wife is pregnant."

As if the infidelity was excusable when Lydia wasn't knocked up, but tacky for those nine particular months.

"We're reporting this together," Jo said, dropping the photographs on Dick's desk.

They landed cockeyed on the clutter of paperwork, the glossies peeking out of the folder, presenting themselves for precisely the close-up Dick gave them.

"Holy ... shit."

"This is nothing that anyone's ever seen in Caldwell before. Or anywhere else." Bill checked his Apple Watch again. "Jo and I are going to investigate this together—"

Dick turned his head without straightening his upper half, his jowls on the down side hanging loose off his jawline. "Says who."

"Tony's still out from the gastric bypass." Bill motioned to the closed door. "Pete's only part-time and he's covering the Metro Council fraud thing. And I've got a doctor's appointment with Lydia in twenty minutes."

"So you wait till your wife's done with the lady doctor." Dick moved the photographs around with the tip of his finger, sipping on his coffee with all of the delicacy of a wet vac. "This is incredible—you gotta get on this—"

"Jo is going down there to the scene right now. My contact with the CPD is waiting for her."

Now Dick stood to his full height of five feet, nine inches. "No, *you're* going down to the scene after that appointment is over, and didn't you tell me it was going to be a quick one? When you asked for only the morning off?" The man motioned around at scuffed walls. "In case you haven't noticed, this paper needs stories, and as a soon-to-be father, you need this job. Unless you think you can get good healthcare coverage as a freelancer?"

"Jo and I are doing this together."

Dick pointed at her. "She was hired to be the online editor. That's as far as she is going—"

"I can handle it," Jo said. "I can—"

"The story is going to wait for *him*." Dick picked up the photographs and stared at them with the eyes of the converted. "This is amazing stuff. I want you to go deep on this, Bill. *Deep*."

Jo opened her mouth, but Dick shoved the folder at Bill. "Did I stutter," he demanded.

✦   ✦   ✦

Mr. F stood in front of the house and double-checked the number that was on its mailbox, not that he knew where he was or why he was here. Looking behind himself, he didn't know how he'd gotten to this cul-de-sac with its seventies-era split-levels and colonials. No car. No bike. And there was no bus service in this part of town.

But more to the point, he had only hazy memory of . . . fuck.

Something that didn't bear thinking of.

He had to go inside this particular house, however. Something in his brain was telling him that he was supposed to walk up the driveway and go into the garage and enter the fake Tudor.

Mr. F glanced around in case there was another explanation for any part of this. The last thing he remembered with any clarity was being under the bridge downtown with the rest of the junkies. Someone had approached him. A man he didn't know. There had been a promise of drugs and the suggestion that sex was involved. Mr. F wasn't that into the grind, but at the time, he had been too dope sick to panhandle, and he'd needed a fix.

So . . . something awful had happened. And afterward, he'd blacked out.

And now he was here, wearing combat pants he'd never seen before, a flak jacket that seemed very heavy, and a set of boots that belonged on a soldier.

The morning was gray and dull, as if the world didn't want to wake up—or maybe that was just Caldwell. Everyone in this neighborhood, however, seemed to have gainful employment and school-aged children. No one was moving around in any of the windows of any of the homes. Nobody in any of the yards. No dogs barking, no kids on bikes.

Regardless of the mood the dour weather put them in, they were all out in the world, gainfully employed, properly enrolled in school, participating in society.

He had grown up in a zip code like this. And for a while, when he'd been married, he had lived in one. He hadn't been back for a lifetime, though.

As he started up the driveway, he was limping, and he knew he'd bottomed for someone. There was also a funny buzz in his veins, a sizzle that didn't exactly burn, but wasn't pleasant. He was not in withdrawal, however, which considering it had been—

What day was it now anyway?

Focusing on the front door, he noted the scruffy bushes and the lawn that was littered with sticks and a stray branch the size of a dead body. The mailbox nailed into the stucco was stuffed with flyers, its flimsy maw open and drooling envelopes, and there were three phone books on the welcome mat, all ruined by the elements. The neighbors must love the neglect. He imagined all manner of frustrated knocking and no answers. Notes tucked into the storm door. Whispers at community cookouts about the bad seeds who inhabited 452 Brook Court.

He didn't go in through the front. A voice in his head told him that the side garage entry was unlocked, and sure enough, he had no trouble getting into the one car. Inside, the crinkled carcasses of dead leaves lay across the oil-stained concrete floor, their entrance granted by a window that had been knocked out by yet another fallen tree limb.

The door into the house proper was locked so he kicked it open, the new strength in his body something that was a surprise, but not reassuring. Catching the panel with his hand as it flew back at him, he stayed where he was, listening. When there were no sounds, he cautiously entered the back hall. Up ahead, there was a small kitchen and eating area, and out the far side, a dining room.

No furniture. No stench of trash or clutter on the counters. Nothing in the living room to the left, either.

There was a lot of dust. Some mouse turds in corners like coins collected. Spiders up around the ceiling and dead flies on the windowsills, especially over the dry-as-a-bone sink.

As he walked around, the floors creaked under the boots that were on his feet. He was sure that the air was musty, but he hadn't been able to smell anything since he'd been tortured at that abandoned outlet mall. Probably a good thing. He had some hazy flashbacks to it when it had been going down, and he remembered retching from the stench. Maybe the shit had killed his nose, too much funk knocking out a fuse somewhere in his sinuses.

Up on the second floor, in what had to be the master bedroom, he found a laptop next to a jar. And a leather-bound book.

The three objects were set together in the corner by the cable TV hookup, the Dell connected to the internet and still plugged into the wall. Everything was covered with more dust, and he wasn't surprised as he tried to turn the PC on that it didn't work. No electricity in the place. Obviously no cable, either.

The jar was weird. Blue-enameled, capped with a pointed lid and in the shape of a vase, it was curvy in the middle, like a woman. As he held it in his hand, turning it, turning it, he found his total lack of sex drive, as well as his complete absence of hunger for food, as troubling as this power in his legs and arms.

Something was inside of the vase, banging on the sides as it was rotated, but the top was sealed, glued into place.

"Leave it alone," he said out loud.

He did not. His feet took both him and the jar into the dim bathroom, over to the sink and the mirror. When he looked at his reflection, he stumbled. The skin on his face was all wrong. He was too pale, but more than that, it was like he was wearing granny powder, his features slipcovered with a matte, waxy outer layer that didn't look right.

And he shouldn't have been able to see this clearly in the darkness.

Absently, he shook the jar. *Thunk. Thunk. Thunk—*

With a slam, he drove the thing into the counter, shattering it. As the shards fell away, what was revealed horrified him.

He was no anatomy expert, but he was well aware of what he was looking at. A human heart. Shriveled and black, the organ that was the seat of humanity, literally and figuratively, had been violently orphaned from its rib cage, the veins and arteries ragged, not cut.

As if it had been ripped out.

Tearing open his shirt, he looked at his sternum. The skin was marked with tattoos, some better than others, but he didn't notice his ink.

He had no scar. There was no evidence that he had been violated. But something had been done to him there . . .

With trembling fingers, he pushed into the sides of his throat. Where was the pulse? Where was *his* pulse?

Nothing. No fragile, sustaining beat in the jugular.

Wheeling away from the mirror, Mr. F lurched back into the bedroom and fell to his knees, dry heaving. Nothing came up his throat. Nothing came out of his mouth. No half-digested food. No bile. No saliva.

He was just like the vase. A container for something that was ruined.

As reality twisted and contorted, revealing a new nightmare landscape his brain could not comprehend, he let himself fall face-first into the carpet.

I just want to go back to before, he thought. *I want to go back and say no.*

The sense that he had been claimed and there was no breaking up with his new spouse was a curse that even all his previous bad deeds had not earned. And what's more, he had not asked for this. Had not agreed to this. A bargain might have been struck, but there surely had been a bait and switch.

Even in his worst moments of being dope sick, he never would have consented to an unholy rebirth. And the one thing he knew for sure about his new incarnation?

It was irrevocable.

You didn't come back from shit like this.

CHAPTER SEVEN

As night fell on Caldwell, Jo was alone in the newsroom and typing furiously at her desk, her coat still on, her need to pee something she had been ignoring for hours now. When her office phone rang, she let it go to voice mail. When her cell rang, she picked it up on the first ring.

"How's Lydia?" She stopped what she was doing. "Everything okay now?"

There was a long pause. Which said enough, didn't it.

"No." Bill's tone was sad and hollow. "They lost the heartbeat. And now she's starting to bleed."

"Oh . . . God, Bill," she whispered. "I'm so sorry. Do you need me to do anything?"

"No, but thanks." He cleared his throat, and then spoke briskly, as if he were determined to be professional. "How's the story coming?"

Jo leaned back in her chair and looked at Dick's closed door. The boss had left at three-thirty, which had been a relief. With all the other staff gone and Bill not at his desk, she'd hated being in the office alone with the guy.

"Good," she said. "I'm about to finally meet your contact, Officer McCordle, down at the scene. And I did end up interviewing the guy who found the body. I also got a non-statement from the Pappalardo family. I'm just spell-checking the update now. Do you want me to send it to you before I put it up on the website?"

"I trust you. And make sure your name's on it."

"It's better to just leave it under yours."

"You're doing all the work, Jo." There was another pause. "Listen, I better go back in there with Lydia."

"Take care of your wife, and tell her I love her and am thinking of her."

"Thanks, Jo. I will. And I'll text you when we're home."

As she ended the call, she stared at her phone. Then she put it face down on her desk. Rubbing the center of her chest, she forced herself to hit spell-check on the file. No mistakes. She spell-checked again. Reread the three paragraphs.

Just before she went through the posting process, she focused on the byline. William Eliott.

The initial story, the one she had written five hours ago and put up online as well as into the printed paper version for tomorrow, had gone under Bill's byline. Even though he was right. She was the one who had typed the initial twenty-five hundred words after doing all the reporting.

Glancing back over at Dick's door, she thought about how much she needed this job. Granted, it wasn't as badly as Bill needed his, especially during this medical emergency, but it was bad enough now that she'd moved into her new apartment by herself.

Whatever. She was doing a favor for a friend—

Her cell went off and she answered without looking at the screen. "Bill, is there something else—" Jo frowned as an unfamiliar voice started talking. "Wait, Officer McCordle? Are you canceling on me?"

"No, I'm leaving the station now." The cop lowered his voice. "But you're not going to believe who they think did it."

"Who?"

"Carmine Gigante."

Jo sat forward. "*The* Carmine Gigante? And is that senior or junior?"

"Senior."

"I don't suppose you have any way of reaching him."

"He hangs out at the Hudson Hunt & Fish Club. But I happen to have his cell phone."

"Can I have it?" When there was a hesitation, she rushed in. "All of my contact with you is off the record. You can trust me. No one will know where I got the number."

"I'd really prefer to deal with Bill."

"I promise. You can trust me."

As he grudgingly recited the digits, she wrote them down and then ended the call. Taking a couple of deep breaths, her hands shook as she started to dial.

The male voice that answered was gruff, congested, and accented with a whole lot of Brooklyn. "Yeah."

"Mr. Gigante?"

There was a period of silence. "Yeah."

"My name is Jo Early. I'm a reporter with the *CCJ*. I'm wondering if you have a comment on what happened to Frank Pappalardo's nephew, Johnny?"

"What the fuck are you talking about."

"Johnny Pappalardo was found dead around twelve a.m. last night not far from that techno club Ten, which I understand you have ties to. Kind of funny for him to be up here in Caldwell, don't you think? Given that his family's territory is down in Manhattan. Rumors have it that he was in town to make peace with you, but I'm guessing that didn't go too well."

"I don't know nothing."

"I spoke with Frank Pappalardo's representative earlier today. In a statement to me, his lawyer said that the Pappalardo family is mourning the loss of a fine young man. Something tells me that's sincere, but hardly the end of it. Do you expect there to be retaliation from—"

"What'd you say your name was?"

"Josephine Early. Reporter for the CCJ."

"Don't call this number again. Or I'll make it so you can't."

"Did you just threaten me, Mr. Gigante—"

As the connection was cut, she took a deep breath and went back to her keyboard. With quick strokes, she revised the update to include the fact that Mr. Carmine Gigante Sr., Caldwell's reigning crime boss, had a no comment when he was reached about the death of one of his biggest rival's close relatives. Another spell-check. And a final read-through.

Putting her hand on her mouse, she paused. Looked at her boss's door for a third time. Returned her eyes to her screen.

"Fuck you, Dick," she muttered as she put one more revision in.

Jo posted the update to the original story, grabbed her purse, and stood up from her chair. As she went to the newsroom's back door and broke out into the cool, clear night, she was not thinking about her headache, her stomach, or her hot flashes.

Who'd have thought it was a relief to get threatened by a mob kingpin?

◆   ◆   ◆

The Hudson Hunt & Fish Club had nothing to do with hunting or fishing, but it was close to the Hudson, about ten blocks up from the river in downtown. As Syn approached the establishment, he was underwhelmed by its unremarkable, windowless front, and that was the point. Nothing about its two-stories-high, shotgun construction was intended to garner attention, the seventies-era rectangle fitting in with the rest of the businesses in the six-block neighborhood. Delis. Locally owned restaurants. Tailors, tinkers. No spies.

Ducking into an alley that was as broad as the eye of a needle, he made quick work through the darkness. Halfway down, a door opened, weak, yellow light spilling out and illuminating the wet pavement.

Well. What do you know. It was his good buddy from the night before, the one with the gun and the racing magazine.

Fates, that nose looked bad, all swollen, and the left eye was black.

"He's waitin' for ya," the guy muttered as Syn entered. "Go all the way to the back."

Syn walked into a bar that was mostly empty. No one at the tables, just three guys at the counter with a bottle of Jack Daniel's and a trio of glasses between them. As he made his way "to the back," their dark eyes stayed locked on him as their hands ducked out of sight into their open jackets.

He hoped they came at him, and he memorized them. One had an eyebrow with a scar through it. Another was missing the top half of both ears, like someone had given him a haircut that had gotten out of control. Number three, who had been called Junior the night before, had a gold pinkie ring the size of a paperweight on his left hand.

In the rear, there was a flap door that led into a hallway that smelled like bacon and eggs. Something opened off on the right, and Syn prepared to take both his guns out.

The man who stepped in his way was your typical barn door, although his stare suggested he was smarter than a flat panel that kept horses inside their collective stalls.

"Stop where ya are," he said around the butt of his cigar. "I'ma pat you down."

Yeah, whatever. Syn got into that brain and flipped some switches.

Promptly, the man took his cigar nub out and nodded. "You're good to go."

No, shit.

Syn entered a shallow passageway with Cigar and then the big guy did the duty with yet another frickin' door.

The office that was revealed was exactly the same as the one from the cement company, making Syn think, stupidly, of a pair of matched socks. And behind the scatter of papers, the old man with the acne scars was pissed.

As he pounded the desk in front of him, the ice in his whiskey glass rattled. "Jesus *Christ*. Answer your *fucking phone*."

Syn stepped forward so Cigar could join them in the cramped space. "I'm here, aren't I."

"Did you see this?" A laptop got turned around. "What the *fuck* is this? You're supposed to be a fucking professional and you do *this* shit?"

The screen was showing the picture of a corpse that was mostly blurred out. Given the amount of pixelated red stuff, it was clear that whoever had killed the poor bastard had had butcher training.

"You were supposed to be quiet." The man picked up a cell phone. "And you know who just called me? The fucking press. The fucking *press*! It's everywhere, goddamn it."

Syn cooled his jets and let the man blow off steam. As this was human world bullshit, he couldn't care less—

"I'm not paying you a fucking dime." The man waved his cell phone. "I got problems I didn't have before you fucked it all up being a fucking show-off last night. So you're not getting fucking paid."

As Syn decided not to remind the man that money had not been the point, on his side at least, that laptop got spun back around and beads of sweat bloomed across that meaty, pockmarked forehead.

"What the fuck are you doing to me!" When Syn still didn't respond, the man pounded his desk and lurched to his feet. "Do you have any idea who I am!"

"Who you are is irrelevant to me," Syn said with utter calm.

Fleshy lids blinked as if Syn had switched up languages on the guy. Then the old man looked at his associate with total shock. "Do you get a load of this guy?"

"Unbelievable," came the response around the cigar.

"You're something else," the old man muttered. "And I don't think I'm making myself clear. Do you *know* who I *am*."

Syn focused on the heartbeat that pulsed on the side of the man's throat. And as his fangs tingled, he knew that the wrong question was being asked. The real question was not *who*, but *what*, and it was about

Syn. But as with the whole money thing, that was hardly a course correction he felt it necessary to make.

The cell phone rang again, and when the old man looked at the screen, he muttered to himself. Then sat back down in his chair and rubbed his eyes like his head hurt.

"You know what, it's your lucky fucking night." Looking at Syn, he crossed his arms over his chest. "I'm going to do you a favor. I'm going to give you a chance for redemption. As opposed to a grave."

"Do tell," Syn said in a bored tone.

"I want you to take care of a reporter for me."

CHAPTER EIGHT

When Syn left the Hunt & Fish Club, he went down the back alley to a rear parking lot that had a dumpster, ten spots for cars of the narrow variety, and no exterior lighting. There was only one vehicle in the square of asphalt, a Chevy Suburban that was parked laterally across many sets of faded yellow lines. As a cigarette flared behind the wheel, it was clear the old man's chauffeur was ever-ready, and as soon as Syn was out of sight of the driver, he dematerialized about twelve blocks up. Upon re-forming, he registered his position with the Brother Tohrment, clocking in for his shift prowling the largely-empty-of-slayers downtown.

He missed the old days. The Old Country. The way things used to be with the Band of Bastards sleeping together like a pack of dogs in the rough, the only rule being that as long as you cleaned up the messes you made, no questions were asked.

But nooooo they had to come over to the New World.

Then again, there had been even fewer *lessers* overseas.

For tonight's shift, he was in the territory next to the Brother Butch's, and he was supposed to be with his cousin, Balthazar—and the latter was a good thing. Balz didn't mind working alone, with the pair of them covering the area assigned without walking side by side. Syn hated that grafted-at-the-hip shit. He was so not a chatter, which was a natural corollary of him not giving a shit about anyone else's life.

Hell, he didn't even care about his own.

Technically, the lone-wolf, on-your-own routine was a violation of protocol. But Balz was a thief with no conscience, so lying by omission was like sneezing to the guy. Plus Syn was god-awful company, and he had the sense that Balz, who was in fact a chatter, would rather be by himself than stuck in a strained silence as they pounded the pavement in search of what they rarely, if ever, found.

The idea that the war was coming to an end was something to herald for everybody in the Brotherhood's mansion. Except for Syn. He was not built for peacetime.

Choosing a random direction to go in, he strode over damp asphalt and used his nose as radar. The fact that all he picked up on was old motor oil and the sweet perfume of gas—thanks to the beaters he walked by—made him worry about the future. As he pictured endless nights of nothing to do, no one to kill, nobody to torture, a cold, numbing despair washed through him—

The falter in his step would have been a surprise if he'd noticed it. He didn't. He was too busy testing the air to see if what he was scenting was right.

Syn's body stopped dead without his brain giving his muscles and joints an order to cease fire. Then his head moved from side to side on its own as he sifted through the shitty bouquet of the city.

Meadow. He was smelling a fresh, summer meadow in the midst of the grime and the trash, the pollution and the exhaust. The scent was so compelling, so resonant . . . so overpowering . . . that he blinked and saw an image of wildflowers in moonlight.

Drawn by what had to be a mistake of his senses, some wire getting crossed between his sinuses and the synapses in his brain, he walked forward like a dog, snout out, body dragged behind. Passing under

fire escapes and by doors locked with chains and deadbolts, he continued along the street. Off in the distance, there were sirens, and then the
dampened beat of a car stereo's subwoofer. Some human on a moped
with a milk crate full of food that was going to be ice cold when delivered swerved out of his way when he refused to divert from his course,
the man barking a curse at him—

And then the wind changed.

Syn stopped and put his arms out like he could fight the thief that
had robbed him of the scent. Circling in place, he tried to catch the trail
again, drawing night air in through his nose like it was his last shot to
breathe before he drowned.

Someone came out of a doorway, took one look at him, and quickly
retreated back into wherever they'd tried to leave. They probably
thought he was on drugs.

Given his sudden lack of control over himself, he *felt* like he was on
drugs.

Unable to regain the scent, he closed his eyes and had to wait before
he could sufficiently calm himself to dematerialize. When he was able,
he ghosted up to a rooftop and prowled around the lip of the drop-off,
looking down, searching, his blood pounding in his veins.

But for once, it was not because he was hungry to kill.

No, this was hunger for a different reason entirely. And it was the
kind of thing he was wholly unfamiliar with.

Yet there was no one he could see in the maze of streets and buildings, his target eluding him in spite of the number of vantage points he
shifted to. And in all his frustrated, frantic searching, he felt as though
he were in a dream, the object of his desire ever out of reach, a figment
of imagination rather than anything of true flesh and blood.

Eventually, he forced himself to stop.

He had obviously imagined it.

As he resolved to get back to work, he was aware of a ringing disappointment in the center of his chest, sure as if he had been cheated out
of a promised benediction.

Then again, for one brief moment, he had had something other than killing on his mind.

Considering the fact that murder and the desecration of corpses had been his only motivator for as long as he could remember, it was a surprise to mourn his return to normal.

◆   ◆   ◆

"Of course Gigante wasn't happy when he answered," Jo said, keeping her voice down. "But that's not a surprise."

Officer McCordle, the beat cop friend of Bill's who she'd come downtown to meet, frowned like someone had accused him of wire fraud.

"Wait, you really called him?" he asked.

"What did you think I was going to do with the number? Play Uno with it?"

The pair of them were about three blocks west of the crime scene, not that it would have mattered if they'd been right in front of where Frank Pappalardo's nephew had been peeled like a grape. The CSI unit had done their thing and cleared the site, and then a commercial cleaning crew had come in to make sure none of the club-goers in the neighborhood took selfies with the aftermath. Not that there had been much blood or guts. But still.

And man, you could smell that bleach.

"Did he threaten you?"

"I'm not afraid of Gigante," she said.

Officer Anthony McCordle had "Good Guy" stamped all over him. Underneath the brim of his police hat, his honest face seemed to struggle to contain the not-happy expression his mood had cast his even features in, and his hand went to the holstered gun at his hip. Like he was protecting her from the mob even though the two of them were alone.

"This is bad." McCordle shook his head. "I never should have given you—"

"There's going to be retaliation, though, right? I mean, I don't know much about the real-world Mafia, but all those movies and books can't be wrong. If you kill your rival's nephew, you're in trouble. Right?"

McCordle looked around at all the not-much-to-look-at. The alley was barren of even trash cans and empty liquor bottles, although that didn't mean it was destined for a Caldwell tourism ad. There was a not-so-thin coating of city grunge on the buildings and the pavement, the whole lot of it like a stall shower that existed in a world free of Oxi-Clean. In contrast, McCordle's shiny new patrol car, which was parked about fifteen feet away, was an example of routine maintenance and care that would never be replicated in this neighborhood.

"Look, I think I'm going to wait for Bill, okay?" McCordle dropped his eyes and stared at the ground, like he didn't want to be sexist, but some internal code of chivalry demanded that he treat women like crystal vases. "I don't want you to get hurt."

For a moment, she was tempted to go Annie Oakley and shoot out his taillight, proving viscerally she was armed and had good aim. The trouble was, Caldwell had an ordinance whereby you couldn't discharge a firearm inside city limits. McCordle thought his conscience was bothering him now? He should see what happened when she put him in the position of having to arrest her for a weapons violation and some willful destruction of police property—or let her go because she was a nice little girl who'd done an oopsie.

"Bill's in the hospital with Lydia. She's having problems with the pregnancy." As the officer's eyes swung back up, Jo shrugged. "So you're going to have to deal with me. It's either that or you go to the national media, and can you really trust them to keep your identity a secret? I'm very sure there's an official CPD policy against leaks to the press, and those CNN and Fox News people won't hesitate to give your name up to your superior if they think it can get them even better access. But you can trust me. I'm local, and I have a helluva lot less to lose than Anderson Cooper does."

Hell, she had nothing to lose. She was just an online editor. But that was not a card she was going to play here.

McCordle's shoulder piece went off with a squawk. As a bunch of 10-Mary somethings came out of the little speaker, he tilted his mouth down and made a response in code.

"I gotta go." He leaned in toward her, as deadly serious as a Boy Scout could get. "Don't reach out to Gigante again, and I'll tell Bill directly that he shouldn't do that, either. That old man doesn't value human life, and he is not afraid of anything. He'll put a hit on you without blinking an eye."

"Don't shut me out, then. I promise not to go near Gigante, but you've got to keep me in the loop."

McCordle walked off toward his patrol car. Given the way he was shaking his head, she had a feeling he was regretting the whole damn thing. Sure he wanted to snag the bad guy, but if he could have run a rewind on getting involved with civilians with laptops and bylines, clearly he would have preferred to make better choices.

"Sorry, not sorry," Jo muttered as she looked over the notes she had made on her pad.

Considering the blue lights that started flashing and the sound of McCordle's siren firing up, the cop had been called in on something serious, and sure enough, she heard the rhythmic thumping of a police helicopter overhead.

Maybe the drama would get his mind off things.

So he would take her call when she touched base with him at the end of the night. And then first thing in the morning.

Someone running down the alley brought her head up and she took a step back. The man who went by her was going fast and checking over his shoulder like he was being chased by something with a knife. He paid no attention to her, but he was a good reminder that she should remember where she was—

"Oh, God, what is that *smell* . . ."

The instant the sickly sweet stench burrowed into her nose, a piercing pain tore through her head and she took another step back, the cold, damp flank of the building catching her and holding her upright.

Roadkill and baby powder. It was a bizarre combination, but she'd smelled it before. She had smelled this before in . . . somewhere dark. Somewhere . . . evil. Glossy oil on a concrete floor. Buckets of . . . blood . . .

A moan rode up her throat and came out of her mouth. But then she wasn't thinking about the stink or the pain. Something else was coming down the alley, heavy footfalls. Thunderous footfalls. A huge body propelled by incredible strength. In pursuit of the thing that smelled so foul.

It was a man, dressed in black leather and wearing a Red Sox cap. And as he looked over at her, his eyes widened in surprise, but he didn't stop. He'd recognized her, however. Even though he was a stranger, he *saw* her.

And she saw him.

As her head ached even more, she wanted to run after him and ask him exactly what it was about her that was familiar to him—

Jo stiffened and looked to the left. Suddenly, the alley seemed darker, somehow. More isolated. The shift came instantly, sure as if the only light in the world had been turned off by the hand of God.

Fear shaved through her.

"Who's there?" she said as she put her hand on her gun.

It was a stupid question to ask. Like whoever it was would answer her?

Up above, the police helicopter came around again, and she wanted to yell up at it to shine a light down to her.

As her heart began to pound, she thought of McCordle's advice about not contacting Gigante. In a wave of paranoia, it felt like she wasn't going to live long enough to take advantage of the sound counsel—

There. In the darkness. Over on the left.

There was a second man dressed in leather.

CHAPTER NINE

S yn stopped where he was, not through conscious thought, but because his mind was too busy taking stock of the female to do anything else with his body. She was tall and she was well-built, dressed in civilian clothes that were of no note except for the fact that they were on her. Her hair was long, or at least he assumed it was. The lengths of what appeared to be red and auburn were tucked into the collar of her windbreaker, the waves ballooning out as if they wanted to be free to flow down her back. Her face was makeup-less, her brows arched in surprise—no, it was more like fear. Indeed, her lips were parted as if she were about to scream, and her eyes, locked on him, were wide, the whites setting off a color he couldn't pin down.

Everything was in a haze, and not just because of the lack of light.

She somehow blinded him. Even as he took careful note of so much about her, his eyes couldn't seem to take all of her in.

And then he realized what she was doing.

He shook his head as he stepped out of the cover of shadow he had found without meaning to, exposing himself to the ambient light that bathed the alley in a glow that might have been romantic had it been in a forest or a field.

"No," he heard himself say. "You're too high."

The female blinked in confusion, and he had a thought that she might not be aware that she was pointing a gun at his face.

"What?" she mumbled.

The sound of her voice went through him as if she had touched him with a tender hand, the simple word rebounding inside his skin and changing his internal temperature—though he would have been hard-pressed to say whether she was cooling his temper, or heating his lust. Actually, it was both.

Syn walked up to her, his eyes locked with her own, some internal warning system telling him to move slowly and try to look smaller than he actually was. He didn't want to spook her, but not because of that nine millimeter she had in her hands. He didn't want to frighten her because, for once in his violent life, he did not want to be who he actually was.

This stranger with the parted lips and the wide eyes made him want to be different. Better. Improved from the base beast that he had been since his transition.

"I'll shoot," she said.

He closed his eyes briefly as the syllables she spoke went into him. And then he felt compelled to respond. "Lower."

When his lids reopened, he was standing right before her, his body having made its own decision about where it wanted to be.

"What?" she breathed.

Syn reached out and took the trembling end of the muzzle, putting it in a better position for her. "Not the head. The chest. You want to aim here. It's a bigger target and the heart is where you can do the most effective damage."

With her gun properly set, he took a step back. "There. Now you can kill me properly."

As he waited with patience for her to pull the trigger, there was such great peace in his capitulation that he was only vaguely aware of a gathering noise above him, some kind of rhythmic thumping sound.

It did not matter. Nothing mattered.

He was hers to command, and if she wished to take his life here and now, he would willingly give his mortal coil unto her. No matter how much it hurt or what his suffering was, it would be a good death, one he had long deserved.

Because this female, who captivated his black soul as surely as if she held his beating heart in her palm, would be the one killing him.

✦   ✦   ✦

On Jo's list of things to do for the night, shooting another human being was not in the top five. The top ten. It wasn't even on her list.

Especially not one that smelled like this. Jesus, what was that cologne of his? It was nothing she had ever run across before. Then again, the same could be said for the man himself. He was enormous, positively gargantuan, and the black leather he was wearing did absolutely nothing to make him seem smaller and less imposing. With a tremendous shoulder span and thick arms, his lower body was likewise developed, heavy thighs holding him upright, big boots covering his feet.

But his face was what really got her attention. It was lean, the hollows under his high cheekbones giving him an austere look, the intelligent eyes sunken in deep, the jaw hard cut and unforgiving—as if he was into punishment over reformation. His hair was mostly shaved, nothing but a three-inch-high Mohawk picket-fence'ing his skull from front to back, and there were no tattoos showing. She was willing to bet he had them under his clothes.

Or maybe he was just acres of smooth skin over all that hard muscle—

Stop that right now, she thought.

Bottom line, the fact that he seemed unconcerned with the gun she was pointing at him made sense. By sheer presence alone, he could have turned a bazooka into a BB gun.

"Leave me alone," she said. "I'm going to shoot."

"So shoot."

Neither of them moved. Even as the rest of the city continued on, its felonies and misdemeanors proceeding apace, its night traffic of deliveries still streaming on the bridges and stop-and-go'ing on streets, its people living and breathing in whatever crammed square footage they rented, between Jo and the big man with the Mohawk, all was still, some kind of fulcrum created between them, around which the world tilted and whirled.

"I'm serious," she whispered.

"So am I."

His big hands went to his biker jacket and he pulled the two halves apart, revealing a vicious pair of steel daggers strapped, handles down, to his broad chest. Then, in a gesture that made no sense at all—not that any of this was in contention for the Yes-this-is-actually-happening Prize—he let his head fall back on his neck, the muscles that rode up the sides of his throat popping out in sharp relief, the jut of his chin the summit to the mountain of his towering body.

It was as if he were submitting himself to her totally.

Giving himself over.

To her—

Up in the sky, the police helicopter made a circle and came in their direction, its icy-bright light skimming down the alley, illuminating the colon created by the buildings that were squeezed in tightly side by side and across from each other. The beam hit the man in his pose of inexplicable supplication, bathing him in what appeared to be, for a brief moment, a sanctification from heaven, as if he were an altar painting of a saint about to be sacrificed for the good of humanity.

Jo knew she would remember the way he looked for the rest of her life—

With a quick jerk, he snapped to attention, focusing on something down at the far end of the alley.

From overhead, a voice piped through a loudspeaker announced,

"Drop your gun. Police units have surrounded the area. Drop your weapon."

Jo looked up at the helicopter in surprise. Were they talking to her—

"We have to go," the man in leather barked. "Now."

She heard what he said, but she was not going to run from the police. She just needed to explain to the nice guys with the badges and the landing gear that she wasn't actually going to shoot this man in front of her. She just wanted to scare him off—

Said man in said leather put his face into hers. Which meant her gun's muzzle was now pressed directly against his sternum.

"You have to come with me." He looked down the alley again. "Or you're going to die—"

"The police are not going to—"

"It's not the police I'm worried about."

As the copter made a tight swoop, the down draft from its rotor blades created a gust that nearly blew her off her feet—and that was when Jo smelled the stench again. That baby powder and roadkill smell.

The man grabbed her arm. "You've got to come with me. You're in danger."

"Who are you?"

"There's no time." He looked to the left one last time. "Keep your gun out. You may need to use it."

With that, he took off—and took her with him. Her legs had no choice but to start running. It was that or she was going to get dragged. And when he took a sharp turn, she lost her stride, her feet tripping. His hold on her forearm was the only thing that kept her up and she recovered as best she could.

In the back of her mind, she knew this was all wrong. She was fleeing the police with the very man she had pulled a gun on.

Talk about out of the fire and into the frying pan.

Or shit . . . something like that.

CHAPTER TEN

Butch closed in on the slayer in front of him, the distance between their churning bodies tightening up as sure as if they were beads on a string. The *lesser* seemed to be tiring, and this, like that heart in that bucket at the abandoned outlets, was a news flash. The fuckers usually had Energizer Bunny endurance in their favor and just kept going, and going, and going.

Unsheathing his black dagger, he didn't know where Z was. The two had lost track of each other when he'd gone after this motherfucker. He knew the brother could handle himself, however, and there was backup called in already. But he would rather have had them stick together.

The corner in the alley came up quick, and the *lesser* skidded on the oil-slicked pavement as he hung a louie, his footing slipping out from underneath him, his body going cockeyed. And that was Butch's cue to skidoo. Leaping up in the air, he flew with dagger outstretched, gunning for the back of the slayer's head. His aim was impeccable. His trajectory sublime. His impact—

Got fucked in the ass when that slayer lost his balance entirely and went down early.

Butch had a passing glance at the skull he had intended to stab as he flew over the sonofabitch—and he was reminded of the truism of SUVs on ice. Four-wheel go did not mean four-wheel stop, and the same was true for nearly three-hundred-pound vampires when they were not in contact with the ground.

Torqueing in midair, he twisted his body and swung his legs out in front of him so they were the bow of his shit-canned ship. The maneuver didn't slow him down, but it made it possible for him to land in a crouch.

Or he would have.

If he hadn't run into the hood of a car that had been abandoned and stripped for parts.

The front grille split him like a wishbone, one leg going north and peeling off the Chrysler emblem mounted over the radiator, the other going south and getting jammed under the front spoiler. His nut sac took the impact and turned him into a soprano, the C note he hit seven thousand octaves higher than any male should ever get near outside of an opera cape.

It was as his 'O Sole M'otherfucker echoed around that the lesser jumped to his feet. There was a split second where he and the slayer looked at each other. Hard to say who was more surprised, but who got back on the boogie train was answered pretty damn quick. Twinkle Toes with the perfectly timed face-plant didn't hang around. He took off, racing past Butch's new avocation as a hood ornament.

Groaning, Butch surgically removed his nads from the car and started after the slayer again. The pain was enough to make his stomach roll and his eyes water, and he had to swing his legs out from ground zero, his gait like a cowboy who'd gotten off his horse after three years in the saddle. Things evened out pretty quick, though, the idea that this could be the one, this could be the final lesser, making him go faster than his crotch would have liked.

Then again, going by how shit was feeling down there? He should be lying on a couch with a bag of frozen peas wrapped around his courting tackle.

Another corner, and by force of will alone, he started to close again.

This time, he wasn't going to run the risk of another crotch-on collision. With his prey in sight, enough with the Matrix shit. He just chugged it out until the stench wafting off the slayer was punching him in the nose, and the huffing and puffing of the undead was as loud as the roar of his own blood in his ears.

Throwing out an arm, he crowbarred his enemy, his elbow locking around the throat, his free hand grabbing onto his own wrist, his body yanking off to one side so that the *lesser* popped off the pavement and maypole'd around. With a practiced move, Butch dominated the ground game that followed, mounting the slayer, palming the back of the head, slamming the face into the pavement.

And that was when he discovered that he'd lost his dagger.

Yanking out his other one, he grabbed onto the *lesser's* short hair, pulled back, and slit the throat from ear to ear.

The undead went slack, and Butch let go and rolled off, disgusted with himself and the sloppy takedown. As the slayer's face flopped onto the asphalt, and all kinds of sputtering and choking rose up, he hung his own head and tried to catch his breath. With the chase over, his adrenaline was ebbing, and oh, God, the pain from his poor, abused testicles took the place of his aggression.

Leaning over, he retched and went between his thighs to delicately rearrange things—not that it helped. Blue balls had nothing on bashed balls.

When he could, he refocused on the slayer. Its arms and legs were still moving, and he thought of a dog in repose, chasing after imaginary squirrels and bunnies, paws twitching as the body went nowhere. Same diff here. Except unless he took care of business, this nonsense was going to go on in perpetuity. Or until some human rode up and went 911 on the situation.

After which, total calamity would ensue as the secret about the vampires and the Lessening Society got out.

Yup, the need for discretion was the only thing that the two sides agreed on.

On that note, he forced himself to get back to work. Reaching out, he grabbed the undead's shoulder and rolled it over. The gurgling sounds got louder, and he stared down at the busted-up face with its wide, secondary smile. That new mouth, below the chin, was drooling black, stinky oil all over the place, but even if the body was drained dry, its motion would continue.

There were only two ways to get a *lesser* gone. One was the stab of a steel knife through the front of the chest, the blade going into the hollow space where the heart had been. Pop-pop, fizz-fizz, back to the Omega it is—at which point, the essence of evil that had been imparted into this once-human body would be returned to the Evil, recycled and put into another vessel.

The second way to "kill" the enemy was the one that was bringing the end of the war, and Butch was the only person who could do it.

Re-sheathing his dagger, he looked up as a police helicopter paddled overhead, its brilliant beam skating past him and the slayer, missing them entirely. Time to move fast. He wasn't taking for granted he'd luck out like that again when it came back around. With a grunt, he planted one hand on either side of the slayer's head. Then he leaned over, his arms bowing out, his eyes meeting the undead's. It was hard to know how much the *lesser* was taking in. Those peepers were wide as car tires, the whites glowing in the darkness. There was no vengeance or hatred in them, however.

It was rank fear. In spite of the fact that the humanity was gone, a very human terror was coming through loud and clear.

"You're not going home," Butch muttered. "I'm going to save you. Even though you don't deserve it."

Although he wasn't so sure about that.

The slayer had run when it had the chance. It hadn't attacked. It hadn't fought back with any weapons. It clearly wasn't trained, and it was alone.

Butch knew this because he could sense the Omega's boys and there weren't any others around. He knew this because, briefly, he had been one of them.

"Do you regret what you agreed to?" Butch whispered.

The head slowly nodded, and a single tear escaped the far corner of one of those bloodshot, swollen eyes.

The mouth, the real one, not the one Butch created with his dagger, moved in a coordinated way: *Too late.*

◆   ◆   ◆

Six blocks over, Jo threw her anchor out and ripped her arm free of the man's hold. In response, there was an immediate holler from her rotator cuff, and he wheeled around just as quick.

"You're not safe here," he said.

In the back of her mind, she noted that he was barely breathing. On her side of things, her lungs were in crisis mode, her rib cage doing push-ups like she was about to be thrown overboard.

"You have to trust me."

"No, I don't," she got out between pants.

He looked in the direction they'd come from, as if they were being chased. Or were about to be.

"I cannot leave you here."

There was an accent to his words. Not quite French, not really German. Not really Italian.

He lowered his head and his nostrils flared. Then he cursed. "You need me—"

Jo stepped back sharply. "Leave me alone—"

"I can't. You're going to die."

Fear curled inside Jo's chest, and it wasn't because she was scared of him. "You don't know me—"

The man cursed again. "You've got to listen to—"

That helicopter crested over the building next to them, the light swinging in a wide circle and heading in their direction.

"The police aren't going to help you," he said. "They're going to arrest you. And I know where to go. You can trust me."

"I'm not going to run from the—"

"They saw you holding a gun to my chest. They know what you look like. Do you want to end up in jail tonight? Or do you want to get out of here."

As Jo looked up, the blast from the blades peeled her hair back against her head. To keep things together, and because she didn't want to be recognized, she yanked the hood of her windbreaker up and tied it in place.

"I don't trust you," she yelled through the wind currents.

"Good. You shouldn't. But I'm all you got right now."

"Sonofabitch," she muttered.

When he took her hand again, she expected to be pulled behind him once more. Instead, he stayed where he was, his huge body tense, his eyes fierce, his aura that of such urgency, you'd have sworn he was rescuing her from a serial killer.

She thought of what she'd look like in her mug shot. Then she pictured how thrilled Dick would be that she'd gotten herself arrested. Finally, she considered her bank account. She might have been the adopted daughter of the grand and glorious Philadelphia Earlys, but the estrangement she had effected with her parents years ago had hit her bank account hard.

"Well," she snapped, "where are we going."

And still he did not move. "I'm not going to let anything happen to you."

"Great, now stop talking and start moving, or I will."

He nodded, as if they'd struck some kind of deal, and then they were off, pounding down the alley, going further into the maze of downtown as the helicopter swung around again overhead. The corners they took were made with decisive turns on his part, as if he knew exactly where he was taking her, and she kept up with him now, the desire to evade the police making her go track star with the running.

Skidding into a right turn, he shot them down a narrow artery between two apartment buildings, and then he—

Took them right into the path of a Caldwell Police Department patrol car.

As the headlights hit them both, he stopped. And so did she.

Maybe it was McCordle, she thought—

"Drop your weapon!" the female officer barked as she opened her
door and stuck her gun out around the jamb of the windshield. "Drop
your weapon—*now!*"

Jo put both her hands up.

And that was when she realized that the cop wasn't talking to the
man next to her. Jo was the one who was armed; she still had her gun in
her palm.

"Guess you don't know which way to go as well as you thought," she
muttered as she ordered her grip to release the nine millimeter.

CHAPTER ELEVEN

Devina, the immortal who wanted to be a woman, put her palms together, stuck out her forefingers, and extended both her thumbs up, making like she had a gun. Aiming her red painted nails at the night sky, she pretended she was leading the helicopter that was circling like a fly trying to land in someone's soup. It was hard to judge whether her extrapolations of speed and direction were correct, however, without actually sending a bullet into that annoying tin can with its loud, thumping rotors.

Her virtue for a handheld missile launcher.

Now that might be fun. And for a second, she thought about conjuring one out of thin air, just for shits and giggles. It would be exciting to see a fireball explode under those rotator arms, and then watch as the twisted, no-longer-flight-worthy carcass careened into a building. Or maybe the thing would pull a Ping-Pong ball and ricochet into a couple of skyscrapers, the flanks of the stone and glass constructions like rackets to send it back and forth.

People would definitely be killed, and not just the pilot. Maybe a transformer would get overloaded and become a secondary source of fun and games. Chaos. Sirens. Humans tripping over each other, trampling puppies and kittens, babies rolling like melons down the street.

Yay. Rah.

She should get right on it.

Or maybe . . . she would just keep wandering.

As she resumed her promenade, she played with her short skirt. It was vintage Escada, a poufy, poppy-colored, polka-dotted flounce that was only long enough to cover her thong. She'd put it on along with a little muscle shirt and fifteen "Like a Virgin" sautoirs, the crosses and beads and chains tangling in a mesh over her breasts. For shoes, she went straight-up Carrie Bradshaw—Jimmy Choos from 1991. In a pink that ever so slightly clashed with the skirt. No purse because she had just plain forgotten, and she didn't need a coat in the cold because, hello, demon.

It was a good outfit. Chosen from her wardrobe with forced care.

An attempt to self-medicate with fashion.

In the back of her mind, she heard Dr. Phil say, *And how's that working for you?*

Not well, Phil. Not at all, actually.

She took another pretend shot at the helicopter, and then her child's version of an autoloader disappeared as she sneezed and had to cover her lower face for decorum. Fuck. That *smell*. It was like someone had tied a dead raccoon to a stick and sprayed the bloated nose-nightmare with drugstore perfume—

Devina stopped, her senses threading out.

In slow motion, her head turned on its spine and she narrowed her eyes on an alley, about which nothing seemed remarkable: There were fire escapes spiderweb'ing down the back sides of some older buildings, a couple of dumpsters . . . and miscellaneous pavement trash that collected in doorways, the city's version of dandruff.

None of that mattered. What held her attention were the two male figures about a block down from the intersection she was standing in. One was lying faceup in a classic pose of supplication, arms flopped out to the sides, boots lolling at the ends of his ankles. The other was bending over as if he intended to kiss the first, but not with passion. It was more like the Grim Reaper coming to claim a soul, menace and death marking the exchange, something consumed from the one who was a victim by the one who was a predator.

As a tingle curled in Devina's gut, the sensation was at once achingly familiar and utterly alien. It had been that long.

And it wasn't just that two men getting it on was awesome.

Something swirled around the tableau of dominance and submission, and it wasn't the stench.

Evil. Pure, high-octane evil was down there in that alley. It was . . . her, but not her, her essence captured and held within the flesh of the one that was on the ground . . . and yet he was not what interested her. No, she was enthralled by the one who was now opening his mouth. Now beginning to inhale. Now . . . drawing up and out of the parted lips of the supplicant a black ether, breath, but not breath.

Devina stepped into the shadows, and cast a spell around herself, ensuring that she was indistinguishable from the bricks and mortar she abruptly had to lean against. Beneath the aggressor, the body of the victim jerked, the chest rising up, the head falling back as if in great ecstasy or great agony. And that was when she saw the slice across the throat and the black blood oozing out of the jugular vein.

Whispers deep in the core of her sex became stirrings . . . which expanded to an honest-to-demon need, the pilot light, long dimmed, flaring to life and heating her body.

The sounds of the transfer, of the consumption, were like the sucking and smackings of a blow job, erotic in her ear, the gurgling, the gasping, the clicking of the dead man's mouth, fuzzing her brain as her blood began to race. Heat pooled between her thighs and did not stay put, the transforming tide washing upward into her breasts, her nipples tightening, her heart racing such that her plump lips parted and she drew in a quick gasp.

The next thing she knew, her hand was under her skirt and between her legs, the rubbing and pressure a compulsion that was sweetly served by her fingers. Meanwhile, the man on the bottom, the one with the slit throat, began to tremble and jerk, sure as if that which was being extracted was presenting some kind of resistance to its removal. The faster and more torturous his quaking, the faster and more rigorously Devina stroked herself—

She orgasmed just as there was a howling screech.

The release made her squeeze her eyes shut, and for a moment, she was so suffused in pleasure, she forgot she was standing against a building in a shitty alley in a not-so-hot part of Caldwell.

When her lids eventually lifted with languorous delay, there was only one man where before there had been two, and the one who had been doing the inhaling listed to the side and fell over onto the ground. Was he dying? He barely breathed, his skin pasty white, his fingers twitching, his legs jerking, as if poison was in his system. Meanwhile, evil emanated from his very pores. He was a resplendent repository for all that was vile and depraved, a black hole of the kind of thing that coursed through her own veins.

He was her twin.

When he seemed to stop moving, Devina took a step forward. And another.

She didn't want to be alone anymore. She was tired of these cold, empty streets, this listless existence, this . . . isolation.

If he died right here? It was too much of a loss to bear even if she didn't know him. She had been an empty shell since she had landed back in the hustle/bustle of this world, wandering the night like a lost soul, pining after an angel who had despised her rather than loved her.

But this man? This . . . whatever he was?

He would not despise her. And she would have him for her very own—

"Cop! I'm here!"

From out of thin air, an entity coalesced and knelt by the man. Devina's man. Before she could kill it, her doppelganger reached for the new arrival with unsteady hands.

"Fuck, V. God . . ."

"I gotchu. Come here."

With impossible gentleness, the entity reached out and gathered her man close, holding him to a chest that was broad and strong. And then a nightmare happened. The two became one, their bodies entwining, as a horrible, awful light began to glow. The illumination was the antithesis of everything Devina had been attracted to, a beneficence that cleared conscience and cognition at once, that eased suffering, that provided miracles too unlikely to even be prayed for. It was the force that returned the lost to the loved one, that rescued the drowning, that gave the first breath to an infant who should not have survived the birthing canal.

Devina stumbled back in disgust.

She was of a mind to murder that interloper, the one who had brought the unwelcomed light to the delicious dark. It was hard not to feel betrayed by his presence, even as she was aware that hers was a very one-sided sense of violation.

The contact between them and the glow that surrounded their bodies didn't last forever. Even though it felt like it persisted for an eternity.

And when whatever process or procedure was done, the evil was gone, only the two men remaining. Except—no. These were not men, were they. They were other.

They were vampire.

Okay, that was fucking hot.

✦   ✦   ✦

Jo had been a rule abider all her life, and it was probably the adopted thing. She had always felt if she didn't do what she was told, she would get sent back to wherever the reject kids got returned to, like a microwave with a faulty latch or an alarm clock that didn't go off or a suitcase that had a handle broken.

And Jesus, when you had a police officer pointing a gun at you? All that yes-ma'am inclination ratcheted up even higher.

"Put the weapon down *now!*"

As her hand followed her brain's command to release, she had a moment when she prayed this wasn't a Quentin Tarantino film where the damn thing would hit the ground and somehow go off into her knee, scaring the policewoman into shooting her full of holes as well—all while some seventies standard played in the background and the man next to her suddenly had wide lapels and a desire to talk about what quarter pounders with cheese were called in Europe.

Except it didn't go down like that.

The man next to her might have kept the lapels of his leather jacket just the same. But he somehow caught the gun before it had dropped more than three inches from her hand.

And nothing happened.

The policewoman didn't start pulling her trigger and there were no more verbal commands from her, either. She just stood where she was, crouched behind the cover of her open door, gun trained straight ahead.

"Come on," the man beside Jo said. "Let's go."

He put the weapon back in her hand and started forward.

"What are you doing?" she said, staring at her gun as if she'd never seen it before.

"She won't be a problem. But we've got to move."

Jo looked up into the stark face of her very questionable savior. He was utterly calm, almost bored—while he had his back to a member of the Caldwell Police Department who two seconds ago had been trigger-happy.

But who now seemed like she'd swallowed an Ambien. Or twelve. Maybe fifteen.

This is my answer, Jo thought. *This man is what I have been looking for.*

As she nodded and they took off again, she was aware that the choice to go with him was a threshold, and having crossed over it, she would be wise not to take for granted that she was going to like the answers she found. This quest thing she had been caught up in had always been frustrated up until now. But sometimes, there was comfort to be had in the unattainable. You didn't appreciate it, however, until you got the kind of information that you only wanted to give back.

Too late, though. She had voted with her feet.

Literally.

The man in leather took her down more alleys, and then, without warning, he stopped in front of a door that looked like it had had a very tough life. The metal panel had multiple boot marks right next to the jamb by the deadbolt, as if there had been a number of frustrated attempts to break in.

On the other hand, somehow, the man didn't have any trouble opening it. Did he use a key and she just not see?

As he went through the doorway, Jo followed, taking comfort that her gun was still in her hand. The interior of wherever they were was so dark that she could see nothing, but that changed when a candle flared.

Ten feet away from where they were both standing.

Pivoting toward the fragile flame, she felt her heart pound—and not from exertion. "How did you do that?"

"Do what?" he said as he shut them in together and then walked past her.

"The candle. The door. The cop."

When he faced her again, he was across a cluttered space, and there was frustration in his expression, as if he were upset with himself. With a grunt, he settled himself down on the floor, stretching his legs out and crossing his arms over his chest. He did not meet her eyes, and she had the strange sense that he was not so much avoiding her, but containing himself while he was around her.

In the strained silence, she looked around because it was a better option than staring at him. The commercial kitchen they'd taken refuge in had been long abandoned, and the exodus from its short-ceiling'd confines had been sloppy and rushed. There was trash everywhere, restaurant-sized, rusted-out cans of vegetables and containers of condiments littering the dusty counters and floors . . . broken plates, bowls, and glassware Humpty-Dumpty'ing in corners . . . discarded aprons and checkered chef pants molding up in mounds stained with food grime.

"Oh, my God . . ." she said as she pulled her hood off. "I know this place."

She had been meaning to come here for months.

"You eat here when the restaurant was open?" he asked.

"No." Not even close. "This kitchen has an interesting story attached to it."

Refocusing on him, she frowned . . . and recalled a funny thing about chaotic environments. The eye noticed the details at first, but not always the pattern. That came later.

"You've been here, too," she said. "Haven't you."

"No."

"Then why are you sitting against a wall in a cleared space that precisely fits the dimensions of your frame?"

"Because it was the only open area and my legs are tired."

"There's a chair over there. And tired, my ass. You aren't breathing hard. You didn't breathe hard the entire time we were running."

"That chair has three legs, and a person can have good lungs but bad quads."

Jo crossed her arms over her chest and shook her head. Then realized she was mirroring his pose. So she put her hands on her hips.

"If you haven't been here before, how did you know where to find this place? And get inside?"

"Lucky guess. And I got you away from the police, didn't I. Why ask questions about the solution to your problem—"

Before he could finish, the sound of a siren flared as what had to be a cop car came down the cramped lane. She prayed it kept going. It did not. There was a screech and then, from the opposite direction, another unit with its own siren going pulled up as well.

Jo focused on the kitchen's battered door as if she could will the thing to stay closed. The trouble was, she knew that the cops were already familiar with this bolt-hole. They'd been here before, when those gang members had been beaten and killed. She'd read the article about the incident in the *CCJ* before she'd started to work at the paper—and then had followed up on it with other sources online, although not because of the deaths or the gang stuff.

Because of the vampire stuff.

It had turned out that a gang member who had survived was convinced he'd been attacked by vampires, and he had been prepared to talk about his experience. Paranormal enthusiasts online were the only ones who had cared about his story of fangs and fright, and she had ended up covering it all on her own blog, Damn Stoker.

There were so many things that didn't add up in Caldwell. So many strange occurrences—

Her head started to hum, and she rubbed her temple with her free hand as her thoughts on the subject ground to a halt.

Whatever. She had other things to worry about at the moment. Like handcuffs and mug shots.

"Are they going to come in or not," she whispered, aware that her gun was still against her palm.

When the man in leather didn't respond to the rhetorical, she muttered under her breath and went over to a section of countertop. Dragging a dishwasher tray stack off to the side, she discovered that what was underneath was less grimy than most of her other options. Plus he was right. On second look, that chair did only have three out of four legs.

As she hopped up on the cold stainless steel, she let her legs swing until one of her feet knocked into a set of pans and knocked them off whatever they'd been balanced on. The clatter made her jump—and pray that the cops who had stopped outside didn't hear the noise.

A moment later, instead of the door opening wide . . . the cars left, one by one.

Jo looked back at the man. "What did you do to them?"

"Nothing," he said in a bored tone.

"What did you do to the other one?"

"Nothing."

"Bullshit." She tilted her head to the side. "Tell me."

His heavy-lidded eyes met hers, and for some reason, the way he stared at her made her acutely aware of his body. His . . . insanely powerful . . . body.

"I'd rather talk about you," he murmured.

"I don't have anything to say on that subject."

"How long have you had the cravings? The hot flashes? The itchy restlessness inside your skin that cannot be explained or avoided."

Jo did what she could to hide her reaction. "I don't know what you're—"

Abruptly, he got to his feet so fast, she jerked back. But for all the speed with which he went to the vertical, he was slow as he came at her, those long, perfectly in-shape legs crossing the distance between them in lazy strides, his boots landing in the trash like the footfalls of a T. rex.

His stare glowed with a light that she refused to understand.

Sex was not going to come into this picture.

Nope.

Jo cleared her throat. And still sounded choked. "I said I don't know what you're talking about."

Dear God, he was enormous as he stopped in front of her, and she had to glance behind herself to make sure she could twist around and bolt—okay, that was a no-go. There was a solid wall behind her. Worse? As her body began to warm in places that she would have much preferred to stay at room temperature, she became concerned that she didn't actually want to get away from him.

"Liar," he said. "You know exactly what I'm talking about."

CHAPTER TWELVE

The shudder of relief that went through Butch when the cleansing was done, when he was emptied out of the Omega's nasty, was similar to when you'd had the stomach flu and your guts finally decided to stop evacuation orders. At first, you didn't believe the calm, figuring that another wave of vile-bile blow chunks was coming. But when that didn't happen, and you started to trust the all-clear, you took a long, calm inhale and followed that up with a tentative fantasy of toast and tea.

His eyes refused to focus at first. The no-sight thing didn't bother him much, though. He knew where he was, and more important, he knew who he was with.

"You okay?" he said with an extra truckload of gravel in his voice.

V lifted his head, and then pushed himself free of the embrace they'd fallen into during the cleansing. As the brother fell back on his ass, he groaned like all of his joints had been beaten with a baseball bat.

"Yeah. I'm good. You okay?"

"Thanks to you."

As their eyes met, Butch dreaded the question that went unspoken. Closing his lids, he braced himself and reached out a sense he did not want to have. The answer about whether there were more *lessers* out there was immediate—

"So it wasn't the last," V said.

Butch tried to keep the disappointment to himself. "No."

"Okay. Then we find another and another—however long it takes."

"I don't think there are many left. And I'm not just saying that."

Bullshit. Of course he was just saying it. He didn't want to do this anymore. He didn't want to be out here, sucking evil into himself, making his best friend get it out of him, all the while praying for the end to come and being denied that prize. His exhaustion with the whole damn thing took the present and made it go on forever.

"Yup," he said with forced bravado. "We keep going. Until the last one—"

As V stiffened, Butch turned and looked down the alley. "Yeah, I sense that slayer, too. You got enough juice to fight now?"

"Shh." Vishous narrowed his eyes.

Butch frowned and shoved his torso off the pavement so he could get at his guns if he needed them. "It's just one *lesser*. I can feel him—"

All at once, the alley went foggy. Except it wasn't fog. *Mhis* was an optical illusion and sensory scrambler that V used to secure the Brotherhood compound, a force field that anyone could penetrate, but nobody could find their way through.

"I'm not that bad off," Butch bitched. "I can still fight."

Vishous got to his feet, but he stayed in a crouch, his attention focused on the enemy that was standing not that far off from them.

"Cop," he whispered. "I need to move you. Right now."

Okay, his best friend was acting weird here. "What exactly are you seeing?"

"Evil. And I *can't* see it. That's what bothers me."

Butch cranked his head so he was staring in the same direction. "Well, I now can't see shit because of the *mhis*. V, I love you. But you're nuts, man—"

"We gotta get you away from here. You're too valuable to lose."

"I can handle myself."

"Not against the likes of this, cop."

"It's just a slayer—"

Butch felt his arm get taken in a rough grip, and his body weight get dragged up off of the pavement. Then there was no further conversation. V hustled them away, and the *mhis* followed him, followed them. The pace that was set was fast, and Butch shuffled along as best he could, his testicular-magedon slowing him down.

"This is waste of fucking time," he muttered into the wind. "We could just be fighting the damn thing."

◆   ◆   ◆

"Don't be afraid of me."

As Syn spoke the words, he saw through the syllables to the lie underneath. This female with the red hair and the green eyes should have been terrified to be alone with him, in a place where no one would hear her scream. But she didn't know about him and what he had done in the past.

This was a good thing.

"You can put the gun away," he said.

Her eyes were leery as she regarded him with a self-possession he respected. "I don't need to be saved."

"Yes, you do."

"So exactly how do you intend to rescue me."

"Listen to what your body is telling you."

"Well, right now, it says I'm hungry. You going to order me a pizza?"

"It's not interested in food."

"Oh, really?" Keeping her weapon in her grip, she yanked her purse into her lap, and with her free hand, she rummaged around in it. "I beg to differ. And how about you don't try to tell a women what her body is doing. Let's start with that."

Extracting some kind of a long, thin packaging, she ripped open the wrapper with her teeth, and took a bite of smoked beef. She chewed with determination, glaring up at him, challenging him to argue with her about what they both knew damn well was going on with her.

"So what now?" she demanded. "You going to put the mental whammy on me like you did the cops? Or does that only work with members of law enforcement?"

Syn shook his head. "I don't want to do that to you."

"So you admit you . . ." She motioned the stick back and forth between them. ". . . somehow hypnotized them."

"I solved a problem for us."

"But how? I don't know a lot about the way it works, but you didn't use a pocket watch, and you didn't ask any of them to count back from a hundred."

Even though Syn tried not to, he found himself watching her mouth as she enunciated her words. Her lips captivated him in ways that had nothing to do with her upcoming transition, and most certainly called into question his Good Samaritan impulses. Indeed, as his body stood before her and his eyes roamed around her face, things that he shouldn't wonder about began to shift his consciousness away from her change.

For example, it was right about now that he noticed her thighs were spread for balance as she sat on that countertop.

He wanted to see what was under her windbreaker.

Under her fleece.

Under . . . her jeans.

As he blinked, a series of images flickered with impossible speed on the backs of his lids. He saw himself moving in closer, his hips splitting her knees even further apart, his chest pushing her back so she was lying against the wall behind her, his hands locking on the hard ridges of her pelvis, one on each side—

Syn took a step back, as if the added distance would help the sex surging in his blood. It did not. He promptly returned to staring at her lips. And meanwhile, she was on a roll with the wordsmithing, talking at him, telling him God only knew what.

It was fine. As long as she was speaking, she wasn't running from him.

This was good. This was better.

Because if she ran, he was liable to go after her, and that was a race he would win. And when he caught her, he would mount her—

Under his skin, a wave of instinct crested, the power thickening his muscles and his blood. As both of his hands curled into greedy fists, he was aware of his breath getting tight.

"I have to go," he said roughly.

That shut her up, her mouth stopping its sensuous contortions. "Running from little ol' me? That's a surprise. Or is it my gun you're afraid of?"

Neither of them moved. Until she took another bite of her whatever-it-was.

"What kind of cologne is that?" she asked softly. As soon as the words were spoken, she shook her head, as if she hadn't known they were going to come out of her. As if she would have taken them back if she could.

"It's not cologne," he replied.

"What is it."

"Me. When I'm around you."

"Why?"

"Why do you think."

The demand wasn't a passive-aggressive move or a fishing expedition for sexual innuendo because he had no game—although the no-game was definitely true. In fact, he hoped that maybe she could sort his intentions out for him. Maybe there was something in his face, his eyes, his stance, that she could see or sense, a warning that he was going to hurt her . . . or an indication that she was safe with him.

He didn't know the answer to that himself.

"I have to . . . go," he mumbled.

"Where do you live?"

"North of town."

"Alone?"

"No."

"Who with?"

"You ask a lot of questions."

She laughed in a short rush. "You come out of nowhere, tell me how to kill you, help me evade the police, and then bring me here. Whereupon you're the one who is leaving. You don't think at least some portion of that is mysterious?"

"I want you to call me when you need me."

As he recited his number, she interrupted him. "What is that, some kind of bat phone?"

"I have to go."

"I know. You keep saying that. So go. You clearly don't have to worry about the police, and something tells me you can handle all those weapons you're wearing under that leather. So you're free, free as a bird."

"Call me when you—"

"Exactly what do you think I'm going to need you for." She closed her eyes. "Actually, don't answer that. I think I know, and PS, as pickup lines go, that is so not very original."

Syn's brain was telling his body to move. His body was ignoring the commands. And as he became trapped, she fell silent.

"You want some of this?" she murmured after a moment. "You keep staring at it like you didn't have dinner."

It took him a minute to figure out she was talking about the snack.

"I don't know what that is," he said.

"You've never had a Slim Jim?"

"No, but I wouldn't mind trying one."

And that was when he kissed her.

CHAPTER THIRTEEN

Back in the alley where the *lesser* had been consumed, Mr. F stumbled from the deep doorway he had hidden in. When he'd sensed the other slayer, he'd come as fast as he could. He needed to talk to someone, anyone, about what the fuck was going on, and for some reason, he had a beacon that helped him track and identify others like himself. If he could only get with one of the previous inductees, surely they had to know more about the ins and outs of his nightmare—the outs being what he was really concerned with.

'Cuz this shit was a bad trip without the LSD.

As he'd closed in on his comrade, or whatever the fuck you wanted to call the other guy, he'd had to stop and take cover. A vampire attacked the *lesser* Mr. F had been after, and he'd braced himself for what he somehow knew was going to happen—in the same way he'd known how to get into that house in that neighborhood.

Except instead of stabbing the undead back to the maker, something else happened.

An inhalation.

The vampire had gone mouth-to-mouth without the resuscitation, taking the essence of the Omega into himself, drawing the evil into his body. Afterward, he had collapsed. That was when the second vampire had showed up and there had been some kind of a light show. But there was no time to think through any part of it. The goateed member of the species, the one in the savior role, looked right down the alley at Mr. F, and that meant it was time to fucking go. Mr. F had learned long ago on the streets not to engage with something stronger than himself if he could avoid the conflict—

Between one blink and the next, Mr. F's eyesight went on the fritz. Everything in front of him became wavy and indistinct, a vague sense of vertigo making him lurch on his feet. Where were the two vampires?

Fuck that. Where was the alley?

Keeping his gun out, he took off running, and it was a relief to find that as he beat feet in the opposite direction, everything he raced past became visually clear: the buildings on either side of the alley. The random trash. An abandoned car that—whoa—had one helluva a dent in the middle of its front bumper.

Mr. F ran for God only knew how long, making random choices of left or right depending on where the police sirens were coming from and where a helicopter with a spotlight was overhead. At least this fleeing thing he had familiarity with. He was used to getting out of the way of the authorities. But the rest of this shit? Oh, hell no. He wasn't a fighter. He wasn't a soldier. Even when he was real dope sick from withdrawal, crazed with nausea and the sweats, head spinning, veins burning, body whacking out, he never aggressed on anyone. He'd never, ever wanted to hurt anybody but himself, and even that brand of ouch was more an unintended consequence of his addiction than anything masochistic or suicidal.

For the last three years, ever since the wife had thrown him out for being a junkie and he'd fallen into homelessness, all he'd wanted was to score what he needed to level out and keep the peace.

That was it.

Rounding a corner, he was aware of not being tired in the slightest, but the endurance was no trade-off for the mess he was in. And anyway, it turned out he had nowhere further to run. A dead end came up at him, seeming to rush right into his face even though he was the one pulling the ambulation routine. And as he skidded to a halt in front of a literal brick wall, he was barely breathing—and it was terrifying that there was no pounding at his temples or behind his sternum from exertion.

He looked down at his chest and thought about what he'd found in that jar.

Ever since he had started on the drugs, there had been few moments of clarity for him and that was the point. Now, however, a thought occurred to him that was so crystal clear, he was momentarily unfamiliar with the cognitive anomaly.

Not it.

This was not fucking it. He still had no solid memory of exactly how he had found himself in this condition, remote-controlled by a third party he'd never met, lost in the familiar streets of Caldwell, chasing after echoes of what was inside himself in the shadows. But he knew exactly what to do about it.

Bending into his thighs, he jumped from the ground, his body propelled up the face of the wall sure as if he had been spring-loaded and set free. Gripping onto the top lip, he swung his legs over as if he were a trained stuntman, and the loose fall on the other side was longer than he would have guessed.

Jesus, he must have jumped up twenty-five feet or more.

Mr. F landed on the far side without breaking any bones in his feet or stressing his knees. And as he started to run again, he had endless reserve.

For a moment, he debated pulling a Forrest Gump and just going west on an endless trail of asphalt.

But he didn't do that. He headed down for the river, to the bridges. To where he belonged.

He knew exactly what he had to do.

✦   ✦   ✦

When the man in leather leaned down toward Jo, she assumed he was going to take a bite of the Slim Jim she was chewing her way through. So as he tilted his head, she went to move the jerky up. But that was not where things went.

His lips found hers without any hesitation on his part—and holy crap, she accepted the kiss without any hesitation on hers. FFS, she should pull back. Push him away. Get out of here now.

She did none of those things.

But she did move. She likewise tilted her head, slightly to the left . . . so that the kiss became more complete. And as his mouth moved against her own, her senses became hyper-aware, although not to the hard counter under her seat, or the musty smells of the cast-aside kitchen, or the sounds of more sirens passing them by.

No, she was all about the velvet brush of an intimate part of him against an intimate part of her. And also about the size of his shoulders, so big that she couldn't see past the heft of him. And then there was that cologne that he maintained wasn't a cologne, and the fact that she knew he was fully aroused. Just by this kiss.

When his tongue licked its way into her, she readily gave him what he wanted—because she wanted it, too, to the point where she had to try to keep a greedy moan from rising up her throat.

Yes, that kind of thing needed to stay put. Letting him know how much she was into this was a mistake—

The moan got out.

And as the begging sound was released into his mouth, she expected him to grab her, push her back, and tear off her jeans.

And what do you know. She'd let him—

The man pulled back abruptly. His pupils had dilated, the black center eating up all of whatever color there was in the irises, and there was a hard, starving cast to his features.

Now, he was breathing heavily.

"I like the taste of you better than anything," he said with a growl. "And now I have to go."

"I don't know your name."

"It's not important. You have my number."

Actually, she didn't. When he'd recited the digits, she hadn't paid attention.

As a sense of thresholding came back, Jo wondered what the hell it was about her life right now that she seemed to keep returning to this precipice theme. Everything felt like it was on the verge of something else.

"Yes," she lied, "I do."

With a nod, as if he were leaving things as he wanted them, the man strode out of the trashed kitchen. When the door into the alley closed behind him, Jo gripped the lip of the stainless steel counter and lowered her head. She needed to make herself stay here for long enough so that it was impossible for her to go after him and find him. So that he was lost to her forever. Never to cross paths again.

It was never healthy to want someone so badly that you forgot they were a stranger.

Especially if they were armed like that. And clearly used to evading the police.

Plus, hello, hypnotist. Which opened up the possibility of things that . . . in spite of all of her blogging about the paranormal . . . she couldn't believe she was even considering.

As the sirens died down again, she wondered if the police had caught whoever it was they were looking for or whether her never-to-be lover had put another whammy on some badges.

Lifting her eyes, she looked around. The kitchen's messy layout was an inconclusive set of tea leaves to read her future in. But other things percolated, and she thought about that gang member.

And what he'd said he'd seen here.

For all the unreliability of her memory lately, there was no need to get out her phone and reread any article or blog post to refresh her recollection of the story. Here in this kitchen, when that kid had been running from the police, he had encountered something that shouldn't have existed outside of the Halloween season—and in spite of his tough street life, he had been horrified by it enough to be incapable of speaking of anything else. Not that the authorities had cared. They'd been intent only on punishing him for the crimes he had committed. None of the felonies had stuck, however. Two had been not-guiltys and one had been tossed out on appeal.

So he'd been free to preach to anyone who would listen about what he swore he'd witnessed here with his own two eyes.

She wished she could contact him now. Not possible. He'd been found dead in an apartment ten blocks from here about three months ago. Suicide? Maybe. Gangbanger life catching up to him? Very likely.

Eliminated because he was a problem that had become too noisy? Also a possibility.

She and Bill had been trying to reach him when his body had been found.

Jo turned her head and stared at the door to the outside. The ache at her temples and across her forehead was back and getting worse by the moment. She had plenty of Motrin at home, however, and the sirens were silent. The man in leather had been gone for a while. And the police were most likely not looking for her. Anymore.

Because she couldn't hear a helicopter overhead.

Shifting herself off the countertop, she picked her way over to the exit, stepping around big dry wall buckets that—

With a groan, she stopped and weaved on her feet. The sense that memories were trying to break through some barrier in her brain dogged her, but she was used to this. The hot flash that heated her body from the inside out was likewise utterly familiar. What was new . . . was the despair that swamped her mood.

As she stepped out into the alley, and hesitated so she could double-check to make sure the police weren't rolling up on her, she was acutely aware that there was no one waiting at her apartment for her.

Nobody to call and connect to. Not a soul who she could unburden herself to.

She had a story to tell about the night, about the man in leather, about how she was feeling, but there was no real audience for it. Even if she put it on her blog under the guise—or maybe it was more like "clickbait"—of him being otherworldly, she was just shouting into a crowd that was mostly focused on themselves. And Bill was her only friend, but they weren't close/close, and besides, he was dealing with Lydia and the pregnancy they'd lost.

Jo's life was nothing but an echo chamber, hollow and dark.

And that reality was the companion that followed her home like a stalker.

CHAPTER FOURTEEN

I t was all so deliciously familiar.

As Mr. F crossed over the packed earth under the massive high-way bridge by the river, he took the first easy breath since he had come to on the concrete floor of that building behind the outlet mall, clothed in shit that wasn't his own, his body stiff and sore, especially inside his ass. He'd been confused and in bad shape, but he'd had too many other things to worry about over his health and well-being.

First and foremost being a compulsion to go out to that house in the 'burbs.

After which, he'd come to, standing in front of the thing.

None of that had made any sense, but this sure as shit did.

"Rickie," he murmured. "What up."

The man in rags sitting on the cardboard pallet waved a gnarled hand at him. "Where you been?"

"Nowhere."

When that was as far as it went, Mr. F was reminded of how much he liked the social rules here in Junkieland, as they called it. Nobody asked for more than you were willing to give. Part of it was respect.

More of it was that everyone under the bridge was in an abusive relationship with their addiction, and wrestling with that monkey on your back took your interest in other people's shit way down your list of things to do.

His eyes went over to where he had always crashed. The junkie who had taken over his sleeping bag and was currently lost to a nod was a guy he recognized. The man was also wearing Mr. F's parka, the rust-colored one with the broken zipper in front, and unless you really knew the difference between their faces, it would have been easy to mistake one of them for the other. Then again, they were brothers, though they came from different backgrounds. Interchangeable they were, their lack of proper nutrition, sleep, and healthcare stamping their features and body types with the mark of kinship. And if that guy died? Of untreated hep C or an overdose? There would be a replacement on that pallet of filthy nylon and fake feathers.

Forcing his brain to turn over, Mr. F tried to replay what had happened to him the previous night, how things had gone so wrong. He had a hazy memory of being approached by someone he didn't know. They'd seemed to be looking for him specifically, and he'd wondered if it wasn't his family finally catching up to him.

And then he'd woken up on that concrete floor in a daze, hours lost to God only knows what.

Walking across to his space, he had to duck down as the wedge of ground rose up to meet the underside of the highway.

The junkie in Mr. F's spot stirred and blinked a lot. "That you, Greg? I was just looking after your shit, you know."

"I'm going to need it back sometime. But you can stay put now."

"Okay. I'll keep it safe."

"Yeah." Mr. F looked around. "So you see Chops tonight?"

"He was here a hour ago. You looking to buy? I got some I can sell you. It's good shit."

Mr. F put his hand into the pocket of the coat he did not own. "I got fifty."

"I can only give you half of what I got 'cuz I'ma need some soon."

"It's cool."

As the man sat up, a whiff of body odor rose up to join the smell of urine and feces and earth. Dirty fingers rummaged through the pocket of Mr. F's own coat, and then a single Baggie the size of a sugar packet was produced.

Mr. F leaned down, aware of a curling anticipation in his gut and a buzzing in his head.

The man recoiled. "Dude. You stink."

Fuck you, Mr. F thought.

Their hands were quick, the transfer of cash and H fast as a blink, and with that, there was nothing else to be said. No thank-yous or goodbyes or see-you-laters. The junkie lay back down to enjoy what was left of his float on a sleeping bag that was not his own, and Mr. F walked off.

He'd gone about a hundred yards before he realized that he didn't have his gear. He needed a spoon, a lighter, and a couple of drops of liquid. Rage rose up at the impediment to his high, but he calmed himself down quick. With his new, super-sharp eyes, he located a used syringe and a bent-up spoon by a turned-over drum that functioned as a communal table. Then he found a discarded Bic by someone's grocery cart of clothes and personal effects. The last piece came together as he walked up on a bottle of Poland Spring that had an inch of mud-colored liquid in it.

The don't-give-a-shit about sanitation or sterilization was as familiar as the landscape of homelessness. He should have cared about the needle being dirty and what the hell was in the bottom of the plastic bottle. He should have cared about the purity of the drug. He should have cared about himself.

But he didn't. He was only focused on what was coming, the promise of sweet relief from the screaming fear and paranoia in his head all that mattered. Everything else that wasn't as-good-as, as-safe-as, as-smart-as, was collateral damage. Background noise. Negotiable to the point of being unimportant.

Even if those compromises were the shit that would bite him in the ass later.

As with all junkies, however, he borrowed against the future, going into an existential debt that didn't have a monthly payment obligation, but rather a balloon at the end of an unknown term that very few could meet. Which was why the repo's happened with such frequency, all those corpses piling up, the OD count growing ever higher as people entered the funnel with that first, tantalizing taste, and then got stuck in the trap, only realizing they couldn't get out when it was too late.

The doorstep Mr. F chose was a familiar one and it felt right to sit his ass down on its hard transom and stretch his legs out. He took a minute to enjoy the view—and by that, he wasn't even seeing the sleeping bags and the clusters of mumblers that were now a ways off. No, he was focused on the promise of no longer feeling anything bad.

His hands shook with excitement as he put the brown nub in the belly of the dirty spoon, poured a little soup on it, and flicked the Bic under the basin. The resulting swill was quick to its birth, but the syringe's draw wasn't smooth, the dried, caked-on grit inside its belly making the plunger fight its retraction. He nearly spilled everything.

But he prevailed over the obstacles.

When the needle was all set, he turned to the crook of his arm, and realized, as he saw that he hadn't taken his coat off first, that he was out of practice even though he'd done this just over twenty-four hours ago. Even though he'd done this hundreds and hundreds and hundreds of times in the last three years. Even though this wasn't rocket science.

The first rule of injection efficiency was that you got your sleeve rolled. You didn't load the needle and then have this kind of delay. But it was an easy fix. Ha-ha. He put the syringe between his teeth and shoved his sleeve up—except that didn't work. He had been scrawny before, his body mass eaten away by priorities that didn't include food. Now, though, he had muscles that he hadn't noticed and that meant shoving what covered his arm up wasn't as easy a move as it used to be.

Mr. F ripped the jacket off, popped a vein by pumping his fist a couple of times, and pushed the needle in.

The plunger went down fine, not that it would have mattered if he'd had to put all his newfound strength into it.

Mr. F exhaled in relief. Leaning his head back, he closed his eyes and opened his senses to what was going to come. He took a deep breath. And . . . another one.

Repositioning himself, shuffling back further against the door, he crossed his ankles. Uncrossed them. Recrossed them.

Anticipation curled in his chest and flushed his face. He couldn't wait for the rush and the float, the buzz . . .

When he opened his lids back up and righted his head, he looked around, his eyes bouncing over the bundles of human flesh that were off in the distance as well as the zombies that shuffled toward the bridge and away from it.

The fury that jumped him up to his feet was so explosive, he turned and punched the door he'd been leaning against, his fist penetrating the panel, breaking through as if the dirty stainless steel was skin. When he yanked his hand out of the hole he made, the ragged metal ripped open his own flesh.

The blood that welled and fell was black like oil and it glistened in the low light. As it dropped off his hand and landed on the dirt at his feet, it was not absorbed into the earth.

It sat there and seemed to stare back at him.

◆   ◆   ◆

Jo walked fast and kept her head down. She might have been raised in a WASPy household in Philly, but she was more than good with the New York self-protection code where you didn't meet people you didn't know in the eye, and thus made it clear that you were not interested in any trouble.

As she went along the street, she held her purse in front of herself and kept one hand in her windbreaker's pocket with her nine against her palm. She was very aware of how many blocks were between her and her car. Not a smart move, but then the last thing she'd thought was going to happen was her doing an after-dark 5k that took her so far away from the damn thing.

The sound of high-heeled shoes coming at her was a surprise, and it was for that reason only that she flipped her eyes forward for a split second.

Well. Her chance of survival just went way up. If anyone saw that package, and had to choose between hitting it over the head and Jo? Easy choice. The gorgeous brunette was wearing some kind of fancy outfit with a brilliant pink ruffle around her tiny waist and ropes of necklaces bouncing on her perfect breasts. Her legs were as long as a city street and shapely as sculpture, and there was nothing apologetic or deflecting about her stride. She strutted like the model she had to be, and to hell with the risks associated with being a 120-pound female out alone after dark.

Then again, maybe she was hiding a whole lot of metal under that skirt—and not of the chastity belt variety, but the point-and-shoot kind.

As they closed in on each other, Jo risked a second glance, and decided that the strut was less model-like and more like ready-to-cut-a-bitch pissed.

Jo dropped her stare as they passed, but she couldn't stop herself from looking over her shoulder.

Yup, the back was as good as the front, that long, mahogany-colored hair so thick, so bouncy, so healthy, it had to be a raft of extensions. Surely no one could have all those physical attributes going for them.

Shaking her head, Jo checked the street sign as she crossed another intersection and then cut over toward where she'd left her VW Golf. The wind came at her now, and it was hard to say exactly when the scent registered. But even with the goal of getting safely to her junker, her feet slowed . . . and stopped.

Copper. She was tasting copper in the back of her throat.

There was only one thing that did that, and there had to be a lot of it for the smell to be concentrated in this kind of stiff breeze.

Narrowing her eyes, she tried to see what was up ahead while she went for her cell phone. Looking behind herself, she couldn't see the woman anymore, and there was no one else around.

Maybe she was wrong. Maybe this was . . .

Even though her instincts were screaming at her to come back when the sun was up, she walked forward, the smell of blood getting thicker until she felt like she wasn't so much breathing it in as drinking it. And then she caught sight of her car, about a hundred yards away—

The dripping stopped her.

Between each of her footfalls, she became aware of a soft *plunk, plunk, plunk.*

Don't look, a small voice inside her said. *Don't . . . look*—

Up on the first landing of a fire escape, there was a tangled knot the size of an armchair, and her first thought was *Why the hell would someone put a piece of furniture up there?*

And then she saw the origin of the dripping sound.

There was a steady stream of something dropping from the knot, and as she went over to the fire escape, light from an exterior fixture some distance away lined up with what was falling to the asphalt.

The stuff was red and translucent.

Stumbling back, Jo covered her mouth with her palm, but then she needed to throw out her arms for balance as her foot knocked into a soccer ball—

Not a soccer ball.

What rolled off to the side was a human head.

As it came to rest, the facial features were angled toward her. The eyes were open and staring sightlessly upward, the mouth lax as if the man had been screaming as he had been decapitated.

Jo's vision went checkerboard and her legs went loose, but she had the presence of mind to dial 911. When the operator answered, the words did not come. She was breathing hard, yet there was no air in her lungs, nothing to send the syllables up her throat and out her mouth.

She focused on her car, and the proximity terrified her. In the back of her mind, she heard Gigante threaten her life.

Run! she thought. Except she was now a witness to some kind of a crime—because there was no way this was a suicide or an accident.

"My name is J-j-jo Early," she said hoarsely. "I'm at the c-c-corner of Eighteenth and Kennedy and I need to report . . . a murder, a killing . . . he's dead. Oh, God, his head . . . is not on his body anymore . . ."

CHAPTER FIFTEEN

B y eight the next morning, Syn was a caged animal as he paced around his empty bedroom. He was not animated by food that he had consumed nor blood that he had swallowed. He was not well rested, either.

The sense that he was needed by that female and could not respond, that he was powerless in the face of the sun's dominance, that he was not strong, but weak, gave him an energy that shook his hands and rattled his teeth. And as a result of the physical quaking, things under his conscious surface, things he had refused to let air for so many years, were threatening to break through.

He fought them back as best he could, but he lost the battle thanks to the bathroom mirror. It was there, standing naked before the sinks, that he bared his fangs—as if to prove to himself he still had them—and it happened.

The present disappeared and the past took him over, a storm unleashed . . .

Old Country, 1687

When Syn lifted his head, blood spooled out of his mouth, falling to the dirt floor of the hut. There was a ringing sound in his ears, surging and retreating by turns, and he thought of the sea that did the same at the base of the cliffs nearby. How long had he been without consciousness this time?

The inside of his nose was stuffed up so he swallowed to be better able to breathe through his lips. As his tongue brushed against where his front teeth should have been, there was a ragged gap, the two—no, four—empty sockets tender and tickly.

He went to try to stand up to see if aught was broken of his arms and legs, but he knew better.

With caution, he looked across to the only bedding pallet. Beneath a carpet's worth of blankets, the great beast slept, the mound of flesh and muscle rising and falling, a gurgle marking the inhales. Even in repose, it had its priorities. A meaty hand protruded out of the woolen layers, the dirt- and blood-caked fingers resting protectively upon the open throat of a bladder of mead.

The snoring was the signal Syn could move, and as he pushed his torso up, he was sore in his shoulders and his ribs. The hut was never clean, never tidy, but after he had been beaten with a copper pot and thrown about like a bolt of cloth, there was more disorder than ever. The only thing that had not been disturbed was the mummified remains of his mahmen, the body, wrapped in its rags, as yet where it had been for the last ten years.

Gingerly setting his seat upon the packed floor, he made sure that the aches and pains were not from serious injury. Verily, his father seemed to know how far he could push the battering. No matter how drunk he was, he did not take the beatings unto death's door. He stopped a hairsbreadth before the point of ne'er return.

The empty belly cradled between Syn's pelvis became something he could not ignore, and not because his hunger was of sufficient urgency. He had been so long starved that the hollow feeling was a natural extension of his body, nothing of note. But the growling sounds it made were dangerous.

He did not want to rouse his sire, although it was hard to know what was worse—when the male was disturbed from his addled state and still of drunken mind, or when he awoke furious at the recession of the mead's soporific properties.

As Syn attempted to stand, his legs wobbled, thin and unreliable beneath his slight frame, and he balanced himself only when he threw out his arms. His father's pallet was set directly afore the heavy skin flap that covered the doorway to the outside, and given that Syn was a pretrans, he could not close his eyes and carry himself off upon the air. He must needed to ambulate about in a corporeal fashion.

Placing his palms upon his stomach, he pressed in whilst he held his breath. On the balls of his feet, he chose his path with care, disturbing naught, and he orientated his safety upon the bladder of mead and the fingertips resting upon it. His sire suffered from an unrelenting unsteadiness of extremity. If he were to awaken, his fingers would tell the tale through movement—

As Syn focused on the back of that hand, he saw something odd in the blood-caked flesh. There was a flash of brilliant white, and he thought that perhaps the strikes of the night—or the day, he knew not which—had been so hard, his sire had broken through the flesh of his knuckles, down to the bone.

But no.

That was not what it was.

Touching the heartbeat behind his upper lip, something stirred deep within Syn's breast. He had no name upon which he could label the emotion, and there was, like so much in his life, nothing he could do to control the feeling.

It was, however, strong enough, insistent enough, that he committed the unthinkable. He approached the beast. Crouched down beside the pallet. Reached out with a hand no steadier than his sire's.

Whereupon he removed a tiny fragment from the flesh of his father.

A tooth.

His own tooth.

As he held the piece of bone with care, as if he were cradling his broken body, he looked over to the remains of his mahmen. He missed her, but he was grateful she suffered no further. Indeed, her remains had not been kept within this horrid hut as a remembrance of love. They were a warning of what came when one did not obey.

Syn put his tooth into the pocket of his ribboned pants, and he glanced around at the floor. He should like to retrieve the other three. Perhaps he would—

"Where'd you think you go the now, young."

Syn jumped back and began trembling. Ducking, he put his arms up and around his face. The response was ingrained. Trained. Second nature.

"I must needs go to get victuals," he whispered. "I go to get food."

There was a grunt from the pallet and his sire lifted his head. His beard was long and gnarled, a rope of coarse dark hair that was indistinguishable from the tangle that grew out from all sides of his skull. Glittering black eyes beneath fleshy brows glared.

"You get them and come back, young. Waste not time. I am hungry."

"Yes, sire."

His father looked down at the hand that was over the mead. A rivulet of blood, fresh and red, had welled and descended unto his forefinger, released by the tooth's removal.

"I shall go the now," Syn rushed in. "I shall beg fervently. I shall—"

Those eyes came back and narrowed. Hatred, like a swill upon the surface of a pond, came to the fore.

"I go now," Syn said.

With a quick shuffle, he skirted around the pallet, but he had to slow at the heavy tarping. As a pretrans, he could survive the sunlight. His sire could not. The hut was backed in against the wall of a cave, its entry point well protected from direct light. But if he did not follow the way things were properly done upon departure, he would be put in the cage and submerged in the river's current.

He would rather be beaten.

"You come back, young." His father's gravel voice was like the curse of the Omega, sly and invasive, with the promise of suffering. "Or I shall become bored and be forced to find something to do. If I haven't already."

Syn nodded and fell free of the hut, his stumble running him into the cave's outcropping of damp stone.

If he hadn't already? *Syn thought.* What had the male done?

Bolting out of the cave, in spite of the soreness in his legs and his torso, he threw himself into the night with all the alacrity he could summon. The moon overhead was low to the horizon and its position terrified him. How long had he been without consciousness? How long had his father been free to roam about the village and environs?

Fates, what had he done?

Fear parched Syn's mouth, and the thirst took him unto the stream where he fell down onto his scabbed knees and put his face into the cold rush. The sting was nearly unbearable, but as he drank, his head cleared. When he righted himself, he wiped his eyes on his torn and bloodied sleeves. The night was cold, but for him, it seemed everything was always of lower temperature than he.

Upon the wind, carried from the south, smoke from a fire wafted unto him. Not just one fire. Several. The village was alive with bustling commerce, trade and service performed and provided during the dark hours before the sunlight brought a halt to it all.

The promise made unto his father called him in the direction of the other vampires. None would e'er take him in for fear of what his sire would do, but there were good souls who took pity upon Syn, recognizing the curses of his existence, remembering what had been done unto his mahmen—and knowing full well what would happen if Syn, weak as he was, did not feed the beast who lurked in that cave, in that hut.

Yet Syn did not go unto the village center. He would, later. As soon as he could.

Instead, he set out upon the forest, crossing o'er fallen trunk and low-level brush, moving like a deer, in silence. He traveled far and tired readily, but he kept going.

None too soon he came unto a clearing, and he was of care to seek shelter behind a thick tree. It would do no good for anyone to know of his proximity, and he wouldnae have come if he could have prevented it.

Across the wildflowers that grew with graceful, unabashed glory, the thatched cottage was modest, yet lovely, and he told himself to trust the lack of commotion. Nothing appeared to be on fire outside of the hearth. There was no bloodshed that he could see or scent. There was—

The wooden door opened wide and the sound of giggling rose like the singing of spring birds, and as with finches flushed from a perch, two figures scampered out. One was short and stocky, the little male running as fast as he could, a pink ribbon streaming behind him. The other was a taller female just out of her transition, her blond hair flying as a flag as she chased after her brother and the prize he had claimed. Together, they ran down to the vegetable garden that had been cultivated in the meadow, and then to the paddock wherein two healthy milking cows were penned.

Syn's shoulders eased and he found he could breathe. As long as the female and her family were safe, that was all that he cared about. She was always so kind to him in the village, and fearless in her regard of him. Indeed, she seemed to notice not his rags and the way he smelled. She saw only his hunger and his suffering, and her eyes did not duck away from that as the stares of so many others, far older than her, did. Nor was she content to merely pity him. She snuck him clothes which, given the scent upon the cloth, she had made for him. He was the now wearing pants she had fashioned from a hearty, thick cloth, and his only coat, the one that kept him warm, but that he had left behind in his haste, had been a coverlet that she created for him.

She was the moonlight in his night sky, and often, the only thing that gave him any ease. Just the sight of her, whether with her basket of weaving wares or as she minded her brother, was enough to give him the strength to carry on.

As the female and her brother rounded by the barn, Syn was content to watch and spin fantasies that wouldnae e'er occur. Verily, he imagined he was the one being chased by her, and he would be sure to allow himself to be caught. In his mind, he went forth into the future, after his own transi-

tion. He saw himself tall and strong, capable of defending her and keeping her safe, his brawn the guarantee against this cruel world that naught would hurt her—

The snap of a stick made him jump.

"Whate'er you do here, son of mine," came a growl behind him.

◆   ◆   ◆

The sound of knocking returned Syn to the present, although the reorientation was neither immediate nor dispositive. Part of him was back in those trees, at the edge of that flowered meadow, and he was grateful for whoever had interrupted his memory-lane'ing. He resented the revisit of his history. There were so many reasons not to dwell on any part of his past, but especially that particular night. Maybe if things had gone differently back then, he would be different now.

Then again, maybe he'd been cursed at birth, everything that happened then and since, predetermined and inevitable.

"I'm coming," he muttered as the knocking started up again and he got over his intermission gratitude.

Whoever was on the other side better have a good fucking reason to disturb all his totally-not-sleeping.

He was even less interested in other people than usual today.

CHAPTER SIXTEEN

Butch finished off the last inch of Lagavulin in his glass, and just as he righted his head from the toss back, the door he was rapping on ripped opened. On the far side, Syn was obviously not a morning person, his glare right out of the Hulk's playbook, his big-ass naked body the kind of thing that could do serious damage to anyone with an alarm clock. Cheerful greeting. Piece of toast.

The Bastard had a case of the cranky-wankies.

"Well, well, well," Butch said. "If it isn't sunshine personified."

"What do you want?"

"Right now? Ray-Bans to shield me from the glare of your happiness."

Balthazar stepped up, putting his solid wall of a body between the two of them. "Let's relax, cousin."

Leaving the blood relations to sort out the welcome wagon issues, Butch barged his way into the completely bare set of rooms. Syn lived like a monk, which was his call, but come on. Like you wouldn't take advantage of a pillow top mattress when they were available to you? But no, we gotta be Old Country hard-ass on the floor.

"So," he said as he strolled around, the remaining pain in his groin from his case of Chrysler-itis something that was briefly eclipsed by the job he'd come to do. "You wanna put some pants on or are you okay airing your junk out like that?"

Balthazar was the one who closed the three of them in together, and the Bastard stayed right by the door, as if he knew there was a chance his cousin could vote with his feet.

Syn put his hands on his hips. "Do I make you uncomfortable?"

Butch laughed. "You have no idea what my roommate's into. So no, I'm good. But you, my friend, are causing some problems for yourself. And not just in a draft-on-your-shaft kinda way."

"How so."

"I think you know." Butch took the hard copy of the *Caldwell Courier Journal* out from under his arm. "You read the paper this morning?"

"Cover to cover. And did the crossword."

"Did you." Butch looked for a place to put his glass down and ended up setting it on the floor. Then he flipped the front page open and faced it toward the guy. "Curious, did you think something like this wouldn't get noticed?"

Syn's eyes didn't dip down to the black-and-white crime scene photograph that took up most of the top half of the fold. And given that the Bastard didn't have a computer, and wasn't on Fritz's paper-boy delivery list, it was impossible to believe he'd read anything—and to hell with the crossword bullshit.

"No comment?" Butch murmured as he jogged the pages. "'Cuz I'm afraid that's not going to be good enough."

Syn's shrug was not a surprise. Neither was his dead calm affect or the hostile light in his eyes. The Bastard was like a torch of aggression as he stood there, all banked natural disaster—and for a split second, Butch kind of wanted the guy to do something spectacularly stupid. A good fistfight might actually burn off some of his own nervous energy.

"See, this is interesting to me." Butch refolded the paper and put it back under his arm. "I thought you'd want to take credit for your work.

Otherwise, why leave the body out in the open like that? And hey, considering you managed to skin this guy alive on the street, that is impressive. I mean, complications aside, it's nice work with a dagger. Like shucking corn, was it? Or ripping the slipcover off a couch."

"You're not judge and jury for me."

"Oh, you're wrong about that." Butch shook his head. "So what do you have to say for yourself."

"Nothing."

"Again, not really an option."

Balthazar cursed softly. "Syn, you and I talked about this. This is the New World—"

"I know where I am. I don't need you to give me a bloody geography lesson."

"So, I'll do the teaching." Butch stepped forward, getting tight with the guy. "You're going to get deported back to where you came from if you keep this up."

"I didn't skin that man."

"You don't have any credibility."

"So why are you here. Why bother talking to me at all?"

"Because I need things to be clear between you and me. Consider it a professional courtesy between soldiers."

"Last thing I heard, Wrath was in charge. Why isn't he here?"

"First of all, you're not that special. And second, I'm the dumb fuck who's in charge of dead bodies. Granted, it's less of an official position and more of a calling leftover from my days as a homicide cop—but I think we can all agree that the last thing anyone needs to worry about is what you're doing with a knife on your off-hours as we come down to the end of the war. We want the humans to chill and stay out of our business. So you've got to go if you can't curb this shit."

Syn finally looked at his cousin, his Mohawk turning to the side.

Balthazar spoke up. "Come on, Syn. You know this has been a problem. You've got to channel your *talhman* somewhere else. Or at least not do it so publicly."

"And what about the other one?" Butch said. "The corpse they found twisted around that fire escape early this morning."

"Fine." Syn shrugged again. "I killed him. I killed the other one. I killed everybody."

Butch ground his molars. "See, why you gotta do me like this? You could just be honest."

"I am. You got me dead to rights. I skinned the one and then I beat the other senseless on a fire escape—because I was bored."

Narrowing his eyes, Butch kept his voice level. "Guess you were really bored, cutting those legs off."

"Both of them. Can we be done here?"

Butch glanced around the room. There were holes in the wallpaper where picture hangers had been taken out of the plaster, and he imagined the fact that things hadn't been properly retouched drove Fritz insane.

He kept his curses to himself. "I'm trying to help you, Syn. You can choose to make this easier on yourself by cutting this out as of today. Right now? This is just me running it up the flagpole. If Wrath gets involved, there's no wiggle room left for you. He's going to get rid of you and you'll be lucky if it's only packing you off on a fucking boat. He won't hesitate to put you in a coffin."

"You're assuming that would be a loss to me."

"We do *not* need this complication. Don't be something we have to solve."

"Duly noted."

Butch gave the guy a chance to say something else. "You're not doing yourself any favors here."

Syn pegged his cousin with hard eyes. "And everybody can stop talking about me anytime they're fucking ready. *Anytime.*"

Balthazar crossed his arms over his chest. "The way you are is not your fault. But you need help—"

"Don't tell me what I need."

Now Butch was the one putting his body in between two males.

"My guy, I don't get the games you're playing here, and considering the shit that's on my plate right now, I really don't have time to fuck around with you. Stay in your lane, or I'm going to make it so Wrath puts you back on your side of the highway. I'm really trying to be decent to you—although I'm wondering why in the fuck I bothered."

On that note, Butch limped out, and when Balthazar came with him, he was surprised. He expected a heart-to-heart to happen between the cousins, but clearly that wasn't on the menu. Then again, as the door clapped shut, there was the sound of glass shattering against the inside panels.

"Guess I won't have to go back and get my empty," Butch muttered as he headed down the hallway of the new wing that had been opened.

"You hurt your ankle?" Balthazar said.

"Wish it was that. You remember those protective bras people used to put on cars? Like, back in the late eighties?"

"Not with any great particularity, no."

"Well, then you lucked out. But tonight, I saw fit to actually make a front grille need one. With my nuts."

The Bastard was still making wincing noises of consolation as they entered the second-story sitting room. There was a bar cart off to one side, and Butch went right over to the liquor. No Lag in the truncated lineup of bottles, but he was thought up enough to settle for bourbon. After he poured himself some I.W. Harper over ice, he motioned the diamond-cut bottle toward the other male.

"Thanks, but no," the thief said. "Your roommate's given me a new habit, so I'm good with that."

As Balthazar lit up one of V's hand-rolls, Butch faced off at the Bastard. "I don't get it. You're all in my ear about what Syn's capable of, and I have no reason to doubt you. But Boone told me what happened a couple of months ago. Syn copped to attacking that human who was castrated, but Boone was the one who did it. Why's your cousin saying he killed people he hasn't?"

"I don't think he's lying now." Balthazar exhaled a stream of smoke in frustration. "And Boone thing aside, Syn's never had to lie before because the bloody knife was always in his dagger hand."

"Look, I don't mean to call you out." Butch swallowed half his bourbon. "But you brought this to my attention, and I appreciate the open lines of communication, blah, blah, blah. I just don't want to keep accusing this guy of shit he didn't do. It's not helping."

"He admitted what he did, though."

"He just told me he cut the legs off of a guy whose pins were still very much attached when he was taken to the morgue. It was the head that had been liberated. So he's lying."

Balthazar frowned. "That doesn't make any sense."

There was a pause as Butch finished what he'd poured. And went for a refresh. "I need you to be honest with me."

"Always."

"Do you have something against the guy? Are you trying to screw him or something? 'Cuz from where I'm looking at things, it seems like you're trying to set him up."

◆   ◆   ◆

Two and a half minutes after Jo came into work, her fingers were flying across her keyboard at her desk in the empty newsroom, her eyes locked on her computer screen, the edits to the article update being made so fast, she prayed that they made sense. When her cell phone went off, she answered it curtly with just her last name and tucked the thing into her shoulder so she could keep going.

In the back of her mind, as she listened to McCordle's latest intel, she realized she was actually a reporter. And that felt good.

"Right. Yup. I got it. Thanks."

She ended the call and kept on typing—

"What the *hell* are you doing."

As she looked up, Dick threw the current copy of the *CCJ* down on her keyboard. Jabbing his forefinger at the front page, at the article Jo had researched, written, proofed, and typeset, along with the picture she had chosen, blocked, and set into the columns, he barked, "I thought I made myself clear. And where the hell is Bill."

"Lydia lost the baby last night," Jo said. "So he's taking a personal day."

Dick paused. But only for a split second. "Then I want Tony on this. And I'll take care of that personally."

As he lumbered off to his office and slammed the door, she had the image of a kid kicking apart their brother's Lego set.

Jo looked at her screen. Spell-checked what was on it. And put that shit on the Internet.

Under her sole byline.

Then she got up from her chair and walked into Dick's office without knocking. He was looming over his desk, dialing a landline, going back and forth between an old fashioned Rolodex listing and the keypad on the phone.

When he didn't send a glare her way, she couldn't tell whether he was ignoring her or if he was just focused on trying to get the numbers right without his reading glasses.

He looked up sharply when she cut the call by depressing the receiver's home button and holding it down.

Before he could start yelling again, she said calmly, "You're going to let me continue to report on Johnny Pappalardo and also the dead body found nine hours ago on that fire escape."

The ugly flush that rode up Dick's thick neck suggested that getting pissed off at her was the only exercise he'd had for the month.

"Don't tell me what you're going to do—"

Jo leaned in and lowered her voice. "It turns out I'm a helluva reporter. You know what my next story is going to be on? Sexual harassment at the CCJ by its editor-in-chief. How many women do you think will take my call on that? I figure I'll start off by telling them my own story, the one about that business trip you asked me to take with you?

That long weekend away—where you made it clear that if I didn't go, I wasn't going anywhere at this paper? How many other women who used to work here have a similar story, Dick?"

Her boss slowly shut his mouth.

Jo released the button on the phone, the dial tone loud in the silence between them. "Thinking of what kind of quote you're going to give me? Make sure it's a good one, one that your wife'll understand. Her family owns this paper now, right? Plus, I'll bet the story'll have national reach, and you'll need another job after she kicks you out of the house and you get fired here. So you better try to put yourself in a favorable light in twenty-five words or less."

She gave him an opportunity to respond. When he put the receiver back in its cradle, she nodded.

"That's what I thought," Jo said as turned on her heel and left his office.

CHAPTER SEVENTEEN

Butch entered the Pit from the underground tunnel that connected the mansion site to the training center. As he opened the steel-reinforced door with a code, he kept quiet. V and Doc Jane were doing some work down at the clinic, so they weren't home, but Marissa had come back to read in bed right after Last Meal, and he didn't want to disturb her. Her work at Safe Place was demanding, and if she were sleeping, he wanted her to log those hours of rest.

The domestic abuse center that his *shellan* ran was the first of its kind for the species, and not unlike her brother, Marissa had a strong service side to her nature. She was driven to help other people, but it also turned out she was a terrific businesswoman. She coordinated everything at the facility, from the females and their young, to the treatment plans by the social workers, and also the budgets, the supplies, the food, the clothing. She was amazing at her job, but leading a compassionate cleanup crew for vulnerables who had been beaten, abused, neglected, and worse, was exhausting.

It was hard stuff to take, night after night.

Of course, her commitment to her work just made him love her more. Except he also worried about her when she looked as tired as she had been lately.

Closing himself in, he glanced at the racks of clothes that choked the hallway leading down to the pair of bedrooms. It was time to start putting his winter stuff into storage, and liberating his spring collection. Usually, he would be psyched for this annual ritual, and so would Fritz, but it was going to be a one-sided party on the butler's part this year.

Butch was too distracted with the prophecy shit.

Walking out to the common area, he took off his jacket and laid it on the arm of the leather sofa. The cottage where he and V, and their mates, lived was the pebble to the mansion's bolder, done in the same architectural style, but filling out a fraction of the square footage. It was also not decorated the same. The big house was like Tsarist Russia meeting Napoleonic France with a flash of Hogwarts. Butch and V's crib? Try frat house crossed with bachelor pad: They had this couch, a foosball table, a TV the size of a soccer field, and V's Four Toys, a.k.a. his computer setup. But at least here had been some refinements since their *shellans* had moved in. Courtesy of Marissa and Jane, gym bags were no longer coughing up jock straps and running shoes like they were choking from the smell, the issues of *Sports Illustrated* were in a tidy stack on the coffee table, and the half-eaten bags of Doritos and sour-cream-and-onion Ruffles were kept to a minimum. There were also no more Goose and Lag bottles laying on the floor like they were the ones passing out or ashtrays full of hand-rolled dead bodies or, even more to the point, BDSM shit that sometimes Butch hadn't been sure was for the B, the D, the S, or the M.

In the galley kitchen, he threw out what was left of the bourbon in the sink and rinsed his glass out. Drying the inside with a paper towel, he poured himself three inches of Lag, and as he took a drink, he sloshed the hot stuff around his mouth to wash the taste of the Harper's away. I.W.'s efforts at alcohol were an acceptable substitute. But when you wanted Sprite and you got seltzer, the disappointment inevitably soured your palate.

Glancing at the bottle of Lagavulin, he was surprised to find it was three-quarters of the way empty. He'd only opened it the day before and no one else drank the shit.

"You're back."

Butch was already looking up as Marissa spoke, his bonded male called to attention by her presence—and oh, what a presence it was. His mate was dressed in a silk nightgown that brushed the tops of her pretty bare feet, the color a blush pink that looked like it had been created especially for her and a select few tea roses. Her blond hair, which she had cut shoulder length a while ago, was growing out, at his urging, and the thick locks curled into spirals that were now down past her collarbones in front and her shoulder bones in back.

He took a moment to study her face. Word had always had it that hers was the greatest beauty in the species, and he knew this to be fact, not rumor. Ever since the first moment he had seen her at Darius's old place—back when he'd been a human and had no idea what he was getting himself into—she had struck him stupid. Except for him, it was not her looks that created such a compelling, compulsive attraction. It was the soul behind the lovely eyes, the voice that came out of those perfect lips, the heartbeat behind the curves.

Her soul was what really did it for him.

"Are you okay?" she said as she came forward. "What's wrong?"

The silk nightgown flowed behind her with the grace of contrails in the sky, and he was reminded, not for the first time, that he wished he brought better things to her life. He had a brutal job with little good news and much bloodshed, and then there was his side gig as the Omega's buck-stops-here.

"Same ol', same ol'." They kissed as he held her close. "You know."

"Not with the way you're hitting that scotch."

"You're too good at reading my tells."

"It's not that hard."

On that note, he finished the Lag in his glass and had to force himself not to pour another. Man, he wanted to manage his emotions better. Going the yoga and meditation route seemed so much more virtuous, and then there was his alkie history to worry about. But somehow, the booze was where it was at.

"Come here," he said, taking his *shellan*'s hand.

As he drew her over to the sofa, she asked, "Your limp is still pronounced. What happened? You didn't tell me at Last Meal."

"It's not important."

"Should you see Doc Jane?"

Sitting down, he grunted—then winced and tried to rearrange himself in his slacks, although he didn't think any particular position was going to help his nads. He felt like they were swollen ten times their normal size, and nightmare scenarios of them exploding in his boxer shorts like overinflated balloons made him look at the bottle of Lag he'd left on the counter.

"It's fine." He turned and tucked her hair behind her ear. "But you're right, I feel like we didn't get to catch up properly during dinner."

He didn't like the way she stared at him, like she had lifted his a okay curtain and was seeing the hot mess of garbage he was hiding.

"You haven't been sleeping and your eyes aren't focusing on anything."

"Untrue." He smiled a little. "I couldn't take them off you as you came in here and I don't want to look anywhere else right now."

"You can tell me anything, you know that."

"I do."

Marissa shook her head like he was frustrating her. "So how about we start with how you got hurt."

"I ran into a car." Butch let his head fall back against the cushions. When he'd been talking about "catching up," it had been more about what her night had been like. "No big deal."

"What if your leg is broken?"

"It wasn't my leg."

"Where did you get hit then?"

He tilted his head toward her. "Little Butchie took it like a man."

Marissa's eyebrows went up. "Oh, my God. I'm so sorry . . . I, ah, exactly how did it happen? Did you run into the hood ornament?"

"I became the hood ornament. I turned a Chrysler LeBaron into a LeBrian."

"That's horrible!"

"I stopped—" He was going to say "pissing." "—peeing blood about four hours ago."

"You need to go to the clinic, right now—"

Butch caught her hand as she went to stand up. "I'm just fine, now that I'm with you."

Crossing her arms, she set a level stare on him, like she was taking his vitals with her eyes. "I overheard V telling Jane that he needed to cleanse you tonight. That's three times in the last week."

Annnnnnnd Butch went back to staring at the counter again, like the scotch was his best friend. "Was it that much? I don't think it was—"

"Yes. Three times."

Closing his eyes briefly, he said, "Please don't take this the wrong way, but I can't talk about work right now. I just can't. There are eleven hours between this moment and when I have to leave to go out into the field again. I need to spend this precious time thinking about something, anything, else than the war."

Assuming that was even possible.

After a moment, Marissa resettled beside him and tucked her feet under herself. Leaning into his chest, she tugged his heavy gold cross out of his shirt.

"I love how this gets warm when it lays on your skin," she murmured. "It makes me feel that you're protected."

"I am. God is always with me."

"Good." As her eyes became teary, she blinked fast. "I know you don't want to talk about this . . . but I love you and I don't want to live my life without you. You're everything to me. If something were to happen—"

"Shh." He covered her hand with his own, so that they were both holding the symbol of his faith. Then he leaned in and kissed her mouth. "Don't think like that. Don't talk like that. I'll be fine."

"Promise me that you'll . . ." She looked deeply into his eyes, as if she could pull something out of him by will alone. ". . . be careful."

He had a feeling that she wanted to make him vow to get through the *Dhestroyer* Prophecy alive. But the sadness in her face told him she was confronting the fact that that was not his call. Being careful with himself? That was within his control to some degree. Being upright in his boots at the end? Way above his pay grade.

She cleared her throat. "Do you remember when they found you, after the Omega got ahold of you and did . . . what he did to you?"

"Let's not talk about—"

"They brought you to my brother's clinic, the one he had before the raids." She carefully tucked the cross back inside his shirt, as if she wanted it closer to his heart, closer to his soul. "I remember when V told me where they were keeping you. I ran to that isolation room. I was relieved you were alive, but horrified by the condition you were in—and you didn't want me in there with you."

"Only because I couldn't have you infected with the evil. And that's still true to this day."

"I know." Marissa took a deep breath. "The thing is, I've been through a lot in my life. All those centuries as Wrath's unclaimed *shellan*. The trip across the ocean from the Old Country when I didn't think we were going to make the crossing alive. Being judged by the *glymera*, by my brother, by the Council. Things only got better when I met you. You made me feel alive . . . you were such a revelation. And then I almost lost you."

"Don't go back there—"

"That's my point. I don't want to ever mourn you again."

"You aren't going to have to."

In a small voice, she spoke the very thing that worried him most. "The prophecy only provides that you eradicate the Omega. It doesn't say anything about what survives."

Butch stared somberly at his mate. "With everything I am, and all that I will ever be, I swear, I will come back to you."

Eventually, she nodded. And she was looking at where the cross hung under his shirt when she did.

"Let me hold you," he murmured as he drew her against his chest.

Making circles with his palm across her back, he felt his love for his female take on a new dimension ... but not for a happy reason. The sense that their time together could be cut short deepened his emotions to a painful degree, and in the overwhelming quiet of their home, he felt true fear. It was as if their separation was in the wind, a leaf falling through the air. Whether it landed on his grave or not, no one knew.

"I just have this bad feeling," she said against his pec.

Butch kept his mouth shut on that one, closing his eyes and running through some Hail Marys in his head. It was the only thing he could think to do, and that reality made him feel his vulnerability more than anything else. His faith was strong. His love for Marissa was even stronger. His control over destiny? Big nope on that one.

After a moment, she stirred against him, her lips pressing into the front of his shirt at his sternum. Then she released a button and kissed a little further down, on his diaphragm. Then ... she shifted her body between his legs, sliding off the sofa so she was kneeling in front of him. As her hands traveled up his thighs, he felt things stir in a place he'd been a little worried about ever working right again.

A rumble rose up his throat. And he repeated the sound as her hands went to the Hermès belt he wore.

"I'm sorry you were hurt," she murmured as she undid the supple leather strap. And started working on the button of his fly. And the zipper.

Butch's pelvis rolled and he braced his arms, his hands sinking into the soft cushions. "I'm not *that* hurt."

Marissa eyed the enormous erection that begged for any morsel of her attention. "So I see. But how about I kiss it to make it feel better anyway?"

"Fuck ... yes, please ..." he breathed.

✦   ✦   ✦

The St. Francis Hospital System's Urgent Care facility was only about ten blocks from the medical center's campus, eight blocks from the CCJ's newsroom. So it was a toss-up. Given how tired Jo was, she couldn't decide whether she should walk or drive, but the day was sunny and warm for March. Under the theory that scurvy was a possibility after the long winter in upstate New York, she decided to hoof it. Unfortunately, she forgot her sunglasses in her car, and halfway between her office and the doc-in-a-box, she came to a decision tree. Did she go back and get them? Or soldier on?

You're going to die.

That mysterious man in leather's bald statement, spoken in his deep, accented voice, spurred her on in spite of the way the sunlight stung her eyes—sure as if her mortal hourglass was running out of sand, and she needed to go faster to make it to medical help before she went into multi-organ failure.

Not that she was catastrophizing at all.

Nah.

Wincing up at the sky, she cursed and put her hand up to her aching forehead. Screw her liver, kidneys, heart, and lungs giving out. She was liable to have her head explode, parts of her gray matter becoming airborne shrapnel as the tumor she was clearly growing under her skull like a fat August tomato spontaneously quadrupled in size.

By the time she pulled open the glass door to the clinic, and stepped inside its Lysol-scented air, she was nauseous, a little dizzy, and a whole lot convinced it was cancer. Of course, the fact that she hadn't slept since the night before, and she'd seen her first decapitated corpse, and she was sad for Bill and Lydia, was likely not helping her hypothetical CNS non-Hodgkin's lymphoma.

Thank you for that differential diagnosis, WebMD.

Offering a wan smile to a receptionist who seemed absolutely uninterested in receiving anyone, Jo wrote her name on the lined sheet that read "Sign In Here" and then gratefully sank into a plastic chair directly under the TV. There were two other people stationed at quarantine-like quadrants around the waiting area, as if no one was sure who had what communicable disease, and therefore, nobody was taking any chances catching something they didn't already have.

She closed her eyes and breathed through her nose. When that did nothing to quell the rolling swells atop the bilious green sea in her stomach, she tried cracking her lips and redirecting her inhales and exhales through that route.

"Ms. Early?" the receptionist said some time later.

After checking in with her driver's license and her insurance card, it was back to waiting, and then she was finally in a room. The male nurse who took her weight, her vitals, and her temperature seemed nice enough, and she prayed she didn't throw up on him.

"So," he said as he entered her blood pressure into her electronic chart, "tell me a little about what's been going on."

"Is my blood pressure, okay?"

"It's on the low side. But your oxygen stats are great and your pulse is fine. You're running a low-grade fever, though."

"So I'm sick."

He stopped typing into the computer and faced her. He was probably thirty, and he had a good haircut, a precisely trimmed beard, and eyes that were not anywhere near as tired as she felt.

"What have your symptoms been?" he asked.

"I've been feeling sick. Fatigued. Headachy."

"Hmm . . ." He went back to typing. "There's a lot of that going around. Flu season is heartier than usual this year, it seems. So how long has this been going on?"

"Three months. Maybe four."

He stopped again and looked over at her with a frown. "Since November, then?"

"I mean, I'm sure I'm fine." Which, of course, was exactly why she was sitting in this exam room, telling herself not to barf on the guy's white uniform. She was just GREAT. "Really."

"Okay." He typed some more. "Anything else?"

"I haven't been losing weight, though. Kind of a bummer, really."

"So you've always been . . ." He scrolled up and read a number.

"That's what I weigh now?" When he looked at her again, she waved her hand like she could erase the question. "I mean, it's fine. I've lost a little weight, but it's no big deal."

"How much did you lose?"

"Ten pounds. Fifteen at the most. I'm tall, though."

Okay, for all the sense she'd made while drafting the online article on that decapitated body on the fire escape, she had now apparently lost her ability to think. Because she was making no damned sense.

Unless she'd also made no sense with the article and just hadn't known it.

"I'm sorry, but I think I've wasted your time." She made like she was going to slide off the examination table. "I'm fine—"

The nurse put his hand out like a crossing guard's stop sign. "Take a deep breath."

Figuring it was medical advice—and also a good idea—Jo followed directions. Twice.

"Okay." He smiled, but she wasn't fooled. That was not the casual one he'd given her as he'd wrapped her biceps in a cuff or shoved a thermometer in her mouth. "Good. Why don't you talk to the doctor when she comes in, okay? Dr. Perez is really easy to speak to. Just tell her what's been going on. Maybe it's nothing, but she'll be able to think the symptoms through with you and give you some options about further diagnostics if she believes it's warranted. Sound good?"

Jo nodded because she felt like a fool. And because she was suddenly very terrified.

She'd been thinking about going to a see a doctor for a good month and a half, maybe two months. And she'd decided to finally follow up on the impulse largely to give herself something to do as she waited for McCordle to check in again. Anything was better than sitting in that empty newsroom with Dick steaming pissed at her behind the closed door of his office—

Oh, who was she kidding. Someone she didn't know had spoken her biggest fear out loud to her last night. And she was here to find out if she was dying.

As if that man in leather was a fortune-teller.

"Have you been under a lot of stress lately?" the nurse asked.

"I accused my boss of a pattern of sexual harassment about a half hour ago."

The nurse whistled under his breath. "That counts. And I'm sorry that happened to you."

"And last night, I saw my first dead body." As his eyes bugged, she figured she'd keep the head-as-bowling-ball stuff to herself. "And I'm working on my first big story as a reporter—now that you mention it, things have been a little intense."

All of that was child's play, though. That man she'd run from the police with? Who she'd kissed in that abandoned restaurant? He was the real stressor, the first-in-line. Which considering the list of stuff he'd beaten for that coveted pole position was really saying something.

Jo took a deep breath again—but this time, she relaxed some as she exhaled. "You're right. This is all probably stress."

The nurse smiled again, and she was relieved that the Medical Professional Expression was not on his face anymore.

"I'll send Dr. Perez in as soon as she's done with her current patient." He extended a card from his lapel, swiped to log out of the computer, and got to his feet. "You take care now."

"Thanks," Jo said.

After he stepped out of the exam room, she swung her feet as they hung off the lip of the table—and remembered doing the same thing the night before in that kitchen. Stopping herself, she looked around and noted the pamphlets on depression, insomnia, and melanoma. The first two applied to her. The last one? She'd never really been into tanning, but redheads were not known for hearty skin.

There was also an anatomy chart on the far wall, the human skeleton on one side, the human muscular system on the other. The latter made her think of the skinned corpse, of those photographs that Bill had showed her.

And then she was back on the man from the night before, the one in leather, the one she should have been afraid of. She could picture him clear as day, sure as if he were in the room with her, and for some reason, the smell of his darkly spiced cologne came back to her—

As her phone went off in her purse, she snagged the thing out of the sea of Slim Jims like God was calling with the answer to a prayer. Sure enough, she didn't recognize the number, and as she hit "accept," her heart pounded, but not from fear. Nope. More like hope that it was that man, although that was not only impossible, it made no sense.

"Hello?" she said.

There was a pause. And then a tinny, falsely real-person'd voice said, "Hello, my name is Susan. I'm calling about your student loans—"

Stupid marketers.

Cutting the connection and cradling the cell in her palms, she found herself wishing she had memorized that man's phone number when he'd given it to her. But where did she think dialing him up was going to get her?

Well, she knew at least one answer to that.

Focusing on the door, she saw that hard, lean face, those deep-set eyes, those wide shoulders in that leather jacket. Then she felt his lips on her mouth, the leashed power of his tremendous body, the possibility of—

A woman in a white coat opened the way into the exam room and entered with a calm smile. Her stare was direct, her manner brusque yet not cold, her attitude one of competence and kindness.

"Good morning, Ms. Early," she said as she closed them in together. "I'm Dr. Perez."

She didn't go to the computer and sign in. She came over and shook hands. And even as her dark eyes were making a sweep of Jo's face, like she had one of Bones McCoy's scanners implanted in her head, she wasn't impersonal about it.

"Let's talk about what's going on. Matthew gave me some idea, but I'd like to hear everything again from you."

As she smiled, Jo smiled back.

Yes, Jo thought. *This* was the kind of person she wanted to get answers from, not some guy who was a stranger she should not trust—as if the repertoire of replies to the question "What the hell is wrong with me?" varied depending on who was supplying them.

Whatever. She was feeling better already.

"I'm really glad I came," she said. "So, it started probably back in November . . ."

CHAPTER EIGHTEEN

At nightfall, Syn materialized downtown without telling anyone where he was going. As he re-formed, his cell phone was
vibrating like it was having a seizure, and he took the thing
out so fast, he sent it sailing and had to pull a two-handed catch before
the Samsung Sam-shattered all over the pavement.

Finally, his female was calling—

Oh, for fuck's sake. Not her. But instead of letting things dump into
voice mail, he answered. "Relax, I'm taking care of it."

The old man with the cement company on the other end coughed
like the carcinogens from his cigars were setting up a campground in
his lungs. "What's the fucking holdup? And I told you, you keep it quiet
this time—"

Syn cut the call and contemplated throwing the phone at the building in front of him. Except then his female couldnae reach him, at least
not during the dead zone between when the unit broke into a million
pieces and the split second later when he got a new one. So yeah, fine.
That mobster wanted that reporter dead? No problem. Syn had a fuck
of a temper going on, and this was a killing-many-birds-with-one-stone

situation. He could burn off his bad mood, let his *talhman* stretch its legs with the guy, and get that fucking human he'd used to find himself a good victim to stop calling his ass.

Win/win, motherfuckers.

Stepping back so he was shrouded in shadows, he cased the parking lot of Caldwell's local newspaper. There was only one car there, a Volkswagen of some sort, and the compact was parked in a spot marked "Reserved for CCJ Employees Only." He glanced at the back door into the building. There was a sign reading "CCJ Staff Only" next to it, and through the chicken-wire'd windows, he could see somebody moving around and shutting off lights in the interior space.

Good. Whoever owned that car was going to tell him where the hell he could find Joseph Early—or they were going to be used to whet his appetite.

Cracking his knuckles, he willed the exterior security lights off, the fixtures going dark one after another until the parking lot was too dim for human eyes. In the other buildings around, there were only a few offices still glowing with illumination, but no one was in them that he could see. Not that witnesses mattered to him—

The steel door opened and the light streaming from behind the egressing person made it impossible to see their face.

But he knew who it was.

Syn's spine straightened like his ass had been hooked up to an electrical charge. Flaring his nostrils, he tested the air to make sure his sinuses weren't playing tricks. They were not. He'd recognize that scent of meadow flowers anywhere.

What was his female doing here?

Frowning, he stepped forward, intending to reveal himself to the person who he'd been waiting to hear from all day long. But he'd killed the lights, and she was distracted texting on her phone . . . so it wasn't until he put himself in her path that she stopped short. Looked up. Did a double take.

"It's . . . you," she said.

God, that voice. He had to close his eyes and consciously keep his balance as it went through him.

Then they both spoke at the same time.

"What are you doing here—"

"Do you work at the paper—"

As they fell silent together, he re-memorized her features, and found that his recollections of her were spot-on. He'd managed to remember everything about her with precision, yet the images he'd stored in his brain were nothing compared to the real thing: The three dimensions of her body. The smell of her skin. The sight of her red hair teased by the cold spring wind.

And most especially the way her green eyes pierced through his skin and bone, and went somewhere so much deeper.

"Are you okay?" he asked.

She seemed too distracted by his appearance to answer. But then she nodded. "Yes. I'm good. You?" Then she laughed in an awkward burst. "I feel like we're at a very strange cocktail party right now—"

"I'm talking about what you saw last night. On the fire escape."

She frowned. "Wait, did you follow me after you left?"

"I just wanted to make sure you got back to your car okay."

Those resplendent eyes of hers closed and she shuddered. "Yeah, that didn't happen. Guess you know that."

"You shouldn't have to see such things. Ever."

She shook her head. "No one should—"

The sound of a bullet being fired came from the left, and Syn yanked her behind him so fast, she stumbled. Catching her fall while blocking the shot with his own body, he got out a forty and pointed it at a junker that was traveling down the lane next to the parking lot.

Just as he pulled his trigger, his female pushed his arm out of alignment and the bullet ricocheted off a building flank, a spark flaring bright before being consumed by the darkness.

"What's wrong with you!" she hissed. "It's just their exhaust back-firing!"

Ignoring her, he kept his eyes on his target, and brought his arm back up. This time, he wasn't going to miss, and he didn't give a shit what the cause of the noise was. Bullet or backfire, those fucking humans deserved to die if only for their failure to Midasize. They'd startled his female. That was more than enough justification to pump them full of lead.

Especially in his current mood.

◆　◆　◆

This time, when Jo tried to move the man in leather's arm position, she got absolutely nowhere. She hung her entire body off his elbow, and still that gun stayed pointed at the old Civic. In a panic, she looked toward the car and could make out the profile of the driver, the man clueless that he was about to be blown sky high.

"Please . . ." Her voice cracked. "I can't take any more death today."

The gun lowered instantly, allowing the Civic to safely round the corner and drive out of sight.

And then it was just her and the man in leather in the damp, rushing spring air, standing in the darkness behind the CCJ newsroom.

As Jo started to shake, she dropped her bag on the pavement and put her hands to her face. "Oh, God."

The trembling got so bad that she threw an arm out blindly, and the man with the gun was the one who caught her, pulling her against him just as her legs lost all their muscle tone and turned into pipe cleaners. His strength was such that he didn't seem to notice the addition of her weight, and before she knew what she was doing, she put her arms around him, holding on as if he were the rope drawing her out of the cold, greedy lake she was drowning in.

As she fell into the weakness that claimed her, Jo turned her head to the side and put her ear against his heart. The strong, steady pump calmed her, and the scent of him was heaven in her nose, and the warmth emanating off of him revived her as nothing else could. So yes, even after she could feel her legs again and stand properly on her own, she didn't step back.

It had been so long since she had felt safe.

Just a little longer.

She would stay . . . a little longer.

"Where can I take you?" he asked.

His voice vibrated through his chest, and she liked the feel of it. Hell, she liked the feel of all of him. And that cologne, dear *God*, the cologne.

But they couldn't stay like this forever.

Prying her body off of his, she forced herself to step away from the warmth of him. Then with a quick tug, she pulled her jacket down and cleared her throat.

Like that would call her brain to order.

"Ah, nowhere," she said. Because it was the right answer. "I'm good. I'm fine—"

"Have you eaten?"

Jo blinked. "Eaten?"

"Yes." He mimed a fork going back and forth to his mouth. "Food?"

And that was when his expression registered. In spite of all his leather and his weapons, and the fact that he very calmly and deliberately had been about to shoot and kill someone with a bad muffler, he seemed . . . sheepish. Shy. Nervous.

Jo laughed in a burst. "Oh, my God. Are you asking me on a date?"

"I . . . ah . . ."

Alarm marked those hard features of his. In fact, he looked downright spooked.

"I, um, I thought you might be more comfortable in a public place," he blurted. "You know. With public around. In a place. That serves . . . you know, dinner things."

She started to smile. 'Cuz sometimes that was all you could do.

"There's a bar with bad fried food about two blocks from here. They also have a beer menu that's three pages long."

"I don't drink."

"Okay, like anything? Because that's not compatible with life."

"Alcohol."

"Well, you can order a tap water and a straw then. How about that?" As he started to nod, she pointed at his gun. "But that stays in your pants. Or . . . yeah, that sounded dirty. But the point is, no shooting anything or anybody. I don't care if the waiter drops a tray right behind you or a fight breaks out and you get beer splashed in your face. Agreed?"

The way the man nodded was like a Doberman who'd been schooled for piddling on the rug.

"All right," she said. "Let me put my bag in my car—wait. One more thing. The bar is where most of the cops go to hang out. Are we going to have a problem with that?"

It was a test. Public places were one thing. But given this guy's point-and-shoot proclivities, she wanted to go somewhere especially safe—and if he were a wanted man? A violent felon? He wasn't going to volunteer to get ID'd. Oh, and as for herself and that helicopter from the night before? There were a thousand redheads in this city, and chasing an active suspect through the streets via spotlight was a very different proposition than identifying her in a bar twenty-four hours later.

Facial recognition was good. It wasn't that good.

Besides, she'd had the hood of her windbreaker up most of the time.

"That's not a problem for me," he said without blinking.

Ignoring the relief she felt, Jo hefted her bag up on her shoulder and headed for the Golf. As she walked, she could sense him behind her, and she glanced back. He was scanning the parking lot, the lane, the buildings around them.

And he hadn't put the gun away yet. It was down by his thigh—

As her phone went off, she put her palm up at him. "Just my cell. Don't fill me full of holes."

He shot her a no-shit-Sherlock look.

Whoever was calling wasn't in her contacts, but she answered anyway. "Jo Early."

Out of the corner of her eye, she noticed that the man did a double take. But then she had to concentrate on what McCordle was saying.

"Wait, wait," she interrupted. "So Frank Pappalardo's definitely put a hit out on him? You're sure?"

CHAPTER NINETEEN

Butch pulled his roommate's R8 up to Safe Place, but he did not cut the V10 engine. As much of a gentleman as he was, there was no walking his *shellan* up to that door. No males were allowed on the property, and definitely not close to the entrance or in the house. The females and young who were finding safety and treatment inside were on a continuum of recovery and stability. There was no reason to make them any more uncomfortable than they had to be, and surprise, surprise, the aggressors who had hurt them were all males.

Marissa leaned over the console and he met her halfway. Kissing his mate, he lingered with their mouths together, his hand sneaking up to the nape of her neck.

When they finally pulled back, he smiled. "I'll come pick you up at four."

"I love driving in with you."

"I love being your chauffeur."

Marissa gave him one more peck, and then she opened her door and shifted her legs out. As she extricated herself from the low-level car, he wanted to pull her back in. Then he wanted to drive off and keep going.

Instead, he tilted over into the passenger seat and looked up at her. "I'm counting the hours."

"Me, too."

Marissa blew him a kiss, closed the door, and went up the front walk-way. On her way inside, she gave him a last wave, and then the heavy, rein-forced oak door was shut. Butch took a deep breath. Then he put the car in M1S and hit the gas, manually shifting the DCT as he left the neigh-borhood. It was a good ten or twelve minutes to get downtown, and he enjoyed the swerving in and out of lanes, the seventy-eight miles an hour in M4S . . . the dropping down into third gear, hammering the accelerator, and taking the Audi up to a hundred just before he got off at the North-way's Trade Street exit.

Some blocks down from where he dumped out onto the surface roads, he ditched the R8 in the garage where Manny parked the mo-bile surgical unit when it needed to be downtown on standby. Out on the street on foot, he strode along with his senses threading through the darkness. He immediately sensed a couple of *lessers,* but they were blocks and blocks away. Frustrated, he gave their approximate locations to the group that was on rotation, and hoped that tempers would hold and nobody would get too stabby before he could come on scene.

The instinct that he was being followed was a gradual one, the kind of thing that snuck up on him . . . as someone snuck up on him.

Triangulating the direction of the wind, he made a left, a right, and then another right so that the breeze coming off the river rode up on his back, carrying the scent of his little friend upon it.

Not a slayer. Not a vampire.

And was that . . . Poison by Dior? Shit, his nose had to be playing tricks on him. No one wore that perfume from the eighties anymore.

Stopping, he pivoted around, not bothering to hide his Hi, how're ya.

The woman was a good twenty feet away from him, and she was surrounded by light, sure as if the ambient illumination of the city was drawn to her. And yeah, he could understand why. Considering all the grime that downtown had to offer, she was certainly more worthy of a glow than a dumpster or an MSD truck.

Long brunette hair. Ridiculously good legs, like a thoroughbred. Tiny waist. Boobs that were perfect, but proportional, which, according to his male brain, meant that they might well be real. All in all, a package done up in runway-worthy clothes that, prior to his bonding with Marissa, would have caught his attention and then some. But he didn't fall into those kinds of feels. He was, after all, and in spite of the many questionable choices he'd made in his past, a good Catholic boy who had no interest in adultery.

Plus, hello, his *shellan* was all he wanted anyway.

The woman kept walking toward him, and she did that model thing, where the high-heeled shoes swung out and came back in with every step, the hips counterbalancing the exaggeration, the hair all bouncing to the rhythm of "Sexy Can I."

This show couldn't be for him.

Her eyes, however, told a different story.

They were locked on his, and Butch glanced over his shoulder, figuring a tour bus full of rappers, ballers, and tech billionaires had to have rolled up behind him.

Nope. She was coming for him.

When she stopped, she was about five feet away, and damn, her foundation was either the spackle they used at the end of *Death Becomes Her* or her skin was just fucking perfect. And those eyes. There was a king-sized bed with furry handcuffs attached to the headboard behind each one of those glittering black irises.

"Can I help you," he said dryly. "Because you've obviously mistaken me for somebody."

"No, I've been looking for you."

As her words came through the air at him, he weaved on his feet, his brain shorting out for a brief second. But then, like the electricity came back on in his skull, he was perfectly fine save for a lingering headache.

He rubbed one of his temples. "Look, sweetheart, you need to keep moving on—"

"Dontcha recognize me? I'm a friend of your sister Janie's."

Butch froze. And not only at the words, but the Boston accent that came through loud as a marching band in those syllables. "What did you say?"

Those eyes never left his, and as he stared into them, he felt as though he were falling, even as he stayed on level ground.

"Your sister Janie. I went to school with her and you." The woman pointed to her bodice. "Melissa McCarthy—and who knew that name would ever mean anything outside of Southie, right?"

Butch narrowed his stare. "Melissa . . . McCarthy?"

"You know, we lived on Bowen and F Street. I had braces back then, but you gotta remember me."

"Your brother was . . ."

"Mikey. Remember they named the five of us with M's? Mikey, me, Margaret, and Molly, the youngest. Megan, who shoulda been the baby of the family, didn't make it when she was born."

"Holy . . . shit, Melissa." He closed the distance between them. "What the fuck you doin' up here?"

His accent, long suppressed by his years in Caldwell, rebounded in his mouth like something that had been vacuum packed.

"We ain't that far from Boston."

"Far" was "Fah." "Boston" was "Bahston." And he loved it.

"Look, Butch," she glanced around, "I didn't mean to ride up on you like this, but it's just too crazy a coincidence. I mean, I was just talkin' to Joyce the other night. She had her second baby—but you know that, right?"

"Ah, my mom, she mentioned something."

"So ya still in touch with some of your family, huh."

"Just Ma. But she's, you know . . ."

"Yeah, in that nursin' home. I'm real sorry about that, Butch. Anyway, yeah, so Joyce was invitin' me to the baptism back home. She said she hadn't seen you, and when I told her I was livin' up here, she said I should see if I could find you. No offense, but I don't think she really meant it. It was kind of a bad joke."

"That's Joyce."

"But yeah, so I was heading over to that club, Ten? Do you know it? Anyways, I seen this hot car go by and park in this garage. Then you came out the door. I was across the street—I couldn't tell for sure it was you. But . . . it was. Is, I mean. You."

They stared at each other for a while.

"It's good to see you, Butch," Melissa said in a voice that got shaky. "You got people who miss you, you know? I mean, where you been these last couple of years? And what's with the clothes. You look like some kinda hard-ass now."

Butch glanced down at his leathers. Opened his mouth. Closed it.

"Listen, whatever's between you and your sistah?" Melissa shrugged. "It's none of my business. I'm not . . . I mean, if you don't want me saying nothing to her, that's fine. And if you don't want to talk to me, I understand. I know what it's like to have to leave things behind. It's not fun, no matter what side of the exit you're on or the reasons why you have to go."

Melissa wrapped her arms around herself and shivered a little, her eyes drifting away as if she were trying to stop her own memories from knocking on her frontal lobe.

"You shouldn't be out here walking alone," Butch heard himself say. "It's not safe."

She seemed to snap back to attention. "Oh, I know, right. Did you hear about those two bodies they found? What the fuck?"

"Why don't I walk you to the club. That way, I know you're safe."

Melissa's smile was shy, and very much at odds with her beauty.

"Come on," Butch said as he offered her his arm. "Allow me to escort you."

"Such a gentleman." She linked a hold on him. "Hey, why don't you come inside with me? Or we could go somewhere quiet."

"I gotta work." The sound of their footsteps rose up from the pavement, the heavy impact of his boots balanced by the staccato clips of her high heels. "And listen, I'm married."

Melissa stopped. Stamped her foot. "Get out. You are? Joyce said you weren't ever going to settle down."

"You meet the right person, that's all it takes."

"Well . . . shit." She recrossed her arms and looked him up and down. When her eyes came back to him, there was a sly light in them. "But married isn't always . . . you know . . . married, necessarily."

"It is with me." He took her elbow and started walking again, drawing her along. "But come on, someone like you, I'll bet you're beating 'em off with a stick."

"You'd be surprised," came the dry response.

"You know, I don't remember you looking . . ."

"So good?" She smiled at him and put her head on his shoulder. "Go on, you can say it and not violate your vows."

"Fine. I don't remember you being this hot."

"Plastic surgery is expensive," she murmured with a laugh. "But the shit works."

"Clearly." He nodded down at her black, sparkling outfit. "And is this ensemble Chanel or am I crazy?"

"It is! How'd you know?"

Like anything else came with all those interlocking C's? he thought.

They chatted about the past during the walk back by the garage where he'd left the R8, and he was surprised how good it was to plug into those memories of growing up   and by that, he didn't mean the shit in his household, with his father hating him and his mom being flinchy about everything. He meant the kids stuff. The friend stuff. The school stuff. Not all of his childhood had been bad.

At least not until Janie was abducted and murdered and raped. In that order.

"So you're not married?" he said.

"Nah. There was someone, but it didn't work out."

"I can't imagine any man walking away from you."

"You say the sweetest things." Mel gave his arm a squeeze, but then cursed under her breath. "He found someone he liked better."

"Hard to imagine."

"She was nothing like me."

"Well, his loss." He looked over. "Was it recent?"

"Yeah. Very. I'm just getting my feet back under me again. I feel kinda lost."

As they came up to the club, he took Mel right to the head of the wait line. When the bouncer looked her up and down, it was clear that she was going to get in without a problem, but just to be sure, he made a little arrangement with the guy's gray matter.

"You sure you can't come in with me?" she asked.

"No, but thanks."

"Let me give you my number. Tell me yours so I can text it."

"You know, it's been nice catching up, but I'm going to leave you off here."

He debated whether to go into her mind and clear the memories, but he found himself not wanting to be a ghost to everyone from his past.

"I won't tell her," Mel murmured. "Joyce, that is. It's pretty clear you don't want to have contact with her. Or you woulda."

"It doesn't matter. You do you. Goodbye, Mel—"

"Maybe we'll run into each other again."

"Maybe." She seemed rootless and floundering as she stared up at him from out of her beautiful face, and he felt bad for her. "True love's out there, okay? I promise you. Hell, I never thought I could find it, and if the shit can happen for a loser like me? You're going to be a piece of cake."

When she launched herself at him and gave him a hug, he lightly patted her shoulder blades and then stepped back.

"Go on," he said. "See if your new man's waiting for you in there."

"What if I've already found him."

Butch frowned. But before he could say something on that, she gave him a wave and strutted into the strobe-lit check-in area.

The club's door closed, but Butch didn't immediately step away. Lifting the sleeve of his leather jacket to his nose, he breathed in. Poison by Dior was all over his sleeve.

Like he'd been marked.

CHAPTER TWENTY

McGrider's was indeed a local establishment that served a lot of cops and firemen, and, back in the heyday of newspapers, Jo imagined that most of the CCJ's staff ate here as well. The vibe was scuffed convenience, everything worn down by generations of patrons, the beer signs in the windows Bud Light, Michelob, and Pabst. And as she and the man in leather settled into a wooden booth—or, rather, she settled and he squeezed—her eating companion didn't seem bothered in the slightest by all the uniforms in the place. Just like he'd said.

"So you have to tell me your name," she announced. "Before anything else happens."

Yeah, 'cuz God forbid she chow down a cheeseburger in front of someone she hadn't been properly introduced to. Evading a police helicopter, fine. But dinner? She had to draw the line.

Rolling her eyes at herself, she said, "What I mean is—"

"Syn," he interjected.

"Sin." Jo tilted her head to the side. "As in not a virtue?"

"No, with a y."

"What's it short for?"

"Syn."

His dark, glowing eyes calmly stared back at her across the table, like he was prepared to field a credit check if she wanted to Experian his ass. And the juxtaposition between all that open-book and the sheer size of him wedged into the booth was a contradiction she was grateful for. The fact that he didn't seem to have anything he was hiding from her made him so much less dangerous.

Plus, again, there was a whole squad of cops around them. If she needed 911, all she had do was pull a "Help!" and a sea of blue would ride up on the guy.

Then again, if he'd wanted to hurt her, he'd had plenty of chances already.

"Can I ask you something?" she said, leaning forward. "And I don't want to offend you."

"You won't offend me."

"You don't know what I'm going to ask."

"It doesn't matter what it is. You will not offend me."

As he continued to look over at her, the commotion of the busy bar disappeared on Jo. Between one blink and the next, there were no waiters buzzing around with trays of drinks and pitchers of beer. No plates of onion rings or chicken wings being delivered. No men with badges laughing loudly or women with badges telling stories. Privacy bloomed around them, an illusion created by how she felt as he stared at her like that.

Jo cleared her throat. What had she been—oh, right.

"Are you a pro wrestler or something?" she blurted.

"Wrestler?"

"You know, the WWE. Hulk Hogan, although I guess he was doing that in the eighties. I know of him through reality TV. And that lawsuit over the sex tape years ago, thank you, TMZ." As Sin with a y just continued to meet her eyes, she shook her head, aware she was babbling. "Have you heard of any of those things?"

"I know what a sex tape is, though I've never seen one."

"That makes you party of nobody else," she said dryly.

"Why would I want to watch someone I don't know having sex? Or someone I do know, for that matter."

Now her eyebrows went up. "You have single-handedly disavowed the porn industry, then."

Make that left-handedly disavowed, she amended to herself. And she would have made that joke out loud, but she didn't know him well enough. Maybe he was really religious?

"It's just not of interest," he said.

"You've never watched YouPorn."

"What is that?"

"You're not from here, are you." As if geography might account for him being the one person in the bar who wasn't familiar with that URL?

"No, I'm not."

"So where are you from?"

"Not here."

When she waited for him to fill that one in and he did not, she sat back. "Europe? I mean, you don't sound American."

"Yes. Europe."

Tick-tock . . . no amplification on that, either.

All right, he might have been open to answering anything, but he clearly wasn't going to help her much on the Easter Egg hunt.

"So you're not a wrestler—are you a weight lifter? Wait—a Cross-Fit guy?"

He shook his head. "No."

"So how are you this big?" She shook her head. "What I mean is—"

"Genetics," he said remotely.

"See, I have offended you."

"No, I just don't like where I came from."

In the pause that followed, a waitress walked up with a pad and pen. As there were no uniform requirements for the bar, the twenty-something was rocking a hipster vibe with mud-colored clothes, a tat-tooed sleeve down one arm, and some piercings in her face.

"What can I getcha to drink?"

That she only looked at Syn seemed right. Jo would have done the same in her shoes—hell, she *was* doing the same. Of all the people in the place, he stood out—and yes, the men and women in uniform and plainclothes had noticed him, too. And at least nobody was springing forward with a Taser and some cuffs.

"Water," he said.

The waitress pulled an "And you?" without glancing in Jo's direction. Her eyes were too busy roaming around the span of Syn's leather jacket and the breadth of his chest and what little she could catch of his lower body. Obviously, she was doing sexual math in her head and solving the equation of him naked with all kinds of yes-please.

"I'll take a Sam Adams in the bottle, no glass," Jo said.

"You got it. Menus are in the holder."

Syn didn't seem to notice the woman's departure any more than he'd bothered with her arrival, and Jo told herself not to be complimented.

"You're not going to take your jacket off, are you?" she said as she shucked her own coat.

"I'm not hot."

Ohhhhhhh, don't be too sure about that, she thought to herself. And besides, she knew the lack of outerwear removal was less about his body temperature and more about the guns and ammo he was hiding under all that leather.

"I was hoping you'd call me." Syn linked his hands and put them on the table, like he was a choirboy in spite of his nickname. "But I'm glad you're all right."

She thought of what he'd said the night before. About death. "Actually, I went to the doctor's today."

"They won't help you."

She froze in the process of folding her coat on the seat. "I beg to dif-fer. That's their job. That's what they do when people are sick."

"You're not sick."

"Then explain that to my flu symptoms," she muttered. "And you and I are going to have to agree to disagree on whether I'm ill. FYI, given that I'm in my skin, I have more credibility on this topic than you do."

"What is Jo short for? I heard you say your name when you answered your phone."

"Josephine."

The waitress brought his water over and the bottle of Sam Adams. Then she lingered, like she was enjoying the close-up more than the panoramic view of him—and even though it was inappropriate on so many levels, Jo felt like hissing as if she were a cat. As if both of them were a cat. As if two cats were—

Frickin' metaphors.

To keep herself from doing something stupid—or something that would land her with a flea collar—she tried her beer. The first draw on the open neck was heaven, so she took another.

"I'm surprised you're so comfortable in here," she murmured as the waitress finally left. "Given all the metal on you. But I guess everything is properly registered."

"I have nothing to fear in this place or any other."

Jo eyed his thick neck and the heft of his shoulders under that leather jacket. Then she remembered what his body had felt like as she had wrapped her arms around his waist. He was hard as a rock, no fat on him, just muscles on top of muscles.

Even though she didn't want to, she found herself following in the footsteps of the waitress, her mind going to places that involved no clothes and lots of exercise.

"That I believe," she said remotely.

◆   ◆   ◆

As Mr. F aimlessly walked the streets in the darkness, part of his life was the same. He had been a wanderer in and around the city for much of the last three years, returning to the bridge's underworld when he needed a fix or the weather was bad or it was time to crash. Back before whatever had happened to him at the outlet mall, the constant motion had been because he enjoyed the movement after the intense part of the nods faded, and also because he'd always had an internal, ticking nervousness right under his skin.

Now, though, he got nothing out of his numb ambulation, the pavement under his feet passing like the minutes and the hours, unnoticed, unaccounted for. He had walked all day long, randomly making big fat circles through the neighborhoods of downtown while the sun rose, peaked, and fell back into the horizon. In spite of his marathon of miles, there was no pain in his feet or legs. No blisters. No need for food or drink or the bathroom. And he mourned the loss of all of those inconveniences, the absence of the nagging aches and pains of humanity. As he continued further, he realized he no longer had the sense that he was, in spite of his lack of assets, status, and success, exactly like all the other men and women who strode by him, drove by him, flew in planes above him, worked in buildings around him.

Then again, he was no longer human, was he.

The disconnection from everybody else made him feel as if things were closing in on him, although he wasn't sure exactly what the "things" were, and had no idea how to avoid them. This lose/lose created a buzzing in his head that was something he had previously been able to needle away, and the fact that his addiction was no longer an option made him feel his dislocation and anxiety all the more acutely. As he struggled to keep it together, he realized that the drugs had been an artificial, but highly reliable, horizon for him, a far-off land that was always available whenever he felt boxed in or cornered—which had been, and continued to be, most of the time.

No more travel for him, though. His passport had been revoked.

When his boots finally halted, he was surprised, and he looked down at them with the expectation that they would explain themselves. There was no answer coming, however, and when his brain gave them a nudge to keep going, they stayed where they were.

It was as if he were on autopilot, and the person in charge of his remote had punched a button—

His head tilted up, sure as if there was a puppet string attached to his eyebrows and the guy running this Muppet version of himself was getting him ready to say a line of dialogue.

Well. What do you know. He was on a narrow street that was littered with big trash: soiled mattresses, a kitchen sink, a refrigerator with the door removed. Somebody had clearly decamped out of an apartment and wanted the city to take care of their shit. Or maybe it was a renovation job, although in this kind of zip code, demolition was more likely.

In the dim light, which did not compromise his vision at all, a figure stepped out of a shallow doorway two blocks down. Mr. F immediately recognized them, though they were a stranger: It was like seeing a distant family member, one who you couldn't put a name to, but who you recalled from weddings and funerals when you were young.

He *knew* this other man. This other man *knew* him.

Not that either of them were men anymore.

And the one controlling Mr. F was insisting they interact. They hit Mr. F's Go Forward toggle, and like any battery-powered device, his body was ready to do what it was told. Meanwhile, the other *lesser* seemed to be waiting for him to do something, say something—and that was when Mr. F got real with himself. He hadn't actually been pacing in random directions all day long. He'd been avoiding the others, shifting among the streets in a defensive fashion so there was no chance of intersection.

Like the asphalt grid of downtown was a radar screen and the other blips warships he had to steer clear of.

As his right foot started to lift, he forced it back down onto the pavement, and when the boot came up again, it was bizarre to find himself not in control of his own body. Then again, after years of heroin addiction? Like he wasn't used to being a servant to a master outside of himself?

Forcing his body to obey his brain, not this external will, he took a step backward. And another.

The other slayer seemed confused at the retreat—

The attack on it came from the left, the airborne vampire pile-driving into the *lesser*, taking it down so hard, there was a crack that had to have been its skull or spine.

The impulse to join the fight, to defend, to conquer and kill, was as foreign as sobriety, and as compelling as the promise of a nod, but Mr. F fought to back himself out of the way, flattening his shoulders against whatever building he bumped into, gripping the bricks, holding himself in place against the draw to intercede in some hand-to-hand he had not been trained for and had no experience in.

The conflict did not go well for his comrade.

The vampire took control of the ground game, pinning the slayer in place, a length of chain swinging out to one side. But instead of strangling the slayer with the links, the attacker let the momentum wrap them around his fist. Then the beating began. That reinforced set of knuckles pounded down into the face of the *lesser* over and over again, black blood splashing the killer as bones were crushed and features gave way.

Mr. F stayed where he was, even as the vampire finally sat back and caught its breath. After a moment of recovery, the thing turned to its shoulder and spoke into a receiver of some sort, the words too muffled to hear—

Abruptly, the wind changed directions and came around, hitting Mr. F in the face.

No, that wasn't right. It wasn't a force of weather. It was more as if a vacuum had appeared behind him, a sucking vortex drawing the air molecules toward whatever had created the flow and caused the strange breeze.

Slowly, Mr. F looked over his shoulder.

Something had opened up in the night . . . like a hole in the fabric of time and space. Of reality itself. And the pull of the inexplicable phenomenon was undeniable, stray newspapers skipping along toward whatever it was, the clothes on Mr. F's body drawn forth in the same way, the hair on his head teased into his face.

And then . . . an arrival.

A swirling fulcrum bloomed in the center of the alley, a dust devil without the dust.

But definitely the devil.

The evil was so dense that its presence created its own gravitational field, and Mr. F recognized his master by what was in his own veins, his body a tuning fork for what appeared. And he was not the only one who noticed. Over the body of the *lesser*, the vampire with the facial piercings and the tattoo of a teardrop under one of his eyes was likewise focused on what had joined them.

"Motherfucker," it muttered.

That just about covered things, Mr. F thought as the dense, roiling hatred took shape.

The white-robed figure was of modest height and modest build, but it made no sense to apply standards of human size and strength to the entity. Beneath the shroud—which Mr. F noted was stained and frayed at the bottom and torn up one side—the evil was a dense promise of suffering and menace and depravity.

"Have you no words of greeting for your master," came a warping voice.

Then the evil looked past Mr. F, at the vampire. "And greetings to you, mine enemy."

CHAPTER TWENTY-ONE

S o tell me honestly," Jo said as she put a French fry in her mouth. "What do you really do? Not wrestling, I know. And I'm thinking you're not in the military at the present. And you can't be a drug dealer or you wouldn't be so comfortable in here."

"I am a protector."

She thought about his response to that Honda Civic with its backfiring. "Okay, I can see that. Like a bodyguard? For who? Who do you guard?"

"There is a male." Syn took another precise bite of his cheeseburger and wiped his mouth. "He and his family."

"Would I have heard of him?"

"No. I live with him and I am not the only one who watches over him."

The waitress came back over with more water. And no offense, but the woman needed to give it a rest with that damn pitcher of hers. Every time Syn took a sip, Ms. Tap Water felt the need to re-level his damn glass.

Jo took a deep breath and told herself to quit it with the territoriality. She didn't even know the man's last name, for godsakes.

"Can I get you more ketchup?" the waitress asked him.

I swear to God, Jo thought. *I will cut a b—*

"No, thank you."

"Thanks, we're good," Jo emphasized.

When they were alone again, she muttered, "Do you always get this kind of service in restaurants?"

Syn finished his burger and wiped his mouth. "I don't eat out usually."

"Neither do I, but it's because I'm cheap. I've got to be frugal with money. It's just me at the end of the day."

"How long have you been on your own?"

"Since after college."

"What of your parents?"

"I was a social experiment that failed them." She glanced over at a table of laughing cops. "Actually, that's not right. I don't think they adopted me because they wanted to do some poor unwanted kid a solid. I think my mom felt like she needed a daughter. It was an accessory to go with her estate and her husband and her lifestyle. I was an accessory."

"They do not watch over you?"

"You have a funny way of phrasing things sometimes." She shrugged. "And it's fine. I can take care of myself."

"Do you not have male relations who you can go to?"

"Like I'm living in a Dickens novel?" Jo smiled. "And I don't want to go to anyone. I don't need to be rescued from my own existence. I've handled things okay this far and I'm going to keep the trend going."

"We all need support."

"So who do you go to?"

Syn frowned and shifted in his seat. Shaking his head, he took out a cell phone that had a privacy guard on its screen—not that she would have peeked. As his eyes moved slowly over whatever had been texted, she had a thought that he might be dyslexic.

"I have to go," he said.

Jo nodded. "Okay. Yeah. Of course—" When he started to get some twenties out of his pocket, she put her hand on his arm. "Nope. This is my treat. I'll cover it."

He froze and stayed that way. To the point where she removed her touch. Maybe she had offended him—

"I don't want to leave you," he blurted.

Something about the way he said the words made her feel warmth in the center of her chest. Or maybe it wasn't the way he said them. It was the fact that he said them at all.

I don't want to be left by you, she thought to herself.

Knowing that she only had another couple of seconds to stare at him, she drank in his face, that hard, harsh face that she knew she was going to see in her dreams—assuming she ever slept again.

"Who are you?" she whispered. "Really."

"I'm a friend."

Ouch, she thought as she sat back.

The pain that shot through her rib cage made her realize that sometime between when he'd been prepared to shoot at some innocent Civic owner to keep her safe, and the ordering of their cheeseburgers and fries, she'd made a decision she wasn't prepared to look too closely at. But it seemed like that was a door being shut on his side.

Well, he'd have sex with her. It wouldn't mean anything to him, however. Friends, benefits, all that.

Syn slid out of the banquette, and now he got serious about the water. He took the glass and downed everything that was in it. Even the ice.

"Are you going out to fight?" she said.

"What's your number? I'll call you."

Jo had a thought that she didn't want him to die. Which was hyperbolic and silly. Then again . . . two dead bodies in as many nights? Kind of made catastrophizing look like a sensible attitude to take about life.

"Are you married?" she asked.

The recoil he pulled would have broken the neck of a lesser built man. "No."

Okay, that was a relief. At least she wouldn't be fantasizing about someone else's husband. Not that she was going to be imagining anything. Nope. She might be reckless, but she wasn't a masochist.

I'm a friend.

The three most crushing words in the English language when you were attracted to someone. Then again, given that she shouldn't be with someone like him anyway, maybe they were a lifesaver.

"Take care of yourself," she said softly.

Syn nodded his head, and then he was gone, striding out of the bar, out into the night. As if he hadn't really wanted her phone number. As if the fact that they wouldn't see each other again didn't matter.

Where did all those only-I-can-help-you's go? she wondered bitterly.

And P.S., how come she was turning into a chick? Real women didn't wait for Prince Charmings to come along and give their lonely, spinster existences meaning. Chicks did, though. They got doe-eyed in the wake of departures and they finished their dinners by their lonesome in mourning and they waited to be called.

Reaching up to her lips, she thought of the kiss they'd shared.

"You're just going to get hurt if you go after him," she said.

Jo lasted another second and a half.

Shoving her hand into her purse, she grabbed some cash. Tossing however much it was on her half-eaten cheeseburger, she took her coat and jogged through the tables, through the patrons, through waiters. Breaking out into the spring chill, Syn's name was on the tip of her tongue.

She didn't let it fly.

Looking left . . . looking right . . . looking straight ahead, she saw nothing but an empty four-lane city street, and sidewalks without any-one on them, and a parking lot across the way that had two cars in its slots and a kiosk without an attendant.

"Where did you go?" she whispered into the night wind.

◆   ◆   ◆

The evil is here. Oh, Jesus . . . the evil is here.

Butch ran as fast as he could, blocks of city streets flying under his shitkickers as he skidded around corners, and tore down straightaways. He was breathing like a freight train, his fists clenched and pumping, his leather jacket flared out and flapping behind him, his weapons moving with his torso in their holsters.

As he rounded a left-hand turn, he ran into some kind of a human and shoved them out of his way. When they shouted at him, he didn't bother to apologize.

Faster, for fuck's sake, he needed to be faster—

Peeling onto Eighteenth Street, he ran up a car that was parked on the sidewalk, pounding over the hood, the roof, and somersaulting into the air above the trunk. He landed in mid-stride and kept tooling, a bar-rage of self-inflicted criticism spurring him on.

Fucking half-breed, motherfucker, loser, piece of shit—

The last turn was one he lost traction on, the treads on his boots pried loose thanks to the centrifugal force of his body weight at an angle. As a result, he skidded into home on his ass, his feet out in front of him, his torso and legs continuing the trajectory while his head cranked to the side in the direction of what had called him.

The Omega was front and center in the middle of the alley, the evil's presence like a stain on the night itself, the density of the bad news so great there was a warping of the air around it. Yet the mas-ter of all *lessers* was actually second on Butch's list of things to worry about.

Qhuinn was a mere fifteen feet away from the Omega, standing fro-zen over the body of a slayer, his attention fixated on the dark deity like behind his mismatched eyes he was considering a defensive response—or worse, an offensive one.

As Butch did the math on any confrontation between the two, the only thing he thought of was those kids, Rhamp and Lyric . . . those beautiful kids that the brother shared with Layla. If Qhuinn died right here, right now, at the hands of the Omega, the adults of the Brotherhood household would mourn and move along, eventually. But that sweet little girl and that sturdy little guy? They would never know their sire. They would grow up with only the memories of other people filling the void of who their brave, strong, incredible father was.

Fuck. That. Shit.

As Butch back-flat'd into Qhuinn, he jumped up in the midst of his momentum, grabbed the brother by the jacket, and yanked them face-to-face.

"Get the *fuck* out of here," Butch hissed. "Now!"

Qhuinn started to argue, of course. But nope. Not up for discussion. Shifting their bodies around, Butch made sure Rhamp and Lyric's father was behind him—and then he torqued with every ounce of body weight and power he had, sending the huge male pinwheeling through the air away from the juncture of an alley, a vampire Frisbee.

There was a crash—like some trash bins had been bowling ball'd—and then Butch barked into his shoulder communicator.

"All clear," he said. "All clear. Repeat . . . *false alarm.*"

Qhuinn stood up down the street and Butch glared at the guy, sending all kinds of GTFO in the male's direction. And what do you know, something must have clicked. The brother dematerialized.

"Repeat, all clear," Butch stressed as he refocused on the Omega—

Oh, looksee, looksee, there was another slayer right by the master, the *Fore-lesser*. A BOGO.

"Isn't this lovely," the Omega said in a voice that weaved through the unnaturally still air. "We meet again."

"That's a line from a bad movie." Butch unsheathed both his black daggers. "I expect more from the likes of you."

"Such credit. I'm tickled. And I've missed you."

"Can't say the same over here."

"You downplay your emotions."

"Not when it comes to hating you."

The Omega drifted over, leaving the *Fore-lesser* behind. "You know, you are one of my few regrets. If I hadn't made you, you wouldn't be such a problem."

"We're almost done here. The prophecy nearly complete." Butch knelt by the slayer Qhuinn had taken down. "You come any closer, I'm going to go to work. And not with these daggers."

The Omega paused. "Do as you wish. I like to watch."

"If you leave, right now," Butch said, "I'll stab this piece of shit back to you. You hang around? I'm going to suck him down like a milkshake on a hot summer night. And something tells me by the look of your robe you can't afford to lose much more."

An unholy growl rose up, emanating from under the dirty white folds. "You mortal scourge—"

"Enough trading insults." Butch leaned down, putting his mouth over the still moving *lesser's*. "So what's it going to be?"

"You need to learn the real meaning of power."

With surprisingly quick reflexes, the Omega curled back an arm-like extension, and cast a dense, shadowy projectile through the air, the buzzing sound of its flight like that of a wasps' nest riled up, the dark magic coming fast and on-target. The force hit Butch like a ton of bricks, throwing him off the gurgling, useless pile of slayer, slamming him against the building behind him.

There was no time to recover. Before the Omega could pitch a second strike, Butch surged forward, grabbed the mangled face of the *lesser*, and made out with the oily mess of anatomy, inhaling like he had been underwater for a half hour, like not only his life depended on it, but like the lives of every single one of the brothers and the fighters who Qhuinn was going to drag here in the next thirty seconds would be saved by the suck.

The Omega let out a high-pitched howl that was so loud, it knocked out Butch's hearing and went straight down his spine.

But he did not look up. Did not stop. Did not slow down.

It was his only shot . . . to save his brothers who were going to come running, regardless of that all clear he'd sent.

CHAPTER TWENTY-TWO

Syn re-formed a block away from the coordinates that had been sent out by Qhuinn, but the instant he resumed his physical form, he received a contradicting message that all was clear from Butch.

Flaring his nostrils, he scented the air.

The stench of *lesser* was so loud, it could only be explained by a juicy kill. So maybe Qhuinn had brought one down, but been worried about backup on the slayer side or something? Only to have Butch take care of round two?

Beneath his skin, his *talhman* surged, and it was the need for bloodshed that sent him forward at a jog—just like it was the need for a kill that had made him get up from that table at the bar, when he hadn't wanted to leave Jo. He was desperate to release his inner burn, however. Overdue to let his bad side express itself.

Maybe there was something left over for him to play with. Maybe there would be others. Maybe this wouldn't take long and he could go back and find Jo—

Syn came around a tight corner and stopped dead.

Even as his eyes focused on the figure in dingy white robing, and his instincts told him what it was, his brain refused to believe the conclusion he drew.

Yet the draped figure with evil spilling out from under its hems could be one, and only one, entity. And the Omega was in attack mode, its form reared back as if it were gathering strength to throw something . . . at Butch.

Who was inhaling a slayer like he was trying to draw a tire through a straw.

Syn didn't hesitate.

With a powerful surge, he bum-rushed the evil, taking three huge strides and throwing all his body weight at the damn thing. And the Omega, for all its omnipotence, didn't seem to notice him—at least not until Syn was on the entity, his body tackling the master of all *lessers* off its feet.

Or whatever held it up off the ground.

Everything went in slow motion at that point. As whatever spell or magic the Omega had been aiming at Butch went haywire and blew a car off its tires, Syn was aware of a horrible feeling swamping through his body, waves of sickness and death and toxic, snarling pain going through him. And then Butch looked up from the slayer and yelled something, his arms reaching out as if he were trying to save someone.

Probably Syn. But no time to think about that.

The Omega slung Syn away like he weighed nothing, and the landing was rock hard as he bounced on his pecs and his palms, just barely keeping his face from being his tarmac as he went head-first toward a brick wall. Putting his hands out, he front-bumper'd the building just before he got his skull cracked open.

After which . . . silence.

Syn tried to lifted his head, but he was curiously weak, his body lax as a damp towel. The best he could do was roll over and try to get his eyeballs to work properly—and that was how he discovered that the alley had only two people in it.

Well, three if you counted the hot mess of the slayer Butch was still straddling.

No Omega.

Before Syn could say anything or check for injuries, his own or Butch's, he was overcome with nausea. Turning back onto his stomach, he propped his hands and threw up what he'd eaten with Jo—and then kept going until he was dry heaving and seeing stars.

Hands reached out to him. Someone talked to him—Balz, his cousin. And then there were lots of people around.

He couldn't hear anything, though, the rushing of the blood in his ears like nothing he'd ever experienced before. And meanwhile, his heart was doing bad things in his chest, its rhythm uneven and way too strong. As his awareness zeroed in on what was going on behind his sternum, he had an image of a boulder bouncing down a rocky hillside, *boom!*, *ba-boom!*, *ba-ba-boom!*—and then dizziness came on him like it was a physical force with three dimensions. As the world spun so badly he keeled over onto his side, he got a terrific close-up of his cousin's shitkicker.

From a vast distance, he watched Balthazar holler at somebody, and Syn had a thought that his cousin was a good male, in spite of the thief stuff. Sure, the bastard might have a more narrow conscience than most, but that didn't mean—

A dark-haired guy in surgical scrubs came running over and crouched down.

Well, this was handy. It was Dr. Manny Manello, the human surgeon mated unto Payne, V's sister.

Syn was so knocked out, he almost greeted the healer. Which was a strange impulse as he was more of a Fuck-off than Cheerio-ol'-chap kind of person. Then again, he wasn't in his right mind at the moment, and the doctor seemed to agree, shaking his head and holding up his hands as if there was nothing he could do.

Huh, Syn thought. Looked like he might be dying.

Driven by an impulse he couldn't deny, he forced his arm out and

slapped the pavement in front of Balz's shitkicker. The male's face immediately came down to level.

Syn started talking. At least . . . he thought he was talking. He
still couldn't hear anything—his cousin's ears seemed to be working
okay, though. The male's face went from worried . . . to confused . . . to
shocked.

Whatever. All that mattered was . . .

From out of nowhere, the brightest light Syn had ever seen coalesced right in front of him, and even in his delirium, he knew what it
was. It was the Fade, arriving to claim him, and somehow, that was the
biggest surprise of all. He had assumed he would go unto *Dhunhd*.

Then again, having just made the acquaintance of the Omega,
maybe the evil didn't want his sorry ass—

As he was bathed in the heavenly illumination, the relief that suffused his body was so complete it was unfathomable. It was as if the
sickness inside of him was erased, and in its absence? An exhausted
peace and calm, like he had come to the end of a long trial.

But that had been his life. A slog that had seemed infinite on a good
night, and a curse on a bad one.

Giving himself up to the death, he waited for the door he had heard
about to come through the light unto him . . . the door that ancient wis-
dom said you opened and stepped through, finding yourself in an eternity with your loved ones. Would his *mahmen* be there?

Would Jo be allowed there as a human?

Panic shot through him. He was leaving his female undefended; his
death was not going to get her out of danger. Gigante would send someone else to kill her—

All at once, the light retracted, Syn's vision cleared, and his ears
came back online. Looking up, he wasn't sure what he expected to see . . .
but the Brother Vishous kneeling down with a torch was not it—

Wait. That wasn't a torch. It was the male's hand, the one that always had that black leather glove on it.

Maybe the illumination hadn't been the Fade.

Maybe those rumors about V being the born son of the Scribe Virgin weren't bullshit.

Maybe he should be nicer to the motherfucker, assuming he didn't want to be turned into a s'more.

Syn pushed himself off the pavement, and as he cautiously got up on his feet, he expected the world to go around in circles again. It did not. And that was when he realized the Brother must have done to him what he did to Butch.

"You *tackled* the Omega?" V said. "What the fuck were you thinking, you crazy sonofabitch."

Vishous punched Syn's shoulders—and then Syn was being yanked forward against that huge chest, the embrace as unexpected as the Brother breaking into song with "Achy Breaky Heart."

'Cuz V didn't like anybody.

Guess if you saved his best friend's life, it got you on his Good Guy list.

Syn felt himself get set back, and then both of his cousins were talking to him. *Everyone* was talking to him, the Brothers who were on site and all the other fighters. It was a blur, and he had some thought that they were making a hero out of him for no good reason. He just wanted to kill something, anything, and he wanted a good fight. The Omega was tailor-made for that shit.

"Where's Syn?" he heard somebody demand. "Is Syn okay?"

Butch broke through the rugby huddle that had formed, and the former cop, former human, seemed to fall back into his role as civil servant. He was all about the Good Samaritan as he approached.

"Jesus, that was brave and stupid. But thank you. I'm serious."

Syn met the hazel eyes of the Brother and shook his head.

Butch nodded, as if he knew what Syn was thinking, but Syn could guarantee he did not.

And to cut any further gratitud-inal shit, Syn tried to walk in a circle to get a sense of how steady he was. Yay. He didn't weave. He didn't throw up again. His body and strength were, like, five on a scale of ten.

Whereas before V had showed up with that searchlight of a palm? Try not even on the damn scale.

"Where are you going?" Butch asked.

Am I leaving? Syn wondered.

"I'm on rotation," he heard himself say. "I'm going out to fight."

Dr. Manello jumped in like he had a chip in the back of his neck that alerted him to dumb decisions. "Nope. You're taking the rest of the night off."

"I'm not injured," Syn said as he motioned down his body. "And I'm not sick anymore. You have no reason to deny me."

As V lit up a hand-rolled, the Brother looked over the cup of his hand. "Let him go. He's more than earned the right to fight if that's what he wants to do. Besides, I took care of him. There isn't anything of the Omega left in him."

Syn pegged the doctor in the eye. "I'm just going to go out anyway. No matter what you tell me."

More conversations, especially as another round of Brothers arrived, Tohr, Z, and Phury needing to catch up on what had happened with the Omega.

Hoping to dematerialize out before his part in the story got more airtime, Syn took a step back from the crowd. And another. When Balthazar glanced over like he was going to put the brakes on the retreat, Syn glared at his cousin and dared him to get involved. When the guy just lit up one of V's homemade cigarettes and cursed, it was clear the message was received.

His kin was not going to get in the way of him getting gone.

◆   ◆   ◆

As the alley turned into a brother-convention, Butch went back over to the carcass of the *lesser*. He hadn't gotten far into the inhale before Syn decided to play bowling ball with the Omega and there was a job to be finished.

And fuck no, he wasn't going to honor that promise to the evil of stabbing the damn thing back to its master.

"You don't have to, cop. You can take a break tonight."

He looked over at V. The brother's clear, cold eyes were like fresh air when you were sick to your stomach. And inside Butch's head, thoughts started to spin, careening into each other, making hash of any logic.

"Cop, you just went through some shit."

"Yeah, and the only way out of this whole thing is to do my fucking job."

Butch dropped to his knees, and angled his face over what was left of the slayer's mashed-in features. As he braced himself to take one of those long, strange inhales that he'd been pulling ever since the Omega had gotten into him, he thought—not for the first time—that he didn't know how it worked. He didn't understand the metaphysics of how he could drain the essence out of its vessel.

Then again, an explanation wouldn't change reality and he wasn't sure he really wanted to know the particulars. Besides, he had other issues to worry about . . .

"The Omega should have been able to kill me," he said as he glanced up at V. "It was throwing shit at me . . . the magic should have blown me apart. And then there was its presence. I mean, I've been right up close with that thing before. I know how powerful it used to be. Not anymore . . . it's dying."

And you'd think he would have gotten a second wind—natch—from the bald evidence of his success. Instead? He only felt more exhausted.

V knelt down and exhaled over his shoulder. "That means it's working. The prophecy is coming true."

"Yeah." Butch stared at the glistening mess of the slayer's face, the cheekbones white under the inky stain of the black viscera. "I feel like a competitive eater in the last thirty seconds of Nathan's Famous."

V put his gloved hand on Butch's shoulder. "We have time. It doesn't have to end tonight. Send him back and let's go home."

Butch shook his head at the *lesser*. "The Omega should have been able to kill me."

When another pair of shitkickers entered his field of vision, he glanced up. Qhuinn had come over, and the brother was white as a sheet, his hands trembling at the ends of the sleeves of his leather jacket. The male lowered himself down. His blue-and-green eyes were red-lined and watery, and he was blinking them like he had a fan right in front of his face.

"Butch, you saved my life," the brother said. "And you're spent. Let me stab it, and we'll all go home."

Butch wanted to do that. He was tired in a way unrelated to physical exertion. He wanted to call Marissa and hear her voice, ask her to cut work early, and just lie beside his *shellan*. He wanted to know that his brothers and the other fighters were on the mountain and behind the *mhis*, behind the thick stone walls of the mansion, behind the fortress Darius had built over a hundred years ago. He wanted to be certain that, if only until nightfall the following evening, everybody was safe.

But that was the thing, wasn't it.

Safety was an illusion if it only lasted twenty-four hours. And those precious kids in that house, not just Lyric and Rhamp, but all of them, deserved to have their parents beside them. Hell, all of the *mahmens* and sires of all of the species should have that guarantee.

As long as the Omega was on the planet, normalcy was a fragile privilege for vampires, not a basic right.

Butch refocused on the slayer. It was still moving, the fingers flexing and curling on the asphalt, the legs churning in slow, faint motion.

Opening his mouth, Butch had to force himself to start inhaling.

So he could take the evil into his body once again.

CHAPTER TWENTY-THREE

Jo stood outside McGrider's on the sidewalk, watching a car pass by. Stepping aside as two guys in what had to be plainclothes went into the bar. Checking her phone, even though who cared about the hour.

The next time Syn asked for her number, she was going to damn well give it to him.

Assuming she ever saw him again.

The night seemed especially cold as she walked back toward the CCJ offices—positively Baltic, in fact—and it was funny, she hadn't noticed the temperature on the way over with Syn. And as she went along, she became aware that Caldwell had suddenly emptied out of life-forms. In spite of the people behind the wheels of the cars that went along the city streets, and the patrons she'd left behind at McGrider's, and even her misogynistic boss, and dear, sweet Bill and Lydia, she felt post-apocalyptic alone, the sole survivor of a nuclear catastrophe.

Then again, someone significant could take everyone else with them when they left—

Okaaaaaaaaaay, time to put away the melodrama. This was not a grown-up episode of *My So-Called Life*, with her as Angela and Syn as Jordan Catalano.

"Hormones," she muttered as she came up to the front of the CCJ building.

Instead of walking all the way round to the back, she took out her pass card and went in a side door. The sense that she wasn't going to be working at the paper for much longer was both part of her weird emotional state, and not that big an extrapolation. And it sucked. The last forty-eight hours had been full of the crazy, but she was starting to love reporting. Blackmailing her boss to let her work was not her gig, though, and she wasn't going to kid herself about Dick. She'd forced his hand for now, but that was sandbags against a storm surge. Sooner or later, the hold was going to break and he was going to find a way to fire her.

She hit the bathroom because she was in no hurry to go sit home alone—although the idea of binge-watching Angela Chase's love life wasn't a bad B plan to the prospect of sitting at her desk until dawn. After she came out drying her hands, she checked her email to see if the other photographs McCordle was going to send from his phone had come in. They hadn't.

Before she started cleaning her desk out, and not because she was firing herself, she decided this was ridiculous. She couldn't stay here all night. Putting the back exit to use, she ducked her head and hustled quickly to her car, aware of a ringing paranoia in her blood. Glancing around furtively, she didn't unlock the Golf until she was four feet away from the driver's side. But come on, like someone was going to sneak into her back seat otherwise? Throwing herself behind the wheel, she shut the door on her coat and left it there as she locked things back up.

Cranking the sewing machine engine over, she pulled her seat belt across her chest, put the gearshift in reverse, and hit the gas—

Jo slammed on the brakes.

In her rearview mirror, bathed in the red illumination of her taillights, a huge figure with a Mohawk was standing right behind her rear bumper.

Jo shoved the engine into park and jumped out.

A quip about long time/no see died in her throat.

"Are you okay?" she asked as she got a load of him.

When he nodded, she didn't believe him. He was pale and shaken, and at the base of both sleeves of his leather jacket, his hands were trembling.

"I need a shower," he said.

"What?"

"I don't smell good."

"Your cologne is all I can smell."

"I need . . ."

She had the feeling he had no idea what he was saying, and she wanted to know what the hell had happened during the twenty minutes between when he'd run out of the bar and now. It couldn't be second thoughts about leaving her. That wouldn't leave a hard-ass like him in this dazed, disordered state.

Before she was aware of making a conscious decision, she went to him and took his hand. She meant to say, "Come with me." But his skin was so icy, she worried about hypothermia.

"We need to get you warm."

"Am I cold?"

She led him around to the passenger side and opened the door for him. "Sit."

You know, in case he didn't know what to do—although how in the hell was he going to fit his big body into that seat—

"Guess you're retractable," she muttered as she shut him in.

Going around the front bumper, she put herself back behind the wheel, aware that her heart was pumping hard and her blood was rushing. As she put the car in reverse for a second time, she glanced at the man she'd picked up off the street like a stray dog.

He barely fit into her car: "Retractable" was an overstatement. Cantilevered was more like it. His knees were practically up to his earlobes, his arms wedged in between his legs, his far shoulder squeezed against his door. He didn't seem to care. Then again, he didn't seem to know where he was.

"My apartment's not far from here," she said. Well, not compared to someone who lived in Vermont. "I mean . . ."

Syn stared straight ahead. As if he were in a different world.

"Seat belt?" she prompted.

When he didn't move, she hit the brakes and reached across him to—

In the cramped space, he moved so fast, she couldn't track him. One second he was like a full-length coat crammed into a shoulder bag. Then next, he had grabbed her around the throat and was looking at her with blank, unseeing eyes.

True fear shot through Jo's chest. "Please . . ." she croaked out. "No—"

He blinked and focused on her properly.

"Oh, shit . . ." He immediately dropped his hold. "I'm sorry. You took me unaware."

Sitting back against her seat, she put her hands up to her neck. "I'm not going to do that again."

"It's just because . . . I'm somewhere else. I'm not going to hurt you, I swear."

As he shuddered, he seemed to have trouble breathing right. And even though he was physically strong and clearly a tough guy, she felt an overwhelming need to take care of him. He looked broken.

"It's okay," she told him. "You be wherever you are. I'll handle the rest right now."

◆   ◆   ◆

"I knew I couldnae trust you."

As Syn's father spoke, Syn put his back to the sweet cottage, to the young female and her little brother, to the innocents who ran with abandon and unknowing bliss through the wildflower meadow.

His sire took another step forward, another fallen branch cracking under his horrible weight. "And I knew where you would go. Care you not that

I hunger? You were to get something to sustain me, but it looks as though I must find something myself."

Glittering black eyes shifted to above Syn's head, and they tracked the fragile prey that had been marked. As his father's lips parted, the tips of his stained fangs descended, and his body lowered into an attack stance.

Syn moved without thinking. He burst forth and bit the back of his sire's hand, the one that had previously held his front teeth within its flesh. As his molars found home, his father's roar was so loud, it rebounded through the trees, and Syn prayed unto the Scribe Virgin that the female and her brother heard it and ran for safety.

There was no waiting round to see if his entreaty unto the higher power was granted.

His sire turned upon him with a vengeance that was madness and aggression combined. And Syn made sure that he stayed within range of the punishing blow that came down with the swiftness of a hawk upon a lemming. At the moment before impact upon his face, he ducked and scampered back. His sire took the bait, lurching forth, swinging again, stumbling, for he was as yet in his mead though he had stopped his imbibing long before.

Syn kicked his father in the shin and went further back. Then he took an off-kilter punch to the side of the head and went another step back.

He knew he had provided a sufficiency of challenge and affront when an unholy red light, emanating from his father's eyes, bathed him in the color of coming death.

It was then that Syn ran.

And he ran fast, but not too fast.

He had no idea where he was going. He knew only that he had to draw the monster away from that family if it was the last thing he did. And indeed, it would be. He was going to die in this, but hopefully the female and her kin would take heed of his broken body and protect themselves—and mayhap this was the best solution for all. He would be over, and that young female would be, if not safe, then safer, for surely Syn's sire would be cast out of the village by the elders?

Another thing to pray for, not that he had time to entreat the Virgin Scribe once more.

With the red light of his father's violence streaming behind him, the forest was lit in a murderous manner, the trees and brush, the trail that Syn found himself upon, the deer that were flushed from their stands, illuminated in the fashion of the blood that would soon be shed.

Syn's thin legs pumped as fast as they could, and the only thing that allowed him to keep the lead was his father's prodigious weight. Verily, the hoarse breathing, the huffing and puffing, was like a dragon that labored upon the ground in a canter when it should have taken unto the air. His sire did not have that skyward option, thank Fates.

The clearing arrived without preamble, the forest's arboreal obstacles of trunk and bramble ending with sharp delineation, and for a moment Syn couldnae fathom where he had taken the chase—except then he recognized the landscape. 'Twas the start of his father's verdant fields, the ones he rented out to the farmers for their horses, cattle, goats, and sheep to graze and take of the river water.

Up ahead, here was a post-and-beam construction, open on all sides, for the animals to find shelter under, and Syn headed there, hoping for some kind of protection from the attack. As he closed in, he noticed a stand of hay rakes propped up against one of the roof supports, and the strangest thing happened. His palms tingled and his body flushed in a manner not related to exertion or fear. Within his mind, he knew with abrupt clarity what he would do with the potential weapons and the precision of his plan shocked him—although not because of its violence. It was because the images held such certainty that it was as if the actions he would take had in fact already been taken.

Mayhap he could survive this.

Allowing his instincts to guide him, he gave himself up to a deadly purpose, relinquishing control to this unfamiliar underbelly of his consciousness. The effect of submission was otherworldly. Within his mind, he receded until he became separate from his body, an observer witnessing himself from off to the side rather than looking out from behind his own eyes.

It all flowed like water.

Adding speed to his spindly legs, he put some distance between him and his approaching sire, coming upon the meadowing tools with promptness. His small palms found the well-worn, sweat-stained handle of one of the rakes and he set the length vertically against his torso, keeping it out of sight as he waited for his sire to come unto him.

The hulking footfalls slowed as soon as Syn halted, and the breath was so heavy and pronounced, his father sounded as a charging bull.

Syn awaited the approach, the thunderous, earthquaking approach, and he began to breathe as did his sire. When he looked down at his hands gripping the rake's pole, there was a red wash upon them, and he wondered when he had started bleeding—

No, it was not blood. It was his own eyes glowing as his father's did.

But he couldnae wonder about this.

As his sire closed the final distance, Syn's mind worried over when to swing, what angle was required, whether he would be able to lift the weight of the rake that was a feather to his father and a boulder to him. But his body knew the answers and had the power. Even as he wondered the when and how of it all, his arm and torso abruptly coordinated together.

The arc of the swing was too exact for him to believe. And he didn't know who was more surprised, him or his sire. His father's jowled face turned and regarded the clawed metal spikes coming at his head as if he didn't recognize what they were.

Syn had little strength and the rake was heavy. However the teeth and tongs were unforgiving. Before his sire could raise an arm or duck, they scored deeply into his father's ruddy, angry features, moving across his temple, his cheek, his nose. As the tool came out on the other side, blood flared and spooled in the air.

His father bellowed in pain, his filthy bear paw hands coming up to where he had been scratched so deeply. And then, on the far side, the rake was carried upon its own momentum, swooping down to the ground, landing like a bird of prey, talons gripping the earth as its perch.

Syn yanked against the handle. Pulled with what might he had. Threw his weight back against the abiding hold of the tool.

He looked at his father and froze.

His sire had straightened and dropped his hands. One of his eyes had been pierced and was hanging by some kind of threaded, bloody ligament, the orb upon his cheekbone, the vacated socket dark as a cave. His face was contorted in a mask of horror and vengeance, the mouth with the rotten teeth wide open, the fangs extended fully.

The rake came free from the earth, and as if of its own choosing, flipped in Syn's grip, the tongs trading places with the blunt end of the handle.

Without thinking of what he was doing, Syn surged forward and thrust the wooden grip's tip upward into the socket. He put all his strength into the penetration, and was horrified and relieved that the tool's home was found as if it were an inevitability.

Another howl of pain rippled through the night, and his father blindly reached for Syn, paws swiping at the air, the sleeves of the filthy tunic whistling by Syn's head and face. Relinquishing the hold upon the rake, Syn ducked between his sire's legs. As he emerged through to the other side, he spun around, arched back, and caught himself upon the ground with his palms. Kicking upward with the soles of his feet, he punched his father's backside.

The push was enough to send the weight that was already off-balance into a free fall, and his father landed face-first on the rake, the handle penetrating deeply into his skull, yanking his head to the side, popping out, popping free.

As his sire continued unto the ground as deadweight, Syn's eyes went to the knife mounted upon his father's wide leather belt. With the beast as yet stunned by the injury, Syn rushed forth and unsheathed the blade. The hilt was too thick for his palm, so he applied two hands unto the gripping. Raising the dagger over his head, he buried the sharp point in his father's thick coating. He didn't know whether it went in enough, however. His father, writhing in slow motion, seemed not to notice the fresh assault.

That was when Syn saw the rock. Flat. Broad. About the size of his chest.

It weighed almost too much for him. But fear and fury combined to strengthen him immeasurably. He waddled the stone over and brought it down upon the top of the hilt, once . . . twice . . . three times.

He hammered the knife in until its guard prevented any further progress.

Stumbling back, he fell upon the hard dirt patch created by a congregation of hooves around the shelter. He was breathing so hard his throat hurt and his eyes were blurry. When he went to clear them of whatever was upon them, he realized he was crying—

With a groan, his father rolled over and sat up, a ghost from a grave, except very real, and very capable of still doing damage. The injury to his eye was horrific and blood flowed freely, covering his features upon that side with a gloss that made Syn's stomach lurch.

When it appeared as if his sire would stand up and fight anew, it was clear that he was drunk and did not feel the injuries sufficiently. Or mayhap the soul that animated him was just that hardy and evil.

Terror clutched at Syn's heart and he jumped up to run—

◆   ◆   ◆

Sometime later, much later, centuries later, Syn's awareness returned unto him. Which was a strange thing as he was not aware of it having left.

Everything seemed quite blurry, so he rubbed his eyes—

A sting made him frown, and as he blinked . . . he realized he was sitting cross-legged upon the dirt patch in a puddle. Had it rained?

No. It was not water.

It was blood. He was sitting in a congealed puddle of blood.

Syn frowned. Lifting one of his hands, he found that it was covered with more of the same. Indeed, there was blood all upon him, staining his ragged clothes. Was he hurt? Had his father attacked him and—

"*Dearest Virgin Scribe.*"

Syn jumped and raised his eyes. The figure standing over him was one that his mind told him he should recognize. Yes, he should know who this is.

The pretrans male knelt down before him. "Please . . . give me the dagger."

"What?"

"The dagger, Syn."

"I dinnae have a dagger—"

"In your palm."

It was as Syn lifted his hand to prove to this familiar stranger that he had naught within his grip that his sight informed him he was the one in the wrong. There was a dagger against his palm. How had he not noticed? And abruptly the identity of the pretrans came unto him. It was his cousin, Balthazar. He recognized the male's face the now.

"The dagger, cousin. Give it to me."

Syn looked to the left and saw the first body part by the broken handle of the rake. The second was impaled on the rake's tongs. The next was . . . over by the fence.

There were many more, and the largest, the torso, had been field dressed. His father had been torn apart by someone. Who else had been . . . here?

"Syn, give me the blade. Now."

His hand was unresisting as the weapon was removed from it. And then Syn looked into his cousin's eyes as reality began to dawn, an ugly, unbelievable sunrise. "I think I did this, cousin."

"Yes," Balthazar said grimly. "You did."

Syn stared at a severed hand that lay upon ground as a fallen soldier. "He was going to hurt her."

"Hurt who?"

"It matters not."

With focused effort, Syn managed to rise his tired bones from the pool of blood. As he weaved on his feet, he lurched toward the river, seeking out the cool, rushing waters. Wading into the current, he squatted down and cupped *his hands, splashing his face over and over again. Then he drank of the stream, dousing the fire that ran down his throat and into his gut.*

When he tried to stand up once more, he faltered and fell, catching himself upon slick rocks. Lifting his head, he found that his skull weighed as much as his entire body, and fast upon the heels of that reckoning came a wave of dizziness. Followed by a burst of heat that bore no relation to exertion.

"Balth . . . azar?"

His cousin hitched a hold under Syn's arm and pulled him up and out of the water. "Oh, no, Syn . . ."

"What?"

Balthazar looked around frantically. "The change. You're going through the change—"

"No, I'm not—"

"There is steam coming off your skin, you are boiling up."

Syn looked in confusion at his arm, at his feet, at his ankles. Steam was in fact rising from his body, and he did feel a strange, certain heat. But . . .

All at once a vast incapacitation tackled him, sweeping his legs out from under him, taking him from the hold of his blooded kin. As he landed in a heap, the fire in his body trebled, and trebled again, and then his limbs began to hum.

"Dearest Virgin Scribe," Balthazar groaned. "We need to get you shelter, and a blood source."

"Nae," Syn said through gritted teeth. "Leave me. It is well enough for me to go unto the Fade—"

As the bones in his legs strained, and his forearms felt like ropes being twisted, he lost the power of speech and laid his head down. Breathing shallowly, he recalled what he knew of the transition: Without the blood of a female, he was going to die, and he wondered how long it would take—

"I shall help him."

At the sound of the words, Syn forced his eyes open. When he saw who it was, he shook his head. "No, no . . ."

It was the female, from the meadow. The one who had always been so good to him.

"Balthazar," he said urgently. "Take her away, she mustnae see—"

The female walked forward. "I know what he did to protect me and my kin." She kept her eyes down, as if she were deliberately not witnessing the damage he had wrought. "I know . . . and I would help him the now."

Syn shook his head weakly. "No. No, I am unworthy . . ."

CHAPTER TWENTY-FOUR

Unworthy?" Jo asked as she pulled into a parking space in front of her apartment building. "Unworthy of what?"

As she spoke, Syn did not seem to hear her. He was sitting stock-still in that passenger seat, hands on his knees, eyes staring straight out the front windshield like he was watching a TV. He seemed totally calm. Or . . . maybe he was dead? He wasn't blinking.

"Syn?"

Well, one thing was certain. She was not about to touch him as she shut the car off—

Slowly, his head turned to her, and his expression was vacant, as if he were in a trance. But then he cleared his throat. "Sorry."

"It's okay." Even though she didn't know what exactly he was apologizing for or what precisely she was forgiving him of.

He nodded. Then contradicted himself. "No, it isn't. None of it was."

Jo glanced around him to the front of her apartment building. "Do you want to come in?"

Was it going to be yes, with a head shake? Or another no/nod combo? she wondered.

"Or should I take you home?" Wherever that was. "I can take you home."

"I don't want to go back there right now."

Was he talking about where he was in his head? Or where he stayed?

Whatever the reply to that question might be, Jo didn't want him to go. She wanted some answers. About what he thought he knew about her. About who he was and where he came from. About why the connection between them seemed so undeniable.

She eyed the thick thighs straining those leathers.

Okay, fine. She had a clue about that last one—

"Yes," he said as he opened the door.

Wait, had she asked him anything? He must be talking about the invite into her place.

Jo got out as well and met him on the other side of her car. As they walked up the cement path together, she wondered how her digs compared to where he was living. Probably not well, given that he was bunking with his boss—or whatever a bodyguard called his employer. Meanwhile, the modest little apartment she'd moved into was housed in a building that was just four stories high and split in two, with units stacked on either side. The outside was cheap brick veneer, the inside common areas utilitarian, but clean. Her neighbors were grad students, medical residents, and a couple who were pregnant and moving out soon.

"I'm over here," she said as they went through the second set of entry doors.

Her one-bedroom was right there on the left, and when he walked into it, he stopped dead as if he'd run out of gas on the highway. She turned on some lights.

"I don't have much furniture." She thought of her parents' fancy mansion. "I don't have much period, but everything in here is mine."

She closed the door. And took her coat off because she had to do something.

"Can I offer you a drink?" she asked. "I have . . . well, four bottles of Sam Adams, and a bottle of cheap red wine that my coworker made me take home with me after I . . ."

"I don't drink," he mumbled.

"Oh. Right. Sorry." Well, she certainly was going to after the last couple of days. "But if you don't mind, I'll just help myself to a beer."

Syn turned to her. "I'm sorry. I shouldn't be here."

"I'm glad you are. No offense, but you don't look well."

Glancing down at himself, he lifted his arms as if he expected something unsavory to be dripping off of them. "I really do want to take a shower."

Jo's heartbeat quickened as she pointed to an open doorway. "It's right in there. Fresh towels are hanging on the rods because I did laundry when I couldn't sleep early this morning."

"You should have called me if you couldn't sleep."

"I didn't want to bother you."

"You didn't write down my number, did you."

Leaving that one alone, Jo motioned at the bathroom. "Hot water is through there. Then we can talk."

There was a pause. And then Syn nodded and went where she told him to go. As he passed by, his sheer size was unbelievable. Out in more wide open spaces—like the back alleys of Caldwell's downtown or the parking lot at the CCJ—his height and weight didn't seem as big a deal. But in here? In her little seven-hundred-square-foot crash pad? It was like someone had driven an eighteen-wheeler indoors.

As he closed the bathroom door behind himself, she wondered if he showered with his weapons on—and then promptly got a mental picture of a whole naked accessorized by Smith & Wesson.

And jeez, that really shouldn't be as hot as she imagined it to be.

When the water started to run, she rubbed her aching head and thought about the empty pit of her stomach to avoid any more hypotheticals involving Syn's birthday suit: She was still hungry. Then again, she'd eaten less than half of her meal at the bar, and she knew she had to do something to make up those ten pounds—fourteen, actually—she'd recently lost.

Pizza was always good, right?

Determined to be a proper hostess—thank you, Mrs. Early—Jo went over and knocked on the bathroom door. "Hey. I know it might be overkill, but I'm going to order some Italian food. Would you like any?"

The last thing she expected was for him to open things up.

And yeah, wow, Syn had apparently turned the water temperature up to Scorched Earth, and given that the hot water heater was right next to the shower stall in the closet, it took no time for things to get toasty. Accordingly, a great swirl of humid air wafted around behind him, setting him off like he was a mystery centuries old—but that wasn't the half of it. He'd taken off his jacket—and also whatever arsenal he wore under it—and then removed the skintight Under Armor shirt he seemed always to wear.

So his pecs were on full display. His abs, too.

As well as the pair of wing-shaped hip bones that flew above the waistband of his leathers.

"Whatever you want is fine with me."

Or at least, that's what she thought he said. It kind of sounded like "Lwibekew ksb icbe ls owbd bakd ow." Because, hello, her hearing had gone on the fritz.

Oh, and if those were the words he'd spoken? Well, then she had a few things she'd like to order, none of which were going to be helpful in this situation, and all of which had him taking his leathers and whatever underwear he had on down to the floor.

Commando? she wondered. *Dear. God.*

"I was thinking pizza." Liar, liar, drop those pants on the fire—that was not even *close* to what she was thinking about. "What do you like on it?"

And P.S., she now had a pretty damn good idea of how men felt when a woman wore a low-cut blouse. It was taking nearly an act of Congress to keep her stare at his collarbones.

"Whatever you like," he said—and re-shut the door.

Jo blinked as she faced off at a whole lot of fake wood paneling. "Sounds good."

+   +   +

On the other side of the bathroom door, Syn turned around and leaned back against the fragile barrier between him and his female. After a moment, he sensed her moving away, and then, over the falling water of the shower, his keen ears picked out her dialing her phone and ordering something that had pepperoni on it. Closing his eyes, he told himself he needed to leave her in peace, but it was an internal argument he'd already lost the second he had gotten into her car.

For the first time in his life, he did not want to be alone.

Actually, it was worse than that.

He specifically wanted to be with Jo.

He wanted to tell her that he'd just jumped the Omega in a back alley, even though she didn't know who that was or why that kind of reckless shit was a bad idea. And he wanted to tell her that the people he lived with were going to think he was a hero for saving Butch's life, even though she had no frame of reference for the Black Dagger Brotherhood or the *Dhestroyer* prophecy, and even though that altruistic crap had not been his motive for his attack. And he really wanted to confess that he killed people to regulate his emotions, not because he had a monster in him, but because he was a monster himself.

Just like his father.

And yup, all of this winning personality and character of his? He'd brought it and a bag of chips right through this poor female's door. In the middle of an impending personal crisis for her that she had no idea was coming.

He was such a fucking hero, wasn't he.

With hard pulls, he shucked his leathers off his legs and then he put himself under the blistering hot water. The nerves in his skin immediately flared with agony, and he had to bite his lower lip to keep from cursing at the pain. But he wanted the punishment. He had earned it.

For never being the hero.

Syn used whatever soap she had, running the bar all over his body and his hair and his face. After he rinsed off, he stood there under the slicing heat to make extra sure he was clean, and then he cut the boiling spray and stepped over the lip of her plastic tub. Using one of the two towels that hung on the rod by the toilet, he wanted to tell her she should burn the thing after he was done.

He felt as if he was contaminating her entire living space with his mere presence.

When there was nothing left to dry off, he stared down through the lazy, swirling mist at the pool of black leather and moisture-wicking nylon formed by his discarded clothes. He did not want to put them back on his soaped-and-rinsed skin. Not while he was under her roof. The set had been worn when he had slaughtered *lessers* who had deserved his killing, as well as a number of humans who had begged for mercy that hadn't come unto them. His togs were bloodstained, sweat-soaked, and carrying the residue of gunpowder and death.

And yet she spoke of cologne.

Humans clearly had inferior noses—

The shriek outside the bathroom was high-pitched and could only have come from Jo.

Syn grabbed the gun that he had put within reach on her counter, ripped open the door, and jumped out with the muzzle up and his finger on the trigger.

Over by the door, Jo and a teenage human male both froze. Then the delivery boy's eyes popped wide and his hands went up. Jo, who was bent to the side and holding a pizza box awkwardly, looked like she would have done the same if she could have.

Then her eyes dropped down.

And . . . not to his weapon. As they peeled wide, she was clearly shocked at his nakedness.

"I just dropped the p-p-p-pizza," the teenager stammered. "I swear. That was all."

Jo moved slowly, righting herself. "I was taking the change from him at the same time—"

"—that the box slipped—"

"—out of his hands."

Syn breathed in and smelled absolutely no fear at all coming from his female. Putting his weapon down by his thigh, he nodded.

"Y-y-you want a refund?" the delivery boy asked. "I can give you a refund. I mean, I messed up—"

"Whatever she wants goes," Syn said as he stepped back into the bathroom and shut the door.

Hanging his head, he wondered what the hell was wrong with him.

Oh, wait. He knew that list all too well.

And one of the entries was that a gangster had ordered Syn to kill the very female . . . he had insisted on going home with.

CHAPTER TWENTY-FIVE

Mr. F ran in a straight line. He ran fast. He ran quiet.

With the speed of a sprinter and the endurance of a marathoner, he went deeper into the rough areas of Caldwell, to the places where he wouldn't have trod back when he'd been on his wanders as an addict. He passed by apartments and then tenements and then crack dens that sprouted like weeds in abandoned buildings. And still he kept going, his breathing even and steady, his legs churning, his feet landing solidly.

No, no, no—

The word banged around his head to the rhythm of his footfalls, and every time it hit the inside of his skull, he saw an image of those dirty white robes, that spilling shadow under the hem, the menace that contaminated the night air with its arrival. He did not know its name, yet he recognized who it was.

The one who had found him under the bridge. The one who had taken him to that abandoned strip mall. The one who had drained him and filled him with something terrible—

The end of the alley arrived with no preamble. One minute Mr. F had an endless, shitty road ahead of him through the forest of tenements and drug houses. The next, his path was blocked by a twenty-foot-high chain-link fence littered with plastic bags, off-kilter "No Trespassing" signs, and random pieces of faded, dirty clothing. Like the thing was a strainer in a drain.

At least he knew this flimsy barrier wasn't going to be a problem.

Taking a running jump, he sprung some ten feet up and gripped a hold into the links with fingers like steel cables. Hand over hand, he climbed for the coils of barbed wire at the top, his upper body strength so great that he could allow his legs to hang free—

A hand clamped on his ankle.

And as soon as the contact was made, the wash of feelings that went through Mr. F was horrible, every sadness he had ever felt, all the fears he had ever had, each regret that had ever dogged him, coalescing in the center of his chest, a pneumonia of emotion. As strangled gasps came out of his mouth and he pulled at the fencing, trying to get himself free, tears came to his eyes.

Because he knew who had come for him and he knew he was not getting out of it. And not just the grip on the bottom of his leg.

He had made a bargain, and the fact that it had been one-sided and he had not known what he was agreeing to, was not going to matter—

"Did you honestly think you could run from me?"

The voice didn't come from under Mr. F's feet. It came from back in the alley proper behind him. Craning a look over his shoulder, he saw the dingy robes standing some thirty feet away, and there was nothing corporeal that he could see on his ankle. Yet the grip was even stronger now, pulling him down, dragging him back to the asphalt, back toward the evil.

"Truly," the warping voice said. "Did you think you could get away from the likes of me, your creator. Your master."

Mr. F fought the drag with everything he had, his fingers ripping down the links, the fence rattling, a black stain streaking on the vertical as his skin was broken. Losing purchase, he crashed down to the pavement and was dragged backward through dirty puddles and oil stains. With his bloody fingers, he fought the claiming and got nowhere—

All at once he was up off the ground and spun around. Suspended in midair, his feet dangling to a point, his arms were pinned to his sides and his body became immobile, though there was nothing on him.

The robed figure didn't walk to him. It drifted, hovering above the filthy ground.

"I chose you," it said in that weird voice, "because you were the only one with a brain. This may have been a mistake on my part. Brawn usually works better. One would think I would have learned that after all these centuries."

With a flick of the wrist, the evil sent Mr. F flying through the air, and the momentum stopped only when he slammed face-first into the side of a tenement, his nose busting wide open, the impact of his chin such that it nearly dislocated his jaw joints. Pressure on his back increased until he couldn't draw a breath, and he had some thought that he should be suffocating. He didn't, though the pain made him see stars.

The voice of evil closed in on him as he was once again dragged down to the ground, the rough brick wall shaving off layers of skin on his cheek. "You are a summary disappointment."

As his feet registered a return to the asphalt, he strained his eyes to see what was behind him.

"I shall give you one more chance to dazzle me," the evil said in a bored tone. "And then I shall move on."

Mr. F squeezed his eyes shut. "Let me go—"

A hand palmed the back of his head and pushed so hard, he could feel his cheekbone start to give way against the brick.

"I will not let you go. And you need to be punished for your transgressions—"

"Against what?" Mr. F gritted out.

"Against me!"

"How have I transgressed..." A toxic sickness flooded into Mr. F's body, and he told himself to stop talking, but his mouth wouldn't listen. "I have done nothing—"

"And *that* is your transgression." The horrible voice was right next to his ear. "You are supposed to serve me."

"How?" Mr. F groaned. "You never told me how. I don't know what I'm supposed to do."

The evil relented some of the pressure, as if it were briefly reconsidering the condemnations it leveled. "Listen to your mind, it will tell you what I want. And in the meantime, I know what you can do to service me now."

There was a pause.

And then something was driven so far into him that Mr. F screamed from the pain.

◆   ◆   ◆

Back at the Brotherhood's mansion, Butch was in the process of opening the door into the vestibule to leave when a gloved hand slammed the thing shut on him and stayed put like it was a car parked grille into the wood.

"Where do you think you're going," V said grimly.

Butch pivoted around, and had to catch himself to keep on his feet. "I'm picking up Marissa."

V looked confused. "What?"

"I'm going to go pick up Marissa."

Those diamond eyes narrowed. "You think you're picking up Marissa?"

"That's what I said."

"Not even close, my guy." V linked an arm through Butch's. "And you're going nowhere this drunk—"

Butch meant to separate himself from his roommate, but it was

weird. The mosaic floor seemed to be made of liquid, everything shifting under the soles of his loafers. As he went off-kilter, he ended up
pulling himself back to rights on V's biceps.

"I have to go pick her up at work."

"You mean pick her up from work? It's not four a.m."

"Yes, it is?"

Now Butch was the one frowning. And things got even more con-
fusing as he lifted up his wrist and looked down at his Audemars
Piguet. The Oak's famously eight-sided dial was all smudged, and the
numbers appeared to be moving instead of the hands.

"I think my watch is broken."

"You wanna try that again?"

"Is your hearing bad?"

Vishous gave him a bored look. "If what you just asked me was
whether my hearing is a problem, I think it's more your mouth. 'Cuz
what just came out of it was something like 'Ian Ziering mad.'"

"Huh. Weird. Maybe he is mad, though. They're not doing any
more *Sharknado*s."

"Gimme that."

When a tumbler half-full of brown liquid was taken out of his
hand, Butch wondered where the thing had come from. Then again,
everything felt like a mystery.

"You're done with that."

Butch released his roommate and tugged his jacket down. "Probably
right. Feeling a little loozy. Loser. Loosing? Goosing. Gosling, Ryan, not
Reynolds. What was the question?"

By way of answer, Vishous started walking him to the billiard room,
but that was a no go. Butch protested by throwing out his anchor.

"No, I'm going to get Marissa."

"I told you, it's not time."

"I'll sit and waiting. Wait. For four. For her—"

"I'm not letting you drive drunk."

"I'm not drunk." Butch stopped as he heard the slur in his words. Holding his forefinger up, he changed tactics. "I'm getting sober up. By the minute."

"Then you better chill here for about ten hours."

Determined to win the argument, Butch explained, calmly and concisely, how he didn't need that much time, and then capped that theory of relativity off with another move to the big-ass door—which would lead him out through the vestibule, which would let him get to the R8, which was parked in the courtyard, which would give him the wheels he needed to go down off the mountain and go into town and find Safe Place's neighborhood—

"Butch. I'm not letting you drive a car like this."

V leaned back against the vestibule's door—which was kind of a surprise. Last time Butch noticed, the guy was standing with his back to the archway into the billiard room. Guess they'd moved.

Whatever. Butch opened his mouth—

"You argue about this anymore and I'm going to give you a nap."

"I don't need a nap." Butch cleared his throat so he didn't sound like a five-year-old. "I need to go be with Marissa."

As the name of his *shellan* came out of his mouth, he had to fight the emotions in his chest. Had to fight the shit in his brain, too. Something about confronting the Omega had hinged him loose in ways he didn't seem to be coming out of well—but at least he knew the solution. He was going to go be with his female. Even if all he could do was sit in a parked car outside of her work for four hours, six hours, before she got off, that would be enough.

He was untethered. She was his harbor. So the math was obvious—

"No," his roommate said. "Not when you're this drunk."

"Will you drive me then?"

"You need to stay home. That was way too close with the evil, Butch. I need you to stay in the *mhis* for right now."

"What are you talking about?" Butch snatched the tumbler back and took a gulp. And the fact that he felt absolutely no burn in his throat at all should have been a red flag concerning his current level of intoxication. But fuck it. "I'm not a prisoner here."

"Just until we can get a team around you."

"A team? Fuck that. I'm—"

"The Omega came out to find you tonight, Butch. Unless you forgot what magically appeared in front of you in that alley?"

"It didn't come for me." As V shot him a yeah-right, Butch shook his head. "The *Fore-lesser* was standing right beside it. The evil came for its subordinate, not for me. It was just a coincidence I was there."

Butch took another draw on the glass, and as he reflected on the way he'd corrected his roommate's version of events, he congratulated himself on speaking so much better. Not that he had been bad at it before, no matter what V had said.

"It was after you, Butch." V shook his head. "And if the *Fore-lesser* was there, it was because it was working to get to you, too. The pair are always aligned, that's the way it works."

"Don't talk to me like I don't know what the fuck is going on."

"You're not thinking straight."

"I am perfectly fucking fine. Now get out of my way."

Things got a little wonky at that point and Butch wasn't exactly sure about the sequence of events. The outcome was clear. When he tried to force his way out of the vestibule so he could get behind the wheel, V ended up taking the glass away for a second time. And then he seemed to look apologetic.

"I'm sorry about this, cop."

"Sorry about what—"

The right hook came sailing through the air with the greatest of ease. And as it hit Butch solidly in the jaw, kicking his head back like a baseball struck for the stands, he had a thought that he didn't feel a thing.

In fact, he went on a nice little float, during which the entire mansion, in spite of its size, weight, and foundation, went on a tilt such that, as he stood on his feet, he managed to look straight ahead at the foyer's dome ceiling three stories up.

Wow, those warriors on their steeds sure looked like they know what they're doing, he thought.

And then, just as V promised, it was naptime.

zzzzZZZZZZZzzzzzzzZZzz.

CHAPTER TWENTY-SIX

You want to talk about some *Jeopardy!* theme playing? As Jo gathered two paper plates, a beer for her, and some napkins in her kitchen, she was counting down the seconds. And when she heard the bathroom door finally open, she had to force herself not to wheel around and check to see what had come out.

And not because she was worried about there being guns involved again.

No, it was because she was hoping there was just going to be a towel. Or maybe even less—

Oh. He was dressed.

To cover her internal conversation about naked things that were none of her business, Jo bustled over to the coffee table, all Suzy Home-maker without any dirty thoughts in her head at all.

Nope. Not a one.

"So how about we try this eating thing again."

It was a good goal. An appropriate one, given that it did not involve body parts (his) or hot thoughts (hers.) Still, every time she blinked, she saw him scaring the crap out of the delivery boy, that body of Syn's so spectacularly nude, that gun in his hand so steady . . . that dead stare in his eyes the kind of thing she wasn't afraid of, but maybe should be.

So naked. So much smooth, hairless skin. So much muscle. So much . . .

Um. Length. And, um. Girth—

Okaaaaaaay, she really needed to stop this—

"Stop what?" he asked. When she looked at him in confusion, he sat down on her sofa. "What do you need to stop?"

Well, for starters, it would be great to quit thinking of you lying faceup on that rug right there and me riding you like Annie-frickin'-Oakley until your six-gun goes off in my—

"Oh, God." She went to cover the flush on her face with her hands—and ended up smacking herself with the plates and the napkins that she forgot she was holding. "Ow—okay, right. I gotta get a grip here."

"On what?" he asked.

Don't say it, she told her mouth. *Don't you dare answer that question.*

Delivering the eating accoutrements that had assaulted her to the coffee table, she opened up the pizza box and discovered that the pepperoni and cheese had had some very bad plastic surgery, all the features of the pie's face horribly rearranged, the molten cheese and toppings slopping over part of the crust.

"Nico's is just around the corner," she explained unnecessarily. "It always comes superhot so that's why . . ." She cleared her throat as she passed him two slices. "Do you want some water?"

Focusing on her empty plate, she put a slice on it and then cracked open her Sam Adams.

"Is there something wrong?" she asked as she realized he wasn't eating.

"I do not start to eat until you do."

She blinked. "A tradition of yours?"

"Yes."

As Syn just sat there, she picked up her slice, nodded to him, and took a bite. When she swallowed, he finally followed suit, and the man ate like he'd been assigned the consumption of the pizza for a class he was taking: precise, controlled, neat, and efficient.

Unlike him, she only managed two bites before her stomach revolted. So when he asked if he could keep going on what was in the box, she nodded.

As Jo sat back and nursed her beer, she watched him while trying not to look like she was watching him. His jaw was going up and down, the hollow under his cheek appearing and disappearing. She had to admit she was surprised he ate all of it. Then again, with that body of his?

Well, actually, thinking of the utter, stupid perfection of his two-arms, two-legs and a torso routine, he should be taking Tren on a regular basis, eating lean meats and low carbs, and pumping weights at the gym twelve hours a day.

Jo took a deep breath. He was back to staring straight ahead, that haunted cast to his harsh face making her wonder what exactly he was seeing behind his eyes.

"Where does the PTSD come from," she asked quietly. "Is it from what you saw overseas?"

As he glanced at her in surprise, she shrugged. "A lot of servicemen and -women have it when they come back from Iraq. Afghanistan. Wherever they've been. It explains a lot."

When he lowered his eyes, she sighed. "Yeeeeeah, and here I am, talking like I know anything. I've never been in the military—"

"Do you always have that gun on you?" he asked.

You mean the one that you had me point at your chest? she thought.

"If I'm out on the street, yes."

"Keep it with you always." He looked at her with serious, steady eyes. "Don't ever have it out of reach. Do you sleep with it next to you?"

She frowned. "Any particular reason why you're bringing this up?"

"It's a dangerous world. You need to protect yourself."

She thought of Gigante. And the body she'd seen wrapped like a bow around that fire escape. "Yes, it can be. But I don't believe in being paranoid."

Liar. But she was trying to front so he'd respect her.

"Paranoia keeps you alive."

"Has it done that for you?"

"Are you a reporter?"

"Nah, I just hang out at the *CCJ* office, twiddling my thumbs." She smiled a little. "Actually, I'm in the middle of my first story now. I was doing online stuff before that. And I'm still doing the online stuff." She tilted the beer bottle toward him. "How about some quid pro quo? And you choose the topic."

There was a long pause.

"Well, tonight . . . I saved someone's life for the wrong reason," he said softly.

Jo felt the urge to sit upright and go *Why? How? Who? Where?* in rapid-fire succession. But she sucked all that back.

Keeping her voice quiet and level, she said, "How is it ever wrong to save a life?"

"I just did it because I wanted . . . to fight."

"The end result was good, though. And how do you know it was just for fighting."

"Sometimes that's all I want to do." His shoulders tightened, as if in his mind, he was remembering specific conflicts. "Sometimes that's all I have in me and I have to let it out."

Jo slowly sat forward, compelled by the mask that covered his face. She needed to know what was under there with an intensity that had bad idea written all over it.

"You can trust me," she whispered. "With your secrets. I'm not a reporter in my personal life."

"If I thought for one instant you were not trustworthy, I wouldn't have come here." His eyes shifted over to hers. "You were the one person I thought of."

"What happened. You weren't gone very long."

"It isn't how long something takes."

As he receded away from her again, she had the sense that he had sought her out for some kind of help which she was not qualified to provide. So Jo gave him what she could.

Reaching toward him, she put her arm around the span of his massive shoulder. "Come here," she whispered.

She expected him to fight her. Instead, Syn's huge, hulking torso caved into her lap, as if he were past his capacity to hold up the burdens he carried with him.

Running her hand over the rock-hard contours of his bicep, she felt him shudder and saw his thick lashes lower onto his cheek.

"You're exhausted," she said.

"More than I can ever explain. Or recover from."

Jo's heart went out to him. She knew exactly how that felt. "You can sleep here tonight, if you want."

◆   ◆   ◆

Syn focused on the slow, magical circles that his female made on his arm. She soothed his whole body just by her touch, and he gratefully sank into the peace she gave him. He knew it was not going to last. Sooner or later, and certainly before dawn, he was going to have to leave her—and he mourned the loss of her even as he was in her lap.

After a while, he turned onto his back and looked up at her. When her eyes went to his mouth, he knew what was on her mind, and not just because of what she was focused on. Her scent changed, and with every inhale, he took her arousal into himself, his body instantly responding, his cock thickening in his leathers, his blood starting to pump. Hard.

"Will you let me pleasure you?" he said in a deep voice.

As her eyes flared, he made no move to touch her. He wanted her to freely choose her way. Freely choose him.

Although how freely could she have him when she didn't know what he was?

In time that would be solved, though, he told his conscience as he inhaled her scent even deeper. In time, they would be the same when she went through her change.

And after that? Well, he was deluding himself if he thought they had a future. No female would be with the likes of him for long.

But they had this moment right here, right now.

"How about we both get pleasure," she murmured.

Reaching up, he touched the length of her red hair, running his soldier's callused fingertips down the locks that fell, softer than water, more beautiful than moonlight, even rarer than gems and gold, upon her shoulder.

Tilting up, he put his lips to hers and stroked her mouth with his own. He went slow, and not because he wasn't desperate. He was panting for her and they hadn't even started yet. The truth, however, was that he wasn't sure how to do this, where to put his mouth, his hands, his body. He had touched females before, back in the nights when he'd been mining the depths of his impotence, trying to find the end of it—before he'd realized it wasn't who he was with, but himself, that was the problem. Back then, he'd never worried about being suave, or having moves, or even about pleasuring the one he was with. They had always taken what they wanted of him, and not one had been bothered when he had told them he couldnac finish. He had been used, and he hadn't minded the using.

To be offended by the likes of that, you had to have self-respect.

"What do you like?" he said as he sat up and switched their positions, shifting her over and settling her across his thighs.

As Jo sprawled in his lap, he liked the way her hair licked over the leathers that covered his lower body. He liked the swell of her breasts beneath her simple shirt. He liked the way her legs stretched out. He liked the fact that there was much to look forward to.

Such as undressing her and mounting her.

"I like kissing you," she said.

"Then we shall do more of it."

Syn eagerly complied with her request, and as their lips met once again, he allowed his hand to do what it wanted—which turned out to be travel down her throat to her collarbone . . . to her shoulder . . . to her waist . . . to her hip. As he further learned the sweetness of her mouth with his own, he took his time with the lushness of her body. He knew they were building something resplendent in this intense, quiet space, a construction that would shut out the world, if only for a short time. Upon this desire they shared, they would layer upon layer a temporary sexual fortress against the pain and strife of the outside, of the past . . . of the future.

For he knew that theirs was not a longtime thing.

He wasn't made for that.

Losing himself in sensation, his fingertips went to the top button of her shirt, and as he started to unfasten the disks, she arched up and sighed into his mouth. It was hard to keep from ripping the blouse apart, but he wasn't going to do that. For her, he would be different than he truly was—

Oh . . . dearest Virgin Scribe.

The shirt halves fell open, exposing creamy curves covered by exactly the kind of sensible bra he knew she would wear. She didn't need lace. She didn't need frills. She didn't need anything but what was underneath to be sexy. Erotic. More than he could ever want.

Syn was careful as he took her shirt off, because he was very aware of how delicate she was compared to him. She was not weak, but he was brutally strong and he would never forgive himself if he hurt her or any of her things.

The purr in the back of his throat was a surprise to him. And when she laughed in satisfaction as the sound rumbled out of him, he felt warm in places that had nothing to do with sex.

But then he refocused. Particularly as she released the front clasp of her bra.

And that was when things changed.

No more slow. No matter what he told himself.

With a growl, he lifted her up so she could straddle him, and taking his lips from hers, he nuzzled into the side of her throat—and kept going. Driven by sexual instinct, he went down, down . . . to the swells that were tipped pink and tight, just ripe for his mouth. Sucking her nipple in, he tightened his hold on her waist as she gasped and grabbed the nape of his neck.

As his fangs descended fully, Syn wanted to score her flesh and suck something else in, but he couldn't go that far. One taste of her blood and there would be no control left in him—and even if she knew what he was, and she did not, it was far too close to her transition to risk drawing anything from her vein.

To distract himself from his thirst for her, he put his hand on the inside of her thigh and inched, inched, his way up—

She cried out when he cupped her through her slacks, and he released her nipple so he could see what he did to her. Fuck . . . *yes.* She was undone, her head falling back, her neck deliciously exposed, her hair a cascade of luxury. The sex had taken her to another place in her mind, a place where there were no dead bodies and nothing to fear, no one sent to kill her, nothing for her but him and what he did to her.

It was exactly what he wanted to give to her. And there was more to go.

Syn worshipped her breasts as he undid the button of her fly and unzipped her pants. She was the one who swept them off, kicking them free—along with her panties. And then she stood before him, her eyes shy and commanding by turns.

"You are beautiful," he said in an alien voice.

"This is not . . . something I do." She motioned between them. "You know . . . randomly. You're different."

"No," he said softly. "We're the same. That's why this is different."

When he held out his hands, she came to him like a blessing from above, all warmth and mystery, a goddess in the flesh appearing before him from out of a dream. And soon enough, she would disappear on him, as all dreams did, but for now . . .

As she straddled him once more, Syn pressed his lips to the skin of her shoulders and ran his palms over her hips, down onto her thighs . . . then up through to the core of her, to the sweetness and the heat, to the heart of everything that made her female.

"Syn," she groaned.

The feel of her slick sex made him close his eyes, especially as his body went live wire, his cock pounding with its own heartbeat. Still, he knew better than to believe any of that promise as it related to his own release.

Not that he mattered in this. She was the only thing on his mind. In his heart.

"Come for me," he breathed into her mouth.

Penetrating her with his fingers, he stroked the top of her sex with his thumb, and a split second later, she stiffened and jerked against him. With care, he rode out her orgasm, giving her body every chance to fully enjoy the sensations—and meanwhile, he enjoyed the view of her.

Syn watched it all. And with greed, he memorized everything about her in the moment, from the undulations of her bare breasts, to the flush on her face, to the flicker of her jugular from her pounding heart. He breathed in deep, loving her scent, and he ran his eyes down the length of her naked body, from the cradle of her hips and the quiver of her thighs to the flex of her toes. He couldn't see the cleft of her sex because his hand was there.

His hand never wanted to leave there.

When she finally stilled, he didn't want to break their connection.

He wanted to keep going. He wanted to be a normal, fully function-ing male who could use what had just happened to her as a preamble for what would become something shared. But that was not possible. That would have to be part of another dream, a different one that would never be lived, at least not for him.

And he was okay with his reality. As long as he had this moment with her, nothing else mattered.

As he retracted his fingers, Jo's heavy-lidded eyes lifted to his.

She didn't speak. She moved.

Tilting her head, she kissed him deep, her hair flowing over him— and greedy for more contact, his hands skated up the back of her thighs and tightened on her backside, kneading the flesh there. Distracted by the feel of her, he at first didn't notice where her own hands went.

They were between their bodies, at the front of his fly.

He should tell her no.

God . . . he should tell her to stop. But then he realized that was just to keep himself from the physical pain that would come later, and that was bullshit. She could ride him and he could feel her—

The first touch of her hands on his bare cock made him thrust up with his hips.

But then she was cursing. "Condom. I need a—do you have one?"

He shook his head. "I can't give you anything. I don't carry viruses or diseases of any sort."

Because he was a vampire.

Jo frowned. "Aren't you afraid I might have something?"

"No, because you don't."

"How do you know."

"Do you?" When she shook her head, he shrugged. "So I'm right."

And he would have explained it all, but he couldn't. The problem was, she might just linger in the almost-there of transitioning. Half-breeds were known to do that, the change never truly arriving, the hor-mones going dormant after they tried to surge all the way but could not complete the transformation.

He didn't like to think about that outcome.

He didn't want them on opposite sides of the species divide.

"We can just stop here," he said. "It's okay."

There was a hesitation. "I'm on the pill. For regulating my periods."

"You're not ovulating now, but it wouldn't matter if you were. I won't . . . I can't get you pregnant."

There was an awkward pause. Like she wanted more information on that one. "Oh."

"It's okay," he said as he reached up and stroked her face. "We can stop."

"But I don't want to."

Without hesitation, she stood him up and sat herself down upon him, joining them properly, his erection buried deep in her tight, tight hold. In response, he jacked his head back and squeezed her thighs, his arousal kicking inside of her.

Before he could move, she moved for him, her hips rolling in a wave, her hands holding on to his shoulders, her breasts coming up and receding back, the nipples brushing his pecs as her head fell loose on the top of her spine. Without thought, he echoed her rhythm, thrusting hard, grabbing her waist and working her up and down on his shaft. Gritting his teeth, he felt urgency to the point of pain, the sensitivity of his cock so great, he shook from it.

And then she orgasmed.

Squeezing his eyes shut, he held himself still so he could memorize the tightening of her core against his shaft. The sensations were so incredible that he felt as though he was gaining on the cliff of release himself, the lip edge so close, he braced his awareness for the final part of the sex act to culminate after all these years.

Only with her, he thought. It made sense somehow that it was her—

Jo slowed.

Then she stopped.

As she collapsed onto his chest and breathed heavily, he began to pant. Surely it would happen . . . now . . .

His hips jerked. His cock spasmed. His hands tightened so much they dug into her pelvic bones.

But no.

Syn remained on the verge, and the pleasure soon soured into pain, until the smallest move she made was like a dagger into his cock, the icy hot agony stabbing his sac.

His female lifted her head. And there was a smile on her face that, under different circumstances, he would have taken great satisfaction in.

The smile didn't last. As she moved, he winced and hissed.

"Are you okay?" she said.

CHAPTER TWENTY-SEVEN

J o might have been enjoying an amazing post-best-sex-of-her-life glow, but she wasn't completely out to lunch. Then again, it was so obvious that something was seriously wrong with Syn that she'd have to be knocked out cold not to notice. Underneath her body, he was sitting stone still on the couch, sweat beading his forehead and his upper lip, his chest pumping in short bursts, the veins running down his biceps and into his forearms standing out in sharp relief.

Oh, God, were they going to end up on an episode of *Sex Sent Me to the ER?*

"What can I do?" she asked.

"Get . . . off . . . me . . ." he gritted.

Pushing up from her knees, she felt his rock-hard erection slip out of her, and as the length bounced on his lower belly, he hissed again and flared his fingers out straight from his hands like they were channeling the pain he was in. And then he just sat there.

"Do you want me to help you—"

"Don't touch it." Syn's eyes were squeezed shut so hard, his whole face wrinkled, his lips pulling off his—

Jo gasped. And it was at that moment that his lids rose up.

As he stared at her, she told herself to get a grip. Those weren't real fangs, for godsakes.

Cursing under his breath, he seemed to force his features into a semblance of composure. "I just need a minute."

"Okay, sure." Moving off the sofa slowly, she grabbed for her clothes. "Take your time."

Concerned for him and embarrassed by . . . oh, so much, really . . . Jo made quick work of pulling on her underwear and her pants—and as she got herself back together, she was very aware of how much he was not moving. Well, that wasn't exactly true. His fingers were now curled into fists, that flex traded in for a tight-knuckled crank. And then there was the breathing.

She looked at his lips, which were now firmly locked in place over his teeth. Maybe she'd imagined those canines?

"Do we need to get you to the ER?"

"What?" he grunted.

"For the Cialis." Clearly, that was the problem here. "Or the Viagra you took."

He lifted his head and looked at her myopically. "What?"

"For an erection lasting longer than four hours, you're supposed to get medical help. It's on the ads for those pills." When he still seemed confused, she covered her hand discreetly and pointed downward to what was still very much going on at his hips. "You know . . ."

Syn re-shut his eyes and let his head fall back against the cushions once more. "I don't have any idea what you're talking about."

"Listen, you can be honest. I'm not going to judge. Men take these things, I guess, to make sure they can . . . be at their best."

The image of that ad with a man and a woman sitting in porcelain tubs and holding hands in front of a sunset made her wonder what in the hell her life was turning into. But then she already knew the answer to that.

And it rhymed with "trapper."

"I know it hasn't been hours," she said, "but you're so uncomfortable, maybe we should just go get this taken care of?"

As he swallowed with obvious difficulty, his Adam's apple went up and down like it was having trouble doing its job. "This is just what happens to me."

Wait, so staying hard wasn't a problem for him? "Then stop with the pills."

"What pills?"

As her cell phone started to ring, she went over and took it out of her purse. When she saw who it was, she looked through into the kitchen, to the digital clock on the microwave. You know, just in case her iPhone was wrong about the time.

But nine o'clock wasn't that late. And how was it only nine? It felt like four in the morning.

With that thought in mind, she answered in a low tone. "McCordle, I can't talk right now." *There's an erection on my sofa.* "Let me call you back."

"Just want you to know the FBI is going to subpoena security tapes from both the Hudson Hunt and Fish Club and Gigante's back office gambling den at his cement business. They've got probable cause on an unrelated RICO charge. They're going to let us see what's on 'em. I'll let you know when I can."

"That's great. Thank you."

Bracing herself, she turned around as she ended the call. Syn was up on his feet and had pulled his leathers into place, somehow stuffing his anatomy in behind the fly. When she considered the logistics on that one, she wondered why he wasn't passed out on her carpet.

Or why the buttons weren't going airborne.

"Let me take you to the ER," she said. "You should be sensible about this."

Yeah, it's not like she waited four months to go see a doc.

"It's not what you think," he muttered.

"It's not what *you* think." Putting her phone back in her purse, she knew he had to have lied about the Cialis thing. "But you're a grown man, and you can do what you want—"

"I can't . . ." He motioned over his hips. "You know, I can't . . ."

"Enjoy your baritone singing voice right now? I don't mean to make light of this, but—"

"Finish."

Jo frowned as she felt herself go still. "I don't understand."

Syn lowered his eyes to the floor. "I can't ejaculate."

"Ever?" She shook her head. "I mean, you orgasm, but you don't—"

"No, I don't find a release."

"At all?" As he shook his head, Jo cradled her purse against her chest. "Have you gone to see someone about this?"

"No reason to."

"There is every reason to. You're suffering, and maybe . . . what happened? Were you hurt?"

"It's just the way it is for me."

He went over to the bathroom doorway. Without her noticing, he'd set his leather coat down just outside of the door, and given the bulges under it, she had a feeling he had hidden things of a holster variety under there. Without further comment, he picked the load up and went into the loo, closing the door behind himself. A moment later, he re-emerged, jacket on.

"You don't have to go," she said.

"It's best that I do—"

"May I take you back to wherever you live?"

"No, I can do it—"

"The nearest bus stop is a quarter of a mile away. I'll take you there."

"That's okay. I'll walk."

Jo found herself speaking quickly because he was clearly in a hurry to leave, and she didn't want him to go for a whole lot of reasons: "Let me walk you out, then—"

"It's just cosmetic stuff, by the way."

"What is?"

Syn pointed to his mouth. "The teeth. They're caps. Don't worry about it."

Jo blinked. "Okay."

When he nodded, she expected him to come over and hug her. Give her a kiss. Hold her for a minute. Instead, he walked right out her apartment door.

Jo stayed where she was as she imagined him exiting the building. Going down the sidewalk. Heading toward—

She hadn't told him which way the bus stop was. Did he know? Or—

Rushing out of her apartment, she jumped through the vestibule, and punched her way out into the chilly spring night. Under the bright moonlight, she looked left. Looked right.

There was no one walking down the sidewalk, no huge-shouldered man with a long stride heading away, no solid boots making heavy sounds on the cement.

Syn had up and disappeared.

Again.

CHAPTER TWENTY-EIGHT

Syn rematerialized downtown, taking shape across the street from the Hudson Hunt & Fish Club. The place was dark, no slivers of illumination showing around the seams of the front door or the painted panels of the windows. There was someone in there, however. A blacked-out Chevy Suburban was parked face out in a narrow alley alongside the building, steam rising from its tailpipes. Behind the wheel, the figure of a man with broad shoulders was a dense, solid shadow, and from time to time, when the chauffeur took a draw on his cigarette, his face was illuminated on a flare.

A car passed between Syn and the SUV. Then another.

Reaching behind to his belt, Syn took one of his two suppressors from its holstered position at the small of his back. Then he drew one of his forties. As he screwed the cylinder onto the end of the barrel, the metal on metal made a soft, pliant sound.

Dematerializing, he re-formed behind the Suburban.

In silence, he proceeded down the length of the SUV, keeping his back flat to the steel panels and the panes of glass. When he got to the driver's side door, he knocked on the window.

The man put the thing down. "What the fuck do—"

The gun made a huffing sound as Syn pulled the trigger. The bullet went directly into the frontal lobe and came out the far side, thunking into the back seat.

As the driver started to slump, Syn caught him before his forehead hit the horn. Forcing the deadweight onto the center console, Syn reached in, popped open the door, and unlocked everything else. With hard hands, he dragged the dead body out, and carried it around to the rear where he stored it into the cargo space in the back.

Returning to the driver's seat, he got behind the wheel, put up the window most of the way, and sat with his gun on his thigh.

His phone went off in his leather jacket, the subtle vibration transmitting through the pocket and onto his chest wall. Getting the thing out, he cut the power to the unit and put it back. When another rattling sounded, he looked down. A cell phone was slotted into a drink cup holder, and he picked it up. The text notification on the screen read: *ETA 2 mins. Home next.*

Precisely 120 seconds later, the side door of the squat, concrete building opened, and a piece of meat with a set of jowls like a St. Bernard's came out. Syn recognized the guy from when he'd entered the place the night before last. He'd been sitting at the bar with the younger version of the old man.

And what do you know, behind the bodyguard, Gigante lumbered out of his establishment, his cigar shoved into the corner of his trout mouth, his jacket open, his big belly exhausting the structural integrity of the buttons down the front of his shirt.

The bodyguard walked ahead and opened the door to the back seat, letting Gigante get in first.

"Sal, you can't keep this car warm, huh?" Gigante said as he hefted himself up. "I hate the fucking cold. What's the matter with you."

The bodyguard shut the door. And Syn turned around to the back seat and discharged two bullets into Gigante's huge chest. The old man gasped and clutched his sternum, his ham hands fisting up his shirt, the cigar falling out from between his lips and throwing up sparks as it bounced off his leg.

The bodyguard opened the front passenger door. Syn pointed the gun at his face and discharged another pair of slugs.

The man fell to the ground in a slop of limbs.

Syn refocused on Gigante. The mobster's eyes were wide, the whites flaring around the dark irises as he gasped for air.

"I don't have a problem killing females," Syn said. "Or anybody. But I'll be damned if you hurt Jo Early. Say good night, motherfucker."

The final bullet went into the front of Gigante's throat, the torso jerking in response, a splash of red arcing forward and speckling the side of the bucket seat in front. Struck by a bored hunger, Syn reached out and ran his forefinger through the stain on the leather; then he brought the blood to his mouth. As he sucked it down, he loved the taste of his kill and stared into the man's eyes for a little longer, listening to the gurgling, the gasping.

The sound of screeching tires brought Syn's head around. Another car was turning into the alley, summoned by someone, something.

Syn dematerialized out of the driver's seat, ghosting away, leaving the carnage behind. Death had been coming fast for Gigante. He would not last long.

And even if the man did, Syn didn't give a shit.

His female was safe. That was all that mattered.

✦ ✦ ✦

Jo took her time throwing away the paper plates they'd used, the napkins that had been wadded up, the empty box that was stained in a circle in the center and had cold cheese clinging to one edge. As she topped off the Hefty trash bag in her bin, she felt as though she were dismantling something she'd imagined. Packing up a fantasy. Putting a puzzle that had been completed away.

And it was for what could have been that she moved slowly and sadly. In her kitchen, standing over her trash which now had to be taken out, she had the thought that she wished she'd used two of the four mis-matched plates she'd taken with her when she'd left Dougie and the boys' apartment. If she'd used washable plates, she could have at least kept what he'd eaten on.

Which was pretty pathetic, really. And God, this was too much of a profound loss for what was really going on. That man was nothing but a stranger coming and going out of her life, a storm passing after an in-tense sexual experience that had ended on an unsettling note.

Yeah, so where was the post-hurricane renewal?

Her phone ringing held little interest, but she went back over to her purse because she could use a distraction.

When she saw who it was, she answered fast. "Bill? Bill?"

"Hey," her friend said. There was a pause. "I'm sorry I've been kind of out of touch."

"Oh, no. Listen . . . how is Lydia?" Jo went over to the sofa and sat down. "How are you? Is there anything I can do for you guys?"

"No, I think . . ." Bill cleared his throat. "We are where we are, you know? The doctor says we can try again after waiting a month. And you know, at this early stage of things, it was probably a chromosomal prob-lem that . . . well, was incompatible with life. That's what they called it."

Okay, compared to losing a child, the fact that Jo was in a funk over some guy seemed downright offensive.

"I am so sorry," she said, her voice cracking. "Children are a blessing."

"They are." Bill took a deep breath. "They sure are, Jo."

There was a long period of silence, and Jo closed her eyes as she thought about her birth parents, the mother who had brought her into this world and the father who had been in on the miracle at the ground floor, so to speak. When Jo had been growing up, she had given into the temptation to think the pair of those parental hypotheticals were totally different from the Earlys who had adopted her. She convinced herself that living in her real parents' home would have been one long birth-day party with balloons and cake and presents every day and all night.

No more cold, drafty house with too many rooms. No more stiff, formal dinners in the dining room. No more sense that she was a nuisance, un-welcome in spite of the fact that her entering Mr. and Mrs. Early's lives had been a willful, deliberate act on their part.

But yes, the stolen-princess narrative had been one she'd spun as a youngster, her true, virtuous parents out there somewhere in the world, swindled out of their rightful place in her life, mourning her loss as they fruitlessly searched for her.

She had waited for a rescue for so many years. So many. But now that she was an adult? She knew that there was no castle waiting for her on top of a mountain. No "real" parents still searching for her. No one that truly cared, one way or the other, about her future.

Which was why she had to be the hero in her own life.

"Jo? You still there?"

Shaking herself back into focus, she cleared her throat. "Sorry. I'm just . . . yes, I'm here."

"I know this is awkward."

"No, it's not. What happened to you and Lydia is painful and very sad, and even though we haven't known each other for very long, you've both been great friends to me." Actually, they were her only friends at the moment, so there was that. "I just wish there was something, any-thing, I could do for you and her. But I can't, and I hate this feeling that I'm failing you. And then there's the suckage that you're good people and this shouldn't happen to good people."

Bill's voice got hoarse. "Thanks, Jo."

"I won't say you're welcome because I wish I didn't have to say it at all."

"Amen."

They talked for a little bit longer, and then they ended the call. Bill was going to take the rest of the week off as personal time, and that was the right thing to do. And when he came back? Jo told him she was ready to co-author everything she was working on.

Putting her phone down, she stared at the door. And thought about how she had made love to a stranger right where she was currently sitting just a half hour before.

Funny how losses were as much of a currency as happiness in life. Somehow, they were noticed more, though.

Jo got to her feet and went back into the kitchen. In a drawer by the refrigerator, one that might have held cutlery if she had any, she kept a manila folder she hadn't gone into since she'd moved in.

There had been so much going on. And she hadn't been feeling well. And—

Well, she just hadn't had the energy to deal with one more thing.

But she took the folder out now, and unsheathed the glossy photograph of a man with dark hair and dark eyes. Turning the image over, she read the block printing that had been done in Sharpie.

Dr. Manuel Manello, Chief of Surgery. St. Francis Medical Center.

Bill had given her the picture. And had typed up a report on what he'd found when he'd looked into her birth mother, who had died during birth.

It was a mystery solved. Kind of. And the dark-haired man? He was her brother . . . who had strangely disappeared off the radar over eighteen months before.

Never to be seen or heard from again.

"I'm getting really sick and tired of people who disappear into thin air," she muttered to herself.

CHAPTER TWENTY-NINE

Even though Butch was a tried-and-true Red Sox fan, he was mature enough to appreciate that there were certain things that came out of the enemy's home state that were not all bad. Not that he was in a big hurry to admit this, even to himself—and yet, as the sun came up, he reflected how much difference a good USDA Prime New York strip steak could make in a man's life. Just the ticket.

On that note, he leaned even further back in the French settee, and repositioned the piece of meat on his black eye. As he let out a groan of relief, someone sat down next to him.

"I'm sorry I had to do that, cop."

Butch opened the lid that worked and looked at V. "S'okay. I woulda done the same thing."

"How's your head?"

"What's that old expression? Kicking like a mule?"

He closed his eye again, and listened to the sounds of the Brotherhood, the Bastards, and the other fighters, filing into Wrath's study. When everyone was accounted for and the meeting started, he would sit up, lose his cold pack, and pay attention, but right now, between the hangover and the damage from that right hook of his roommate's, he had about all he wanted to handle.

"Can I get you some Motrin or some shit?" V asked.

"You really do feel bad, huh."

"I didn't enjoy that."

"Because I wasn't in a leather thong?"

V laughed in a crack. "If I light up, will it make you feel worse?"

"Short of you punching me in my other eye, I think I've hit rock bottom."

There was a *shcht*, and then the familiar scent of V's Turkish tobacco wafted over. When Butch felt up to it—okay, fine, he wasn't up to shit, but he didn't want to be antisocial—he pushed himself higher on the cushions and dropped the steak in his lap. Fritz, well familiar with the requirements of people who had swelling in places where it was unwelcome, had been thoughtful enough to slip a ziplock over the meat so there was no facial cleanup to worry about. Not that Butch would have worried about that.

Not that any of the males or females in the room would have worried about it, either.

And as for crowds gathering in common spaces? All in all, you could not get a more mismatched pairing than the decor of the French blue, French antique'd study, with its morning glory-colored walls and its Aubusson rug and its foal-legged furniture and frilly drapes ... and the legion of hard-ass'd, hardheaded, heavy-bodied boneheads who somehow managed to repeatedly wedge themselves into the four-walls-and-a-ceiling without breaking anything.

Then again, they had been doing these little think tanks here about all things Lessening Society-related for over three years now, ever since the Black Dagger Brotherhood and the First Family had taken up res in this gray stone ark of a mansion. So at this point, it would have seemed strange not to be sitting delicately on all of these spindly love seats and socialite-worthy armchairs talking about life and/or death.

Proof positive that whatever you were used to was normal no matter how weird it might have been without the habit part.

"Where's the big man?" Butch asked as he glanced over at Wrath's vacant desk.

"He's coming." V took another drag and talked through the exhale, the smoke briefly obscuring his goateed face. "I think he's stealing candy from a couple of babies to warm up for what he's going to do to us, true?"

"Least he's not kicking puppies."

"They're the only ones who get a pass."

As Butch tested out his eyesight by focusing on Wrath's desk, he thought that at least there was one set of furniture in the room that made sense. That old-school throne that the last purebred vampire on the planet took a load off in was exactly the kind of thing you'd expect the great Blind King, the leader of the species, to set his leather-covered ass on. Word had it that the carved oak heavy weight had been brought across the ocean from the Old Country by the Brotherhood, back in the days—nights, natch—when Wrath had refused to lead his kind.

There had always been the expectation, the hope, that the male would finally assume the mantle of his birthright—

The double doors, which had been shut after each entry—because there were children in the house now, and none of them needed to hear the cursing carnival that was small talk among the fighters—broke open, and not by a set of hands. They were willed apart.

As a hush fell over the room, Butch thought, *Well, the race had gotten itself a leader and a half, hadn't it.*

"Be careful what you wish for," he muttered dryly.

"Like anyone would order that out of a catalogue?" V shot back.

Standing between the broad jambs, Wrath, son of Wrath, sire of Wrath, was a seven-foot-tall scourge of non-human humanity in his stack-heeled shitkickers. With black hair that fell from a widow's peak to his hips, and a face that looked like it belonged on a serial killer who happened to have a blue-blooded pedigree, he was the kind of thing who even fully armed brothers would cross the road to get out of the path of. Especially when he was in one of his moods.

Which was pretty much anytime he was conscious.

And especially after a night like tonight had been.

As he walked into the room, his face never changed position, his wraparound sunglasses straight ahead and not varying as he wound his way around the bodies who were standing, the people who were seated, the furniture, the everything. His ability to circumnavigate the space was not just the result of memorization. By his side, George, his golden retriever service dog, brushed against his outer calf, guiding him through a set of subtle cues invisible to those outside of the symbiotic relationship between owner and animal.

They were a hell of a pair. Like a sawed-off shotgun and a home-made quilt. But it worked—and you want to talk about true love? Sometimes that dog was the only thing that kept Wrath's temper in check.

So yup. Everyone in the household was a huge fan of George's.

The doors to the study closed in the same way they opened, without the benefit of a hand—and hey, at least they didn't slam hard enough to rattle the hinges.

Although again, that was only because it would have scared the dog.

Over at the desk, Wrath lowered his three-hundred-pound, 0% body fat, mesomorphic bulk down on his throne, the old-growth timber bearing his weight with a tired groan. A lot of the time, George got picked up and settled in his lap. Not today.

Butch put the steak back in place and waited.

Three . . .

Two . . .

. . . and—

"What the *fuck* is going on out there," Wrath yelled.

Boom!

In the silence that followed, Butch looked over at V. Who looked at Tohr. Who slowly shook his head back and forth.

"Am I sitting in here alone?" Wrath demanded. "Or did all of you check your cock and balls at the door."

"You know, I wondered what that basket was for," someone said.

"Mine are so big they wouldn't fit in it—"

Wrath slammed his fist into the desk, making everyone, including the dog, jump. "Fine, I'll fill in the blanks for you bunch of pussies. The Omega shows up in a back alley, and *you*—"

Butch closed his eyes and shrank into the settee as the wraparounds swung in his direction.

"—decide it's a great idea to call an all clear even when you needed backup." Wrath's face then swung around in the opposite direction, at Syn. "And then *you* decide that tackling the evil is the right move." Wrath then looked around the room. "After which all of *you* arrive on scene and circle jerk each other."

Butch raised his hand even though no one was going to call on him. "I had a plan."

The Oakleys of Death came back at him. "Oh, really. What was it? Getting killed? 'Cuz Jesus Christ you almost pulled that off with room to spare—"

"Save the father at any cost."

Wrath frowned. "What the fuck are you talking about?"

"Qhuinn." Butch shifted himself on the petit point throw pillows, and decided that the last thing his aching head needed was that blind stare boring into him. So he shut his peepers and prayed like he was back in parochial school and one of the nuns had heard him cuss. "Save Qhuinn, that was my plan—and it worked. He had just taken down a slayer when I sensed the Omega coming in for a landing. I knew Qhuinn wasn't going to leave me so I did what I had to to get him to go." He kept quiet about his little bargain with the Omega. "You think you're pissed off now? Imagine how you'd feel if we were having a mourning ceremony at the Tomb for Rhamp and Lyric's dad instead of this thoroughly enjoyable little holler session in here."

Over in the corner, Qhuinn rubbed his face. Next to him, his *hellren*, Blay, put a supportive hand on the brother's shoulder.

"I'd do it again," Butch said as he reopened his eyes. "So am I suspended or something? I mean, V was already talking like I was going to be put on lockdown, like I'm some kind of lightweight who can't take care of myself. Is that where you're heading with this? Or are you going to let me live up to the Prophecy bullshit? Huh? What's it going to be?"

A loooooooot of stares moved his way, everybody in the room giving him the hairy eyeball with a combination of respect and oh-boy-this-was-going-to-hurt.

Wrath stared at him for a long moment, during which Butch figured he was probably going to need a lot more strip steaks.

"Now I know what she meant," the King muttered.

"I'm sorry?" Butch asked. "What?"

"You and the fucking questions. I always wondered why the Scribe Virgin refused to let us ask questions of her. Now I know." Before Butch could throw out another one, in the form of a "why," Wrath answered the unspoken. "Because it's *fucking* annoying, that's why."

✦   ✦   ✦

Standing off to the side, with Balthazar next to him like the bastard was holding the leash of a hungry bear, Syn wondered why he was at the meeting. It wasn't that he didn't care about the ass kicking Wrath was warming up to. He kind of liked it when the leader of the vampires got all riled up. It made Syn feel like he was working with someone he could understand and respect.

After all, he'd grown up around a male with a temper. He was familiar with the ranting and the raving, and in a sick way, he was comfortable with it—although in Wrath's case, the hellfire was backed up with a formidable intelligence and a strong sense of right and wrong. Sure, the Blind King had a tongue like a sword, and had been very, very aptly named, but Wrath was a true North, the kind of thing you could bet on to be fair even when he was furious.

"I'm not staying indoors like some kind of little bitch," Butch said from over on a dollhouse-sized sofa. "I'm not going to do that."

The Brother had clearly been in a fistfight since Syn had faded out from the alley where the shit with the Omega had gone down. Butch's left eye was the color of one of Rhage's grape Tootsie Pops, and that piece of beef in a plastic bag he kept putting on the bruise seemed like excellent first aid. Plus, hello, you could cook it up and eat it once the cool had faded to room temperature—and who could say that about commercial-grade ice packs.

"And the lockdown is not even necessary," the Brother said.

"Bullshit," Wrath shot back from over on the throne. "And I've got four centuries of fighting with the Omega under my belt to prove you wrong."

"The evil is not what it used to be." Butch sat forward. "And I've had the close-ups under *my* belt to prove *you* wrong. Unless I need to remind you about how you and I came to know we're related."

"He's right."

As the eyes in the room reoriented in Syn's direction, he was surprised to find that the two words had come out of his mouth.

Shrugging, he muttered, "I should have been incinerated or blown into chunks when I tackled the fucker."

"Which brings me to my next agenda item," Wrath said dryly. "What in the hell were *you* thinking?"

"I wasn't. I came on scene and I was ready to fight. That's it."

"So you picked the evil on a just-'cuz? Ambitious—or self-destructive, depending on how you look at it."

"Both."

"At least you're honest."

Butch spoke up. "I'm going back into the field at sunset, and I'm going to keep doing what I'm doing. We're so close—" The Brother made a pinchie with his thumb and forefinger"—and that's why it's safe for me to go out there."

"*I will tell you what you can and can't do,*" Wrath cut in. "Unless you think this big-ass chair is a prop?"

"This is our shot." Butch looked around the room. "And I'm not going to be the one who blows it."

"But you need to be protected," V gritted.

As arguments popped up in all corners, Syn let the various debates recede into the background. He already knew what the outcome was going to be. Butch was going to be allowed to go out into the field—because he was right. They were getting close to the end and the King knew that. No one wanted to put somebody as mission critical as the fucking *Dhestroyer* at risk. On the other hand, how the fuck was the cop going to be able to fulfill the prophecy if he were cooling his heels at home like he was made of cut glass?

The meeting broke up sometime later. Maybe it was five minutes. Maybe it was an hour. Syn didn't care. And guess what. Butch was free to do his job, even though V looked like he wanted to file a protest to that royal decree with a dagger.

Syn never waited for anyone, and with his position close to the double doors, he was the first out.

As he headed to his room to crash, the footfalls in his wake stuck with him as he passed through the second-story sitting room—and were still hanging tough when he entered the corridor that led down to his suite.

"Syn."

He just shook his head and grabbed for his door.

"Syn," his cousin said, "we gotta talk."

"Nope. We don't."

As he went to slam the panel shut, Balthazar caught it. "Yeah, we do."

Syn gave up fighting over entry control and headed for his bathroom, shedding clothes as he went, letting them fall on the floor. "I think the meeting was self-explanatory. I didn't take notes if you're looking for a review of it—"

"Who's the female."

Syn stopped in front of the dual sinks. Lifting his eyes to the mirror, he looked at his cousin. Balthazar was standing just inside the bath, his jet-black clothes loose and comfortable, his flexible, non-heeled shoes the kind of thing you could climb up the outside of a building with. Syn recognized the uniform instantly.

Guess the thief been working a little side hustle of his own at the end of the night.

"Been brushing up on your perishable skills, cousin?" Syn drawled.

"Who's the female."

"What did you steal?"

"Don't play games with me."

"If I ask you to empty your pockets, what's in them? Necklaces of the diamond variety? Cash? A couple of expensive watches?"

When Balz just stared at his reflection, Syn recognized the steady-Eddie expression for what it was: evidence that the goddamn bastard was prepared to spend as much time as it took to get what he wanted. The tenacious fucker.

Syn started the water running in the sink and soaped up his hands like he was a surgeon about to amputate a leg. Or maybe that was just wishful thinking on his part.

"I don't recall," he said, "there having been any discussion about a female at the meeting. Then again, I wasn't really paying attention."

"Back in that alley earlier. Who is this female you want me to get ahold of in the event of your death."

Syn looked down at his soapy hands. Because, hello, cleanliness was next to godliness, and who wanted to be a dirty bird. "I don't know what you're talking about."

"Yes, you do."

"I was delirious."

"You can't be trusted with females, Syn. Not like you are right now."

"I'm naked." He indicated his body. "So they're perfectly safe. Unless you think my . . . difficulties . . . have resolved themselves. Which I assure you they have not."

Shit, that thing with Jo. He hadn't wanted it to end like it had.

"We're coming down to the end of the war, Syn. We don't need your kind of complications right now."

"And again, I say unto you, I dinnae know what you're talking about."

Balthazar stared at him. "There are limits to what I can clean up, Syn."

"Then don't play *doggen* for me. Pretty simple solution there, burglar mine."

When the male cursed and walked off, Syn met his own eyes in the mirror. As his cousin's words rebounded in his head, his thoughts went back to the past—and though he tried to fight it, the memories were stronger than his resolve to deny them.

✦   ✦   ✦

'Twas three nights following the death of his sire and the onset of his transition that Syn stood in the hut that had been the only home he had ever known. As he looked at the pallet where his sire had slept, and the remains of his mahmen, and the pathetic valuables that were nothing more than containers for rope and fur, and bladders for mead, he knew what he had to do.

"You're leaving?"

He pivoted to the heavy tarp flap. Balthazar was standing just inside the doorway, the male's pre-transition face grown up in spite of the immaturity of the features.

"I dinnae hear you come in, cousin," Syn said.

"You know me. I'm very quiet."

Outside the cave, the cold wind howled, a harbinger of autumn. Summer was indeed over, and Syn felt in his bones that it would never come again.

Not that it had ever been there for him, no matter how warm any night was.

"Thank you," Syn said as he went over and picked up one of the discarded bladders of mead.

"For what?"

As Syn sniffed the open neck, he grimaced and knew he would ne'er drink such. Ever. The memories that came with the scent made him cringe. Tossing the empty aside, he went to find another, sifting through the discord.

"Getting the female when you did," he said. "I would have died."

"She came on her own."

Syn looked up with a frown. "How did she know then?"

"You saved her life. Did you think she wouldnae come see about you?"

"She should have stayed away."

"She had the choice to or not only because of you. She told me what you did. She saw your sire in one of his moods, on the verge of their property. You drew him away. She was home alone with her brother. Fates know what would have happened."

Syn grunted, for he couldnae speak any further of her, especially as both he and his cousin knew exactly what his sire would have done to such a delicate beauty.

Leaning down, he at last found a bladder that was half full. Lucky. His father rarely left them with anything in their confines.

"You saved her life," Balthazar said. "She saved yours."

"Not a fair swap," Syn said as he took the cork out of the neck. "Not by any distance at all."

Walking around, he poured the strong, fermented alcohol out, the smell making him choke. Since his transition, his senses were painfully acute, and his body did not feel like his own. He was so tall, his limbs flopping about, his feet too large for even his sire's old shoes, his hands broad and long-fingered.

He didnae know what his face looked like. He didnae care about that.

"What are you doing?" Balthazar asked.

Syn paused as he came up to the feet of his mahmen. "Why did he keep her here? He didnae care for her."

Even as he asked that of someone who wouldnae know, Syn himself had the answer. The remains were a visceral reminder of why doing what he was told was his only chance for survival. His sire had had to ensure Syn's submission. There were many nights and days when the male was too drunk to be able to forage for food. He needed to be attended.

And he had wanted to be obeyed.

Syn murmured something to his mahmen and then he proceeded to pour the mead upon her, the dark liquid sinking into the layers of blanketing that surrounded her skeleton.

When he had emptied the bladder, he tossed the thing upon the pallet.

"Are you burning this down then, cousin?"

Dearest Virgin Scribe, he couldnae stand the stink of the mead. It took him back to nights he had been smaller. Weaker. Glancing behind himself, he saw a broken chair and remembered how he had been thrown into it, his little body splitting the arm and one of the legs.

At least his full set of teeth had come in during his change. His father had only knocked out the little ones.

Syn turned to the fire and picked out one of the logs that was alit. "You need to leave."

Balthazar frowned. "Were you not even going to say goodbye to me?"

"You need to go."

There was a long pause, and Syn prayed that the male didnae fall victim to emotions that were best left unexpressed.

When his cousin merely stepped out, Syn looked around one last time. Then he tossed the burning log onto his mahmen's remains. As the flames flared and spread quickly, he thought of the heat that had torn through his body during his transition. He remembered little of what had happened with any clarity, but he recalled the heat. That and the snapping of his bones as they had grown inches in the course of hours.

He couldnae believe he had lived through it. Or that that lovely, generous female had fed him from her vein until just before dawn. With the approaching sunlight, she had had to go so that she wasnae caught in such deadly illumination. Balthazar, meanwhile, had strung up tarping around *the shelter to shield Syn as the transition had continued, his body maturing to its current, unfathomable size.*

He had been so weak after it was all over. He could remember lying with his cheek on the hoof-trodden, packed earth, and feeling as though he would never cool down. But eventually, as the sun had gone behind the horizon and the day's warmth faded, so too had the burn within his torso and limbs.

When he had finally emerged from the shelter, he had braced himself to see the blood of his sire, blood that Syn had shed, the gore and the remains all that was left behind of his father. There was none. It was all gone, as if it had never been. He had asked Balthazar if he had smelled the burning during the daylight. His cousin had said yes, he had.

And after that, Syn had recovered herein this hut for the three days and nights.

Now, as flames flared further and began to spread, Syn closed his eyes and said his goodbyes. He knew not where he was going. He knew only that he couldnae stay in the village for one more night. He had no possessions and only his feet to carry him forth. But there were too many ghosts here, too many . . . people, here. He needed to find a destiny away from who his father had been and what he had done to the male as a result.

The village would know all by now. The female would surely have had to explain why she was gone for as long as she had been whilst feeding him through the change. And as for Syn's father? The male's brutish presence would not be mourned, but it would be very much of note.

Syn stepped out of the hut and—

Balthazar was standing just outside the cave, the reins of two strong horses well laden with supplies dangling in his hands.

"I'm coming with you," his cousin said. "I may not be through my transition yet, but I am fast of hand and smarter than you. You will not survive without me."

"I have already survived much and you know this," Syn countered. "I shall be well enough."

"Then just let me go with you. I need to get away from this place, too."

"Because you've already stolen from everyone in the village and there are none who are not wary of you?"

There was a pause. "Yes. Exactly. Where do you think I got these steeds?"

"From the squire?"

"Aye. He didnae care for them well enough. They are better off with us." As one of the horses stamped a hoof as if it agreed, Balthazar held out a set of reins. "So what say you, cousin?"

Syn didnae reply. But he took what was offered to him.

As he mounted up, Balthazar did the same. Smoke was rising from the hut, and the crackling of the fire within made the horses twitch. Soon, the blaze would eat through the thatched roof, and orange flames would lick their way out of the cave, reaching up to the heavens.

He had turned the horrible and sad home he had known into a pyre for his mahmen, and somehow, that seemed fitting.

Before they reined off, his cousin said, "Are you not going to say goodbye to the female before you go?"

Syn pictured her in that meadow before all had transpired, running free with her brother, her laughter rising, like the smoke was doing now, up to the stars.

"We are even, she and I," he said. "It is best to leave things with this resolution."

Spurring his horse forth, he knew he loved her. And that, more than anything else, was the real reason he didnae go unto her family's land. It was also the true reason he was departing the village.

When you deeply cared for someone, you did what was best for them. His father had taught him that lesson by lack of example. So the kindest and most necessary thing for Syn to do was to leave the now.

And ne'er darken her doorstep ever again.

CHAPTER THIRTY

M r. F sat gingerly on the bus seat, staring out the cloudy window as the gentle rock of the loose-cannon suspension lullaby'd him and the other four people riding the route out to the suburbs. Rain was falling, a soft, winsome dew drifting out of a dove-gray sky, and as the piss-poor aerodynamics of the public transport wicked the moisture down its injury lawyer advertising wraps, the water coalesced in rivers over the slick topography of the glass.

When his stop came, he got to his feet and shuffled down the center aisle. No one paid any attention to him. The other passengers were on their phones and not because they were talking to someone on a call, their heads tilted down, their eyes locked on little screens that provided them a virtual world vitally important yet made of less than air.

As he disembarked, he envied them the manufactured urgency of the useless information they were sunk into.

Mr. F had real problems.

There was no one waiting in the Plexiglas bus stop, and he cautiously ambled away from the pitiful shelter, his boots treading over the sidewalk that eventually took him by some small-scale apartment buildings. The units were short stacks of three and four stories that were split in mirrored halves, and only some of them had dedicated parking lots. These dwellings soon gave way to neighborhoods of small houses, and Mr. F continued as his feet took lefts and rights on their own.

When he arrived at the untended-to fake-Tudor he'd visited days before, he noticed that there was a new flyer in the mailbox, something orange. He imagined it was for a lawn service. Maybe a roofing company. Pavers looking for work, perhaps. It was the kind of advertisement that would have showed up at his parents' house back when he was young, back when he didn't have to worry about adult things. Not that he had done much of that sort of worrying when he'd reached adulthood. He'd always thought he was better than all that average Joe stuff. He'd been convinced he was going to be a rocker à la Kurt Cobain. A real badass poet with a pocketful of guitar riffs.

Reality had proven to be so much less inspirational—although he'd lived up to the drug standard, for sure.

And now he was here.

Going through the garage, he stomped the rain off himself, leaving a dark splatter on the cement floor. Inside the house, he took a moment to focus. Then he started rifling through cabinets, closets, and drawers. He opened them in the kitchen. In the downstairs half bath. In the built-in shelving of the family room and in the front hall. He went upstairs and opened them in the master suite, and the two bedrooms, and the full bath that was supposed to be shared at the head of the stairs.

Anything he found, he put in an empty box he'd taken from the hall closet.

Back on the first floor, he set the box down on the dusty kitchen counter, and before he did an inventory, he went into the basement. Nothing there except for a washer and dryer, three paint cans that were open and dried up, and a box of Bounce dryer sheets that had mouse turds in it.

In the kitchen once again, he sifted through his bounty. Two sets of Ford-branded car keys, only one of which was accompanied by a remote—which suggested the other vehicle was an older model. A house key that, when he tried it in the front door and the back door, did not fit the house. An autoloader with no bullets. A magazine that did not match the gun. A pair of handcuffs with no key. Four cell phones that were out of juice and did not have chargers.

The laptop and the book he was already familiar with thanks to his first visit here.

Plugging the laptop in, he got nowhere. No power in the socket. No battery life left. It was probably password protected anyway, and there was nothing he could do about that. He had the IT skills of . . . well, a junkie.

Mr. F put both palms on the countertop and leaned into braced arms. Hanging his head, he felt the remnant aches of the internal injuries the Omega had given him and thought of the do-nothing H he had shot up under the bridge. The two realities formed a north and south pole, his existence trapped and rotating on the axis between the pair.

Taking the book with him, he found a spot in the living room on the unvacuumed rug. As he settled his back against the wall, he opened the cover of the book.

The words were dense, made out of small letters that were squeezed in tightly, like commuters on a morning train. His eyes refused to focus at first.

The sense that he had to find his way in this new prison he'd ended up in was what made him start to absorb what was on the page.

In the Omega's world, the only asset Mr. F had was himself.

◆   ◆   ◆

Jo parallel parked her Golf across the street from the police barricades and the news crews that surrounded the Hudson Hunt & Fish Club. Getting out, she frowned up at the drooling sky and put the hood of her windbreaker over her head. On a jog, she crossed to the other side of the road, and skirted the crowd that had gathered. As she shuffled behind a newscaster with a camera rolling on him and a microphone up to

his mouth, Jo was glad she could cover her face. No reason she needed
to be seen here.

The front entrance of the concrete block building was a no go and
so was the side door where, according to the news conference that had
been held at nine a.m., the assassinations had occurred. Three were
dead. Gigante, his bodyguard, and his chauffeur. Gigante had been shot
three times, twice in the chest and once in the throat, his body found
slumped in the back seat of an SUV registered to his cement company.
The chauffeur had been shot once through the forehead and then folded
up and stuffed into the rear compartment of the vehicle. The bodyguard
had been shot twice and collapsed on the ground just outside the open
passenger side door in front.

Jo camo'd herself in the crowd of spectators and checked her watch.

Five minutes later, McCordle came out the side door of the building. When he caught her eye, he nodded over his shoulder, away from
the commotion.

Holding her bag against her body, Jo jogged past the hair salon
next door and went down its length, her breath tight in her chest. As
she came out around the rear, McCordle was stepping free of the bar-
ricade, and he double-checked the parked squad cars before striding
up to her.

"Let's go over here," he said, leading her back out of sight by the
beauty parlor.

"I'm surprised you wanted to meet me here," she whispered. "Are
those the crime scene pictures?"

When she pointed to an envelope tucked under his arm, McCordle
nodded and gave the thing over to her. "Listen, we need to talk."

"Yeah, that's the plan."

He took her arm and squeezed it. "I'm serious. One of our sources
says that Gigante may have put a hit out on you."

Jo frowned. "But I don't have to worry about that anymore. Gigante's dead."

"The hit man working the contract isn't going to worry about that.

He's going to want his money and he'll get paid by the family only when you're . . . you know."

"Dead. You can say the word. I'm not afraid of it."

"You should be. This is no joke." When there was a shout, McCordle put himself between her and the noise. After a minute, he started talking again. "It's only exciting on the outside, Jo. On the inside of a situation like this, people get hurt, even if they're innocent."

"Do you know who the hit man is?"

"Not yet. My source is looking into it—and maybe something will show on the tapes."

"So the FBI hasn't turned them over to the CPD yet."

"My department is putting every pressure we have on them. In the meantime, you need to be very careful—"

"You said 'may have,' though. A hit on me is unconfirmed so it could just be a rumor." Before McCordle could lecture her some more, she cut him off. "About the scene here. What have you found out since nine a.m. this morning?"

"Forensics didn't get anything in the SUV that wasn't expected. No fingerprints apart from Gigante, the bodyguard, and the chauffeur. No foreign hair samples. They've got the bullets and the casings, but there's no gun."

"Who called the murders in?"

"Passerby."

"I know, but your captain didn't give the name during the news conference."

"It's a minor so we're not releasing it. It was a seventeen-year-old going to a six a.m. athletic practice. He was on his bike. He said he always cut through the alley on his way to Jefferson High in the morning, and he called the situation in without taking pictures and posting them on the internet. All is not lost with this younger generation."

"Has Frank Pappalardo released any statements about all this?"

"We're bringing him in for questioning. But no, and he's not going to say a word. He's old-school."

"But this is the payback. For Johnny Pappalardo's murder. Right?"

"Looks like it. And this is why I'm telling you, you've got to be careful. You have my cell phone number. You call me if you see anything suspicious around you or the paper or where you live."

"Speaking of which, did you find any cell phones in the SUV?"

"Jo. Are you listening to what I'm saying?"

"Yes. Any cell phones in the SUV?"

McCordle glanced over his shoulder like he was cursing in his head. "There was one found. We're not sure who it belongs to, but it's not Gigante's because he was known to hate them We're getting the texts and photographs that were on it."

"What happens next? Does Gigante's crew put a hit out on Pappalardo's hit man?"

"Jo, will you please—"

"I don't get a lot of time with you. I need to get these questions in. What about payback for the payback?"

"It's probable. These things roll downhill until one of the higher-ups calls a détente meeting. It's going to be a tennis match of dead bodies before it stops, though, especially with Gigante's son in the mix. Junior's going to want to avenge his father."

"Has he given any kind of statement?"

"Jesus, are you even listening—" When she just stared at him, he muttered. "Junior has had nothing to say. And given that he was being groomed by his father, it's likely he'll let his gun do the talking."

"Will he take over here in Caldwell?"

"There'll be a power struggle first. Then we'll have to see." McCordle glanced toward the scene again. "I gotta get back. Promise me you'll call if you—"

"Yes, of course. I'm not going to be stupid about this."

There was a pause. "Jo."

When he didn't go any further, she said, "What."

"I get that you want to do your job. And you're a really good reporter. But you need to leave town until the dust settles. Nothing is worth your life."

"You'll let me know if you hear anything for sure about me."

"I will. I promise."

"Looks like we'll be in touch again, then."

Tucking the envelope under her arm, Jo gave McCordle a nod and then she went back around the hairdresser's and across the street to her car. Before she got in, she looked over the crowd. The sense that this was not the end of the story, and she had the inside track on the situation, made her flirt with self-satisfaction. And it was that ego-driven nonsense that hounded her as she went back to the newsroom.

It was dangerous to think you were above things.

When she pulled into the parking lot of the CCJ, she went for the first available open spot. Putting her car in park, she opened the envelope and slid out the glossies.

Grimacing, she recoiled at the sight of a man squeezed into the back of the SUV. His face happened to be turned toward the camera and his eyes were open, as if he were alive, even though she knew that wasn't the case: There was a black circle in the center of his forehead, about the size of a pencil eraser, and a tendril of blood leaked out of it, traveling down at a slant until it joined his eyebrow. The trail didn't go any further than that.

She was surprised there wasn't more gore.

She got that with the Gigante picture. God . . . it looked like a font of blood had come out of the front of his throat and waterfall'd down his fat-belly shirt.

The sense that she was being watched brought her head up and she burrowed her hand into her bag, finding her gun. Heart pounding, she looked around the lot. The buildings. The lanes. No one was moving, but would she see someone who had taken cover—

All at once, her headache came back, the sharp, piercing pain cutting some kind of mental connection. Some kind of—

It was a memory of feeling like this in her car before. Yes, she had felt *exactly* this kind of fear-based adrenaline sitting behind this wheel—and it hadn't been a distant-in-time thing. It had been recent. It had been . . .

Groaning, she had to stop following the thought pattern, but the amnesia was frustrating, the conviction that what she was reaching for, in a cognitive sense, was close at hand and yet out of reach, taunting her.

Fumbling to slide the pictures back into the envelope, she grabbed her bag and got out. The rain was still falling in a gentle way, and she felt an urgency to take cover that had nothing to do with the weather. She flat out ran for the rear door of the newsroom's building.

With a shaking hand, she swiped her card and all but jumped inside.

Pulling the solid steel panel closed behind herself, she leaned back against the wall and tried to catch her breath.

Maybe McCordle was right, she thought. Maybe she needed to get out of all this—

A memory that had no obstructions in front of it came to her mind. She saw Syn jumping out of her bathroom, prepared to shoot the pizza delivery guy. Contrasting that image with McCordle in his uniform, putting his version of brawn between her and that shout at the scene?

No offense to the officer, but she'd pick Syn every time in that race.

And P.S., she didn't need a man to watch out for her, anyway.

Putting her hand on the side of her bag, she felt the hard contours of her gun, and decided Syn was right. She needed to keep this weapon close, 24/7.

She didn't want to end up a crime scene photograph.

CHAPTER THIRTY-ONE

Day transitioned into night, and still Mr. F read on, turning pages one by one, his eyes skipping nothing of the book's incredibly uninspiring prose. From time to time, he took a break, although not to get up and stretch or go to the bathroom or find food. And it remained an eerie revelation that none of that was necessary.

No, he stopped just because he felt like it was something he would have done before: When he'd been studying in high school. When he'd been on the grind in college during the year prior to him dropping out. It seemed important to connect to who he'd been, even if the old him had no more substance than a reflection in a mirror.

Fanning the remaining pages, he remembered that scene at the end of *Beetlejuice* where the father is sitting in his study, trying to get through a copy of *The Living and the Dead*.

This thing reads like stereo instructions.

Mr. F should be so fortunate. What he had in his palms read more like the Dead Sea Scrolls trying to explain how to hook up a seventies-era record player.

244 J. R. WARD

But he had learned a lot. Some twelve hours after he'd started, he now had the basics about what happened during induction, and what was in the jars that had to be guarded against pilfering by the Brotherhood. He knew how slayers were killed with a stab through the empty heart cavity with anything made of steel. He understood the process by which, thereafter, the essence was returned to the Omega, as the master was called. He also had a history of the war with the vampires, including the original conflict between the Scribe Virgin, who'd exercised her one act of creation to bring those with fangs into being, and the Omega, who was her brother and suffered from what sounded like standard sibling jealousy. Further, Mr. F now knew about the Black Dagger Brotherhood, and the great Blind King, and the different social strata of vampires.

And then there was the shit about his own role. There were chapters on the previous incarnations of organization within the Lessening Society, and a section devoted to what the *Fore-lesser* was supposed to be and how he was supposed to act, including a primer on troop mobilization, training, and provisions.

Not that that last one seemed relevant anymore. Assuming there were a couple more of these outpost houses scattered around the suburbs of Caldwell—hello, those keys that did not fit the lock here—the pathetic, ill-matched bunch of war knickknacks he'd found during his search of this place were no doubt no better than he was going to get at any of the other properties.

As he glanced around the empty living room he'd camped out in, he had the sense of a power structure left to rot, and, like a body that through a combination of age and disease no longer properly functioned, he wasn't sure a revival was coming—or even possible.

He'd been hoping for light at the end of the tunnel with all the packed prose he'd been wading through. Now that he was coming to the final chapter, he was worried he wasn't going to get one. For all the knowledge he'd gained, he still didn't know what to do.

That changed in the last four pages.

Like the finish line of a marathon, the solution arrived only after he had expended assiduous effort through the twists and turns of an uphill slog. And at first, when his eyes traced the words, he almost kept going.

Something drew him back, and as he reread them, he realized it was only because they were set in the middle of the page, the lines indented, each one of them.

Stanzas. Like it was a poem.

There shall be one to bring the end before the master,
a fighter of modern time found in the seventh of the
  twenty-first,
and he shall be known in the numbers he bears:
One more than the compass he apperceives,
Though a mere four points to make at his right,
Three lives has he,
Two scores on his fore,
and with a single black eye, in one well will he be
  birthed and die.

An end before the master? Or an end of the master?

Mr. F thought back to the night before, to the Brother who put his mouth over that slayer's and started to inhale, the Brother who the Omega took on as an enemy of special importance. Mr. F wasn't sure what to make of all the passage's threes and fours, two scores and the single black eye, but he knew what he'd witnessed. The Omega and that particular vampire were tied together, and the strings that linked them were in these stanzas.

If *lessers* that were stabbed with steel sent their evil back to its source . . . maybe that male vampire with the prodigious set of lungs circumvented that process. Maybe he was the reason the Omega that was described in this book was so diminished in person.

Mr. F thumbed through the pages he'd read. The master as depicted here was an all-powerful scourge, capable of great and terrible things.

What had shown up in that alley? Mystical, sure. Magical, yup. But all-powerful? Not in that dirty robe. Not with whatever the master had thrown at that vampire.

That shit had only knocked the Brother back.

If you were really the root of all evil, if you were truly the powerful demigod in this book? You would have blown your enemy apart, little bits of flesh and tiny slivers of bone all that were left to drift down onto the pavement, mortal snow to fall from the sky.

Not what had happened.

Mr. F closed the book. He was not a strategist by nature. But he knew what he had read. He knew who he was in this game, and he knew who controlled him. He also knew how he and the Omega were connected.

So he knew what he had to do.

He had to pull all of the slayers together here in Caldwell. And they had to find that Brother from the night before.

It was the only way he was going to come through this. Besides, according to the book, it was all but preordained.

◆　◆　◆

St. Patrick's Cathedral was some real Catholic majesty, Butch thought as he sat in a pew in the back-back, as he'd called it when he was a kid. The church was the seat for Caldwell and many surrounding towns, and the stone building could handle the responsibility. With Notre Dame-like stained windows and arches, and the seating capacity of an NFL dome'd arena, it was exactly where he liked to go to services, take confession, and enjoy moments like this where he just sat with his hands folded in his lap and his eyes on the great marble altar and the statue of Jesus upon the cross.

It was important to feel small and insignificant when you talked to God.

Taking a deep breath, he smelled incense and lemon-scented cleaner. There was also the faded pastiche of the colognes, perfumes, and fabric softeners of everyone who had left the midnight service that had concluded about forty-five minutes ago.

He should probably head out, too. In spite of V's shut-in proposal, Butch was allowed to go into the field tonight. He was allowed to search for *lessers*, and he was going to be on hand if any of the brothers or the others found any. And every time he inhaled one of those sonsofbitches down, they were one step closer the end—

Butch winced and focused on the depiction of Jesus's downcast face. "Sorry," he whispered to his Lord and Savior.

You shouldn't cuss in church. Even in your head.

Taking a deep breath, he exhaled long and slow. In his mind, he pictured himself standing up. Hitting the center aisle. Going out into the narthex. Going out into the night. Going over to the R8 in the parking lot.

At which point, he would head downtown and—

The creak of the pew refocused him, and he jumped a little as he realized he was no longer alone. A nun had joined him, taking a seat about three feet away. Funny, he hadn't noticed her walking in.

"Forgive me, Sister. Do you need me to leave?"

The nun had her head lowered, the hood of her habit falling forward so he could not see her face. "No, my son. You stay as long as you wish."

The voice was soft and gentle, and he closed his eyes, letting the peace of the place, of his faith, of this woman who had given her life in service to the church and to God, wash over him. The resulting cleanse of his anxieties was similar to what Vishous did for him. The strengthening, too.

It made him feel like he could handle what was coming. Later tonight. Tomorrow night. Up until the last moment.

"What do you pray for, my son?" the nun asked him from under her habit.

"Peace." Butch opened his lids and stared at the altar which was draped in red velvet. "I pray for peace. For my friends and my family."

"You say that with a heavy heart."

"It will not come easy, and there's a lot on me alone. I wouldn't have it any other way, though."

"What is on your conscience?"

"Nothing."

"A pure heart is a blessing. Mostly because it does not require us to tarry after services for this long."

Butch smiled a little. "Sister, you are right."

"So speak unto to me."

"Are you from Italy?" He looked over and found himself wishing he could see her face. "The accent."

"I am from a number of places."

"I'm from Southie. Boston. In case you can't tell from my own accent." He exhaled again. "And I don't know if it's something on my conscience. It's more like I can't control the outcome."

"We never can. That is why our faith is important. Do you believe, do you truly believe?"

Butch took his gold cross out from his shirt. "I truly believe."

"Then you will never be alone. No matter where you are."

"You're so right, Sister." He smiled again. "And I have my brothers."

"Then you come from a big family?"

"Oh, yes." He thought of Vishous. "And I can't do ... what I have to ... without them."

"So you worry about them?"

"Of course." Butch rubbed his cross, warming the solid gold with the heat of his mortality. "My roommate in particular. I literally cannot do this without him. He is ... well, it's hard to explain. But without him, I can't go on, and that is not hyperbole. He is integral to me. To my life."

"It sounds like a close relationship."

"He's my very best friend. My other half, in addition to my *sh*—my wife. Even though that sounds weird."

"There are many different kinds of love in a person's life. Tell me, you say that you worry about him. Is this because of your relationship or because he is in danger himself."

Butch opened his mouth to answer that which had seemed to be expressed as a rhetorical—and then closed things with a clap. As his mind started to connect some dots, he saw a pattern emerge that was so obvious, he should have noticed it before. Other people should have noticed it.

And somebody should have fucking—*frickin'*—done something about it.

Butch burst up to his feet. "Sister, I'm so sorry. I gotta—I gotta go."

"It is all right, my child. Follow your heart, it will never steer you wrong."

The nun turned her head and looked up at him.

Butch froze. The face that stared at him was no one face. It was a hundred female faces, the images shifting on top of each other, blurring into an optical illusion. And that wasn't all. From beneath the black folds of the habit, a brilliant, cleansing light pooled on the floor, making the prayer stools glow.

"It's . . . you," Butch breathed.

"You know, you always were one of my favorites," the entity said as the faces smiled together. "In spite of all the questions you asked me. Now go, and follow your impulses. You are correct in all of them, especially the one involving my son."

Between one heartbeat and the next, the Scribe Virgin disappeared, but she left the glow of her goodness behind, the beneficent illumination of her presence remaining for a moment before it faded.

Left alone once again, there was the temptation to replay the interaction, mine it for more clues, bask in the fact that he had been sitting right next to the creator of the vampire race.

That of everyone, she had come to see him.

No time, though.

Shuffling out of the pew, Butch went for his phone as he hauled ass out of the sanctuary and through the narthex. The number he dialed was in his favorites. He prayed that it was answered.

One ring . . .

Two rings . . .

Three rings . . .

For fuck's sake, Butch thought as he burst out of the cathedral's heavy main door. V was downtown right now. Looking for *lessers*. And the Omega wasn't stupid.

The evil had to know how the prophecy worked because no mortal entity, vampire or human or combination of the two, could survive taking a part of the Omega inside of itself. There had to be a way to get the evil out of a mortal, and there was.

The Omega's nephew, Vishous, was the key. And surely this was going to dawn on V's uncle. Any tactician would put the two and two together at some point, and the fact the Omega hadn't done so already meant the dawn-on-Marblehead, switch of strategy, was long overdue.

"Pick up, V," Butch muttered as he broke out into a run down the stone steps. "Pick the fuck up."

Butch wasn't the one who needed to be kept off the streets in safety.

His roommate was.

CHAPTER THIRTY-TWO

A s Syn re-formed in the damp, cold night, he was frustrated. Twice a year, all fighters had to have physical exams down in the Brotherhood's training center. It was a colossal waste of time. If you were upright and nothing was in a sling or a cast, or had been stitched back together within the last twenty-four hours, you needed to be out in the field. For fuck's sake, back in the Old Country, you fought as long as your dagger hand was steady. Here? In the New World? People worried about things like biomechanics, nutrition, performance.

Such snowflake bullshit.

Especially when he had things he had to do before he could go downtown into the field.

The back end of Jo's apartment building was quiet. Just like the front had been when he'd looked for her car, and been reassured to find it was parallel parked three spots down from the sidewalk that led to the front door. She was safe. She was indoors. She would be as such until dawn.

He had no more business here.

He'd had none as soon as he'd arrived.

Why had he come back here then—

Syn frowned as his palm found the butt of his gun and he crouched down. He was behind a commercial-grade dumpster off to the side of a small, common area terrace—so he had cover, both optically and olfactorily. And he was going to need it.

He was not alone.

Flaring his nostrils, he scented the wind that had abruptly changed directions.

About fifteen feet away, a tall, powerfully built figure in black was standing outside Jo's bedroom window, its back to the building, its eyes trained on the glass if it were trying to see between her venetian blinds without giving its presence away. Light slicing through the slats created enough of a glow so that its goatee and temple tattoos were obvious to someone who had seen them plenty of times before.

What the fuck was Vishous doing here?

As Syn's fangs descended and his upper lip peeled off his teeth, he had to force himself not to trade his gun for his dagger. Guns were for when there was an emergency. Daggers were for when you wanted to stare your kill in the face as you took their life from them.

And he wanted to murder the Brother. Straight up.

Hell yeah, he respected the male in the field. How could anyone in the fighting business not value Vishous's kind of backup? The Brother was no joke with that glowing palm of his, and even better, he kept to himself except for the occasional, spot-on, sarcastic kick in the mouth he was always ready to give anyone who deserved it.

But all of that shit didn't mean a goddamn thing when the male was lurking next to the private sanctuary of Syn's female.

Not a goddamn thing at all—

V shoved a hand inside his leather jacket. Taking out his cell phone, he cursed and stepped away from the window. As he answered whoever was calling him, he kept his voice low, but Syn's ears caught the syllables just fine.

"Butch, lemme call you back for fuck's sake. I'm just checking on that half-breed to see if she's any closer to her trans—" Vishous frowned. "Wait, what? Cop, slow down—what are you talking about?"

During the silence that followed, the Brother frowned so hard, those tattoos around his eye distorted. "You saw *who*? My *mahmen*? What the fuck."

Syn closed his eyes. When he reopened them, he discovered that he had indeed swapped weapons, and as the steel of his dagger flashed, he thought of the number of times V had sharpened it for him. Vishous sharpened everyone's blades. At first, Syn had thought it was yet another ridiculous, fussy centralization of function, the kind of thing people worried about when they knew where their next month's meals were coming from. For shit's sake, he'd been doing his own blades for centuries, as had the other Bastards.

All it had taken was one treatment and Syn had gotten over himself.

V took that grinding and polishing to another level and you had to recognize the skill. The benefit was not an issue of safety—Syn didn't give a fuck about that—it was an issue of efficacy. You were more lethal with what V did to those sharp and shiny weapons.

So yup, killing him tonight was going to be a bummer.

"—no, no, we're not discussing a damn thing. I'm not the *Dhestroyer*. You are. You're the one who should be kept indoors—"

The venetian blinds parted, as if Jo had heard the talking. And as Syn caught sight of the dark outline of her head and hair, his heart stopped. And redoubled.

He looked down again at the dagger in his palm and considered the way his body had taken things, literally, into its own hand. As he thought about the fact that he had armed himself, and was ready to go against an ally—and someone who would absolutely, positively be missed? And who absolutely, positively hadn't done shit to Syn?

It was clear what was going on.

Fuck.

He'd bonded with Jo.

◆   ◆   ◆

Jo let the blinds on her window fall back into place. Stepping away, she put her hands up to her head. As her heart pounded, she thought about calling 911, but what was she going to say?

Help, there's someone talking right outside my bedroom. At least, I think they are. At least . . . I think I heard a male voice.

It wasn't an emergency to hear whispers. More to the point, it wasn't an emergency to *think* you heard whispers.

Sure, ma'am, we'll send someone out with a flashlight to do a perimeter search. All those people who've been in car accidents with drunk drivers or the victims of crime can wait.

Going out into the living area, she walked to the main door of her apartment and back. Even though it was after midnight, she was fully dressed, with her coat on. She had been putting on her ground-grippers, as she called her boots, when the low-level noise had registered.

Her backpack was right by the exit. And hey, there was a flashlight in it.

Plus her gun.

"Screw it," she muttered.

Going over, she double-strapped things and locked her apartment up as she left. At the building's outer door by the mailboxes, she hesitated again, trying to see into the pitch-black night beyond the security lights while her breath fogged up the glass.

Even though she was paranoid about so much, she'd planned to go out anyway. She was exhausted, but antsy, and there was no amount of Netflixing that was going to chill her out. It was like she was a car with the gas and the brake on at the same time. So she'd already decided on a destination when she'd heard the murmurs outside her bedroom.

No doubt it was best to not go look into them. She needed to stick to her plan—which had not included playing welcome committee to someone sent by the Caldwell mob to kill her.

Cursing again, she shoved open the door, ducked down, and scrambled for her car, wondering if she shouldn't be crossing the lawn in a zig-zag pattern so she was a harder target. As she came up to the driver's side, her body was shaking.

And yet she stopped.

Looking over her shoulder, she searched the darkness beside her building.

"Syn?"

It better be Syn, she thought. Or she was a sitting duck for someone who—

"I'm not stalking you," came a familiar voice out of the shadows. "I swear."

"Oh, thank God, it's you." Jo sagged against her car. "I was . . . well, never mind."

And actually, she'd expected to see him earlier. She'd thought he might be waiting for her in the parking lot again as she'd left the newsroom. Then she'd anticipated the ring of her doorbell at any moment as soon as she'd gotten home: through her after-work shower, through dinner—Slim Jims and M&Ms, mmm tasty—through the debate on whether to get into bed or get out of the apartment.

And now he was here.

Syn walked forward, emerging into the illumination thrown by the light fixture mounted on the corner of the building. As he came over to her, her eyes were greedy and so were her hands. She indulged the former. Kept the latter to herself.

"Hi," she said as she stared up at him.

"Hi."

There was a long silence. And then she grabbed his arm and gave it a shake. "Before we say anything else, what's your phone number? And I promise, this time, I will remember it."

When he didn't start spitting out digits, she frowned. Then she closed her eyes.

"Right," she said with defeat. "So you've come to tell me that last night was a mistake that should never have happened because you're married."

"What?"

"I gotta go." She turned back to her car door. "Take care of yourself—"

Now he was the one detaining her, his big hand landing on her shoulder. "Where are you going? It's late—"

"Why do you care?" She glanced at him. "And I'm not being obnoxious with that. I've spent all day thinking about what happened between you and me—and what didn't. Guilt has a funny way of dimming a man's performance, and you clearly don't want me to contact you."

He shook his head as if she'd switched languages on him. "I'm not following what you're—"

"You lied to me, didn't you. You're with someone."

"No. I'm not mated."

Jo rolled her eyes and shrugged out from under his heavy palm. "Married. Whatever—"

"Where are you going?"

"I really don't have to answer that. If you can't even be honest with me about where you live, what you do for a living, who you really are, and who you're with? I don't have to tell you a goddamn thing about myself—"

"I don't want you to know the truth about me."

Jo froze where she was. Then blinked. "So I was right. And I'm afraid that I've got to go. I don't have the energy for any of this, especially not being the side piece to your significant other—"

"I'm not mated." Syn put his hand on the jamb of her door, preventing her from opening it. "And you're in danger—"

She put her forefinger right in his face. "I am getting *really* frickin' tired of men telling me that tonight."

A frown landed on his forehead like it had jumped off a bridge. "Who else said it?"

"It's not important—"

"You will answer me right now."

"*Excuse me?*" She stepped in real close. "You don't use that tone with me. *Ever*. And you can take that demand and blow it out your ass."

His eyes gleamed with anger. "Do you think this is a joke?"

"No. I think you are."

Syn didn't move. She didn't move. And it was not sexual tension that kept their faces so close together.

All at once, that headache of hers came back and she groaned as she put a hand up to her temple. "Just leave me alone, okay."

"You shouldn't go out there by yourself," he said remotely.

"What?"

Syn looked away. "This is a fucking mess."

Before she could give him another push-off, he released her door. "Let me come with you. If you let me . . . ride along, I'll tell you everything. Everything."

Jo crossed her arms over her chest. "How will I know?"

"That I'm with you?"

Like that *isn't going to be obvious?* Jo thought.

"That you're telling me the truth," she said in a bored tone.

"You have my word."

Great, for whatever that was worth.

"If you lie to me, I'll know." She leveled a stare at him. "I'm a reporter. I'm going to make it my business to find out what's going on with you one way or another, and if you lie to me tonight? You better never come around me again. You taught me where to best shoot someone, remember?"

"Yes," he said gravely.

"Good." Jo wrenched open the driver's side door. "Because thanks to you, I know how to kill a man."

And boy, that sounded like a *really* great idea at the moment.

CHAPTER THIRTY-THREE

S o start talking."

As Jo put the command out, Syn pulled his seat belt free of his chest and then let the strap come back into contact with his pecs. The fact that they came up to a red light seemed apt.

When the thing turned green, she didn't hit the gas. "Well."

"I don't know where to start."

"Pick something random—like birth," she said dryly.

"I fear your knowledge of me." He looked out of the side window. "I want a better story than the one I have to give you."

The beep of a car horn behind them had her moving them forward. "We all want a better story. But that's marketing, not reality."

Syn thought of the hut he had lived in with his sire, the one he had burned down. He thought of the fact that he had slept next to his *mahmen*'s dead body for a decade, after it had rotted with a terrible stench for three months. He thought of the drunken, slobbering, abusive tormentor he had had to endure until he had sliced the male into pieces and let the sun do the work of ashing the remains.

Maybe start with the present, he decided.

"I'm a soldier. You're right about that." He looked at the local shops that they passed, and reflected how he would have so much preferred to be detailing a life where going into a store and choosing which gift, which bottle of wine, which piece of cheese, to purchase was the most strenuous decision and consequence faced. "I'm a soldier and some other things I'm not proud of."

"Being in the military most certainly is something to be proud of."

"It's not what I've done when in service that I want to apologize for." He took a deep breath. "It's true that I'm a bodyguard. Of a very powerful male—man. An extremely powerful one who has many enemies."

"That explains how you acted with the delivery guy."

"It's my nature. And my training. Sometimes . . ." He cleared his throat. "Sometimes both conspire to get the best of me."

"And you really do live with him? That man you guard."

"Yes, in his home, with his wife and his child. He has a number of personal guards and I am one of them."

"Who is he?" She glanced over. "Unless you can't tell me that?"

"I am paid to be discreet. I'm sorry. And I can't take you to where I live for the same reason." He looked at her pointedly. "But I'm not lying about this. I am telling you everything I can—and maybe, in the future? I might be able to tell you even more. Not the now, though."

They continued on, going into the commercial part of town. No more mom-and-pop stores with homey themes best suited for Instagram snapshots and baby showers. Now there were tile stores, and carpet stores, and places that sold electronics, tires and cars.

"Is that why you're downtown so much?" she asked. "Helping your boss."

"A lot happens there. It's a dangerous place."

"True." Jo glanced over, and in the light glowing from the dashboard, her face seemed reserved, but no longer angry. "That's why you said what you did to me that first night, huh. About me being in danger. About me dying."

"You need to be careful."

"Women can take care of themselves."

"They shouldn't have to."

"Which brings us to my next question." She refocused on the road ahead, her ten-and-two grip on the wheel tightening. "What's up with your wife."

"I told you." Syn shook his head. "I don't have one."

"I don't believe you."

"That is the one thing you can be completely sure of," he said bitterly. "You know that I have a problem when it comes to sex. What female would have me? I cannae get her pregnant."

"There's more to a relationship than having children."

"Not for most females, and who can blame them. Besides, it's never been a priority for me."

"Sex?"

"Marriage."

There was a long pause. "Were you injured?" she asked as they came up to another traffic light. "You know, while fighting overseas? Is that why you can't . . . I mean, I'm no medical expert. I don't know how these things happen or work."

He recalled his first rutting. It had been with a female of the species who he had paid to allow him to take her vein. Evidently, she had found him attractive and had mounted him while he had been feeding from her. He could still picture her riding up and down on his hips, her stained peasant blouse open, her pendulous breasts swinging back and forth on her chest like saddlebags on a galloping horse.

It was common for males to become sexually aroused when they indulged their bloodlust. He'd learned this over time. But that did not mean they wanted to have sex. Or, in his case, when he'd lost his virginity, consented to the act. After it was all done, she had kissed him and dismounted with an air of satisfaction. Taking the money, she had left him on the cot, her juices drying on his hard cock, a dirty feeling staining the inside of his skin.

The sense that she had taken something from him had persisted for nights.

"It's not an injury," he said tightly. "It's just the way it's always been."

"Have you been checked out by a doctor?"

"Sure," he murmured so she'd stop asking questions on the topic.

"And there's nothing they can do about it?"

"No."

"I'm really sorry."

Syn took a deep breath, and as he let it out, he hoped the exhale took some of the sting in his chest with it. "I don't spend any time thinking about it."

"Have you ever been in love?"

I've bonded with you, he thought to himself.

"So tell me about her," Jo said softly. "And don't deny she exists. I can see it in your face."

"I'm looking away from you," he pointed out as he deliberately focused on a Panera restaurant. Then a Ford dealership. Then a Sunoco gas station.

"Fine, I can hear it in your voice."

"I didn't say anything."

"You are now. And I can tell."

Syn was not about to go into the bonding thing with her. So in his head, he moved on to that female from the Old Country, picturing her front and center so that all other considerations were hidden—even though, as much as he had always been told, humans couldn't read the thoughts of others.

So it wasn't like Jo could get into his skull and see what he was skirting.

"That female was not meant for me," he said. "So I don't think I ever loved her in the way you mean. We were never together."

"How did you know her?"

"She lived in the same village I did. Back . . . home. In the Old Country. I knew her because I was—" He swallowed. "Anyway."

"What," Jo said. "Please, just tell me. This is really helping."

There were streetlights mounted up high on poles, and as they passed them by, the illumination came through the sunroof's transparent panel. As the gentle strobing bathed he and Jo to a slow beat, he found that he was glad they were in a car and she had to focus on the road ahead. On the other drivers out with them, though there were few. On the red lights and the intersections.

There was no way in hell he could have gotten through any of this if she'd been staring him in the face.

"I was poor," he said. "Not the poor where you want things you can't have. Not the poor where you're bitter about what other people are doing or what they own. Poor like you don't know if you're going to be eating at nightfall. Like you aren't sure whether there will be clothes for you to wear. Like if you get sick, you're going to die and you're okay with that because all you know is how hungry and thirsty and tired you are."

"God, Syn—"

When she reached over and put her hand on the sleeve of his leather jacket, he moved away sharply. "No. I'm going to get through this once and then I'm never speaking of it to you again. And you're not going to touch me when I'm talking."

"But I feel bad—"

"I don't care." He looked over at her. "You want a pound of flesh, fine. I get it. Hell, it's even a fair thing to ask. Do *not* pity me, though. You can fuck off with your sympathy. I'm not asking for it and I'm not interested in it. Are we clear?"

There was a brief pause. And then she nodded with a sadness that was palpable.

"Crystal clear," she said quietly.

CHAPTER THIRTY-FOUR

Inside the downtown garage bay, Butch paced back and forth across the space where Manny's surgical RV chilled out when it wasn't in use in the field, transporting someone to the clinic for treatment, or being worked on back at the training center.

He checked his watch. Paced some more.

The garage was a nifty bolt-hole on the edge of the field, and the two-story, steel-girded lockdown was stocked with all kinds of supplies: Medical crap. Mechanical crap. Food crap.

Crap, crap, crap—where the fuck was V?

Muttering to himself, Butch walked over to where he'd parked his roommate's car off to one side, popped the trunk's release, and went to the four rings on the hood. Lifting up the panel, he shrugged out of his suit jacket, took off his silk shirt, and put on his long-sleeved base layer. In the warmer months, he wore muscle shirts, but they were not there yet with the temperature. It was still cold as balls out there as far as he was concerned.

As he undid his belt and dropped his slacks to the tops of his loafers, he sensed he was no longer alone.

Kicking off his shoes, he said, "It's for your own safety, and where the hell have you been."

"I had to go back to the Pit for smokes. Something told me I'd need them." There was a *shcht* as V lit up. "And that whole safety argument did not fly with you. What makes you think it'll work on me?"

Butch stepped to the left and picked up his pants, folding them precisely down the creases and putting them with his good clothes, a sandwich of Armani. "Because you're smarter than I am. Always have been—and if you try and deny this, I will remind you of alllll the times you've felt compelled to point the happy fact out."

Grabbing his leathers, he pulled them into place, hopping on the balls of his feet to get them over his bare ass.

"You shouldn't be out here alone, cop."

"There are about twenty other people who can back me up." He turned around and tucked in his shirt. Then buttoned things up down below. "There's only one who can Simonize me."

V exhaled a stream of smoke and leaned back against a counter that had a tool box and six silver jugs of Valvoline Full Synthetic Advanced 0W-20 motor oil on it.

"That metaphor doesn't work. I'm not buffing and polishing you."

"Oh, my God." Butch clapped his hands. "This is *exactly* what I'm talking about."

"Excuse me?"

"See? You're smart enough to know about that metaphor thingy not working out. Therefore you are smarter than I am. Henceforth, the logic of you staying the fuck home is more immediately apparent to the likes of you because you're a fucking brainiac."

"FYI, you don't get more points for your argument by tossing around 'therefore' and 'henceforth.'"

"It's the only recourse an idiot like me has."

"And the last time someone used the word 'brainiac' in a sentence was when Flock of Seagulls was hitting the charts and AT&T was ordered to break up."

"Thank you, Alex Trebek." Butch bent down and picked his chest holster up out of the trunk. "And by all means, let's keep talking. It's just making me look dumber which is a big help to my side of this debate."

V seemed nonplussed for a moment. "Are you aware of what you're saying?"

Strapping on his daggers, handles down, Butch shook his head. "Not a clue. Which is what stupid people do, right? Not smart people. Like you."

He put his ammo belt around his waist. Stocked the guns on either side. Checked his bullets. Then he put his leather jacket on.

"What about your boots?" V muttered.

"You know, unless you'd mentioned them, I would have forgotten to put them on."

"Don't you dare sit your ass down on the front of my car."

"Not to worry. I might be dumb, but I don't have a death wish."

Shutting the hood, Butch parked it on the concrete floor by the front air dam and drew socks on. Put his feet in shitkickers. Laced things up.

He grunted as he went back onto the vertical. Jogging everything into place, he put his hands on his hips and stared across the vacancy of the garage.

"You wanted to kill me the first night we met," he said.

"Still do."

"But we're a long way from that now. And if I'm going to do what I need to out there, I can't be worried about you."

As V started to look around, Butch went over to a table and picked up a half-full bottle of Coke. "You ash on the good doctor's floor, he's going to operate on something you can't grow back."

When he cracked the top, there wasn't a fizz to be heard or seen. "Here."

V took what was offered and tapped his hand-rolled over the open neck. "I'm not going to let you die out there."

"The Omega is going to come after you. That he hasn't already makes no sense."

"Maybe he's not that smart."

"You know that's not . . ." Butch rubbed his temples as they started to ache.

"What?"

What had he been saying? "Anyway, you know how your mom left us? The species, I mean."

"No. I forgot—tell me more. And we shoulda gotten her a fake gold watch for her retirement. Cake that read 'The Golden Years Are the Best.' Bouquet of fucking flowers with a card." V shook his head and spit out a flake of tobacco. "Helluva female, true? Creating all this shit and leaving it in the dust like none of us matter—I mean, the race. Like the race doesn't matter."

"But what if she left because she had another job to do."

V frowned. "Like what."

"Protecting you." As V rolled his eyes and started cursing, Butch put up his palm. "Hear me out. The first rule in conflict is finding the weakness in your opponent and exploiting it. The Omega knows what I do and he knows about you. His very existence is at stake. You think he's not going to do the math and put a target on your back? Eliminate you and what I can do to him is out the door. Problem solved."

"You're suggesting that the Scribe Virgin took off so she could watch over me?" V laughed in a short burst. "Yeah, right. My *mahmen* doesn't think about me or my sister."

"I don't know if I believe that. I think she's more involved than we know, and I think she came to me to send me a message about your safety."

"Trust me. It was not about that."

"Then what the hell was she doing in a Catholic church tonight?"

"Not talking to me, that's for sure." V ashed into the soda bottle again. "And let's put this conversation aside, so we can keep fighting about the topic at hand. One argument at a time."

Butch shook his head and walked across to stand in front of the brother. Putting a hand on the side of V's neck, he cut the bullshit.

"You can dematerialize to me, anywhere I am. I can't do that. I'm stuck with the ground game. You can be covered by a legion and so can I when we're together. But if we lose you? It's all over for me. We are both equally important, but what I do has to be in the field. What you do can be done anywhere."

V stared down at the tip of his hand-rolled. "I'm feeling some kind of way about this."

"It's the truth and you know it."

"Motherfucker."

Butch leaned in and put his forehead on V's. "I'll call as soon as I need you."

"You die on me, I'll resuscitate you just so I can kill you all over again."

"Fair enough." Butch straightened. "Now get the fuck back home."

"I don't agree with this."

"Yes, you do or you wouldn't be leaving." Butch nodded to the exit, even though that would not be the way Vishous ghosted out. "Go on—"

"How did my *mahmen* look?"

"I'd never seen her face before."

"That makes one of us," V said bitterly.

"Mothers are complicated."

"You don't say." V dropped his hand-rolled into the soda bottle, a little sizzle rising up. "You call me. I'll come at any second."

"Or they'll bring me to you."

"I'd prefer the former." V rolled his eyes. "Guess I'm going to go clean my room."

"You think Fritz is going to allow that?"

"You think he's going to have a choice?"

V was shrugging as he dematerialized, and Butch stared at where his best friend had stood for a moment. Then he locked up the R8, and texted to everyone on rotation that he was heading into the field.

He didn't make it.

As soon as he stepped out of the garage, he stopped dead in his tracks from shock. "Jesus . . . *Christ.*"

◆   ◆   ◆

Behind the wheel of the Golf, Jo tightened her grip and was tempted to tell Syn to stop talking. But that was a whole load of bullcrap. He'd had to live through his past. She was just having to listen to it.

And when he didn't immediately go any further with his story, she was not about to prompt him. She just kept driving them along.

About a mile later, he started talking again. "That female I cared for fed me when I was starving. She clothed me when I was all but naked. She warmed me with her smile when I was cold." He paused. "She was the only thing in my life that didn't cause me pain."

I would have helped you if I could have, Jo thought.

"She sounds like a very good person," she said.

"She was."

"Was? Is she . . . has she passed?"

"I don't know what happened to her. I moved away from my village, and I understand that eventually, she came over here as I did. I also understand she got mated and had some young. Two, I think. Which is a blessing." He rubbed his eyes. "After everything she did for me when I was a young, I just wanted her to have a good life. A long, happy, healthy life."

"So you did love her."

"I told you. It wasn't like that."

"No, I mean—you loved her as in she mattered to you."

"She did." The breath that came out of him was sharp and short. "But enough about her."

"Okay."

He cleared his throat. "I was a natural born soldier. I was good at . . . what I did. So I was recruited to fight the enemy."

"Was this just after nine-eleven? You must have been so young. I mean, how old are you? And what country did you fight for?"

"In times of war, you do what needs to be done. And it was the best use of me. Before the structure of my . . . unit, I guess you'd call it, I was doing contract killing. My cousin was the one who got me into the service—"

"Wait." Jo glanced over at him. "Contract killing?"

"Yes." He looked at her. "Don't make a hero out of me, Jo. It won't serve you well."

"Do you ever regret what you did? What if you killed someone who was innocent?"

"I didn't."

"How can you be sure?"

"Because I only accepted certain kinds of jobs."

"I can't imagine taking someone's life."

"Sometimes it's easier than you think. If someone threatened you, your immediate family, your blooded kin? You'd be surprised what you can do in that moment. Civilians can turn into soldiers pretty damn quick in those circumstances."

"You definitely see things like a military man," she murmured.

"Always. And I will defend me and mine against all comers. It doesn't matter who they are or how otherwise virtuous they may be. If you are a danger to me? To my brothers? To those I serve? You will submit to me. I will take the payment for your indiscretion out of your flesh. And when I am finished? I will never think of you again—not because I am troubled by what I have done, but because you do not matter to me and neither does your death."

A cold fear curled in Jo's chest. "I cannot fathom those deductions. That conclusion. I mean, a life is a life."

"Then you haven't looked into the eyes of someone who is going to kill you solely because you are not like them. Because you do not believe the same things they do. Because you are living a different kind of life. Wartime is not the same as peacetime."

Jo shook her head. "Anyway, so you said your cousin got you into the military? What branch? Or was it, like, Special Forces?"

"Yes, something like covert ops. We fought for . . . years over in the Old Country. Then the focus of the conflict changed course and I came to America with the leader of my squadron. After some . . . reorientation . . . we fell in line with the powerful male I work for the now. And that brings us up to date."

Jo thought of the flash of attraction she had felt when she had seen him in all that leather, with all those weapons on his body. He had seemed so thrilling and mysterious. Now, she confronted the reality of what the guns and knives were used for. What they did. What his body had done to other bodies.

"What would you be doing with your life if the war hadn't happened?"

There was a pause. "I would have been a farmer." He shifted in his seat. "I would have liked to have a plot of land I could cultivate. Some animals to care for—horses to ride, cows to graze and milk. I would have liked . . . to be one with the earth."

As Syn seemed to become steeped in sorrow, he lifted his palms and stared down at them, and she imagined he was picturing his hands in good topsoil, or traveling down the flank of a healthy horse, or cradling a newborn calf.

"A farmer," she said softly.

"Aye." He put his palms down on his thighs. "But that is not how things went."

They were silent for a while. Then she felt compelled to say, "I believe you. Everything you said, I believe."

He leaned to the side and rooted around inside his leather jacket. Taking out a slim wallet, he presented her with a laminated card.

"Here's my driver's license." When she shook her head, he put it up in front of her. "No, let's do it all. That's who I am, but the address is an old flophouse where I stayed with my brothers."

She glanced at what he held out. The name listed was Sylvester Neste. And the street was like "Maple Court," or something equally all-American.

He took the license back. "As I said, I'm living with the male—man, I mean, and his family. I've got no wife, no kids, and never will. So you know everything about my current status."

Jo opened her mouth to say something, but he cut her off. "And here's my telephone number."

He recited seven digits. Twice. "You want me to write it down for you? There's a pen right here."

Taking her Bic out of the drink cup holder, he bent down and fished around the Slim Jim wrappers at his feet. Wrote his number on the back of a Hershey's wrapper. Tucked the number into the drink cup holder and put the pen back where it had been.

"Any questions for me?" he said evenly as he tucked his wallet away.

Jo looked over at him. "I'm not going to pretend to be comfortable with some of the things you stated. But it's . . . they're the reason I think you're being honest, though."

"I withheld nothing."

"I feel like I should apologize for forcing you to talk."

"Don't worry about that. I'm a stranger and this is a dangerous time. There's nothing wrong with taking care of yourself." He brushed the top of his Mohawk. "Also, I have no Facebook page. No social media anything. Who gives a shit about all that. I also do not have an email address, and I do not put money into the banking system."

"At all? So how are you paid?"

"In cash, and I will not apologize for being off the grid. No one should trust the government."

She laughed dryly. "I don't judge you on that."

"It is what it is—and feel free to verify everything. I'll give you my Social Security number if you want? But I'll tell you that it's one that was bought and paid for on the black market. I don't really exist in the records of the world you live in."

"Syn." She briefly shut her eyes. "I didn't mean to turn this into an inquest."

"Do you want my Social Security number?"

"No. I don't."

As they came up to a four-lane byway, she braked at a red light and took a right. She didn't expect him to say anything. Ever again.

"I'm not a hero, Jo." He put his elbow on his window's jamb and propped his hard chin on his knuckles. "I have no future, and a past I don't waste time thinking about. I've got this moment here and now, and even when it comes to that, I'm only halfway present. You spoke the truth. I'm a joke."

"I didn't mean that," she said sharply.

"Yes, you did. And I'm not hurt by the truth. Why should I be hurt by the reflection of myself in the mirror of your eyes?"

"Syn . . ."

Jo looked over at his profile. With his Mohawk and his hooded eyes focused on the road ahead, he looked like exactly what he'd told her he was. A military man who had seen the very worst of humanity, been at the mercy of governments and greedy politicians, and learned that trust was a luxury he couldn't afford.

"I'd like to tell you I'm sorry," she said.

"No sympathy, remember?"

"I didn't express any." She briefly took both hands off the wheel and held them up. "I only said I *wanted* to tell you that. I also wish I could tell you that you're anything but a joke, and that I'm grateful you talked with me. Somehow, I don't think you talk much about yourself and I can see why. I'm very sad about your past." As he opened his mouth, she shook her head and cut him off. "I didn't say any of that, though. I'm just expressing what I *wish* I could say."

His mouth twitched on one side, like he was trying not to smile. "You're exploiting a loophole."

"Next time define your terms better, then."

"Aye." He looked over at her. "I shall do that."

After a moment, he reached over and gave her a little squeeze on the knee. When his hand stayed put, she covered the back of it with her own.

"I'm truly sorry," she whispered softly.

Syn pulled his arm back, removing the contact, and then he cleared his throat.

"So where are we going?" he asked brusquely, as if he were closing a door.

And throwing a dead bolt on the thing.

CHAPTER THIRTY-FIVE

Outside of the Brotherhood's downtown garage, Butch grabbed onto his dead sister's friend's arm to keep her from collapsing onto the dirty sidewalk. Mel McCarthy was badly beaten, in a way no woman ever should be.

"What the hell happened to you?"

Mel grabbed onto the lapels of his leather jacket with torn-up hands. "Oh, God, Butch . . ."

As she looked up at him, blood dropped out of her nose and landed on the bodice of her pale pink bustier, widening the bright red stain that had formed over her left breast. There was also a nasty abrasion on the side of her face that was likewise leaking, and around her throat, ligature marks were a ruddy band in her pale skin. And the injuries continued from there. A dull scratch ran from her collarbone into her cleavage, and below the waist her black skirt was off-kilter and her black fishnet stockings were ripped, more blood running down the bare skin of her thighs from cuts and scrapes.

"Come here," he said, holding her up. "Let's get you out of the cold."

Opening the door into the garage, he helped her inside, holding her up as she limped on the one stiletto that still had a heel. There were a pair of stuffed armchairs off in an alcove, next to the refrigerator and the space heater, and he took her over to one of them. As she eased down onto the padded cushion, her wince told him more than he needed to know about where else she'd been hurt.

Leaning to the side to turn on the heater, he opened his mouth to say something, but struggled to put together anything coherent. Too much of him was focused on wanting to find whoever had done this so he could kill them.

Mel put her head in her hands, her tangled hair falling forward. "I am *so* stupid. So stupid to have been alone with that guy—"

Butch crouched down and took her palms from her face. "Hey, hey. Stop that." He brushed a strand of her long, brown hair back behind her ear. "We need to get you to the hospital." And to a rape kit. "And we should call the police—"

"No!" She wiped a tear off her cheek and winced. "I'm not going to do that—"

"Mel, this was a crime."

"I don't know his name—"

"That's okay, we'll give a description to the CPD, and we'll make sure they have a DNA—"

"I'm not going to the police."

Butch gripped her hands. "Mel. I can't imagine what you've just been through. But I know for certain there are people who can help you—people who can also make sure that the piece of shit who did this to you will get what he deserves."

Her eyes were luminous with tears that trembled on her lashes. "I can't. I just want to forget this ever happened—"

"Caldwell has a SART program, and I can put you in touch with them. They're really good and they—"

Mel sniffled. "What's a SART?"

He thought of his *shellan* and how much he had learned from Marissa as she'd studied how humans deal with violence against females. "It's a sexual attack response team. It's a multidisciplinary approach that is all about the survivor. It's medical people, law enforcement, social workers, all coming together to support you as you seek justice. I promise you, they're good folks, and—"

Mel's eyes went down to their linked hands. "I can't go to the police."

Butch frowned. "I know that it will be hard. But I swear, you'll be taken care of—"

"You don't understand." Her stare came up to his own. "It's really not an option for me."

And that was when her meaning sunk in. As the implications became obvious Butch released her hands and sat back on the cold concrete floor.

"I don't want you to think any less of me." She sniffled again and cleaned her tears with the back of her arm. "But yeah . . . it's not going to happen."

"I don't think less of you."

"You sure about that."

"Absolutely, I am. I just . . . it's not where I expected—" Butch cut himself off. "But enough about that—"

"You didn't think I'd end up an escort?" She held out her short skirt and moved around the hem, as if she were looking for tears in the fabric. "Neither did I."

Getting to his feet, he got a roll of paper towels off the top of the refrigerator. After spooling free some sheets, he folded them and knelt back down again. Gingerly patting her cheeks and under her nose, he grit his teeth at the fucking animal who had done this to her.

"It doesn't matter what the circumstances were when the two of you met up," he said. "This is an assault. It's illegal."

"I've already been popped twice down in Manhattan. That's why I had to come up here. I don't want my family to find out how I'm making my money. I'm more afraid of that than going to jail for solicitation. Prostitution. Whatever they call it in this jurisdiction." She took ahold of his hand as he tamped her tears. "And I don't work the streets or any-thing. I'm expensive."

"Pinch your nose with this." He gave her the paper towels. "We need to stop the bleeding."

She did as she was told, her words coming out muffled. "I feel like if I tell you that you won't think I'm a common whore."

"Don't use that word."

"It's what I am. What I've become."

He thought back to what he remembered of her and Janie, and the center of his chest hurt. "You're still exactly who you've always been."

"I sell my body, Butch." She took the paper towels away and stared down at the red stain on the white twist. "What else would you call me."

"If you're trying to get me to judge you, it won't work."

"I feel like I should be judged. Ten commandments and all."

"That doesn't matter." He looked up into her face. "*You* matter. Your choice of what you want to do with your body is not an issue. It doesn't change a damn thing."

Mel touched her cheek where it was abraded. "How badly am I hurt? Do you think any of this is permanent?"

"No," he said. "You're still beautiful."

The defeat in her eyes aged her. And the bruises and cuts, the blood and swelling, made him furious and despaired by turns.

"Listen, I know a doctor." He cleared his throat. "She could come and check you out. She's totally discreet."

Mel shook her head and squeezed one of his hands. "I'll take care of myself."

"You really should have a doctor—"

"You think this is the first time something like this has happened?"

Butch closed his eyes briefly. "Shit."

Releasing his palm, she pushed herself to her feet with a wince and lurched to one side. As she looked down at her shoes in confusion, she mumbled, "My heel broke off. I didn't notice."

"Let me take you home, at least? And is there someone we can call? Someone who can sit with you?"

"I shouldn't have come. I just ran out of the club, and the next thing I knew, I was here. I just wasn't thinking right."

"Will you let me drive you home?"

She looked at the R8. "This is not how I imagined seeing you again."

"Fate has a strange way of working things out."

◆   ◆   ◆

Behind the wheel of the Golf, Jo kept driving along, leaving the strip malls and the car dealerships behind, and proceeding into more open spaces where cemeteries, the community college, and part of SUNY Caldwell's campus was. Things had been silent inside the car for a while now, and they were closing in on their destination. She couldn't decide whether this was a good thing or not.

A part of her just wanted to drive around until dawn. As if everything on his mind, and all that was on hers, would maybe run out of gas before the VW did.

"So what about you?" Syn asked.

Jo cleared her throat and found it hard to know what to say; her thoughts were still bouncing around the details he'd shared about his own life. So it was on autopilot that she ran through her dossier.

"I was adopted. I grew up in Philadelphia in what would be considered an old family. I'm not close to either of my parents, I have no clue where my birth parents are, and I came to Caldwell for a job after I got out of college. Not married. Wouldn't mind it, but it's not a priority. Just moved into that apartment after living with some frat boys. Um . . . I've only just started reporting on things at the paper. I was hired to be the online editor. And I have a feeling I'm going to be out of work again soon."

"Are things not going well for the *Courier Journal*?"

"You could say that." She took her foot off the accelerator and let the Golf coast to a stop in the middle of the street. "And there's one other thing."

With a strange feeling in her heart, she looked up at the dilapidated entrance to the Brownswick School for Girls.

"Oh?" As Syn noticed where she was staring, he sat forward in his seat. "And what's this?"

Jo tried to find the right words, but there were none. At least none that could guarantee him not to jump to conclusions about her mental health.

"I . . . ah, I've got a hobby, I guess you'd call it. I investigate supernatural things in Caldwell."

When he just nodded calmly, she thought of his cosmetically altered teeth.

"But you maybe get it, right?" she said with hope.

"Does this place have something to do with your hobby?"

Jo let her eyes roam over the off-kilter wrought iron gates and the broken-toothed fencing that stretched in both directions, separating the shaggy grounds from the sidewalk, the road, the tended-to environs of the rest of the area.

"My mother went to school here. Back when it was a going concern."

"Are you looking to speak with her ghost? Has she passed?"

"She was never really there in the first place." Jo shook herself back to attention. "Sorry, I mean, she's alive. She and my father still live in the house I grew up in."

"Do you see them often?"

"No. We don't have anything in common except for the first eighteen years of my life. They're very nineteen fifties, if you know what I mean—traditional sex roles, old money, stiff upper lip. It was like growing up in a Spencer Tracy–Katharine Hepburn movie, except my parents weren't actually in love, and I'm not sure they even like each other."

Jo hit the gas, as if she could drive herself out of where her thoughts went. It didn't work.

As they passed under the archway, she pictured the campus and buildings not as they were, everything ill kept and decaying, but as they had been, with rolling lawns, brick buildings with bright white trim, and trees that were picked and pruned, not left to nature's seasons. It was not hard to imagine the students in their Sloane Ranger attire, pearls paired with muck boots as they went to ride their thoroughbreds at the stables.

"My mother is still all about the sweater sets. You know, shoes always match the bag with Sally Field-in-*Steel Magnolias* hair."

"What's that?"

"Sprayed into a football helmet." As she followed the lane that rolled up a rise, she thought of her old roommate, Dougie, because it was so much easier than dwelling on her mother's buttoned-up version of femininity. "Anyway, she's not why we're here."

At the top of the hill, Jo stopped the car again, and this time, she shut off the engine. Turning to Syn, she said, "Look, I'll be honest. I've been worried about myself for the last few months. I've had all kinds of weird symptoms, the worst of which being these headaches I keep getting, especially as memory problems seem to go with the pain. Like, all of a sudden, I'll just . . . not be able to remember where I've been or what I've done."

She looked out through the front windshield. "And there's been other strange things that have been happening. For example, I've got this blog, and it keeps getting taken down. I don't know why and I don't know who's doing it. But I have the rough drafts of all the posts and my research on the subjects. Tonight, because I couldn't settle myself, I started going through my files, and I found an email Dougie, my former roommate, sent me at my old work. It was about him and this video about something that occurred on this campus . . . in the clearing down there. A dragon with purple scales. I have these vague memories of talking about it with Bill, my friend at the paper. So I thought maybe if I came back here, something would jog my memory. I mean, Dougie's a druggie—hey, that rhymes—so he thinks he sees a lot of strange things. Like, during no-shave November last year, he was convinced one of our roommates was Abraham Lincoln. But he's not good enough at editing videos to put dragons in them, you know? He certainly managed to misplace the original file and any copies of it, though. Like, where did it go? Where has all of it gone for me?"

Shrugging, she popped open her door, and as she stood up, she felt foolish.

"Or I don't know." She looked around the brush and the darkened windows of the building she'd stopped by. "Maybe this is all just the product of an anxious mind."

Syn got out and came around the car. "Well, whatever it is, we'll go together."

As he offered her his hand, she hesitated. And then she took his palm.

"Come on," he murmured, "let's see what comes up for you."

Jo smiled a little. And then she nodded, the pair of them starting off through the brambles, explorers of a landscape that felt utterly foreign and vaguely hostile.

Jo was not surprised as her headache came back and settled in.

But she was surprised about how much it meant to have this man by her side.

CHAPTER THIRTY-SIX

A s Mel stopped in front of what obviously was the entry to her place, she unlocked a dead bolt and there was a hollow echo in some kind of big interior space. Butch didn't focus on either. He was too busy wondering about the damn door. The thing seemed to be made of the same cast iron panels that were used on Navy ship hulls, the bolt heads fat as a man's knuckles, the horizontal and vertical reinforcements making him wonder just what the hell was on the other side.

And he frowned as she put her shoulder into the bulk to open the way in.

"You want some help with that?" he asked.

"I've got it."

When she continued to struggle, he put his palm on the cold metal and pushed. The hinges, which were as big as his damn forearm, squeaked and groaned, and all that was revealed as the thing broke away from its reinforced jambs was a whole lot of pitch black. Like she lived in outer space.

Glancing over his shoulder, some instinct made him note the details of the basement hall—not that there was much to memorize, just blank walls, a low ceiling, and a black-and-white linoleum floor. Serviceable fixtures mounted at regular intervals were stocked with the new kind of lightbulbs that threw dull, listless light.

The building they were in had been a surprise. It was mostly commercial space, with this cellar underground just a bunch of storage areas with corporate names in plastic plates next to each unit. And P.S., none of the other doors were like Mel's *Game of Thrones* prop.

"At least I know you're safe here," he said dryly.

"It is my sanctuary."

On that note, she walked into the interior, her body swallowed down by the darkness's gullet. Just as he was getting worried about her, there was a flicking sound, and then light bathed an interior that had a totally open floor plan.

Mel motioned with her hand. "Come in, please."

Butch stepped over the threshold. "Holy . . . shit."

The door closed of its own volition with a banging sound, and he almost jumped—but that would have been a pussy move. And then he was distracted by the crib. The walls and floor of the three thousand or so square feet were painted black, and four concrete pylons kept the ceiling from caving in, making him feel like he'd shrunk and was standing under a coffee table. A sitting area was delineated by a large area rug, with a sofa, three chairs, and a coffee table—in all white leather—arranged on it like a glamorous Hollywood meeting was about to happen. There was also a king-sized bed over against one wall, with black satin sheets and a throw blanket of some fur-like persuasion slipping off one corner of the mattress. The bathroom was likewise fully in view, a Victorian claw-foot tub set next to a sink and a toilet, all of which were white. Oh, and the galley kitchen was directly across the way, the refrigerator, stove, and sink running down the wall and fronted by a barrier of white countertop.

But none of that was what stunned him.

Clothes took up at least half the square footage. There were tall racks with evening gowns. Medium ones with slacks. Shorter sets of blouses and skirts. Shelves with forward tilts displayed stilettos, wedges, boots, and flats. Birkin bags, and Chanel purses, and Judith Leiber minaudières sat on Lucite tables, their cloth storage bags folded under them, the boxes they'd come in like thrones for their glory. A modern era, floor-length, store-worthy mirror—the kind with the wings on the left and right that you could angle to inspect the rear of yourself—was set upon a white shag carpet.

"I have a shopping addiction," Mel said sadly. "It started when I was a model."

"This is epic." He walked over and pulled out a blood-red *crêpe de chine* gown from its lineup of colleagues. "Dior?"

"Early eighties. I love vintage."

"Me, too. Although I know more about men's designers, of course."

"So I don't have to explain to you how someone from Southie ended up in love with fashion?"

"Not at all." He wandered around, checking out Valentino skirts, and Chanel blouses, and Gaultier bustiers. "You have great taste."

"Thank you." She cleared her throat. "Do you mind if I take a bath? I'd like to get clean."

"I should go." He turned back to her. "And I still really think you should talk to the police."

"I know." Mel's voice was that of a little girl who didn't want to disappoint a parent. "Um, listen, can you stay while I wash up? I would feel better if someone was here while I get in and out of the tub. I'm a little woozy."

Butch glanced over at the bathroom area. That tub on its riser seemed to be spotlit. On a stage. With a full orchestra.

"You won't see anything, I promise," Mel said with exhaustion. "I just don't want to slip and fall and have no one around to know about it."

Butch put his back to her and jacked up his leathers. All he wanted to do was leave. "Okay."

"I won't take long."

"I'll keep looking at your clothes."

The sound of rushing water made him glance at the heavy door they'd come through. The locking mechanism was not a bog-standard dead bolt. Hell no. It was a bifurcated iron bar with a crank mechanism in the center. When you rotated the gear, the horizontal pegs plugged into brackets mounted on both sides of the jambs. Nobody was getting through that setup. Not unless they came with a battering ram.

Mounted on the front of an Army tank.

"How did you find this place?" he asked as he checked out some slacks. "I mean, is this living space even legal? It's in a commercial building."

"I am allowed certain—" She hissed on an inhale. Then cursed softly.

When she didn't say anything else, he glanced behind himself. She was by the tub and facing away from him, struggling to unhitch the fastenings on her bustier with hands that were cranked around back to her shoulder blades. As a result of her contorted quarter-turn, the swell of her breasts and the drift of her hips was obvious . . . but that wasn't the half of it. She had taken off her ruined panty hose and her skirt, nothing but a slide of black silk covering her bottom.

Butch looked away. Rubbed his face. Stared at the industrial door.

"Do you need help with that?" he asked roughly.

◆   ◆   ◆

Technically, Syn was out in the field.

As he and Jo walked around a flat clearing large enough to host multiple games of soccer or football, he had springy, winter-dead grass under his boots, and there was a cold breeze in his face, and across the meadow bare-limbed trees stood at attention around the edges of the acreage.

Sure, okay, fine, it was just *a* field, instead of *the* field, but beggars/choosers/all that shit. Besides, he didn't care if it was a playing field, a park lawn, or this scruffy, crappy expanse of formally-used-as at this abandoned school, he was not leaving Jo's side. Slayers could be any-where, and they would recognize her for what she was, even though she didn't have a clue about her nature.

Yet, he reminded himself. She was going to turn and then . . .

Yeah, and then what? he thought. Happily ever after for the pair of them? Hardly.

"This is a waste of time," she announced as she stopped and made a three-sixty.

Fuck.

When she put her hands up to her head, he said, "You seem ex-hausted. How about we go back?"

"If I could only get my brain to stop." She dropped her arms. "I mean, there's nothing here. I don't know what I was thinking."

"Let's go back to the car."

Jo looked over at him and a breeze teased out a strand of her hair. "You must think I'm nuts."

"Not in the slightest."

Her green eyes drifted to a ruined structure of some kind, its roof torn up, one wall collapsed into a collection of rotted, loose lumber that looked like a set of bad fangs.

"In the video," she said, "something like that was attacked by the dragon. It was a shed, or . . . and . . ."

Syn had sworn to himself he wouldn't touch her. He broke that vow by putting his arm around her waist and steering her away from what troubled her.

And, to be fair, what troubled him as well. He knew exactly what had attacked that out building. Rhage's beast. But he couldn't tell her that.

"You're cold," he said.

"Am I?"

"Your teeth are chattering."

As he started them back up the hill, she touched her lips. "They are?"

He nodded and kept them ascending at a steady pace. He hadn't minded the walk around with her. They had plenty of privacy, and his instincts, which he trusted more than any other thing about himself, were not firing, not yet: There were no scents on the air that shouldn't have been there. No movement in the shadows that his keen eyes caught. No sounds other than, off in the distance, the occasional passing car on the city road they'd come in on.

But she was clearly out of gas, and at least her car appeared back into view soon enough. When they came up to it, Jo hesitated and glanced over her shoulder. Then she looked at what was ahead of them, the vacated classroom buildings and the dorms.

As her eyes roamed the campus, his stayed by her and tried to be patient. He really just wanted her to get some rest. The change was so brutal on the body, and she needed to be strong.

"It's like I'm blind even though my eyes are working," she murmured.

"You're searching for answers."

"I just don't know the questions I'm trying to ask."

"How about we go back to your place."

"I want to take a look around for a little longer."

Jo started to walk away from him, and he was well familiar with that vacant striving she was motivated by. It wasn't going to release its grip on her until she got what she was actually looking for—the transition. Which would transform her from something that was mostly human with a little vampire in her, to mostly vampire with almost no human remaining.

There would be no peace until that happened and he would take on this miserable prodromal period for her if he could.

"Just a little longer," she said. "I promise."

"It's okay."

As they continued on, Syn's eyes panned left to right to left, measuring the windows in the brick buildings. Checking rooflines. Assessing what was coming at them and what had been left behind. Even though he would have preferred to take her back to her home, he followed her readily into one of the buildings. He wasn't going to force her to leave if she didn't want to.

Prepared to protect her if he had to, Syn trailed her as she went up a set of creaking stairs, and then wandered along corridors that were strewn with fallen plaster from the ceiling and leaf debris that had blown in from broken windows. Given the number of doors they passed, he guessed they were in a dorm, and the skeletal bed frames and wilted, stained mattresses seemed to confirm his assumption.

"I wonder if this was where her room was," Jo said.

"Your mother's?"

"Yes."

"Do you not know where she stayed?"

"I barely know more about her than her birthday and her wedding anniversary."

Jo kept on going, the sound of her boots crunching over the plaster bits loud in the silence of the building. When she came to the end of the hall, the cold breeze drifting in through the busted panes of glass lifted her hair.

And that was when her scent changed.

The arousal was a surprise.

"You're right," she said remotely. "We should go."

As she turned toward him, she ducked her head and dropped her eyes. Putting her hands in the pockets of her coat, she seemed to retract into herself as she went to go by him.

Syn caught her arm. "I know what you want."

Her eyes were shocked as they met his. "I don't—I mean, I just think we should go home. You're right. I am exhausted."

Syn stepped in closer. "That's not all you're thinking about."

"But—"

"And I know what you're going to say." He shook his head. "Use me. Let me give you what you want. I don't care about myself."

Jo shook her head and backed away from him. "That's not fair—"

Syn's body took over, moving into her, pushing her against the corridor's wall. As her breasts came up against his chest, she gasped.

He didn't wait for more commentary. He wasn't interested in talking. Her scent told him everything he needed to know.

Dropping his mouth to hers, he took from her what she hesitated to give him because she didn't want to use him for a one-sided pleasure session. But like he gave a fuck? He had been taken in the past by females he didn't care about—and he had bonded with Jo. Plus she wanted him. Bad. So as she groaned in submission, he took advantage of the parting of her lips, licking inside of her, penetrating her with his tongue. Meanwhile, his hands made quick work of her coat's buttons and then burrowed in to find her waist, stroking down to her hips and onto her backside.

He deliberately brought her lower body into contact with the erection that strained at the front of his hips—

Jo pushed against his shoulders and he reluctantly eased back. The high flush on her cheeks was what he wanted. This pausing thing was not.

"I don't want to do anything if it ends with you in pain."

Syn shook his head. "Don't think about me. Just let me pleasure you, Jo. I can make it all go away. The whirlwind in your head. The anxiety in your chest. Even if it's only for an orgasm or two, I can give you something else."

"But what are you left with afterward?"

"The satisfaction of the satisfaction I gave you." Syn moved a hand up to just below one of her breasts. "Don't you want what I can give you?"

He cupped her through her clothes, his thumb finding her nipple even though there were layers between them. And as he stroked the tip, her eyes closed and her head fell back.

"That's right," he growled. "Just let yourself go. I'll take care of everything."

She murmured something, maybe it was about fairness, maybe it was about guilt, he didn't know and didn't care. And he wasn't going to give her any more chances to think.

With his other hand, he pulled her ass in as he rolled his pelvis so that his arousal rubbed on her. Releasing her breast, he quickly drew the zipper of her fleece down and then he lifted her loose T-shirt up. Her bra had a front clasp and he released it.

Bending to her flesh, he nestled his way in through her clothes, his mouth seeking . . . finding.

As he sucked on what he sought, she gasped and grabbed the nape of his neck, urging him closer to the pillow of her breast. He more than obliged. And it wasn't enough.

He was damn well going to fix that.

She was wearing sweatpants. Which was the best thing that had ever happened to him.

Putting his hand between her legs, he rubbed her sex through the soft folds as he nursed at her. Licked at her. Nibbled her.

As he worked her, she was panting, gripping any piece of him she could get ahold of, saying his name.

Syn let her nipple pop out of his mouth. Then he spun her around so she faced away from him. Grabbing onto her hips, he yanked her feet back and bent her over.

"Put your palms on the wall."

She complied, but seemed to do it blindly, fumbling before she found the brace.

Syn ripped her sweatpants down. And took her panties south with them.

Even in the dim light, her sex glistened, swollen and pink between the pale curves of her buttocks.

It was a glorious sight.

Syn was *so* glad they'd stayed a little longer.

CHAPTER THIRTY-SEVEN

Y es, I need help."

Of course she did, Butch thought. And he should *not* have asked Mel that question.

Keeping the curses to himself, he backed over to where she was standing by the slowly filling tub. He turned around only when he had to, and as he unfastened the bustier, he looked solely at the claw hooks of the garment. He didn't touch her creamy skin and he was not aroused—and God, he hoped she didn't make a move on him. As beautiful as she was, he wasn't tempted in the slightest, and he really didn't want to have to humiliate her by shutting her down.

She didn't need that kind of capper to this night—

The bustier fell off Mel's body and landed in the rushing water.

As she let out a cry of dismay, she bent over, grabbed it, and straightened in a quick movement. Which caused her breasts to swing freely—

Butch wheeled away and went back to the racks of clothes, placing himself all the way across the apartment, the space, the whatever-the-hell this was. A moment later, the faucet was cut off and there was the dunk/dunk of two feet stepping into the deep-bellied basin . . . followed by the hiss of someone who was injured as they sank their sore bones into warm water.

"I'm sorry if I made you feel awkward."

The words Mel spoke were soft and tinted with contrition.

"I'm not awkward." Butch pulled out a black sequined skirt that had a ruffle of netting around the hem. "I know where I stand."

"What do you mean?"

"I'm in love with my wife, and she's the only person I have any sexual interest in." He tucked the skirt back into alignment and continued down the lineup. "So I'm good—wow, check out the McQueen."

"Most of the men I know don't have that kind of discipline."

Butch glanced over at the tub. Mel had stretched out and leaned back into the curve of its far edge, her head propped on the lip, her brunette hair hanging down in thick ringlets that nearly reached the floor. That her eyes were closed with exhaustion made him worried, but at least there was a rosy blush coming back into her cheeks.

"It's not a case of discipline," he said. "You're a gorgeous woman, but it's not about you. It's about who's waiting for me at my home."

Mel's lids lifted and she stared into space for a moment. Then she turned her head and looked at him across the distance he'd put between them.

"Can I ask you something?" she murmured.

Butch refocused on the clothes, pulling out a black leather skirt that was the size of a napkin. "Sure."

"What did she do?"

He frowned and glanced back toward the bath. "I'm sorry?"

"What did your wife do to make you fall that in love with her? Be so devoted to her? I mean, even that first night I saw you, when I wasn't covered with bruises . . . you left me at the club. Most men would have come in and we would have . . . we woulda been together and not because you paid for me."

Putting the skirt back, Butch wandered up to the bags and the shoes, although he didn't see any of the thousands and thousands of dollars of high-end luxury goods. Even as his fingers brushed over the Hermès and the Louis, he was picturing instead the first time he'd seen his Marissa. It had been back at Darius's house, back when the place had just been a flophouse for the Brotherhood. He'd been waiting in an elegant parlor to find out if he was going to be killed by what he assumed was a group of drug dealers—when *bam*! His life changed forever.

Marissa had walked into the archway, wearing a chiffon gown that belonged on a queen, her long, fair hair down to her hips, her clean, ocean scent tantalizing him. She had been so beautiful and so sad at the same time, an ethereal goddess he was not worthy to gaze upon.

And then she had looked at him.

"Nothing," he said in a gravel voice. "My wife didn't have to do anything. She just walked into my sight and I knew. Everything about her was perfect as far as I was concerned, and absolutely nothing—nothing at all—has made me question that perfection since."

"How long have you been together?"

"Three years."

There was a soft sound of water, as if she were moving in the tub. "And you've never had an argument?"

"Not really. I mean, if we disagree, we don't get angry. We both just want to figure out a compromise so we can get rid of the tension."

"Does she dress for you? I mean, is that how she keeps your interest? Does she change her lingerie a lot? Do you role-play for sex?"

Butch regarded the racks of clothes, all the colors and fabrics, the styles and cuts, the eras, represented in the collection.

He shrugged. "She could be wearing a burlap sack. A ten-year-old T-shirt. A pair of long johns or a polyester track suit. It's not about what she has on. And role-play? I want her. Anything else is inferior so why would she dress up for me?"

"She must do something. Her hair—what does her hair look like?"

"You're searching for a physical explanation. Something tangible. You're not going to find it because that's not the point." He touched his cross through his Under Armor. "It's like faith. It just is."

When Mel fell silent, he was happy enough to let the subject drop. Except then the scent of tears got his attention.

He looked back over to the tub. Mel was still staring straight ahead as she cried in silence, her tears landing in the water.

"Mel," he said softly. "Please let me call that doctor friend of mine? It's a female and she's very good."

"No." She wiped her face and looked down at her fingertips. "I just wasn't enough, I guess. For him, the one I love . . . at the end of the day, he just didn't want me. It's a hard truth to accept. And you're right, I'm looking for physical explanations because I'd rather there be something more external for why he didn't love me back. Something less about the inside of me. You can change your clothes and your hair, put on a different lipstick, do your nails a different way. But when it's who you are, you can't really work with that, you know?"

"But maybe it was on him. Maybe he wasn't ready. Maybe there was something wrong with the bastard."

"The one he ended up with is nothing like me."

"So his picker is wrong." Butch went over and sat down in an armchair that faced away from the tub. In that huge mirror, on the left, he could still see her in the bath, though. "I know this is hard. But you're blaming yourself for something that may not have a damn thing to do with you. I know it sounds like wicked bullshit, but it's his loss and I hope he regrets it for the rest of his natural life."

"I just don't know what to do with myself. I walk aimlessly around town at night. I go to clubs and find nothing of interest. I . . . take my mood out on others. I'm not alive. I'm just not here."

Butch sat forward and rubbed his face. "I've been where you are, Mel. I know what that's like."

"You do?"

"Yeah. And it's rough." Driven by commiseration, he got to his feet and turned around. "I'm so sorry, Mel. I don't want this for you. I don't want any of this for you."

More tears fell from her eyes, disappearing into the clear water that covered her body. When she looked over at him, she was so sad, so small, in spite of her beauty.

Sniffling, she said hoarsely, "You really understand it, don't you."

"Yes." Butch would have gotten closer if she'd had clothes on, but he kept his distance. "Mel, I need you to believe things will get better, okay? I mean, if love can happen for me? It can happen for you. You're a good person. You're a beautiful woman. Any man would be proud to have you for a partner. You just need to wake up to the truth that you are enough, no matter what some asshole thinks to the contrary."

"I'm not perfect, Butch."

"None of us are."

"I've done some bad things."

"We are all sinners—and yet our creator still loves us. And if the prerequisite for true romantic love was an unassailable history and character? The shit wouldn't happen for anybody. You're worthy of love. You deserve to be respected and cherished, and to get that, you don't need to be anything different than you are. You have been created for a reason. You're *here* for a reason. You have a purpose, and you have to believe that you'll find someone who will help you in that purpose. And until that happens? All you really need to know is that you don't have to be validated by anybody but yourself. You are enough."

Her hands came up to rest on her cheeks, water running down the backs of them. "What is my purpose, though. I used to think I knew what it was. Now, I'm just so empty. There's nothing there."

"What makes you happy?" He glanced around. "Well, except for buying clothes. I think we can both agree that you're an expert in that, just like me. But that's a surface thing. What really feeds your soul?"

Mel got a far-off expression on her face.

As Butch's phone rang, he ducked his hand inside his leather jacket.

"Do you need to take that?" Mel said remotely.

He silenced the ringer without taking the thing out. "No. You're what matters right now. They can wait."

Mel took a deep breath. Then she covered her breasts with her arms and sat up. Her eyes were grave as they met his own. "You mean what you say, don't you."

"Every word. Or I wouldn't waste my breath on the syllables."

"How will I know," she whispered in a small voice.

"You mean who the right man is?" When she nodded, he smiled. "It'll be because when you look at him and can't look away? He'll be doing the exact same thing at the exact same time. It's in the eyes, Mel. They're the windows of the soul, right?"

She stared across at him for the longest time. And then she nodded once.

"You can go," she said softly. "I'm going to be okay."

"You will be, I promise." Butch took out his phone. "Do you want me to call someone for you?"

"No." She shook her head. "You've been more than enough."

"Can I at least leave you the number of the SART folks? In case you want to report things?"

"I can find it on the Internet if I need it."

Butch nodded. Then he walked over to the reinforced door. Taking one last look back at her, he said, "You take care, Mel."

"You, too, Brian O'Neal. You're a good man."

"I try to be."

On that note, he turned the center crank and the security bar retracted on both sides. Then he pulled open the heavy weight and stepped out. As he pivoted around to shut things, he looked through to the tub. Mel was staring at him.

She lifted her hand in goodbye.

"Just believe in yourself," he told her. "And you can do anything and be anything you want."

Butch shut things up behind himself. And as he walked away, he released a held breath.

But he didn't get far. Stopping, he frowned and looked over his shoulder—even as he had no idea what had gotten his attention or what he was waiting for.

Still, it was a while before he could get his feet to resume the task of taking his body out of the building.

Weird.

CHAPTER THIRTY-EIGHT

As Jo braced herself against the wall of the abandoned dorm, she was breathing so hard that she felt like swords were going in and out of her throat. Not that she cared. Not that she really even noticed. Her awareness was taken up by a short list: Her sweatpants around her ankles. Her bend at the waist. And the fact that her core was completely exposed.

Wait. There was one more thing.

The sounds were soft in nature, but louder than a jet airplane in her head: Buttons being freed from a set of leather pants.

You wouldn't think you could hear such a thing.

When a massive hand planted itself next to her own on the wall, she jumped, and the difference in size between the backs of their palms, the length of their fingers, the thickness of their wrists, made her tremble. Not in fear, though.

And then Syn probed her sex with his free hand, his fingertips stoking, slipping over her flesh . . . rubbing. She gasped and arched her back, pushing into the touch. Moving against it. Begging for what was coming.

Syn's voice was right next to her ear. "I'm gonna fuck you now."

She nodded, her hair swinging free, her eyes opening, closing, her legs loose even as her pelvis was strong and ready.

His fingers left her. Then something soft and blunt replaced them.

The moan that bubbled up her throat was nothing that had ever come out of her mouth before. And then she barked Syn's name—as the hard, hot length of him went in deep, filling her, stretching her. Just as she went limp and would have fallen, his other arm whipped around her stomach and kept her up—worked her against him, too. As he thrust forward, he pulled her back, then he pushed her away and slammed her back into him, all the while using the building itself to hold them up.

Syn worked her like she weighed nothing, and she gave herself up to the sex, the pounding, the way her teeth clapped together and her breasts slapped under her clothes. Unlike him, she lost hold on the wall. Arms flopping, hair tangling, breath sawing, she was at his mercy— except he was giving her what she wanted, what she needed, instead of taking anything from her.

The first orgasm lightning'd through her, the pleasure cracking loose and splintering throughout her body. And another release was fast on its heels. Meanwhile, Syn didn't lose his rhythm as the pulses made her core tighten on his erection. The power of him was almost overwhelming, and yet she only wanted more—and as if he read her mind, he continued until she lost all thought, sensation taking her over, replacing everything.

Except then, without warning, he stopped, pulled out, and spun her around. Looking at him with feverish eyes, she had no idea what he was doing as he got on his knees in front of her.

With a harsh hand, he grabbed one of her calves. "Lift your foot."

"What?"

Instead of repeating the command, he pulled her leg up and the next thing she knew, her boot was off and one half of her sweats was free of her leg.

"Give me," he growled.

Jo's head was too scrambled to do the math, but he solved the confusion by positioning her where he wanted her. Putting her sock foot over his shoulder, he leaned forward, angled his head . . .

"Oh, God!" she cried out.

As her voice echoed around the cold, debris-laden corridor, she fell against the wall. Splaying out her arms, she flattened her palms and held on as his mouth brushed against her sex. Sucked on it. Licked at it. And then he was pushing her up higher, his hands on the backs of her thighs, splitting her around his face as he lifted her up off the floor and onto his shoulders completely.

He worked at her, moving her back and forth as his tongue went into all kinds of places, slick on slick, hot on hot.

Looking down, her eyes burned at what she saw, his Mohawked head between her thighs, her legs parted over his enormous back, her socked foot flopping around, her booted foot and her sweats doing the same on the other side.

As the pleasure became too much, Jo's lids squeezed shut.

She had no idea where she was. But she knew exactly what was being done to her and who was doing it.

Syn had more than delivered what he'd promised her.

All she knew was him, and it wasn't that nothing else mattered to her.

Nothing else even existed.

✦   ✦   ✦

Syn could have kept going forever. But he knew that the abandoned dorm was not as secure as he would have liked, and his phone was going off again in his inside pocket. God only knew what was wrong now.

And yet . . .

Dragging his tongue up Jo's sex, he paid special attention to the top of her core, lolling around, flicking quick. He really wished she were naked, and they were in her warm apartment, and there was a forever ahead of them instead of only an hour. A quarter hour. Ten minutes . . .

Five minutes.

One minute.

As she called out his name again, he reluctantly released her flesh. Then he carefully, gently, eased her off his shoulders and set her feet back on the cold floor.

He took a moment to enjoy the sight of her, her red hair a glorious mess around her shoulders, her clothes all disordered, her thighs twitching and quivering. He especially loved the way her face was flushed and her eyes were glowing.

"Here," he said softly. "Allow me to tend unto you."

"Hmm?"

The fact that she was so undone she couldn't speak made him feel a surge of male satisfaction throughout his entire body.

"Allow me," he repeated as he took the loose leg of her sweatpants and slid it back on over her foot.

It was hard to cover her up, and he led with her panties, drawing the cotton slip into place. Before he went any further, he leaned in and chastely kissed where he had spent his time. Then he took the waistband of the sweatpants and went up, up, over her creamy thighs, re-clothing her.

Sitting back on his heels, he put his palms on the outsides of her knees. "Thank you."

As she stared down at him, he deliberately ran his tongue around his lips.

The groan she let out made him smile.

"Are you okay," she asked in a deep voice.

"I'm perfect."

It wasn't exactly a lie. Yes, he was in pain. Yes, there were going to be aftereffects. Yes, he grunted as he stood up. And he winced. And he cursed as he turned away from her and pulled his leathers into place.

Yeah, sure, stuffing his cock into his pants was an exercise in torture.

But he didn't regret one stroke. One suck. One lick.

When he pivoted around again, Jo was looking worried.

"No," he said patiently. "We had a deal."

"We did?"

"Yup. You weren't going to worry about me." He took her hand. "And now we're going to get you home."

Together, they walked down the hall, and down the stairs, and down the way to the car. When he asked her for her keys, she protested only a little, and then he settled her in the passenger seat and closed her door. Getting behind the wheel, he drove them back out to the gates of the school. As he hit the brakes, he looked over at her.

Jo's head was off to the side, propped against the window, her eyes closed and her breathing even. The flush he had given her was still on her cheeks and there was the lilt of a smile on her lips, the kind of thing that suggested her dreams were what he wanted them to be.

Happy. Safe. Peaceful.

Syn didn't put the directional signal on, for fear that the ticking would rouse her. And he went easy on the brakes and the accelerator as he eased their way home, keeping everything as smooth as possible. When he pulled up to her building, he hated to wake her.

He was still staring at her, the engine running, the heater blowing warmth on them both, when her lids fluttered open. Her eyes, sleepy and contented, a little confused, focused on him.

"Hi," she said.

Syn reached over and brushed her cheek with his fingertip. "Hello, beautiful female."

"Thank you."

"For what?"

"Everything."

Syn had never been a gentlemale. But he shut off the engine and all but bolted around the front of her car to open her door. Extending his palm to her, he drew her out as if he were in a tuxedo and she in a ball gown, and he escorted her all the way to her door like the building she lived in was a castle.

He even opened the way into her apartment for her, pretending to use the key that was on the ring even though he freed the dead bolt with his mind.

But he stopped on the threshold. "I'm going to leave you here."

"Okay." She stepped inside and turned around. "Would it look desperate if I asked when I can see you again?"

Behind her, he eyed the couch they'd had sex on the night before, and decided they needed to test out those cushions again. Also her bed. The floor. Her shower.

Those kitchen counters.

"It's not desperate at all," he murmured as he refocused on her face. "Because I was just going to ask you the same thing."

"Tomorrow night? After work?"

"Yes. I will come to you here—"

"Oh, shoot. The bus isn't running this late. We need to take you downtown—"

"It's okay. I left my car parked around back."

"All right. Good." She glanced down for a second, to where his shit-kickers and her much smaller boots were nearly toe to toe. "Are you sure you're okay, you know, after we—"

By way of answer, he pulled her against him and covered her mouth with his own. Kissing her deeply, he bent her back so that she gripped his shoulders. When they were both breathless, he released her lips.

"Does it feel like anything's wrong with me?" he drawled.

Jo shook her head. "No . . . not at all."

"Until tomorrow." Syn had to force himself to separate their bodies and let go of her. "Shut your door and lock up. I won't leave until I hear that dead bolt go back where it belongs."

"You're so protective."

"Of you? You better believe it."

Jo's smile made him feel like a wealthy male, a curious state given that he had never cared about the material before. Then again, money and assets were not the true way of judging whether someone was rich.

Before she disappeared into her apartment, Jo rose up on her tiptoes and pressed her lips to his. And then she closed her door.

A split second later, he heard the shift and *clunk* of that bolt hitting home.

Turning away, Syn whistled under his breath as he set about his departure. In spite of his colossal set of blue balls, he skipped his way by the mailboxes and all but twinkle-toed his way out into the night.

Amazing what the right female will do for a guy.

CHAPTER THIRTY-NINE

Sister mine.

  The entities had agreed to meet upon neutral ground, in their usual place at which to congress, the grand and gracious Caldwell Public Library. Second floor. Marble colonnade that led into the rare books section where one needed proof of identity and a master's to gain entrance.

  If one were human, that was. If one were not? If one were substance made of air, sound captured within silence, light that cast no shadow and darkness that did?

  Well, then you went wherever the hell you wanted to.

Brother mine.

  As the Scribe Virgin communicated her greeting, she regarded her sibling with reserve. There were conclusions she came unto, but she kept them free of her thoughts. The pair of them were, as many twins were, connected on a deep level, and there were things he mustn't know.

  The Omega floated around before her, hovering above the white and black marble floor, the shadow which was his essence spilling out from under robes that had previously always sparkled with cleanliness, but were now stained and torn.

She was surprised at the sadness she felt over his disintegration. *How fare thee, Brother?*

You know the answer to that. The Omega stopped, the draping that covered his features moving around to face her. *Why must we always meet here?*

When you were allowed to choose the site, you picked a morgue.

A chuckle came out from beneath the dirty white hooding. *I did.*

And then a murder scene.

To be fair, I was working that night.

And finally, a car accident.

That one was perfectly appropriate. The Omega shrugged. *Indeed, Father always says we should do more things together.*

I do not believe that includes being in a car as it careens off a cliff.

We would have had the whole trip down to the ocean to talk. The driver was drunk, he would not have heard us, anyway. And there was plenty of room in the back seat of that SUV.

It was not appropriate a'tall.

You are such a stiff, Sister mine.

Tell me how you are, Brother.

The Omega drifted over to the marble balustrade that ran around the grand, theatrical staircase. The main lights had been dimmed as the facility was closed for the night, but sconces glowed sweetly upon many a wall and the wrought iron chandelier that hung from a heavy chain over the descent of marble steps cast soft illumination.

I am very well, thank you.

You can stop this, you realize. The Scribe Virgin moved closer, but not too close. *This war that was started so long ago can be voluntarily ended upon our agreement.*

Can it? The dingy hood shook back and forth as the Omega seemed to be looking down the stairway, down to the broad and beautiful entrance foyer with its statues upon pedestals and carved messages of intellect. *I do not believe it can.*

Simply stop fighting. Stop attempting to kill what I have created for sport. And then it is over.

Ah, Sister, but what I do is not for sport. It is my nature to destroy. Balance to the force of you and all that, the pair of us created with deliberation by Father. We are the Alpha and the Omega, Analisse. Do you not speak of this truth with some regularity? Surely it is not something I must teach unto you after all these centuries.

The Scribe Virgin backed off and went on her own wander, moving herself across the floor until she reached the closed double doors of the rare book room. Through glass insets that were reinforced with chicken wire, she stared at the collection of leather-bound volumes and felt a draw unto the old oak shelves and the peaceful contemplation offered by so many pages filled with so many words.

She had always loved libraries. Collections of prose. Stories that were based upon real life. And had this congress with her sibling been of different circumstance, she would have touched the glass with a plaintive, yearning hand. But she knew too much of her brother. No appendages should be extended nor weakness shown.

You will be destroyed, she intoned as she faced her sibling.

You sound as though that would be a regret for you.

You are my brother. Of course I would mourn you.

I am your enemy. The Omega rotated around so they were squared off across the polished floor, two opposing chess pieces on a life-sized board of black and white marble squares. *It has always been thus—and further, I cannot exist without you. As well, you cannot exist without me.*

That is untrue. The Prophecy provides so.

No, the Omega corrected. *That stanza states that there is one who would see the end of me. Simply because the wording lacks mention of you does not mean you shall be unaffected. Would you not say that you urge me the now to quit more to protect yourself than out of any familial love for me?*

No, I would not say that.

Then you lie. There is me in you as there is you in me. You can be quite as devious as I can, Sister. Which brings me to my purpose in seeking this audience. The Omega's transmission of words grew deeper in tone, falling an octave. *I expect you to stay out of the conflict. Per our agreement.*

What say you the now, Brother? I am uninvolved.

You most certainly are not *uninvolved. Or do you think I am unaware of your little visit in church with the Dhestroyer earlier this eve?*

The Scribe Virgin felt her ire rise. *I am permitted to interact with my creations.*

You are not allowed to sway them with respect to our conflict. The contest must be fair—you yourself stated this long ago when you insisted we codify our roles and obligations. And this evening, you warned the Dhestroyer such that he has sequestered your borne son from the field. Unfair, Sister.

The Scribe Virgin deliberately shielded her thoughts. *Are you aware that I have stepped aside?*

Stepped aside how?

I have relinquished my role of overseer of mine creation to another. Did you not know this?

Given the long pause that followed, it was evident he did not.

I have, Brother mine. I am no longer in my Sanctuary. I have assigned my authority unto another and I have departed.

The hood moved as if the Omega recoiled. *Whyever for?*

Over the course of eons, I have determined that my strength is in creation. It is not in the maintenance of such creation. She thought of her borne son and daughter. *The act of bringing into being a mortal—or many of them—is not the same as parenting them. One does not know this until it is too late, however. Until one has done damage that is regrettable.*

It was a relief to speak her truth aloud, but she stopped herself. Her brother was hardly a trusted confidant and she had likely given him too much already.

Meanwhile, the Omega tilted his head and drifted by at the balustrade, staring down to the staircase, to what was below. When he came back toward her, she braced herself for some kind of pronouncement. Or a triumphal insult about her lack of fortitude.

Where do you stay the now? he asked instead.

I spend time with Father. But mostly, I drift through the centuries and ob-serve my behavior. I try to see where I went wrong. There is much to review in that regard. An urgency to change her sibling's course made her want to go unto his side, but she kept herself where she was. *And that is why I say unto you, stop this. Relinquish. Depart the field of conflict and save yourself.*

The Omega shrugged beneath his tattered robe. *And then do what?*

Exist. Learn— As the Omega made a dismissive sound, the Scribe Virgin tightened her tone. *'Tis better than not existing.*

I may still win, you realize. The hood turned toward her. *You take for granted the outcome shall be in your favor.*

Surely it is better to concede than to risk being destroyed.

One of the stained robe's sleeves lifted, and the black shadow of her brother appeared to be lifting a forefinger. *Ah, but remember my nature.*

Even if you are the one annihilated? Surely that is a foolish testament to your character.

At least it is my purpose culminated, which is more than I can say for you the now.

The Scribe Virgin shook her head. *Creation is linked with nurturing. Or at least it should be. I have excelled at the former, I seek to discover the skills of the latter. I would say that is a worthwhile pursuit.*

You and I are so different.

Yes, Brother mine. We are.

An evil tone entered the Omega's communication. *I would rather be destroyed than disappear.*

That is, of course, your decision.

And I shall take you down with me. Either way, whether I win or lose, you will no longer be free. In the former, it will be because you mourn the deaths of your precious creation, the prison of your pain an eternity in Dhunhd I will have the perpetual satisfaction of knowing I made manifest. In the latter, it will be because you will implode with me. The universe can-not be unbalanced. Our Father will not allow it, and He will sacrifice your existence to maintain His own legacy, trust me. If I go, you go.

It was strange for an immortal to fear the end of themselves. To brace against the snuffing out. To wish to avoid such an outcome. And the Scribe Virgin kept all of those feelings far, far away from the tip of her consciousness's spear.

That is not up to us, she said. *Father will determine the consequence, if any, if you cease to be.*

Well, He is certainly going to determine one other thing. The Omega's satisfaction colored his words with an arrogance that was another attribute intrinsic to his nature. *You violated our agreement and therefore I am due restitution. You changed the course of the game, therefore I am permitted a redress.*

When did I do that? By speaking with Butch tonight? I most certainly did not change the course of anything. Brother mine, you are unreasonable—

Father has always been our intermediary, at your request. Therefore I shall seek an audience unto him and he will decide what is fair.

The Scribe Virgin kept her emotions in check as frustration surged. *And this declaration is the reason you brought me here?*

Yes. It is.

Your contest of my action is naught but pretense. Nothing in the course of the war has been altered—

Your borne son is now out of the field and heavily protected as a result of your interference, and we both know that he is an integral element of the outcome given his unique importance to the Dhestroyer. So there has been a very material shift in power, one that inures unto your benefit, and that deserves redress.

The Scribe Virgin recognized the aggression being projected unto her for what it was: the thrashes of someone who was greatly diminished and yet avoiding the nature of that reality. The end was near, and her brother's losses were tallying up. He was flailing around, and therefore, so much more dangerous.

Yet she trusted their Father.

Do what you must, my brother, she said remotely.

I always will.

Is this all you require of me at this time?

There was a pause, as if the Omega had expected a stronger response. Had counted on it. Had looked forward to protest and argumentation. He had always loved conflict.

Yes, that is all, he said tersely.

All right, then. I shall expect Father will inform me of his decision when he is ready.

The Scribe Virgin turned away and floated over toward the stairs. There were other ways of leaving, but she did not wish to miss the experience of descending down those grand and white marble steps.

In the event it was the last time she did.

When her brother joined her, it was a surprise, but she welcomed his presence. As always, the pair of them were separated by the brass handrail, him taking the left side, her the right. And as always, she was the one who set the pace, although whether that was him stalking her or adhering to protocol, she never knew.

Well, she could guess.

The Scribe Virgin proceeded slowly as there was another finality that could be occurring. She did not know if she would e'er be in the company of her sibling again. Indeed, this could be the last time for that as well.

At the bottom, he stopped and she was compelled by his halt to do likewise.

You should know something, the Omega said quietly. *I deliberately never went after Vishous. I have known all along that I could, and I am precisely acquainted with how his elimination could be of benefit to my position and survival. But I declined to involve him.*

The Scribe Virgin looked across the bannister. *I must say, this is unexpected.*

He is family, after all. He is my blooded relation through you. And it is as I stated. There is a bit of your goodness in me.

You have my gratitude, she murmured.

Alas, this means you gave yourself a disadvantage for no reason. You did not have to go unto the Dhestroyer *and plant the seeds you did. Your birthed ones have always been off-limits for me.*

For a moment, she was tempted to fight. To point out that she would have made a different choice, if she had known of his reticence. She elected to let the animus go.

Thank you, she said simply.

Upon that note of gratitude, she spirited herself away from her fraternal twin, leaving the Omega to whatever course he was set upon.

Her brother was the autumn wasp wandering upon a windowsill, bathed in the last sunlight of summer, unaware of or refusing to believe of the death that would soon come and carry him unto his back, his legs curled in as mobile became immobile.

His stinger was something of which to be especially watchful.

And thus she would allow him the petty victory he was claiming.

She had concerns of far greater magnitude. She had always taken solace in the *Dhestroyer* Prophecy, assured that however great the losses and the pain sustained by her creation at the merciless hand of her brother, there would be an end.

She had never considered the idea that in that termination there would be repercussions for herself. What if what her brother purported was true? Balance had to be preserved, so with him gone, where did that leave her?

Perhaps she was wrong about the inevitability of her brother's failure, however. She had certainly never seen coming so much of what had transpired.

As great as her powers were, she was not their Father.

The future was not hers to command.

And she had never dreamed of a moment where she might have to choose her own existence . . . over her creation's.

CHAPTER FORTY

The train rocked back and forth, the subtle sway and distant *clickety-clack* of the sets of wheels over the tracks a lullaby that had Jo's eyelids growing heavy. When she had boarded the Keystone Service 701 toward Harrisburg at 8:18 in the morning, she had been fortunate enough to get a row of seats all to herself, but that had not lasted. There were a lot of people doing the go-to-work thing, so she soon had to put her backpack at her feet to accommodate another passenger.

The trip was just over three hours, and she could have driven, but with New York City sitting in the way of the most direct road route, she had opted out of the immovable object that was rush hour traffic.

Besides, there was something magical about a train. On the far side of the broad window, she watched the landscape change, high-rise apartment buildings replacing the sprawl of suburban neighborhoods as they approached Manhattan; then the skyscrapers coming into view; then the Big Apple's bridges rising and falling over the Hudson. After that, there was the descent underground and the slowing and stopping under the great city, with a further exchange of passengers at Penn Station. Finally, they were off again, the air in the car smelling of oil and coal as they proceeded out of the subway system's subterranean tunnels.

Bright light again now, free of the city on the far side, the trees and grass of New Jersey always a surprise given the concrete congestion of New York.

The train pulled into the 30th Street Station on time, and Jo sat quietly for a moment before grabbing her pack and getting to her feet. There was not much of a wait to get off, and as she stepped down onto the platform, she looked around, the hot breath of the hissing engine catching a lick of her hair.

The next thing she knew, she was out of the columned, squared-off building that, with its rows of vertical supports down its glass panels, had always reminded her of a federal prison. Or maybe it was Philadelphia, itself, that made her think things of a penal nature.

Or maybe it was her family.

Using her phone, she got a Lyft to take her out to the house. When she and the driver pulled in between the stone pylons and proceeded up the lane, the guy behind the wheel glanced back at her in the rearview of the Toyota Sienna.

"I thought this was a residence?" He shook his head. "I mean, it's fine. It doesn't matter to me—"

"No, it's a family—well, a couple lives here."

"Huh. You don't say." He looked out to the side, at the specimen trees that were as yet still without buds, and the statuary that remained unchanging through the seasons. "You applying for some kind of a job here or something?"

Jo thought about the role she had played in the household as she had grown up. "I was already hired."

"Oh, congrats. The pay must be good."

Well, it had gotten her through college without any debt. But only because she'd gone to Williams, which was her father's alma mater. She had often wondered how the finances of her bachelor's degree would have gone if she'd only been able to get into a state school. When she'd been accepted into the Yale master's program for English, they'd indicated she'd have to pay for that herself.

So naturally, she'd ended up looking for work at that point.

"Holy crap, look at that house."

"Yeah, it's a big one."

The grand mansion loomed at the top of the rise, although she had a feeling it was the pit in her stomach that turned the place into something threatening, rather than anything behind its leaded glass windows or under the eaves of its regal roofline.

Paying the guy, she got out and waited until the minivan had drifted down the hill. She had a feeling that if there was a car anywhere in view, it would increase the likelihood she would be turned away.

When the Lyft was gone, she took a moment to look around. Everything was in its place, all the bushes draped with hemmed-up burlap cloth to protect them from the cold, the grounds cleared of any debris, the flagstone walkway glowing blue and gray as it cut around the flower beds to the front entrance.

As she stepped up to the gleaming door, she expected some kind of warning bell to go off, the inhabitants alerted that the daughter was on the premises—not that she had been officially kicked out or anything. It had been more a case of tacit agreement that the Early's compulsion into parenting hadn't really resulted in a favorable outcome for the adopted or the adoptees.

The doorbell, when she pressed it, made a muted *drrrrrrrrrrrrrrrrl* sound, neither bell nor alarm. It was an old-fashioned noise, one generated by a mechanism that she imagined was, like the floors and moldings inside, original to the house. She didn't know exactly how it worked or where the thing was within the jambs of the entrance, and she wondered, if it broke, how someone would fix—

The door opened.

"Hello, Father," she said softly. "Surprise."

✦   ✦   ✦

"So are you going to do something with your wardrobe? Or just stand there looking at your shit."

As V spoke up from behind his Four Toys, Butch cleared his throat and meant to move away from the first of his three racks of clothes. Goal denied.

"Cop, seriously. You're beginning to freak me out. You're like something out of *Paranormal Activity*."

"That was about ghosts, not vampires. And I'm fine."

"You've been making like a statue there for fifteen fucking minutes. Sixteen. Seventeen . . . you want I keep this hourglass bullcrap up?"

Butch shook his head and went back over to the Pit's sofa. Sitting his ass down, he went to take a drink from his glass of Lag and was surprised to find the thing empty. Instead of refilling it, he put the sturdy cylinder of crystal on the coffee table.

"So I met an old friend tonight."

V leaned out around the forest of his monitors, one black slash of an eyebrow lifting, his diamond eyes sparkling. "What's her name."

"I didn't say it was a woman."

"You don't have to. That guilty tone is a driver's license with a picture."

"It wasn't like that."

"Wasn't it?"

Butch shot up to his feet and went to the door to the outside. Then he turned around and walked back to the rack. And back to the sofa.

Fucking sunlight.

"Look, cop," V said as he pushed away from his keyboards. "I was just pulling your leg. You would castrate yourself before being with another female. But what's the deal?"

"She was a friend of Janie's."

"Jesus . . ." V crossed his arms over his chest and kicked out thick-socked feet, using one of his subwoofers as an ottoman. "Why didn't you say?"

"I'm talking about it now, aren't I."

V nodded down the hall. "You tell Marissa?"

"No, but it's not a thing." When Vishous just stared across the sitting area, Butch wanted to throw something. Like maybe the Foosball table. "I'm serious. It isn't."

"Sure it's not. Absolutely not. You wanna talk about the weather? What Fritz is serving for First Meal, maybe?"

Butch put his hands up to his hair and grabbed onto the shit. "Her name was Mel. I haven't seen her for like ... I mean, twenty years? Maybe longer." He pictured the bustier he'd helped remove. "She turned out different than I thought she would. She and Janie were supposed to be married by now, like my sister Joyce. Couple kids. Husband who works at a job that pays enough so they can stay home."

"So what happened to her?"

"Not any of that. Not by a long shot—she, ah, yeah, she moved to Caldwell. She used to be a model down in NYC. She collects clothes, just like I do."

"Used to be a model and moved out of Manhattan? She's an escort—"

"I didn't fucking say that," Butch snapped.

"Don't have to."

Butch rubbed his eyes and reflected that his roommate's penchant for piercing insight was really fucking annoying sometimes.

"Did she ask you if you wanted to pay her something?" V said. "And did you say no, but even as your mouth formed the answer, your brain went in a different, more naked direction? One that, even though you would never, ever pursue it in real life, made you feel bad for the mere thought?"

"No." He shook his head. "I have that solace at least. She took a bath in front of me, as a matter of fact. As beautiful as she was, I didn't feel a thing below the waist, and that's the God's honest."

"Well. Look at you being all choirboy and shit. I'm honestly not surprised, true? And listen, you're referring to her in the past tense. Just thought I'd point that out to your overactive conscience."

Butch just shrugged. "I'd first run into her a few nights ago, see. Randomly, downtown. She was on her way to a club, I was coming out of the garage after I parked the R8. And last evening, after you and I talked? She was there on the street when I came out. She'd been . . . hurt. Bad. By a man."

"Shit. Did you send her into the human system?"

"She refused to go." Butch picked up his glass and took a sip from the empty, proof positive that addictions were part biochemical, part muscle memory from habit. "I took her to her home. You know, to make sure she got there."

As images of all those cuts and bruises played through his mind, he winced. "I'm sure she's fine."

"You're not sure, at all."

As wild, paranoid conclusions jumped around his skull, Butch threw them all out, one by one. Or tried to. "I think I'm just exhausted."

"Nah, come on, you look like you've been on a tropical vacation for a month. If you glowed from health any more than you do right now, you'd be a fucking night-light."

Butch let that dig go.

"I'm not seeing her again." He cleared his throat. "I'm just going to forget about her. Besides, she promised she wouldn't tell Joyce she ran into me. It's a non-issue."

"If it's a non-issue, why haven't you told Marissa?"

Butch stared over at the suits hanging from the racks and wondered exactly why he needed so many variations on the color dark blue in his life. "I'm thinking about giving my wardrobe away."

V cursed under his breath. "Did that woman hit you on the head with a brick or something? What the fuck."

"I like the clothes, but I'm using them as camouflage."

" 'Cuz you're hiding what? Other than your meat and two veg."

Butch shot his roommate a flat look. "I'm trying to camo the fact that I'm a piece of shit unworthy of the female who shares my bed every night. I put the good threads on my body and hope she doesn't look any further than the surface of 'em. That's what I'm doing with them."

"You are not."

"Yeah, I am. And I didn't realize it until I was at Mel's place tonight. She does the exact same thing. Maybe it was something in the water in Southie—you know, from when we were growing up." Butch shook his head. "I haven't talked to Marissa about it yet, not because of Mel. But because of me."

He rubbed his eyes. The back of his neck. His shoulder.

"And there was something else," he heard himself say.

Stop talking, a voice inside his head countered.

Abruptly, his roommate sat up straight. "What else, cop."

CHAPTER FORTY-ONE

W ell, Josephine. This is a real surprise. Sit down, will you?"

The breakfast room in her parents' house was an ancillary of the dining room, a circular offshoot decorated with a garden mural that was cheerful as a spring day. The glass table in the center was set upon a pedestal of white iron curlicues, and there were eight white wicker chairs around its beveled edge. A bank of diamond-paned windows, that overlooked the pool and the actual garden, let so much light in, Jo had to blink.

The table was set with only one place, the sterling silver fork and knife as yet unlifted from the folded damask napkin, the *New York Times* and the *Washington Post* still in their mille-feuille arrangement on the right-hand side. The plate in the center of the sterling silver charger was monogrammed, and there was half of a sectioned ruby grapefruit on it. A soft-boiled egg in a cup was next to where the coffee had been poured.

"Josephine?"

She shook herself back to attention and pulled out one of the vacant chairs. As she sat down and put her backpack in her lap, she made sure her knees were together and her ankles crossed under her chair.

"Would you care to have something to eat?" her father inquired. "I will have Maria prepare whatever you like."

Thus far, Jo had not looked at the man, even when he himself had pulled open the great, well-oiled door at the front entrance. His voice had therefore been that of a ghost. Except he was really there.

"No, thank you. I'm not hungry."

"Well." He pulled his own chair out on the short-napped, green-and-yellow rug that had been custom-made to fit the space. "I must confess, this is a surprise."

"Yes. I'm sorry. I should have called. Where is Mother?"

"She is away with Constance Franck and Virginia Sterling. They're on a vacation to Bermuda for a week. Did you know that Virginia and her husband just bought a house there? Your mother was very impatient to check it out. They'll be back on Sunday. Are you sure I can't get you something?"

As if this were a hotel with a restaurant.

"No. Thank you."

Jo was unaware of falling quiet, except then her father cleared his throat. "So," he prompted.

"I don't need money," she said. "I just have to talk to you."

"About what? You know, this all seems rather ominous."

Taking a deep breath . . . she looked up.

Her first thought was that Randolph Chance Early III had aged. The full head of salt-and-pepper gray hair was now far more salt than pepper, and there were new wrinkles around his watery blue eyes. Other than that, the physical impression he made was all as she remembered. The lips were still thin, testimony to the man's predilection for self-control, order, and the absolute denial of any passion, anywhere, and the clothes were the same, the navy-blue blazer, gray wool slacks, white button-down, and club tie the kind of thing he surely had come out of the womb wearing.

Her second thought was that her father was less scary than she had always made him out to be. It was amazing how being financially independent made her feel taller than the five-year-old she reverted to every time she set foot in this house. Not that she was rich, by any means. But she was surviving, on her own, and no amount of disinterest or disapproval from him or anyone else could diminish that.

Unzipping her backpack, she took out the manila folder she'd taken from her kitchen drawer. Opening the front cover, she slid free the black-and-white photograph of Dr. Manuel Manello and placed it on the glass.

"Do you know this man?" she asked as she spun the image around and pushed it across the smooth surface.

Her father dabbed his lips even though he hadn't taken a sip of coffee or a spoonful of grapefruit or any of that egg. Then he leaned in, holding his tie in place though there was nothing for it to brush into.

On the far side of the flap door that the servants used, subtle sounds of a kitchen in full swing percolated, filling the silence. And as Jo's anxiety rose, she clung to the soft voices. The chopping. The occasional scrape of metal on metal, a pan dragged across the sixteen-burner stovetop.

"No, I do not." Her father looked up. "What's this about?"

Jo tried to find a perfect combination of words to explain herself, but realized that there really wasn't one. Besides, what exactly was she protecting him from?

Maybe it was more like she was looking for the combination to unlock her past in the syllables she could shift around.

"He's supposedly my brother."

Chance Early frowned. "That's impossible. Your mother and I only adopted you."

Jo opened her mouth. Closed it. Took a deep breath. "No, he's supposedly related to me by blood."

"Oh." Her father straightened in his chair. "Well, I'm sorry, but I wouldn't know anything about that. Your adoption was a closed one. We have no records on the woman who birthed you."

"Do you remember the name of the agency you used?"

"It was through the Catholic Church. The local diocese here. But I am sure it's been shuttered for years. How do you know he's a relation?"

"I have a friend of mine who is a reporter. He worked back from the hospital I'd been born in. Talking to people there, he discovered that my mother had been given a pseudonym, and that someone with that same name had also given birth to this man, who had been adopted. His name is Dr. Manuel Manello."

"So you already know the story. Why do you need to question me about it?"

Jo moved her eyes to the windows. Outside, in the cold, a man in a dark green landscaper's outfit strode into view with a hoe.

"I just thought that perhaps you or Mother might recall something."

Her father picked up the silver teaspoon by his knife. Digging into the grapefruit, he frowned again as he put a piece in his mouth.

"I'm afraid the answer is no. And why do you want to look into all this?"

Jo blinked. "It's my history."

"But it doesn't matter."

She refocused on the gardener. "It does to me."

When she went to get up, he said, "You're leaving?"

"I think it's for the best."

"Well." Her father patted his mouth with that napkin. "As you wish. But do you have any message for your mother?"

"No, I don't." At least not her adoptive mother. "Thank you."

As she took the photograph back, she had no idea what she was thanking him for. The fact that she had made it to maturity still alive? That was about it.

Returning the folder to her backpack, she re-zipped things, nodded, and turned away. Walking out through the dining room, she paused in front of the portrait of her mother that hung over the sideboard. Mrs. Philomena "Phillie" Early was beautiful in the Grace Kelly kind of standard, a platinum blonde with cheekbones like a thoroughbred.

"Jo."

She looked over her shoulder. Her father had come to stand in the archway of the breakfast room, his napkin in his hand, his thin fingers worrying the damask.

"Forgive me. I have always found that I handle this subject badly. One feels a sense of failure that one could not provide one's wife with a child. I'm sure you understand this."

"I'm sorry," Jo said because she felt like she had to.

"I can give you the name of our attorney at the time. I don't believe he is in practice anymore, but he must have known the real name of the woman as he processed the paperwork with the diocese. Even if whatever hospital she was in gave her a pseudonym for the birth, legally, she would have had to use her given name to relinquish parental rights. Perhaps that would help you?"

"But she died."

"Not as far as we were told."

Jo recoiled, unsure what story to believe. But then she refocused. "I would like that contact information, please."

Her father nodded and walked over. "It will be in my records in the study."

Jo followed him out across the polished foyer and into a wood-paneled room that had always reminded her of a jewelry box. Over at the desk, her father leaned down low.

"You have your own file," he said.

As if she were a car and he were keeping her maintenance records so the warranty held up.

Extracting a thick portfolio tied with a band, he sat down as he dove into the paperwork, and she wondered how it was so voluminous.

"I saved all of your school reports and test scores," he said as if he read her mind.

Why, she wanted to ask. Then again, maybe he thought he might need them if he sought to return her to the hospital she had been born in.

Watching his spindly fingers pick through the pages he had retained, she reflected on how frail he seemed, his thin body bent, his narrow shoulders hunched. For some reason, his physical weakness made her think about all of the propriety he always insisted upon, and how his protocols had defined her childhood and early adulthood, presented to her as a test of morality or worthiness she had to pass. Funny—now, she saw all of the arbitrary rules as the defense mechanisms of a feeble and conflict-averse man, one who had muddled through life with a remarkable lack of personal distinction for all the historical distinction of his pedigree.

"Here," he said. "His name and number."

Her father held out a business card and Jo took it. Robert J. Temple, Esq. With a downtown Philadelphia address and an original 215 area code. No firm name listed.

Putting the stiff little rectangle on the leather blotter, she got her phone out and snapped a photo of it.

"Thank you," she said as she handed the thing back.

"You are welcome."

Jo felt as though she had to wait as the business card went back into the portfolio, and the flap was battened down once again with the band. Her father then returned the collection of documents to the lower drawer and got to his feet. As if the business meeting were over.

"Do give Mother my regards," Jo said.

Now, the man smiled. "Oh, I most certainly will. And she will return them to you, I'm sure."

He was pleased because that was an appropriate thing to say and do. Which would provide him with an appropriate thing to communicate to his wife when the subject of the unannounced visit came up.

"Oh, do you need a ride somewhere?" Chance Early asked. "I didn't see a car in the drive."

"No, I'll get a Lyft."

"From whom? Tom can take you where you need to go."

Of course the man had never heard of Lyft or Uber.

"A taxi, I mean." She one-strapped her backpack. "I'm just going to wait on the front step after I call for it. I will enjoy the fresh air and sunshine."

The relief on her father's face wasn't something he bothered to hide. "Very well. It has been lovely to see you again, Josephine. I look forward to our next meeting."

He stuck his hand out.

Jo shook what she was offered, finding his palm bone dry and skeletal. "Thank you. I'll see myself out so that your breakfast is not unduly interrupted."

"That is most considerate."

As Jo left the house, she got out her phone again. A number not in her contacts had called and left a message, but she ignored the notification as she went into the Lyft app.

She was leaning back against the warm stone of the house, her face lifted to the sun, when a Nissan Stanza pulled up. Getting in the back, she declined mints, control over the Sirius radio, and an alteration—hotter or cooler—of the air temperature. The driver was chatty and she was glad. As he hit the gas, she had the sense she was not ever going back to her parents' house again and she needed a distraction from that conclusion.

Except of course she would go back. She had visited her parents for Christmas just three months ago. And Christmas would be coming back around in another eight. So surely she would return . . .

Jo didn't remember much about the drive back to the 30th Street Station. Or precisely how she came to be on a train again.

At least she managed to get another window seat.

As she settled in and hoped that she would continue to have the car mostly to herself, she took out her phone and checked again to see if Syn had called. She was disappointed to find that he hadn't. Then again, she needed to reach out to him first, didn't she.

Instead of calling him, she went into Safari and did a Google search on the lawyer her parents had used—and found the man's obituary. He had died ten years ago.

Naturally.

To pass the time before the train started moving and she could fall asleep against the window, she played the voice mail that had been left by the unknown number, expecting it to be a scam offer for health insurance or maybe a fake program to help her with student loans she didn't have.

Hi, Ms. Early. This is St. Francis Urgent Care. You were here about seventy-two hours ago? You left us a blood sample? Well, it turns out that it was contaminated in the lab somehow. We hate to ask you to do this, but could you come in and let us take some more? Again, we're really sorry. We've never had this happen before. It must have been a screwup on their part, but they're saying they couldn't read what they had. Thanks. Oh, our telephone number is—

Jo cut the message off. All of that was so not on her list of things to worry about. Besides, she'd essentially been cleared by the doctor and—

Frowning, she rubbed at her nose, a terrible smell invading her nostrils. When there seemed to be no escape from the stench, she leaned out into the aisle. Two men had entered the car at the far end, and it had to be them.

Assuming the pair had strung dead skunks around their necks under their coats.

Jo blinked her eyes and rubbed her nose again. God, she'd never smelled anything so awful. It was like baby powder and roadkill—

All at once, her headache came on with a vengeance, her skull pounding with pain. Clearly, the stink was the trigger.

Nope. Not gonna do this for two hours, she decided. *No matter how rude it is to move.*

Grabbing her backpack, she got to her feet and shuffled up to the next car in line—and thank God that whatever the smell was didn't carry into the other space.

Just as the train bumped and started forward, she sat down at a new window seat and massaged her temples. As the agony continued to build, she refused to submit to it. For some reason, she had the feeling it was trying to distract her. Get her off some kind of thought trail.

Even though that was crazy talk. Anthropomorphizing a migraine? Really?

Still . . . that stench. What about the stench—

Even as the vise cranked down harder on her skull, she probed further the conviction that she had smelled that horrible stink before. Sometime recently. Very recently . . .

Going into her phone, she went to her call log. Without knowing what she was looking for, she checked what had come in on, and gone out of, her phone over the last couple of days. Lot of calls back and forth with McCordle. Then there was Dougie looking for money. Telemarketing bullcrap—

Jo sat up.

What the hell had she been doing, talking to Bill at ten p.m. A number of times?

She'd been home at the time. Or should have been. And yet she had no memory of speaking to him then. Sure, they regularly chatted about their little extracurricular hobby with the supernatural—but not after ten o'clock on a proverbial school night. And not over and over again within such a short period of time . . .

No, wait, she thought. She'd been out somewhere. She had gone in search of . . . something.

Yes, in her car. It had been raining—

Moaning, Jo shut her phone down and had to let her head fall back against the seat rest. As she breathed in a shallow way, she vowed to find out where the hell she had gone and why she had called her friend.

She was done with the knowledge holes in her life.

At least a simple mystery like where she had been when she had spoken with Bill had to be solvable.

It just *had* to be.

CHAPTER FORTY-TWO

Thirty minutes after nightfall, Butch parked the R8 in the downtown garage—and this time, he did not expect to meet with anyone. Not Mel. Not his roommate. Not his roommate's estranged mother.

Yup, he wasn't interested in crossing paths with anybody.

And FFS, it sure would be handy to dematerialize.

Instead, he hoofed it. Stepping out of the garage, he popped the collar on his leather jacket, ducked his head, and started making time. The rest of the Brotherhood were still back at the mansion, doing a weapons check—something he technically should have been involved with. But whatever. He needed a little personal time before—

As his phone started going off, he took it out and killed the vibration without bothering to check to see who was calling. This wasn't going to take long, and as soon as he was finished, he'd hit the home team up, pull a *mea culpa*, and proceed with the regularly scheduled program.

It took him six minutes to get to his destination, and as he stared up at the twenty-story office building, it occurred to him that he had no memory of how he and Mel had gotten inside the night before. She must have had a key. Had it been through the front entrance? That seemed unlikely given that there were revolving doors that had been locked in place because it was after hours.

Around back?

Unease prickled up the nape of his neck, and he palmed one of his guns as he went down the side of the building. In the middle of the block, he found an unmarked entrance, but it was bolted closed with no wiggle room whatsoever.

Hell, the damn thing didn't have a lock to pick or even a card reader. Had to be an emergency exit.

Rounding the far corner and facing off at the back of the property, he hoped for a receiving dock in the shallow parking area—and had his prayers answered. But that was as far as the good news went. He couldn't get into anything. Not the bay doors that were all rolled down tight, and not the three regular doors with their electronic key readers for which—duh—he had no pass card.

He went around the footprint of the building. Twice.

Before he caved.

Taking out his phone, he was cursing as he hit send on the call. No reason to go into his contacts to find the number. The fucker in question had been the last person who had called him. Three times in a row. In the last three and a half minutes—

"Where the fuck are you?" V snapped.

"That's not important. I need a favor—"

"Oh, it's not important. I'm on lockdown here—with Lassiter, P.S., who's going to make me watch *The Munsters* all night long—"

"—I need to get into a locked facility—"

"—when I'm an *Addams Family* kind of male—"

"—and it's got these card reader thingies—"

"—and more to the point, you've clearly skipped weapons inspection—"

All at once, they both stopped and barked, "Will you listen to what the fuck I'm saying!"

Then, also at the same time:

"You're watching TV with Lassiter?"

"You're trying to break into a building?"

Butch fought a wave of exhaustion. "Look, it's not for business. I just need to get into this place, and you're the only person who can help."

"Where are you? And if you say not important again I'm going to punch this angel because he's the closest thing to me."

"Not important—"

Over the connection, there was a muffled *OW! What the FUCK, V!*

"God, that was satisfying," V murmured. "Thank you."

"You're welcome."

Butch looked over the loading dock, locating the security cameras that were mounted on the corners of the bays and above each of the three doors. There was also a refuse bin the size of a railcar and an Iron Mountain records storage unit. Neither of which were going to be helpful.

He cursed. "Don't you have a universal card or something? I don't want to set off any alarms."

There was a rustle, like the brother was getting off a sofa. Then, in a softer voice, V said, "What are you up to, cop?"

"It's not about the war or anything."

"Okay, hold on."

Butch exhaled in relief—then jumped back as V materialized right in front of him. The brother was in leathers and shitkickers—great—except without a single weapon on him. Unless you counted his acid tongue, which was only material in an argument.

Then again . . .

Plus that hand of his. But still.

"What the *hell* are you doing out here?" Butch snapped into his phone.

"Oh, sure," V said bitterly into his own, "it's fine for you to be in danger—"

"Get back home!"

"I thought you needed help, asshole—" V paused. Took his phone from his ear. Ended the call. "So, yeah, we're face-to-face now. How 'bout we scream and yell at each other in person."

Butch dropped his phone from his ear as well. "You're not armed."

"And your weapons haven't been checked."

"Touché. And at least you're not in *Little Mermaid* PJs."

"You'd be surprised at how sexy I look in them." V assessed the back of the building. "So this is our target, huh."

"There's no 'our' in this." When V started striding forward, Butch grabbed the guy's bare arm. "This is too dangerous out here for you. Remember our little agreement?"

"You'd sense if there were slayers around. Are there?"

"Well, no. But there could be at any—"

"So this is *our* target." V went over to one of the loading bays and jumped up onto the concrete lip that was chest high. After he inspected the linked panels, he nodded. "Okay, I think I know what to do."

"I should never have called you."

"Are you even serious? This is so much better—"

With that, V dematerialized in mid-sentence.

Standing by his little lonesome, Butch slammed one shitkicker into the pavement like a five-year-old. Then he froze, waiting to hear an alarm. Then he paced when nothing of the ear-plosion variety occurred.

The clunking sound of the bay's sections going up was loud in the quiet, and V's leather-clad legs and muscle shirt and bare shoulders were revealed inch by inch.

"—than staying home with that angel," he finished as he leaned down and offered his palm. "I swear to God, it was going to be me or him."

Butch grabbed onto the lead-lined glove and was hauled up into a receiving area that was every bit as grimy as the parking area. "I don't get it. You could have just left the guy and gone back to the Pit."

"Fritz is cleaning our place tonight."

As V shuddered and eased the panels back down with a hand crank, Butch whistled under his breath. "Yeah, I'd pick Lassiter over that."

"I swear, that butler would vacuum my backside if he got the chance." Securing them inside the receiving area, V clapped his hands together. "So where are we going?"

Butch glared at his roommate. When V just stood there, patiently waiting, Butch resolved to learn breaking and entering skills from Balz.

"Oh, for fuck's sake," he bitched.

"Is that a department here?" V drawled. "Or just a certain floor."

Grinding his molars, Butch glanced around. Thanks to the glowing "EXIT" signs over the various doorways into the building proper, he was able to assess things well enough. Not that he was inspired. Other than rolling bins for FedEx boxes and a long stretch of counter that looked like a processing station for mail, there wasn't much to go on.

He'd been hoping for a map mounted on the concrete wall or some shit. Hey, the folks who worked here had to know where they were going with the envelopes and the packages, right?

"I need to find the basement," he muttered as he headed randomly toward one of the doors. Before he went more than two steps, he held out one of his forties. "Take this. I know I'm not going to get far trying to make you leave."

"It's like you know me or some shit, true?"

"Shut up, V," he said as they set off together.

◆   ◆   ◆

They had made love the second Syn had come to see her at nightfall.

Is that the right past tense? Jo thought as she hit her direction signal and then put her hand back in Syn's.

Or was it more like, they'd had sex. They'd fucked. They'd screwed. They'd banged, boinked, bumped uglies . . .

Whatever the grammar, whatever the vernacular, they most certainly had been together. Pretty much all over her apartment. But she'd promised herself that enough was enough. Given Syn's . . . issue . . . she just couldn't bear being so selfish as to expect him to service her sexual needs like a stud and get nothing out of it for himself.

And the aftermath for him was so much worse than just nothing.

Next to her, in her passenger seat, he repositioned himself gingerly, and the wince that hit his face told her everything she needed to know about how uncomfortable he was.

So, no, she had not intended to get intimate. All she had wanted to do was see him. Smell him. Hold him—and all of that had happened the moment he had come through her door.

Followed by more of same. Just with a lot less clothing on.

"I can't believe you're willing to go on another of these wild-goose chases with me," she said.

The way he squeezed her hand was getting to be familiar. "I'm off-duty tonight so there's nowhere else I'd want to be."

Before she could think of something to say to that, he leaned into her and whispered, "I love the way you're smiling right now. You'll have to tell me exactly what you're thinking about later."

"Okay and now I'm blushing, too."

"Good."

Except then he moved stiffly again, pulling the seat belt out from his chest and realigning his hips with a hiss.

"Syn, are you all right—"

"Perfect in every way. So where are we going?"

Jo shook her head, but let it go. Having a conversation with only one person participating was difficult, and clearly, he was in asked-and-answered territory when it came to his discomfort.

God, she hated it, though.

"Well, as you know . . . I'm just so sick of these memory lapses I've been having." She debated about whether or not to tell him about her trip to see her father, but like that was relevant? More to the point, she wondered if there was any way to volunteer the visit for her amnesia. "It's a long story, but apparently, I came out to this abandoned outlet mall a couple of nights ago. Bill, my friend, talked to me while I was there, and also on my way home, except I have no recollection of leaving my apartment. Driving anywhere. Seeing anything or doing anything."

"Bill is the one who is mated? Who you work with."

"Yes. He and his wife just lost a pregnancy."

Syn's frown was deep. "For that, I am sorry."

"Me, too." Jo leaned into the windshield. "So yeah, I want to come here and check the site out. The turnoff should be right—yup, here we are."

Heading up a rise in the road, she braced herself for a headache—and sure enough, as she made the final turn and a darkened stretch of one-story shops came into view, the pain hit her right in the frontal lobe.

"You don't have to do this," Syn said grimly.

"I have to do something."

As she let her car roll to a stop, she knew—she *knew*—she had been here before. Done this before.

"I swear to God," she muttered, "it's like someone keeps getting into my brain and stealing things from me."

"Park your car over there."

"Where?"

"Behind that lean-to, and make sure you turn it around so it's headed out. You never know."

"Oh. Of course."

As Jo did as he suggested, she decided there were distinct advantages to having a trained killer around.

When they got out of the Golf, she was further impressed by Syn's direction. Her car wasn't big, and the lean-to, which was a bus stop that had been Adirondack-ify'd, was the perfect cover for it. No one would know they were here—and he was right. If they needed to get gone in a hurry, all she had to do was put that sewing machine engine in drive and hit the gas.

"So Bill told me he was going to come and meet me here." She winced and massaged the back of her neck as they started walking. "He was worried about me being all alone. But he never made it out. He said I called him on my way home and told him I hadn't seen anything. So he turned around and went back to his own house."

"Have you and he ever been together—"

Jo whipped her head around. "Oh, my God, never. He's married. And even if he wasn't, he's not my type."

Syn gave a grunt of satisfaction at that and Jo had to smile. Taking his hand, she bumped herself into him. "You're jealous."

"I am not."

"Really?"

"Nah. I always want to tear people limb from limb. It's exercise, you know." He pounded his pec with his fist. "Develops the heart muscle, the arms. And plus the satisfaction of destroying an enemy is the best trophy there is."

He looked down and winked at her.

"You are incorrigible," she said.

"I don't know what that word means—" As her boot nailed the lip of the concrete walkway, he easily caught her as she fell forward. "You okay?"

Jo laughed. For no other reason than they were together. "Yup. I am."

Forcing herself to focus, she stepped over a chain and proceeded forward, looking into the darkened shops as they went down the promenade. Not much to see. Not much left behind. Not much that would have made her think to come for an after-dark visit.

God, her head was pounding.

At the end of the covered walkway, they stopped in front of the faded stencil of a cow holding an ice cream cone with his hoof. As the wind kicked up, blackened leaves chattered and rushed along the cracked sidewalk, congregating in the corner of an inset doorway with others of their kind.

Pivoting around, she shook her head and felt like a fool. "Bill said I'd

gotten some kind of tip that I'd been vague about. I'd told him it was off
my blog, but there's nothing about this site anywhere on it—hey, there
are stairs over here. Do you mind if we see where they take us?"

"Nope. Lead on, female."

Jo smiled some more and led them down the concrete steps, spurred
on by something in the center of her chest. At the base of the descent,
she stopped and took in the sight of a vacant parking lot—

A gust of wind ruffled more winter-worn leaves across pavement
that had potholes like it was Swiss cheese. And that was when she
heard it. *Creeeeak—slam. Creeeeeak—slam.*

Over in the far corner of the lot, there was a building with sets of
garage doors running down the front of it. A regular-sized door off to
one side was loose on its hinges, and as the wind came up, it opened and
closed on its own.

Wincing and weaving on her feet, she muttered, "Yes. Over there.
I know the sound of that door."

Without waiting for a response from Syn, she stumbled across the
asphalt, blinded by pain, but hyper-focused by the sense that finally, the
mystery was going to be solved. When she got to the door, her breath
caught in her throat and her heart began to pound. With a trembling
hand, she reached—

Syn put his arm out. "Let me go first."

"I can do it."

But he made the decision for her, stepping ahead, stepping inside. A moment later, a flashlight clicked on, and its beam made a slow
circle . . . of an absolutely empty, windowless, concrete-floored maintenance facility.

"Shit," she said as she joined him. "I could have sworn—"

The door slammed shut behind her, making her jump.

"Another wild-goose chase," she muttered as she walked around, her
footfalls echoing.

She was just about to suggest they leave and promise that she
wouldn't have any more bright ideas about nocturnal destinations . . .

. . . when the first of the cars pulled up just outside that slamming door.

◆   ◆   ◆

"I swear to fucking God," Butch said, "it was down here. The door was like something out of a dungeon . . . and she . . ."

As he let the words trail off, he walked back down the corridor, reading the little laminated headers that announced each corporate owner of each storage space behind each absolutely normal-looking fucking door.

"I'm beginning to think I'm crazy." When V didn't say anything, Butch glanced over at the guy—who was standing in front of what should have been the entrance to Mel's apartment. "I swear—"

"I believe you." V put his hand up. "Gimme a minute."

Vishous closed his eyes and lowered his head, becoming so still, it was as if he were no longer a part of the living-and-breathing crew. Meanwhile, Butch found it impossible not to keep pacing.

None of this made any sense—

Well, actually, it did make sense. It was just Butch didn't like where the connect-the-dots was taking him.

"What if she wasn't who I thought she was," he said. More to try the words out than anything else.

V lifted his head. "And you're sure this is the building."

"We can check the GPS on my phone, right? You record where all of us go every night—it's how you found me here just now." Butch got his Samsung and held it out to his roommate. "It should be in the log."

In the back of his mind, he was aware his instincts were going haywire—and it was a little late for that, wasn't it. If he'd been played by something . . . otherworldly . . . whatever it was was no longer here.

"I can get your trail on mine," V murmured.

As the brother went into his own phone, Butch crossed his arms and thought about the strange thing that had happened when he'd started walking away from Mel's the night before. He'd just closed her door and taken one, maybe two steps . . . when that massive locking mechanism with the bifurcated iron bars had slid back into place quietly behind him.

There was no way the woman could have gotten herself out of that tub, across the breadth of that open area, and locked herself in. Even if she hadn't been injured.

And that was the other thing. When he'd found her outside of the garage, she'd been bleeding in a lot of places, bruised and beaten. But when he'd helped her with the bustier? When she'd stared at him from the tub? There had been nothing marring the porcelain skin of her face.

At the time, he'd been too busy making sure he didn't look anywhere he shouldn't to really notice. But now? He knew that kind of healing was flat-out impossible—

"This is fucked-up."

Butch glanced over. "So I wasn't here?"

"No, you were, but last night, there was a helluva misread on your location." V turned his phone around. "This is the map of Caldwell. This is you. Here we go."

V tapped something, and like some old-school Pac-Man shit, a little blinking dot moved through the block maze of streets.

"This is Trade here." V's finger went vertically across the screen. "And now you're on Thirteenth. And . . . here we are, one block from this address."

The dot disappeared.

"Fast-forward about fifteen, twenty minutes at the most," V said. "And . . . here you are again."

All at once, the dot reappeared and moved away from the dead zone. Which seemed to take up the entire block that the building was on.

"What the fuck," Butch muttered. "And who the *hell* was I talking to?"

CHAPTER FORTY-THREE

Not just one car. Many.

As what sounded like a goddamn flotilla pulled up to the groundskeeping facility, Syn put his body between Jo and the door they'd come through. Getting out his gun, he cursed himself as he flicked off his flashlight. There had been no cover that he'd seen as he'd looked around the interior space. Nothing but support beams, the roof overhead, and the oil-stained, concrete floor.

He was getting out his gun when the situation went from bad to deadly.

At first, as the scent of the enemy reached his nose, he tried to tell himself he was imagining it. What the hell would *lessers* be doing out—

"That smell," Jo hissed. "It was on the train coming back from Philadelphia today. And I swear I've sm—"

"Shh."

As she fell silent, he listened hard, threading through the wind and the slamming of that door, waiting for voices. Although what was that really going to tell him?

Grabbing her hand, he took her further into the darkness. Totally no cover. Absolutely no escape. And here he was with a limited amount of weapons and ammo, a half-breed who didn't know what she was, and God only knew how many *lessers*.

Voices just outside the flimsy building now. A congregation. Three? Four of them? It was hard to get a bead on multiple scents this far back.

A blowtorch. What he needed was a blowtorch so he could burn a hole through the metal walling for Jo to squeeze through. But like he could have thought that far ahead? The only other option he had was to leave her in the back here, totally undefended, essentially unarmed, while he went on a blitz offensive, shooting up whatever the fuck was out there. Not appealing. Not by a long shot—or a hundred of the point-blank variety.

What other choice did he have, though? He couldn't call the Brotherhood or the other fighters. If he thought he had problems with the proverbial management already, it was nothing compared to what would happen if he were caught with a half-breed, pretrans female, out in the dark, all by their lonesome.

Besides, she was his. Not theirs.

"Take this," he said as he unholstered the backup forty he kept on his calf. "It's heavier than you're used to, but it'll blow a hole in—"

He froze. And then twisted around to the corrugated metal wall behind them.

Yes, he thought. *That may work.*

"On three, I'm going to start shooting at the wall," he said as he palmed up the other Smith & Wesson on his hip. "They'll take cover, but not for long, so I need you to be ready to run. After we've busted out, we go straight for the wood line. All you have to do is keep up, okay?"

"Who are they?"

"No questions. And no, we're not calling the police. They cannot help us. You have to trust me."

There was a pause. "Okay."

Syn closed his eyes. "I'm sorry."

"What for."

Without answering, he put up both of his autoloaders and pulled the triggers—and got the opposite result he'd been hoping for. The barrage of bullets went haywire, sparks flying as lead slugs ricocheted back at them instead of penetrating through the panels.

He had to stop shooting. If he could keep going, he might be able to sieve shit up enough for him to bust through with his shoulder, but it was too risky. He was going to fill Jo and him full of fucking holes first.

"*Damn it,*" he bit out.

And of course, now those *lessers* outside knew that there was somebody on the property who was armed.

As much as he hated everything in this moment, as much as he dreaded what he had to do, Jo's life was more important than absolutely everything.

Including whatever future he had secretly been deluding himself into believing they might have.

Syn sent out a distress call to all the fighters on duty.

CHAPTER FORTY-FOUR

No, I'm telling you the bruises weren't there." Butch felt like he was pleading in front of a jury. Except given V's nodding head, the brother at least agreed with the version of events being described. "I just didn't notice it at the time—"

"Because you were trying not to notice—"

"So many other things—"

As Butch's phone started to vibrate in his pocket, he jumped and then went on a hand dive to get the thing—while V did likewise without the jerk of alarm. When they both read the same message, they looked at each other.

"The outlet mall," Butch said as he started texting fast.

"Where the induction we cleaned up was."

"What the fuck is Syn doing out there?" Butch grabbed V's arm. "And you're *not* going on this call. No fucking way—"

"There are slayers. So it's time for you and me to go to work—"

All at once, Lassiter appeared, a milkshake in one hand, a TV remote in the other. As he finished sucking the bottom of the old-school soda fountain glass, the slurping noise was loud as—well, Vishous dropping seven f-bombs in a row.

"You rang?" the fallen angel said in a pleasant tone.

"No." V punched at Butch's pecs. "You did *not* text him."

"He did." Lassiter gave the straw another suck. Then he metronomed his head back and forth, his blond and black hair swinging. "He did, he did, he did."

To the tune of *Hocus Pocus*'s "amuck, amuck, amuck."

Vishous jabbed a finger in the angel's face. "I'm *not* going back with you, asshole."

"Okay, that is really hurtful." More with the sucking. "I mean, what'd I ever do to you?"

"Your presence is enough." V confronted Butch. "And you are a traitor."

Butch shook his head and put his phone away. "No, I'm making sure you stick to the plan we agreed to."

"Fuck you both—"

Just as V went to dematerialize, Lassiter closed his eyes and nodded like *I Dream of Jeannie*. All at once, a containment barrier formed around V's entire body, the translucent prison the kind of thing that cut off his yelling and levitated him a good six inches off the floor.

For a moment, all Butch could do was stare at the spectacle of Vishous, son of the Bloodletter, blooded borne son of the Scribe Virgin . . . pounding mutely on the inside walls of his floating mini-prison.

"He looks like a bumblebee caught under a glass," Lassiter remarked.

Butch glanced over at the angel. "I know you're immortal and shit, but you better run like a motherfucker when you let him out."

"You know, I'm inclined to agree with you." Suddenly, the angel's odd-colored eyes got really fucking serious. "You let me know if you need him, though. And be careful. Things are so close to the end, and that's always when the parachute fails."

With a nod, Butch said, "I will be. But can you tell me anything? About where we're at? What's going to happen next?"

Lassiter seemed distraught as he shook his head. "I'm sorry. I can't. It's not my place—and even I have rules I need to follow if I want to stay in the game."

Butch studied those handsome features, usually so lighthearted and laughing. "So it's going to get really bad, huh."

The angel ignored that happy little comment and focused on V. "Come on, Sparky. I'm taking you home." With his open hand, he summoned the V-bubble, and it came forward like it was on a leash. "Should I try and dribble him?"

Butch shook his head as he got a load of the furious flush on his roommate's goateed mug. Plus, hello, there was all that hopping around that was still happening.

"I realllllly wouldn't go there," Butch murmured.

"Yeah, you're probably right. Drive safe."

Justlikethat, both the fallen angel, who was #1 on pretty much everybody's beat-down list, and the Wilson edition of Vishous, up and disappeared.

Butch spoke into his shoulder communicator as to his ETA and then he jogged off down the corridor. He'd gone about ten feet when he realized . . . he had no clue how the fuck to get out of the goddamn building. Lock-and-key expert Vishous was gone.

And with that pissed-off genius, went the exit Butch needed.

◆　　◆　　◆

As Jo stood behind Syn and gripped the heavy gun he'd given her, she grunted through the pain between her temples. Something was rising within her consciousness, a memory that was inexorable even against the barrier that was blocking it. Parting her lips, she breathed in a shallow way, her pounding heart and tingling limbs, the present danger in front of her, everything including even Syn, giving way to a desperate need to know just one thing.

One fucking thing—

Like spring rain bubbling up through the crack in the foundation of a basement, all at once a sliver of memory broke free and made itself present.

She saw herself at the security chain in front of the mall's barren promenade. And she recalled being convinced that things were going to change forever if she continued forward.

Then she remembered lifting her running shoe up and over the links. And moving forward with a heart that beat as fast as hers was now.

"I was right," she mumbled as she had to let the recollection go because of the pain.

Giving up her hold on the image, the thought, the piece of her past, the semi-answer that explained nothing sank below the impassable void that seemed to be consuming events and emotions, the black hole disappearing so much of what was so vitally important.

"Get behind me," Syn said. "And be prepared to shoot if they come through that door."

"I'm ready." Liar. She was shitting her pants.

As they stood together, him in front, both of them poised to use their weapons, she remembered running from the police helicopter with him. That had been the warm-up for this showdown—and none of this should have made sense, but it did. Somehow, this was where she had been heading these last months.

As much as her brain didn't understand anything, her instincts got it all—

The gunfire was not like it was in the movies. It was not some grand explosion.

And it was not inside the corrugated building.

It was outside. *Pop-pop-pop-pop*—

"Are they shooting at each other?" she whispered into the darkness. Even though she didn't know who the "they" was.

"Gimme the gun back now—"

"Wait, what?"

Syn snatched it out of her hand. "I can't run the risk of you killing my reinforcements."

The door to the facility swung open and light pierced through the pitch black. Just before the illumination hit them both, Syn yanked her out of its path—and meanwhile, figures stumbled into the interior, nothing but black outlines that scrambled, slipped, and fell to the concrete floor.

The stench of them made her cough and gag. Just as it had on the train.

As the door slammed shut, there was a shuffle.

"Bolt it from the inside!" a male voice said. "Fucking bolt it—"

"I will! Christ—"

"Who has a weapon?"

Outside, whatever battle was going on continued, and given the echoing sounds of metal-sliding-on-metal, the men had found a way to buttress that metal panel shut.

"Stay here," Syn whispered.

"No!" Jo grabbed the sleeve of his arm. "Don't go—"

"I need to know where you are."

"What are you going to do?" Even though she knew. He was going to kill them by hand. "Don't leave me!"

There was a split second of a pause. And then his lips somehow found hers in the darkness. The contact was too swift—

The explosion registered first as blinding light. Second as a shock wave. Third as a sound so loud that her ears felt like nails had been driven into them.

Jo was thrown back against the wall, her head hitting the metal with a clang, her vision conking out. As she struggled to recover her senses, the smell of the gunpowder or whatever had been combusted was like lead shavings in her nose, and she reached out blindly, trying to find Syn.

He was gone.

Rubbing her eyes, she—

The growling sound about five feet in front of her was not human. It was that of an animal, a wild animal . . . something massive and powerful, the kind of predator that thought of every other living thing as prey.

And then a red tint flared inside the building.

Shock and terror tightened Jo's chest and made her heart skip beats, and both got worse as her eyes came back online. Across the empty space, in the far corner, smoke wafted inside on erratic wind currents, its frothy path illuminated by the light inexplicably flooding in from the outside. No, not inexplicably. Part of the building had been blown apart, the force of whatever had been set so great that the metal was peeled back, the hole big enough to drive a semi into.

It was courtesy of the illumination that she watched the horror movie unfold.

Even as the gunshots and shouting continued out in the parking area, even as there was another explosion somewhere on the property, she forgot about everything else.

As she witnessed three killings happen right in front of her.

The hulking shadow with eyes that glowed red moved fast and low to the ground, taking the men down one by one, and not by shooting. A knife. A dagger—no, two daggers—slashed in a deadly dance, the hazy headlights streaming through the ruined wall of the building showing all of the blood that flew from sliced throats, opened veins, and amputated limbs.

One after another, the three men who had locked themselves in fell to the concrete, writhing, bleeding out, mortally wounded.

Syn was so lethal and fast, it was as if he were a machine, and when he was finished, he braced his feet and sank down into his thighs. With the light shining on the front of him, he was nothing but a black shadow to Jo, his Mohawk a raised stripe on his head that rotated as he scanned the area—

And that was when Jo realized there were no more gunshots out in the lot.

There were, however, the sounds of screeching tires and pounding footfalls.

Jo pushed herself off the wall. As her weight came fully into her boots, she was about to say Syn's name when a high-pitched whistle sounded out in a series of four short bursts. Immediately thereafter, there was a response from another direction, in a different rhythm.

And that was when the roar ripped through the groundskeeping shed.

Jo put her palms to her ears as her body shied away, not from conscious thought, but primordial, survival instinct.

Syn reared back as he released his battle cry, his arms extending out from his torso, his matched set of knives jutting from his brutally hard fists.

And then he put the daggers away. As they disappeared somewhere inside his jacket, Jo had a thought that he was going to come check on her.

He did not. Instead, he marched over to the first man he had cut up. Standing above his prey, he snarled something—

And bent down low.

Syn attacked the man with his . . . teeth. Or at least that was what it looked like as his head went down over and over again, pieces . . . pieces seeming to be torn away from . . . the face. And dear God, the victim was alive as he was torn apart, his legs kicking and his arms flailing, as juicy, gurgling, gagging sounds rose up from the hole in his throat.

Syn did not stop.

When he was finished with the first, he moved on to the next, picking that man up off the floor by the thigh and the neck, and slamming his spine on the top of Syn's leg. The crack was so loud, Jo jumped—

Syn slammed the now-corpse headfirst into the concrete, the sound of a skull shattering even worse than that of the lightning strike snap of the vertebrae.

"Stop . . . stop . . ." she whispered as she held a scream in.

But there was no stopping him.

Especially not as he moved on to the third, taking the slowly churning legs by the ankles and swinging the almost-dead man around in the air like a discus. Once, twice . . . and then Syn released his hold.

Against the spotlight of the high beams that penetrated the blast hole, through the still clearing smoke, the body spun like a Frisbee, blood leaving from its open wounds with a curious grace, floating up on the air.

Defying gravity for a brief moment.

Before crashing down along with everything else.

Including Jo's illusions about who she had been sleeping with.

CHAPTER FORTY-FIVE

With a screech of tires, Mr. F fled the fight, K-turning the car he'd stolen and punching the gas like his immortal life depended on it. The ten-year-old Ford Taurus was like a turtle on a skateboard, and as he careened down the side of the abandoned mall, he ran over something—someone—he didn't know.

"Shit, shit, shit," he repeated.

Keeping his foot on the gas, his eyes shot to the rearview. No one was behind him, but would that change? How had the Brotherhood known to be there?

More tires leaving rubber on the road as he slammed on the brakes and wrenched the wheel to go around by the front of the stores. Another car—low-slung and fast—came at him, and they almost crashed. Both of them instinctively made the right decision, however, swerving in opposite directions—and then he was clear and so was the other driver.

The descent down the hill was the fastest he imagined the POS sedan had gone since it had left its assembly line, and he glanced down at the *Fore-lesser* manual on the passenger seat. But like that would give him another two hundred horses under the hood? Or explain how things had gone down so disastrously? He had called the gathering of *lessers* through the mental connection the book had told him he had with his subordinates. He had intended to get the slayers together and organized. Find out how many of them there were. Figure out what the resources were.

And then give his command.

As he got to the bottom of the rise, he didn't know where he was going. Paranoia made him wonder if there was some kind of tracer on the car, but like a random Ford Taurus that he'd found at the side of the street downtown would have a GPS tracker on it? Tied to the Brothers? Impossible.

He went right just because he went right. And as he punched the accelerator and the anemic engine wheezed, a second car came toward him. As they passed, he looked up again into the rearview. That car took a left to ascend the hill.

More slayers to their "death," such as it was.

Not at all how this was supposed to go. But at least, the further away he got, the more his adrenaline eased up and allowed him to think with better clarity. He had been the second to arrive. And then the other trucks and sedans and two motorcycles had rolled up on the parking area in front of the groundskeeping building. Men had gotten out of the vehicles, dismounted the Honda crotch rockets, and come over to him with expectation on their faces.

No, not men. Not anymore.

They had been reborn into the undead. A servant class that bled stink and had limited free will. An army cobbled together to kill vampires, led by an evil entity who was fucking insane.

Tonight was supposed to have been all of them coming together, meeting for the first time in person in most cases, a ragtag congregation of has-beens, never-was's, and street-smart psychotics with anger issues. Mr. F, not a born leader, had tried to prepare some kind of speech beforehand, but what he'd come up with had been all platitudes, low on inspiration—and he had never gotten to it. Just as he had been about to address his soldiers, such as they were, a hail of bullets had fired up inside the building. Everybody had taken cover, and within moments after that—thirty seconds at the most—warning alarms had started screaming in his head, in his veins. And that was when the shadows had emerged from the tree line. Six of them. Seven of them.

The Black Dagger Brotherhood. And some of their fighters.

He had known exactly who they were.

More shooting at that point, not inside the groundskeeping building, but outside, in the parking lot, bullets ricocheting off of the quarter panels of cars and the hoods and bumpers of trucks. Mr. F had thrown himself flat on the ground, right behind the rear tires of this car he'd stolen. Shitting his pants, covering his head, he had panicked and shut down, his brain going on an ill-timed vacation.

So he had seen the explosion go off in slow motion. One of those flashy motorcycles had been parked by the right corner of the building, like its owner was precious about the bi-wheeled coffin dropper and worried some idiot would open a car door into its tailpipe or something. A stray bullet, one of dozens, found the gas tank. Or maybe it was more than one.

And it shouldn't have exploded. Mr. F had seen the *MythBusters* episode when he'd been in one of his rehabs. But clearly there was something special in what the Brotherhood was shooting.

BOOM!

The force of the combustion had recalibrated the verticality on all kinds of vampires and slayers alike, blowing men and males off their boots, bodies flying backward. Then came the shrapnel, falling to the ground from the sky, metal chunks and pieces of bike skipping across the asphalt in a clatter of applause as if the show of light and force had been approved of.

Mr. F had meant to stay. He'd intended to stay. He'd told himself he was going to stay.

But it turned out the mortal survival instinct was one thing that even the Omega's induction couldn't disappear. With things still dropping from the explosion, he had slithered into the sedan, cranked the key, and thrown it in reverse.

And so he was here. Out on the four-laner that carved a trail through all manner of retail stores and touristy holes-in-the-wall. Every car he passed he wondered whether it was one of his. And every time he looked at the road behind himself, he worried that something with a vampire at the wheel was closing in on him.

As far as his brain had informed him, there had been thirteen *lessers* left in the Society. But he had no idea how many had survived, and it would be a while before he could concentrate and do a recount.

The Omega was going to be pissed at this.

And Mr. F knew what the punishment was going to be.

"Damn it," he moaned.

◆   ◆   ◆

The white landscape—the barren, blinding wasteland of white—drifted away like fog dispersed by a cold wind. In its place . . . awareness. Sounds, smells, tastes . . . and then sight.

The first thing Syn saw when he was able to focus was the one thing he never wanted to see. As the black-ink blood of *lessers* dripped off his fangs and his fingers, off his chin and his clothes, as the still-alive, half-destroyed bodies of his victims moved slowly on the blood-covered concrete, as the smoke cleared and the skirmish quieted . . . he discovered that he had turned to Jo and was staring at her.

Revealing the realest part of him.

To her.

The horror on her face. The hands up to her cheeks. The slack mouth and pale skin.

Yes, she saw him. She saw all of him, including his *talhman*, and she saw everything he did.

Wiping his mouth on the back of the sleeve of his leather jacket, he whispered something. It didn't carry. He didn't want it to.

And then the Brotherhood came rushing in: familiar, heavy boots pounding over the concrete and stopping behind him, breathing that was heavy, scents that were intermingling with the stench, shadows that were long from those headlights shining in through the blast hole.

"Syn," someone said. "How you doin'?"

When somebody tried to walk by him, his arm snapped out and stopped them by grabbing a hard hold.

"Do not touch her," he growled. "She is mine."

Another voice. Different than the first. "Okay, my guy. We won't go near her. But listen, you're leaking, and this is not a secured site. We've got shit we have to deal with and you need some stitches."

Please, he thought at Jo. Even though he didn't know what he was begging for.

Bullshit, he knew exactly what he needed from her. He wanted her to forgive him for being his father. For revealing to her the fact that he was a terrifying killer. For showing her why he didn't care that everyone else knew, but what he wished she had never discovered.

Jo shook her head. Then she focused over his shoulder and her face changed.

"Oh, shit," one of the Brothers said.

"I've seen you before," Jo said hoarsely. "Coffee shop."

Syn looked over his shoulder. Rhage was standing a couple of feet away, and the Brother ran his palm down his face.

"Does she know what's going on?" Hollywood asked.

"No," Syn muttered. "She does not."

"Motherfucker."

"That about covers it."

Syn stepped off and tried to walk around, hands on his hips, head lowered, heart pounding. He didn't get far. His boot knocked into something . . . a torso that was bent backward, its limbs moving in slow motion, like the thing was a remote control robot whose batteries were running out.

Out of the corner of his eye, he was aware that everybody was staring at him, and he knew what the questions were. Too fucking bad.

The only ones that mattered were from Jo, and he had no good answers for her.

The arm of the slayer at his feet flopped over on its own accord, and he watched as the black-stained hands clawed uselessly at his boots.

With nothing to lose, and Jo having already seen the worst, he unsheathed one of his steel daggers, tossed it in the air, and caught the hilt with a smack of his palm. Vicious point down, he lifted the weapon over his shoulder as he dropped onto one knee to stab—

Rhage caught his wrist. "No. We wait for Butch."

CHAPTER FORTY-SIX

Right about the time Syn was trying to shoot his way out of that groundskeeping building, before the explosion, Butch was attempting to get out of the office building downtown. He punched the bar on an interior fire door, breaking the thing open on its hinges. As it swung wide, he burst out into yet another corridor—even though he didn't know what the fuck he was rushing for. He was still going to end up in that mail receiving area with no IT MacGyver flashy shit to get him out smoothly.

Then again, he didn't need to be smooth, right? Did he really care if the whole goddamn building lit up with alarms and the cops came with sirens blaring? He was going to be long gone, running back to the garage, getting the R8 and going 0–60 in 3.2 seconds to the conflict location.

Thank God V got the engine upgrade to the performance—

The smell of fresh air was not good news. As he rounded the final corner before the receiving bay, the scent of the night was a shocker and meant someone had already come in. Cops? Maybe the alarms were silent.

Skidding to a halt in front of the last door, he unholstered one of his guns and back-flatted it against the wall. There were no sounds of anyone moving around on the other side. Nobody talking. But he didn't want to be someone's target practice just because he was distracted and not reading the situation right.

He was quiet about his penetration this time, slipping through the last panel.

"What . . . the fuck?"

One of the bays was wide open, and parked right in front of it, ass in to the building, ready to go with the powerful engine already running . . . was V's R8.

Like Butch was Tony Stark and had summoned the fucking thing with a remote.

"Lassiter?" he said as he looked around the dreary mail room.

Whatever. No time, no time.

Butch covered the distance in three big strides, leaped out of the bay like a parachuter, and would have *Dukes of Hazzard*'d it into the driver's seat of the R8 except for: (1) the window wasn't down; (2) there was no way in hell he could fit himself through the aperture of the top half of the door; and (3) if he left so much as a smudge on the paint, the leather, the trim, the seat, the center console, whatever V did to Lassiter after the containment spell was going to look like a Sandals vacation in Cancún.

Five minutes later, he was out of the congested streets and tall buildings of downtown. Five minutes after that, he was in the sprawling retail-urbs, blowing through red lights and dusting the few cars on the road with him in the passing lane. If he'd met a cop, it would have gotten nasty, but he didn't.

When he made the turn to go up to the Adirondack Outlets Mall, even the Quattro couldn't keep the supercar on the pavement, the heavy back end of the car fishtailing. At the top of the rise, he shot forward to the stores—and nearly bought the farm in a front-end collision with a gray Ford Taurus.

The inside of the older sedan was dark so he couldn't see the driver, but there was no time to follow up on that shit, either.

He went around to the back, as instructed, and got a load of a scene out of a Schwarzenegger movie circa 1987. You want to talk about chaos? There were cars and trucks full of holes, slayers on the ground still moving, gunpowder—and in this case, gasoline, too—thick in the air. Oh, and a whole corner of the building was gone. Slamming on the brakes, he got out, and the stench of *lesser* was so intense, he fell back against V's precious car.

Qhuinn came jogging over. "We got some enemy down on the ground, all ready for you."

"How many?"

"Nine. Maybe ten."

Butch kept his groan to himself. "Any of us hurt?"

"We've got one with a leak—even if he refuses to admit to the shit. Manny's on the way."

"Who's injured?" Butch looked around. "And what the fuck happened to the building?"

"Bike blew up. Oopsie." Qhuinn calmly unholstered one of his guns and put three shots into the head of a slayer who'd reached for his pant leg. "I believe it's being classified as a Honda-plosion."

"I'm going to need Vishous to come in." Butch shook his head. "But I hate to have him so exposed."

"We'll move the bodies, then."

Rhage jogged over, called by the shooting. "Everything okay out here?"

"One of them was getting touchy-feely, but my body, my choice." Qhuinn tucked his gun back under his arm. "And now he doesn't have a frontal lobe or eyeballs so it's not going to be a problem."

"We need transport," Butch said. "You're exactly right. We'll move the slayers to a neutral location where I can do what I have to and V can be right on hand. This place is way too exposed."

Sure, V could throw up some *mhis*, but after that explosion, the scene was bound to be on 911's radar. The last thing anyone needed was a bunch of humans wondering why they couldn't see something that they knew damn well was there.

"And we've got one other problem," Rhage said.

As Butch's phone went off, he glanced at the screen. Then focused on the brother. "Manny's ETA is just six minutes from now. So if it's bleeding, we've got it covered."

"It's not bleeding. And I wish it was the kind of thing the docs could fix."

◆   ◆   ◆

It was as all the men came to stand in front of Jo that she realized the truth she had been after, the trailhead she had been determined to find, the answers she had sought ... was going to be worse than the not knowing.

Seven of them. All Syn's size. All wearing some version of leather on the top and the bottom. None of them spoke. They just stared at her, and their expressions were the same, no matter the features.

Sadness. As if they pitied her.

Because they were going to kill her? Or was it because of something even deeper than that. Death, after all, was a simple, if traumatic, concept. There was a truth in this lineup of huge bodies, however, one that she recognized as very complicated, even though she had yet to learn its dimensions.

Its repercussions.

She looked at Syn, who was standing with his back to her. Who was standing between her and the others.

"Who are you really," she said to his broad shoulders.

When he didn't answer, and none of the others did either, she stared at one of the bodies on the floor. The torso was bent at a right angle— in the wrong direction. The man's head was nearly touching his hips.

And even though his back was clearly broken, and the spinal cord must have been severed, and no part of him should have been moving outside of autonomic twitches in the toes or the hands? The legs were churning and the arms were scratching over the cement.

His head turned to her, and his unblinking eyes stared up.

With pure hatred.

As Jo gasped, more of the sickly sweet stench speared into her nostrils. And as her headache pounded, she put a hand to her temple.

The blood all over the should-have-been-dead man wasn't right. It wasn't red.

None of this was right.

"What are you!" she yelled.

When Syn didn't turn around, and none of the others replied, she jumped forward and punched his shoulders. But even though she put all her strength into it, the impact seemed to barely register on him.

"Tell me! Tell me what this is all about—"

Sharp footfalls came at her. "Easy there," a male voice said in a Boston accent.

Jo wheeled around and recognized who it was in the hazy, disjointed way of a dream. "You . . ." She groaned and weaved on her feet. "I know you . . ."

"Yeah. You do," he said with a strange kind of defeat.

"The blog . . ." Her headache was getting so much worse. "The school for girls. The restaurant that was abandoned downtown. The stories and the photographs, that video feed from the souvenir shop parking lot . . ."

The man with the accent didn't respond. None of them did.

"I was right," she mumbled. "I've been getting too close to the truth. And you . . . you've been taking my memories from me, haven't you. That's the headaches. That's the . . . confusion. The restlessness and the exhaustion. You are a secret that you don't want me to know."

Now Syn turned around.

His eyes were back to normal, but she couldn't forget the way they'd been, flashing with an unholy red light.

There was nothing in the real world that did that. There were also no corpses that were not corpses in spite of the fact that they had been hacked open and drained of blood. There was nothing that smelled like this, or fought like that, either.

"Give me my memories back," she said in a low voice. "Right now. You give me my *fucking* memories back. They were not yours to take, no matter how justified you think it is. They're *mine*."

The one with the Boston accent muttered, "Syn? You know her?"

"Oh, he knows me," she said without looking away from her lover. "Don't you. Or do you intend on taking those memories from me, too."

Someone cursed. Again, the Bostonian. "What the fuck are you thinking."

He was talking to Syn. Then again, so was she.

"I trusted you," she said bitterly. "I let you into . . . my home. I took you in when you were fucked-up. You *owe* me the truth."

"I'm sorry," he whispered.

All at once, floodgates opened in her mind, and like birds released from a cage, images and sounds and smells fluttered forth into flight, revealing themselves as they dodged and weaved in the airspace of her consciousness.

Jo staggered back, putting her hands to her eyes. When she would have fallen, a strong hand took her arm and kept her from landing in the pools of black blood: She remembered it all. The research she had done. The sites she had visited. The pieces she had written on her blog that had been taken down. Conversations with Bill, speculation, questions.

She dropped her palms and looked up at Syn, who was holding her up.

With a shaking hand, she reached to his mouth. And though she expected him to jerk back, step back, push her away, he did not fight her or try to protect himself.

His upper lip gave way under her fingertip.

"This isn't cosmetic," she mumbled. "Is it."

He didn't have to answer. None of them did.

She had started on the trail of the supernatural in Caldwell on a whim, only for the work to become a necessary distraction. But never in her wildest imagination nor in her jumpiest paranoia . . . had she ever imagined she would stand in the presence of exactly what she had been looking for.

"Say it," she demanded. "*Say it!*"

Syn closed his eyes. "Vampire."

CHAPTER FORTY-SEVEN

Balthazar left the battle site and re-formed in front of the Brotherhood mansion. There was *lesser* blood splashed across his leathers and dripping off one sleeve of his jacket. As he shook his arm, a black stain speckled the stone steps and he frowned at the glossy, stinky liquid.

Then he looked up at the great house's gray expanse with its diamond-pane windows and slate rooflines—and thought of the people who lived inside the hundred-year-old walls.

No, he thought. *Not here.*

There should never, ever be any trace of a *lesser* here.

Taking a bandana out of his ass pocket, he bent down and wiped off the old granite. Just as he was finishing the job, a set of headlights rounded the hill from the back side and he squinted into the glare. The box van was white and solid-walled, and as the panel in the middle opened and slid back, Zypher leaned out the front window.

"You good?" he asked.

Balthazar nodded. "Let's do this."

As he got inside, it was shoulder-to-shoulder room only. With Syphon behind the wheel and Zypher riding shotgun, it meant that Blaylock, John Matthew, and Tohr had only the one bench seat to fit on.

"I'll ride in the back," Balz said as he dematerialized into the cargo space and sat his butt on the carpet.

The side door was shut again and Syphon hit the gas. As they started down the mountain, Balz ran some quick math in his head. Blaylock had dislocated his shoulder the night before in the field and suffered a minor concussion. John Matthew's left leg had gotten knee-capped three nights ago, and still wasn't right—har, har—and Tohr'd recently been stabbed in the gut.

But they had to use everybody and none of them complained that they'd been called out of mandatory R&R—

The van came to a hard stop on the decline, Syphon stomping on the brake. As everybody lurched forward and caught themselves on whatever they could, guns were taken out.

"What is—"

"Do you see something—"

"Holy fuck—"

"Who has it," Syphon snapped. As everyone "Has what'd" him, he wrenched around and glared into the back seat. "The Jolly Rancher. Who's got the fucking Jolly Rancher?"

Cue the eye contact between everybody in the van.

"That fake watermelon smell triggers my gag reflex," Syphon bit out. "And I get carsick which is why I have to drive. So if the person who's sucking on that red square of vomit-inducing nasty doesn't spit it the fuck out now, I'm going to make sure I throw up in their lap."

Pause. Longer pause.

And then Zypher cursed, turned his head . . . and spit the candy right out—

Onto the window he'd just put up. Where it stuck like a Post-it Note.

As everyone in the van fell into a chorus of *Ewwwwwwws*, the bastard picked the thing off, put down the window, and flicked it out into the bushes.

"You happy, Penelope," he muttered as he reclosed the window. "Now, do you want to take a Tums and put a hot compress on your forehead, or can we get on with this?"

Syphon ten-and-two'd his hands and assumed the self-righteous composure of a deacon. "Not everyone has a stomach of steel."

"No, shit," Zypher said under his breath as the van started moving again.

In the back, Balz propped himself against the van's side-wall, tucked his arms in, and closed his eyes. A little catnap was just the ticket. As long as Zypher didn't decide to replace that Jolly Rancher with anything else that was artificially fruit flavored.

Lord help them all if he broke out the Starburst.

◆   ◆   ◆

As Syn uttered the word that had been bounding around Jo's brain, she expected to feel fear or be overcome with shock. Instead, a strange calmness suffused her tense body, easing all her muscles. The relief was eerie.

Then again, on some level, she had known all along, hadn't she.

"We don't know about you," she said to them. "So you hide in plain sight and prey on humans—"

Loud curses rang out in the empty building. And then one of them said, "Don't put your human bullshit on us. We're hunted and trying to survive. You are a threat to us, not the other way around."

Somebody else chimed in, "Those movies and books got us all wrong, sweetheart. So don't get judgy until you know the truth we live."

"Don't call me sweetheart," she muttered. Then she shook herself back into focus. "So what are they."

She pointed to the corpses on the ground, the ones with the black blood and the stink. The ones that moved though they should be dead.

"They are our hunters." The one with the Boston accent stepped forward. "And we just want to live our lives in peace. There's none of that biting people and turning them, no soulless defilers of virgins, no garlic or capes or bats or wooden stakes."

"You took my memories . . . I saw you here. Several nights ago. With a man with a goatee—"

"Male, with a goatee," he corrected. "We don't use the term 'man,' and yeah, you did. But listen, here is not the place for this kind of conversation."

"But there's not any place for this talk, is there." She looked at Syn. "You're going to take my memories again, aren't you. Or are you going to kill me here and now?"

Jo was amazed she could be so calm. Then again, when the paranormal became real, it was as if you'd entered a video game. The action was in front of you, but the implications didn't go further than two dimensions. After all, if vampires existed, was death even a thing?

"No," the Bostonian said. "We're not going to kill you."

She looked at the bent-back man on the concrete again and thought of the decapitated body she'd seen wrapped around the fire escape. And then the one that had been skinned alive in that alley.

"But you've killed humans before." She refocused on Syn. "Haven't you. So what makes me different? I've got a lot of memories to erase. It's got to be easier just to slit my throat, especially given how many times you've done that."

No one said a thing.

And her eyes didn't leave Syn.

"Is this what you apologized for?" she demanded.

"Yes," he replied in a gravel voice.

"So what happens next if you're not putting me in my grave?" As she spoke, she was aware she was asking about so much more than just the vampire revelation. "Tell me why I'm different."

Before anyone could answer, a vehicle pulled up outside, the sound of the tires crunching over the debris coming through the hole in the building.

"It's the doc," one of the men—males—said. "And Syn, you need to get treated. We've also got a van coming to pick up the trash."

"And what about me." She wanted Syn to be the one who answered her. "What are you going to do with me."

A vehicle door opened and closed with a *thunch* and then there were footsteps on the approach, a figure appearing in the explosion-created, ragged jambs of the building's newest entrance. The backlighting made it impossible to see his features, but his voice, dry and deep in tone, was crystal clear.

"You guys been redecorating again?" The man—male, whatever— stepped over the threshold. "Can't you do it with something other than C-4?"

When he made a shift in direction, the side of his face was illuminated—

And the world ground to a halt for Jo.

Dark hair. Dark brows. Deeply set eyes. Square jaw, high cheekbones—

"Manuel Manello," Jo heard herself say. "Dr. Manuel Manello, for- mer chief of surgery of St. Francis Medical Center. Missing and unac- counted for."

The man stopped dead. "Do I know you?"

Heart pounding, breath short, head spinning, Jo said roughly, "I'm your sister."

CHAPTER FORTY-EIGHT

A lot can happen in twenty-two minutes.

Right after the second explosion of the evening had gone off—said bomb involving three words as opposed to a gas tank and a bullet with water from the Scribe Virgin's fountain in it—Butch had looked at his watch for some reason. So yup, he was positive that it took exactly twenty-two minutes for Syn to get packed up into the mobile surgical unit with Manny, for the half-breed female, Jo Early, to be driven off by Phury, and for the box van to arrive.

"So where are we going with this load of trash?" Rhage asked as they went over to one of the downed slayers.

Butch took the head. Hollywood took the feet. And then they humped the leaking, smelly, still-moving bag of Omega juice over to the back of the van. While Balz and Syphon did the same. And so did the others.

Nine slayers. And the slowly moving bodies stacked nothing at all like orderly cordwood. To fit them in, they had to close the double doors in the rear and cram the last three in the back seat.

When the job was finally done, everyone needed a bath, and the sound of the limbs moving sluggishly against the inside walls of the van was enough to make the hairs on the back of the neck stand at attention.

Rhage shook his head. "I'll drive. But it's going to ruin my appetite."

Qhuinn came over. "Shotgun."

They all turned to Butch for a destination. Even Tohr.

Kicking his brain in its ass, he tried to think of a good place to go, and he didn't have a lot of time to make the decision. This battle site needed to get cleaned up by V ASAP, for one thing—given that explosion, it was a miracle the human police hadn't shown up already. But even more critically, although he didn't sense the presence of the Omega at the moment, that could change at any time.

He glanced at the van. It was going to take a lot of time to inhale nine *lessers* and he wasn't even sure he could do it all on a oner. V and he were going to need hours—and they had to be in an environment where they would be protected without Vishous putting any effort into sustaining a *mhis* shield. They needed somewhere . . . that already was protected.

Butch looked at Tohr. "The Tomb."

The brother recoiled sure as if he'd been slapped. "Are you fucked-up? We're not taking the enemy into our most sacred—"

"It's the only place that's safe enough. The Omega is getting weaker, and after I'm done with these? He's going to be just about done, only a shadow of him left. The *mhis* that's around the mountain? It's the kind of thing the evil couldn't get through when he was all-powerful. Now? The odds are only going to be worse for him. And V won't have to do anything but cleanse me, and that's going to be a really big fucking job in and of itself."

Tohr was in full head-shake mode. "No, I can't let you do that."

Butch stepped up to his brother and met those navy-blue eyes baldly. "It's the only way. You've got to trust me. You think I want them there anymore than you do? But sometimes the decision is between a bad choice and an even worse one. And Vishous and I exposed while we do what we have to do to end this war? Really, really, really worse-er."

In the silence that followed, the tension rose within the group, thick and fraught in the night air. And as an abrupt wind weaved through the ring of trees behind the busted-up groundskeeping building, Butch looked over his shoulder and braced himself.

But it was not the Omega. Not yet.

"We gotta go," he said in warning. "We need to leave here with the van and get to the mountain."

Tohr cursed. "Can I talk to Wrath first?"

Butch refocused on his brother. "On the way. You go with Rhage and Qhuinn in the van. I need to be kept apart from the slayers in case the Omega shows up. He'll come after me as a first priority, and if I die, you need to take those fuckers to the Tomb anyway and keep them there. You'll want the evil to be as run-down as possible when someone else does the final takedown on the fucker." He glanced at the other fighters. "For the rest of you, let's confiscate these cars and bikes. It'll give V less to toast. He has to come here first while we're driving to the mountain."

"If Wrath refuses access," Tohr started.

"Then tell him to call me. There is no other option."

Tohr caught Butch's arm. "If Wrath says no, you're going to find one."

✦　✦　✦

Sitting on the operating table in the mobile surgical unit, Syn let his boots dangle . . . and thought about the way Jo had sat on the countertop in that abandoned restaurant kitchen. It seemed like a lifetime ago since the pair of them had sought refuge from that police helicopter.

And now they were here. In two separate vehicles. Heading for the training center and God only knew what.

Up in front, behind the wheel, Manny didn't have much to say either as they continued down the highway. Then again, shock'll do that to a guy.

"How did you find her?" the human surgeon asked eventually.

The fact that the man might be Jo's brother changed a lot of things. In the vampire tradition, bonded males always came first with respect to their females—and there was no one around who didn't know Syn's status after the little show he'd put on tonight.

Well ... except for Jo that was.

Fuck.

But the next in line after a bonded male? The eldest male in the bloodline. Which, if what Jo alleged was true, meant that Manny deserved answers to questions no one but he had any right to ask.

Syn cleared his throat and felt obligated to keep all images of anything sexual out of his mind while he replayed the course of his relationship with Jo—which he knew damn well was over now.

God, this hurt, he thought.

"She's a reporter. She was looking into a murder downtown. There were *lessers* around, and I was worried that they'd recognize her for what she is—even though she is not aware she's a half-breed." He decided to edit out the part about her pointing her gun at him. Also the Mafia hit stuff. "There were the human police all over the place, too. She didn't want her presence to be known, so I made sure it wasn't. I've only ever protected her, I swear to you."

Manny twisted around in the driver's seat for a second. "She doesn't know about the change?"

"No. She'll find out tonight, though. Or at least she better. It's so close for her the now."

"Why didn't you tell someone?"

"V already knew about her." Syn did his best to keep any aggression out of his voice. "So she's been looked after."

"They should have brought her in."

There was a long pause. And then Manny said, "I know your reputation."

Rolling his eyes, Syn muttered, "Who doesn't. And she's living and breathing, isn't she. If I were going to kill her for sport, I would have already."

There was an even longer silence that followed that little piece of caring-is-sharing, and in the quiet, Syn went back into his past, thinking of the first female he'd gone after in the Old Country. It had been back when being a mercenary had been his only job, before Balz had gotten him in with the war camp and the Bloodletter and Xcor.

In another case of his reputation preceding him, Syn had been approached in a pub by a farmer whose fields were being encroached upon by a neighboring landowner. As the conflict escalated, the farmer's cows had been poisoned and his lake spoiled. He'd been looking to have the problem resolved.

Syn took the money. Did recon to ensure that the story as represented to him was true. Infiltrated what turned out to be a castle to get a feel of his victim's environs.

And then it was time to kill the male. His *talhman* had looked forward to the moment of blade to flesh, but Syn had waited for the spring festival to commence so there would be chaos and distraction and drunkenness inside those thick walls. Lurking within the castle and seeking the perfect moment to strike, he had followed the master of the estate back to his private rooms. Imagine Syn's surprise when he had attacked and discovered that under the garb of a male there was, in fact, a member of the fairer sex: With her hair shorn, and heavy sandalwood sachets to cover the scent of her, no one had guessed her truth.

When it came to slaughtering her, Syn hadn't cared about which sex she was.

And he hadn't spared her.

He had shed all the blood from her veins until the inlaid floor beneath her bedding platform had glistened with what had kept her alive. He had felt nothing.

No, that wasn't true. The usual rush, the thrill, the sadistic joy he experienced at causing pain, as well as the release from his own buildup of anger and aggression, had all been there.

They were always there.

In fact, that cycle of kindling, target finding, killing, and resulting relative peacefulness was why he had to murder on a regular basis.

His *talhman* was what made him a serial killer. Like an alcoholic needed a drink to deal with stress, he needed to bring death to complete his cycle, and he had not, and never did, regret a thing. But that was because he had rules. The efforts and time spent determining whether his marks were criminal had ensured he was not like his father.

And had also ensured that he got to kill people like his father, over and over again.

That was why the Lessening Society had never been enough for him. That was business.

What he did with his murder kit on his own time was personal, a return to the death he had wrought on the sire who had tortured him and his *mahmen*.

Syn was getting lax about the screening process though, wasn't he. When Gigante had told him to kill Jo, he hadn't looked into whether the target was an innocent or not. He'd been reeling and kill-starved, overdue and therefore prepared to murder a reporter, regardless of their virtue or lack thereof.

Which was very different from a mobster who sold drugs to kids and did fuck-all else.

"I don't want you around her," Manny said abruptly.

"So you've decided to believe her. About your kinship with her."

"Doesn't matter." The surgeon's dark eyes went to the rearview. "Sister or not, she doesn't need you in her life."

Syn looked down at the gauze banding around his thigh. Manny had insisted on packing that wound as well as his others.

"So you're just going to let me bleed out, huh," Syn said.

"No, I'm still going to treat you. I have professional ethics."

Syn lowered his head and closed his eyes. As images of Jo came to him, a relentless onslaught of memories, his instinct to protect her surged under his skin and raced along his veins. Under different circumstances, he might have suggested he and her brother fight it out.

What stopped him was . . . he couldn't disagree with the man's conclusion.

Jo was much better off without him.

CHAPTER FORTY-NINE

"Y ou stole from me again."

As Jo spoke, she stared out of the window of the truck she'd gotten into at the abandoned mall. The last thing she remembered, they were leaving the site of the fighting. Now, they were in a parking garage somewhere . . . God only knew where.

"It's for your safety."

She looked across the seat. The man—male—beside her was Syn's size, but with a long, flowing, multi-colored hair and the calm demeanor of someone who had done so many super-dangerous things that chauffeuring a woman to . . . well, wherever the hell they were . . . was waaaaaaaay down on his list of stressors.

"My safety?" She glanced at the bulk of his leather jacket. "Really. Like I'm not already at risk around you."

He killed the engine and stared over at her with yellow eyes that were beautiful—and so not human. "You will not be hurt here."

"I'm supposed to trust you? When I've lost—" She tapped the digital clock on the dash. "—seventeen minutes. Oh? You mean you didn't think I'd check the time? I knew you were going to do something with my memory, so I've been keeping track of these numbers as they change."

The male narrowed his eyes. "What you don't understand is that there are people who would torture you for the information about where to find us. And they can read your mind and know what you know in the blink of an eye. So yes, it's for your safety."

Jo looked back out the window. There wasn't much to see. Just concrete, asphalt, parking spaces, and no open-air anything.

As he got out of the truck, she followed suit. "Are we underground?"

"Yes." He indicated an unmarked metal door. "And we're heading over there."

Following him—because really, what was her other option?— she ended up in some kind of corridor, going by . . . what seemed to be classrooms. Meeting rooms. And then some medical facilities that looked every bit as state-of-the-art as any hospital she'd ever seen.

He stopped in front of an open door. "I think Doc Jane wants you in this exam room."

Jo crossed her arms over her chest. "I'm not consenting to any kind of medical procedures, FYI."

"Not even a blood test to prove that the man you think is your brother is actually related to you?" When she didn't reply to the rhetorical, the male nodded. "That's what I thought. Manny—Doctor Manello—is right behind us. I know you two didn't get a lot of time to talk at the scene. And then you can meet Jane and find out if you're his kin."

Before she could ask him anything further, he gave her what looked like a little bow and backed out of the room. After he closed the door, she expected to hear some kind of lock get turned. That didn't happen. And a few minutes later, when she tried the knob, she was able to open things just fine.

Leaning out, she looked left and right. The corridor continued beyond the room she was in, and she was surprised at the extent of the facilities. This was not anything cobbled together, and it sure as hell couldn't have been cheap to build or maintain—

Down to the left, the reinforced door she had come through opened and she stiffened. Syn limped in first, and right behind him was Manuel Manello. Both men—males, whatever—stopped dead as they saw her, the heavy panel they'd used shutting with a solid *thunch* behind them.

Jo stepped out, figuring she had every right to take up some space. Then she noticed the huge red spot that had grown on the white bandage around Syn's thigh.

"Are you okay?" she asked as they approached. Which was a stupid question.

"He'll be fine." Dr. Manello stepped between them. "It's nothing for you to worry about. I'm just going to stitch him up and then we'll talk, okay?"

"Yes. Please."

Standing next to the doctor, Syn was a silent, looming presence that kept his eyes lowered and his head down. But just before he went into the treatment room next door, he glanced sideways at her. And then he was out of view.

As she retreated back into her own exam room, she realized she expected him to say something. Maybe break away and come talk to her. Explain . . .

Well, what did she expect him to say, anyway?

Pacing, she made a circle around the examination table. Then she went over to the stainless steel sink and cabinet setup. Opening the cupboards, she checked out the orderly sterile supplies and equipment—

The voices in the room beside her were low at first. But then they got louder. And louder still, as an argument intensified.

Jo went over to the wall and put her ear to the Sheetrock. The doctor and Syn were going at it hard-core—and there were so many reasons to just stay out of whatever the fight was about.

Even though, come on, she could guess.

And because she had an idea what they were bumping heads over, she walked out, hung a left, and ripped open the door to the other treatment room.

"—she's damn well going to go through the transition!" Syn yelled.

"You don't know that!"

"You're human, you wouldn't know—"

"Fuck you—"

The two of them were on opposite sides of the examination table, leaning in, forehead to forehead, arms planted—at least until they noticed her at the same time. That shut them up quick, and the two bags of testosterone straightened, pulled their clothes back into place, and played at total composure.

Like they were choirboys who would never, ever raise their voices.

But she wasn't worried about audio decorum.

Swallowing through a tight throat, Jo had to clear her voice before she could speak. Twice.

"What am I going to go through?" she asked hoarsely.

◆   ◆   ◆

In addition to righteous styling, a fine sound system, and plenty of fucking torque, one of the benefits of the Audi R8 performance coupe was its all-wheel drive. There was also plenty of rubber available for grip on its racing tires, and good braking if you got a little overexcited with the pedal on the right.

Unfortunately, when it came to four-wheeling it through a forest, the car had one great rate limiter.

The thing had the ground clearance of wall-to-wall carpeting.

As a result, as Butch drove the supercar behind the box van, he was fifty-fifty on whether or not he was going to have to give up the ghost and hoof it the rest of the way.

The Tomb was located quite a distance from the Brotherhood mansion, its hidden location born courtesy of a thin fissure in the mountain's granite and quartz superstructure, one that happened to widen into a huge subterranean cave. From what Butch had been told, the site had been in use way before Darius had built the big house, the underground space serving as the *sanctum sanctorum* of the Brotherhood.

Not only were all the *lesser* jars that had ever been collected stored in its ante-hall, but deep in its stony belly, inductions and sacred rituals had been hosted for a couple of centuries, all with the Tomb's special brand of torch-lit, yup-this-some-vampire-shit-right-here.

The R8 gave up the effort about a quarter mile from the site. Or rather, Butch decided that he could run faster than he was going, and given V's little sojourn in Lassiter's bubble of happiness, it was better to stop rolling the dice on that front spoiler: He didn't want to have to explain how he'd peeled the thing like a grape. And besides, he'd made it a good mile farther than he'd thought he would.

Putting the engine in park, he killed the growl and got out, leaving the fob in the slot by the gearshift.

No reason to think the car was going to be five-fingered out here. Not only was the mountain a hard climb, that hard-core, permanent *mhis* obscured everything in the landscape, making it impossible for anyone or anything who was not supposed to be here . . . to be, well, here.

Which was why Wrath had voted yes for proposition privacy. The great Blind King hadn't liked the idea of bringing the enemy to the Tomb any better than Butch or anybody else did. But he'd seen the logic, and made the right choice.

Falling into a jog, Butch scanned the pine trees as he weaved around boulders that reminded him of adult teeth breaking through in a child's mouth. There wasn't much underbrush. The mountain, like all of the Adirondack range, was more rock than soil, the topography carved by the advance and retreat of glaciers that had briefly considered a zip code relocation during the Pleistocene epoch.

This, by the way, was all according to V. Who liked to use big fancy words like "Pleistocene epoch" for "Ice Age" (not the movie.)

And so, yes, now, some eleven thousand years later, Butch was here, running over a spongy mattress of fallen pine needles, hell-bent on welcoming the enemy into the most sacred place the Brotherhood had.

He must be crazy.

The plan had seemed very reasonable when he'd been out at that battle site, vulnerable to humans and the Omega alike. But like a lot of decisions made quickly under pressure, when you got to the consequences part of your bright idea, you ended up with a case of the re-think wobbles. Except it was too late now, and the facts remained the same. Unlike the *mhis* that V threw up from time to time downtown, the shit that blanketed this elevated acreage was impenetrable and permanent.

Sharpie vs. your generic magic marker.

Red wine as opposed to spilled seltzer.

A house, not a lean-to . . .

As he caught up to the box van, Butch wound down his Top 50 list of endurance metaphors. They weren't really making him feel much better about this, anyway. Besides, destination reached. No more hypotheticals.

Rhage got out from behind the wheel of the stink-mobile, bent over, and braced his hands on his thighs. Between slow, deep draws of fresh air, he said, "Fuck those Febreze commercials. There is *no* nose blind for that shit."

Qhuinn stumbled out of the other side of the van, retching. "And I thought switching out the Diaper Genie was bad."

While the pair of them tried to recover their olfactory equilibrium, the full complement of the Brotherhood arrived, the leather-clad males materializing in the darkness, stepping forward one by one. Everybody came. Z and Phury. Tohr, obviously. Murhder. John Matthew, the newest inductee.

V was the last to re-form and he walked over to Butch. "I cleaned the site."

"Good. Oh, quick question. Did you kill that immortal angel when he let you out of the bouncy cage?"

"No, the fucker's fast on his feet. But it's coming, true?"

Butch was about to switch gears and address the group, when one more person arrived.

Wrath walked forward into the clearing and everybody shut the fuck up. It was a shock to see him outside of the mansion—and a safety risk. Not even the *mhis* here seemed secure enough to protect the King. Plus there was no George to guide him.

Not that the male hadn't been here plenty of times over the last three centuries, dropping off the jars of the *lessers* he'd killed, adding to the collection of a thousand or more vessels that were already on those shelves in the ante-hall. Plus there had been the inductions of late. And disciplinary actions. But still.

"Will you stop looking at me like that," Wrath muttered. "Even blind, I can feel your stares. And I'm allowed to fucking be here."

Like anybody was going to argue with the guy?

Tohr stepped up. "Of course you are."

When Wrath glared over at the brother—although, to be fair, that was kind of a pat-on-a-toddler's-head placation—Butch felt the need to intercede.

"Will someone open the gates for us? We gotta move this load."

The refocus worked, Tohr leading Wrath over to the Tomb's hidden entrance. As the pair of them penetrated the fissure, Butch popped the latch on the back of the van and—

During shipping, the stacked and slacked *lessers* had settled right against the double doors, likely the result of the ascension up the mountain, and as a result, they spilled out like fish guts at Butch's feet. Jumping back from the tide of black stank and body parts, he cursed and kicked off some kind of anatomy from his shitkicker—looked like intestines?—before turning to V.

"We shoulda brought a goddamn shovel," he said to his roommate.

CHAPTER FIFTY

Among the truly strange things about destiny . . . fate . . . God's will . . . whatever you wanted to call it, was the location where major shifts in a person's life happened. Sometimes, the place made sense. Like a hospital, where someone was born or died. Or a stage, where you graduated from high school, from college, from grad school. Maybe an altar, where a person got married.

But other times?

As Jo glanced around at the break room, with its vending and soda machines, its self-serve buffet spread, its bowls of fruit and boxes of cereal, she knew she would never, ever forget anything about it. Not the round tables and the chairs. Not this cluster of sofas where she was sitting. Not the linoleum floor or the fluorescent lights in the ceiling or the TV that was up there in the corner, an episode of *The Simpsons* playing mutely.

It was one of the early Treehouse of Horror episodes.

At least that seemed apt considering what she had just learned about herself.

And well, she wouldn't forget anything here assuming they let her keep these memories.

She refocused on Syn. He had been silent most of the time. "So we're enemies if I don't turn."

Considering the fact that she had just learned she might not be human at all, she figured she'd start with some of the more basic realignments. Her brain simply wasn't able to cope with the bigger ones.

Dracula, who? Dracula, what?

"Answer me," she prompted him. When he didn't respond, she feared everything he was keeping to himself.

"He can't." Manny, as he'd asked to be called, shook his head. "The enemies question depends on a lot of things."

After she'd interrupted their argument, cooler heads had prevailed, and the three of them had ended up in this land of consumables. She was glad for the change in location. They were both big guys and those exam rooms were claustrophobic to begin with. Plus, hello, she couldn't remember when she'd eaten last.

Not that she was hungry.

"Like how successful my memory loss is over time, right?" When Manny shrugged, Jo burst up from her chair. "And because no one knows whether or not I'll go through it, I'm being treated as though I'm just a regular human. That's why my memories were taken from me."

"That's right. Half-breeds are wild cards. There's no telling what side of the divide you'll end up on."

"Except you're in this world. And you're still human."

"I'm a special case. And there have been a few others."

"But it's not a run-of-the-mill kind of deal, right?"

"No, it's not. Separate is better, generally speaking. For both species."

She looked over at Syn again. "And that's why you didn't tell me what you are. Because if I don't change, I can't know you."

After a moment, he nodded. And she couldn't decide if it was because he wanted to say more and couldn't because they weren't alone. Or if it was a case of him wiping his hands of the whole damn thing.

Walking over to the vending machine, Jo stared at the Hershey bars lined up in their corkscrewed chute. "So all the cravings I've been having. The restlessness. The fatigue. It's all part of this . . . change?"

"Yes." Manny turned around on his sofa so they could continue to make eye contact. Syn, on the other hand, stayed where he was, staring down at the floor in between his boots. "It's the prodromals. It's an indication that the hormones are waking up. But it's not a true predictor of what happens next. Sometimes they just regress back into dormancy."

"Is that why you're not a . . ." Sooner or later, considering all things, she was going to have to get that V-word out of her mouth. "Is that why you didn't change?"

"I've never experienced what you're going through. But again, everyone like us is different."

Jo thought about that thick file in her father's desk. It seemed bizarre that for all the sheets of paper in there, the real truth had remained hidden. The important truth.

God . . . she couldn't seem to make her head work. Everything was a mess under her skull, half-formed questions about her birth mother and father, her health, her future, like paintballs flying around and staining everything into a mess.

But there was one thing that superseded all of the rest.

Jo stared at Syn. And then she heard herself say, "I want a minute alone."

Manny cleared his throat. "Syn, will you give us a—"

"Not with you." She went back and sat down where she'd been. "With him."

◆   ◆   ◆

Syn expected the dismissal to open the door to another argument with the surgeon. Hell, he'd just learned firsthand exactly how good Manny was at the high-volume, point-counterpoint shit. Turned out the guy was a hot-blooded sonofabitch, and under different circumstances, a male might have respected that.

But not tonight.

And never when it came to Jo.

There was some conversation at that point, and then Manny was peeling off from the sitting area and striding for the break room's exit.

Before he stepped out, he said over his shoulder, "Come find me if he passes out from blood loss. I've still got to stitch him up."

Then they were alone. Because it was hard to meet Jo in the eye, Syn watched the door ease shut as if its repositioning against the jamb held the secrets to the universe. Or maybe it was more that he was hoping the slab of wood could coach him on what to say.

Only one thing was coming to him at the moment.

"I'm sorry," Syn murmured into the silence.

"You keep saying that."

"It's so apt in this situation." He lifted his eyes to hers. "I'm also not good with . . . a lot of things."

Jo was sitting across from him, but he felt as though they were separated by the ocean. She looked exhausted and jumpy at the same time, her heel bouncing on the floor, one of her hands fiddling with the sleeve of her coat. Her red hair was tangled, part of the length tucked inside her lapels, and her face was pale, way too pale.

Her eyes were what killed him, though. They were wide and white-rimmed, frightened as if she were being stalked by a madman with a knife—and though he had not brought her genetic destiny unto her, he sure as hell had delivered a number of other bad news packages.

And she didn't know the half of it.

"I'm scared," she whispered.

Syn jacked forward, and had to stop himself from taking the movement even further. "It's going to be okay."

"Is it? I'm not so sure . . . I never knew who my birth mother or father was, and I thought that was bad." She laughed in a short, tense rush. "Turns out not knowing what species I am is so much worse. I almost can't comprehend . . . anything."

"You're the same person you've always been."

"No, I'm not." She put out her hands and turned them over. "Because I didn't know what I was in the first place."

"Nothing has to change."

"Then why is it called 'the change.'"

Shit. He completely sucked at this.

Abruptly, Jo tucked her hands under her legs, as if she couldn't bear looking at them. "Is this why the urgent care center called me and told me they couldn't read my blood sample?"

"Did you see a doctor?"

"Yes. I already told you. And their office called and said there was a lab error and I needed to come for another try at it. But my blood wasn't contaminated at the lab, was it."

"No. The readings would be off compared to humans."

"I wish I knew whether the change was actually coming."

"I think it is." Syn tapped his nose. "I can smell it. Others of my kind can as well."

"And that's how the other one, the Boston guy, recognized me?"

"Yes."

Her eyes locked on his. "Do you think I've been hunting for vampires because I am one?"

"I think you've been looking for yourself."

"How many memories have you taken from me?"

"None."

Jo was quiet for a time, and Syn found himself getting to his feet and moving over to her side of the divide, her side of the coffee table . . . her side of the conflict. Even though, when it came to her transition, there really wasn't a conflict to be had. Her body was her future, its internal mechanisms of oxygen exchange and heart rate, hormones and DNA, a mystery that was going to solve the mystery. And no one and no test and nothing was going to force the outcome.

But he was with her, no matter what.

"Before Manny left just now ..." She cleared her throat. "He said I was going to have to take a ..."

When she didn't go any further, he finished things for her. "Take a vein. I'm sorry, I know it must repulse you. But if it happens, you need to have the blood of an opposite member of the species or you will die—"

"I want it to be yours." As Jo's eyes glowed with unshed tears, she wrapped her arms around herself. "No one else's."

Syn shook his head as he tried to get over his shock. How could she ever pick him? "Jo ... there are so many better choices."

"Then I'm not doing it. It's you or no one."

"I don't think you understand what's going to happen. Your body is going to make up your mind, not the other way around. Bloodlust is nothing to negotiate with."

"You're the only person in this world I know. I don't want some stranger ..." She squeezed her eyes shut. "This is like a nightmare. I literally can't get my head around any part of this. And you think I'm going to choose a stranger?"

"It doesn't have to be sexual." Syn's molars ground together as the bonded male in him started to scream. "The feeding, that is."

"How will I know? When I have to ..."

"You will know."

"And you did this? I mean, it happened to you?"

Syn pictured the female from the Old Country. "Yes. And there was nothing sexual in that first feeding for me."

"How long ago was it?"

"Three hundred years. Give or take." As her eyes bulged, he nodded. "Our life expectancies are different."

"Will mine change?" When he nodded, she chewed on her bottom lip. "Is the transition dangerous?"

"I'm not going to lie to you."

"So that's a yes."

Syn slowly nodded, fear gripping his chest at the idea he might lose her. Even though she never really had been his.

"Isn't there a blood test or . . . something . . . that can tell me precisely when it will hit?"

"No." He wanted to reach out. Hold her. Ease her in any way he could. "You just have to wait. And again, because you're part human, it could be a while."

"Or it could never happen, right?" When he nodded again, Jo looked around the break room. "Tell me they don't expect me to just sit around and wait here, like I'm some kind of prisoner? I have a job . . . a life . . . to get back to. Especially if this never happens."

"They won't keep you here against your will. They can't."

"You sure about that?"

"Yes." Because he was damn well going to make it so. "I'm sure."

Jo seemed to relax at that, her shoulders easing some.

Except then she pegged him with a level stare. "So are you saying you won't do it? That you won't . . . give me your vein if I need it?"

CHAPTER FIFTY-ONE

Fuck the shovel, Butch thought. What they really needed was a wheelbarrow.

As he dragged the first of the slayers into the cave by the ankles, he was aware that he had cherry-picked his payload. Unlike a lot of the other undead, this one was fully intact, with the arms and legs and the head still attached to the torso. Most of its sieve-like comrades did not pass this basic inventory test, and under different circumstances, he would have felt bad for leaving the lesser-than *lessers* for his brothers.

Except he knew he was going to go back for more. And then there was what was ahead of him.

The inside of the smaller cave behind the fissure was a black hole, but there was an orienting glow around the corner so he had enough to go on when it came to light. As he rounded the turn, his undead followed along with him, that head bumping over the rocky, uneven ground.

Like Butch gave a shit about the back of that skull.

When he came up to Tohr and Wrath, they had just opened the

way into the Tomb, having slid back the rock wall and gone forward to the first set of thick gating with mesh that prevented access to anyone who wasn't supposed to be there.

As the two turned to him, torches flared to life in the corridor beyond, willed to flame by Tohr. Or maybe it was Wrath, even though the King didn't need illumination.

"I wish we didn't have to do this," Butch muttered as he dropped the ankles, the heels of the slayer banging into the packed dirt. "But the good news is, once these fuckers are consumed? I think we only have four left."

"Four?" Wrath frowned. "Four slayers in the Lessening Society, and that's it?"

"There were thirteen on-site or close to it when I arrived. I could sense them. One got away on the bike that was still operational. Another was in a car that I almost had a head-on collision with. And two turned back before they got there. That's four left. All the others we've got in that van out there." Butch looked down at the still-animated remains at his feet. "Plus this ball of fire right here."

"But how do you know that's all of them," the King asked.

"Tonight was a meeting called by the *Fore-lesser*. It's the only explanation for why so many of them were in a place outside of the field downtown. The only other congregations of that size have been inductions, but there was no evidence that anyone had been turned tonight—and more to the point, the Omega never uses the same site twice for that shit. He'd already used that groundskeeping building. No, it was a meeting, convened by the *Fore-lesser*. A gathering of the troops and resources which we found by luck thanks to Syn and that woman—so the count is the count. Thirteen."

"But the Omega could make more. He could be holding an induction as we speak."

As the other brothers came into the cave with more chum, Butch glanced down again at his little buddy with the bleeding problem. "I'm not sure he can anymore. He's got to have enough energy inside of himself to propagate, and he was looking a pale shade of half-dead when I saw him the other night. I don't think there's any strength left for that."

"Four slayers." Wrath shook his head. "I can't fucking fathom it. Did anyone get a bead on the *Fore-lesser?*"

"Not that I'm aware of, and he isn't among the fallen." Butch rotated his sore arm. "I'd recognize him from when I . . ."

As he trailed off, he leaned around the King. And promptly lost his voice to shock.

"What is it?" Tohr asked.

"Cat got your tongue, cop?" Wrath said.

On a sudden surge of panic, Butch pushed Tohr back and jumped in past the gating. Behind him, Tohr said to the group sharply, "Weapons out."

The chorus of shifting metal on metal ushered Butch down the hall.

But he didn't have to go far to be overcome by an unheard-of act of vandalism, the kind of thing that was so shocking, it made him doubt the information his eyes were feeding him.

All of the jars that had been set upon all of the floor-to-ceiling shelves in the ante-hall, well over a thousand, had been thrown to the stone floor of the Tomb's entry corridor and shattered. Every single one.

Butch stopped as his shitkickers crunched over the first of the shards . . . that soon grew into a mountain.

"What is it—"

As Tohr abruptly stopped talking, Butch dropped down on his haunches and picked up a piece of enameled pottery. It looked old, but some of what had been broken was quite new, the sort of vases you could buy at Target.

"What the fuck?" someone else said as they got a look at the mess.

Butch stared up at the shelves. There was not one single jar left.

For generations of fighting, the Brotherhood had collected these vessels from the *lessers* they had slain, taking the hearts that were stained with evil as trophies of triumph. Whether it was a case of lifting the ID off the body before it was stabbed back to the Omega or actively torturing the enemy for information on where they stayed, claiming the jars had always been part of the victory ritual.

When Butch had joined the war, he had done it himself.

"Who the fuck got in here?" another brother said. "And why did they break all of this shit?"

Butch eyed the mound of shards and shrapnel that swelled to a point in the center of the corridor. As the torches on the walls threw strobing illumination on the jagged pile, he couldn't imagine who could have found—

"Oh, shit!" he barked.

As everyone else fell silent behind him, he wasn't thinking straight as he plunged into the pottery and porcelain debris, shifting through the pieces with hands that were cut by sharp edges, digging . . . clawing . . . praying.

"No, no, no . . ." He heard someone saying that word over and over again, and became dimly aware that it was him. "No . . . *no* . . ."

As people started to talk behind him, he ignored them.

Butch went all the way down to the stone floor. All the way down.

Then he gave up in utter defeat, twisting around to his brothers as he let himself fall back on his ass in the clearing he had made with hands that now bled red.

For a moment, all he could do was stare up at the group of males who had been enemies to him first, and then friends . . . only to culminate in blooded brothers. He knew their faces as well as he knew his own, and he loved each and every one of them as much as he could love another male.

And it was because of that love that he was suddenly completely and utterly terrified.

Tohr looked over and held his hands up in confusion, all WTF. "Cop, what's going on here?"

"The hearts are gone," he choked out. "The Omega . . . somehow, he got in here and he took the hearts from the jars."

The response was immediate, voices exploding and echoing around as the brothers—and Wrath—went on an immediate offense with their guns and daggers, like they were about to go hunt down the enemy deeper into the subterranean lair.

"He's not here!" Butch yelled over the din. When they quieted down, he likewise lowered his voice. "The Omega's gone. He took what he needed . . . and he's gone."

V spoke up. "That's impossible. There's no way he could have found this place."

Butch reached out and picked up one of the shards. It was a pale blue circular piece, a base, he guessed—and when he turned it over, it read "Made in China."

Closing his eyes, he rubbed the smooth, flat surface between the pads of his thumb and forefinger. Then he reopened his lids. "No, it was him. I can feel him on this."

"The house," Wrath growled. "The females. The young—"

"No," Butch interjected. "He's not on the property. I don't sense him anywhere here on the mountain and the *mhis* wouldn't affect my read on him. He's not here."

"But he was," the King said.

"Yes." Butch tossed the shard away and got to his feet. As he brushed his bleeding palms on the seat of his leathers, he shook his head. "And we've got an even bigger problem than him knowing where we live."

"What the fuck could that possibly be," somebody muttered.

Butch turned his back on the brothers and stared at the debris. "He's taken the hearts to fortify himself. To reenergize and restrengthen his power. He's just consumed the essence of himself that was in each and every cardiac muscle in those fucking jars."

"So we're back to square one," Tohr said bitterly.

"Or worse," Butch warned.

CHAPTER FIFTY-TWO

Just hold this up for me—yup, right like that." As the doctor crooked Jo's elbow, the female smiled. "I told you I was good with a needle, right?"

"I don't feel a thing." Jo shook her head. "I mean, didn't."

Doc Jane—as she'd introduced herself—rolled herself back on her stool, and tucked the tube she'd filled into the square pocket of her lab coat. Her dark green eyes were full of compassion, and she moved them back and forth between Jo, who was up on the exam table, and Manny, who was in a chair by the door to the treatment room.

"So, thanks to our Sarah," the doctor said, "who is a genius researcher and a bit of a genetics wonk, we now have a blood test we can use to determine family relationships." She smiled at Manny. "As opposed to the old-school ancestor regression, which was very dangerous. As I explained, we're going to compare both of your samples and see what you have in common. We also have a database we've been adding to within the species as a whole. Sarah's done an amazing job with this project, and it's really going to help us when it comes to you two. Do you have any questions for me?"

Manny shook his head. "I don't. Jo?"

Jo had plenty of questions. But not about the test. "I'm good. Thank you."

The doctor got to her feet. Squeezed Jo's shoulder. And left.

As the door eased shut, Jo stared at the man who might be her brother, reading the features of his face, trying to see what they shared with her own. When his eyes swung to hers, she flushed and glanced down.

"I'm sorry," she said. "I don't mean to keep looking at you. I've just never been with anyone who I'm related to—or might be related to."

Manny stretched out his legs and leaned back in his stiff little chair. "That's understandable."

Jo blinked quick and tried to remember where he had left off when the doctor had come in. It had been a shock—and a relief—to find out her birth mother had not in fact died. And there was so much else to learn.

"So you were telling me about you—our . . . father?" she prompted.

"Yeah, sorry." He lowered his forearm and pushed at the cotton ball that had been taped into the crook of his elbow. "Like I said, his name was Robert Bluff. He was a surgeon, and my mom met him at Columbia Presbyterian when she was an ICU nurse. He died in nineteen eighty-three in a car accident. Buried in Pine Grove Cemetery. I can take you to his grave sometime if you like."

"I would. Please."

"They were never married or anything. And she never really talked much about him. Somewhere in my stuff back at the house I've got some newspaper clippings on him and I'll show them to you. And I also have one photograph. But that's it, I'm afraid."

"And she—our mother—is definitely alive, though?"

"Yes." Manny cleared his throat. "She lives in Florida. I bought her a house down there a couple of years ago. She's retired now."

"Do you think . . . would she . . ." Jo shook her head again and tried to ignore the pain in her chest. "I mean, obviously we need to wait for the blood tests to see if—"

"Of course I'll introduce you." He shifted to the side and took a phone out of the white coat he was wearing. "Here, let me show you a picture. You must be wondering what she looks like."

As he scrolled through his cell, Jo was aware of her heart pounding. And when he held out the Samsung, her hands shook as she took the thing.

The image on the screen was black-and-white, and the young woman with the thick, dark hair seemed haunted as she stared at the camera.

"I thought you'd like to see an early picture first. That's actually when she was pregnant with me. Here, let me show you a more recent one."

Jo gave the phone back, and couldn't help but hope there was another snapshot, a couple of years more recent, of the woman . . . pregnant with Jo.

"How old are you?" she asked. When he told her, she was shocked. "So you're much older than me. God, you look terrific."

"Thanks. And here's a more recent one of mom."

Jo braced herself as she took what he put out once again. This time, the photograph was in color, and the years showed on that once unlined face. Not that the woman wasn't attractive—and she still had the thick brown hair. But the eyes remained shadowed and there was still that tension around the mouth and the brow.

"What's her name?"

"Shelley. Shelley Manello."

When Jo returned the phone to him, he stared at the picture, something in his expression shifting.

"I don't have to meet her," Jo said through a tight throat. "I don't want to cause any problems."

"No. I would never keep the two of you apart."

"So what's wrong?" Jo closed her eyes and shook her head again. "You don't have to answer that."

"Hey, siblings, right?" His dark brows lowered even further. "And I'm just trying to remember."

"What?"

"When she was pregnant with you." Manny looked up sharply. "I am *not* doubting anything you said. I just . . . going by how old you are, I'd have been out of the house and in college, but you'd think I'd re-call. Or that later, she would have told me about it."

Jo fixated on the back of the phone as he focused on the front. In the silence, unease trickled down the back of her neck, like ice-cold water dripping from some kind of height.

What if Bill had been wrong with his research?

Her dread that that might be the case told her how much she wanted to be Manny's sister. It was funny how this stranger had made her feel so grounded. Especially given that Syn had left the room.

"But you know," Manny said, "things were tight for Mom and I back then. From day one, she'd been bound and determined that I was going to go to medical school and I was going to become a surgeon and I was going to be somebody. She was a nurse, and she was always taking extra shifts to afford my education. My main memory of her from my child-hood was of how tired she always was. If she happened to have got-ten pregnant again when I was away at school? I mean . . . there was no way she could afford to keep it given my costs." He winced. "You, rather. Keep you. Sorry. I feel like I'm—"

"Don't ever apologize. I'm the disrupter, not you. Besides . . . maybe she didn't want to be pregnant with me." As his eyes lifted to hers, Jo pictured the image of that haunted face. "Maybe it wasn't that it was an unintended pregnancy. Maybe it was the result of . . ."

She couldn't say it.

But given the way Manny squeezed his eyes shut, she didn't have to.

"We could be half-siblings," she suggested sadly. "Maybe Robert Bluff was not my father. Maybe . . . it was someone else."

Manny rubbed his face.

"It would explain why she never wanted to tell you about me," Jo said hoarsely.

Jo unhinged her arm lock and removed the cotton ball and the tape. Beneath the white puff, there was just the smallest of marks, a red dot that was already healing in her skin.

The idea that she had been worse than a mistake . . . that she might have been from some kind of sexual violence? That she could well have been something her mother had tried to abort and failed?

As tears came to Jo's eyes, she looked around for something to wipe them away with.

Manny was the one who delivered the Kleenex to her, reaching to the counter and then extending the tissue box across the space that separated them.

And then he was getting up, and coming over. Hopping onto the exam table with her, he put a strong arm around her shoulders and pulled her in close.

"I am so sorry . . ." she said as she started to sob over the suffering of a woman she had never met.

✦   ✦   ✦

On the other side of the exam room's door, Syn sat on the concrete floor of the training center's corridor. After Manny had properly stitched him up, he had stepped out, ostensibly to give the siblings privacy. In reality, he had needed time to think.

And then he'd heard every word Jo said. Every single one.

As she spoke about the circumstances of her birth—or what she feared might have happened—he knew what the answer to her question about feeding had to be.

Getting to his feet, he turned and faced the door of the treatment room. With a shaking hand, he laid his palm upon the closed panel, as if he could reach inside through the chains of molecules between them, the space that separated them, the distance between his heart and hers ... and bring her something other than grief and chaos and misery.

Manny was the correct one to comfort her. Her blooded brother was a good man, a kind man ... a strong man. She was safe with him. He not only could look after her; he should.

Still, it was a while before Syn could force himself to turn away. And when he finally did, he had to make his body ambulate down the corridor.

Every part of him wanted to stay with Jo. Make sure she was okay. Attend to her every need, bringing her the choicest food and cleanest drink, securing her a warm and dry shelter, along with clothes that were of fabrics and colors of her preference. He wanted to sleep with her up against his body, skin to skin, a dagger in his right hand, a gun under his pillow, a length of chain beneath the bed, to ensure her protection against anything and everybody that would hurt her.

He wanted to service all her bloodlust.

And help her through her transition.

And then ... after a decade, or whatever it was ... attend to her in her needing—

Like a needle derailed on an LP, there was a screeching in his head as the culmination of his fantasy was what decimated the very core of his desperate delusions.

There would be no servicing her in her time of fertility. He couldn't ejaculate.

In the face of that reality, the rest of the building blocks of their hypothetical life together fell away, leaving nothing but devastation and desolation in the center of his chest.

But there was one way he could take care of her.

If the definition of love was putting the object of your affection before yourself, then there was one sacrifice that he certainly could make on her behalf. No matter what it cost him.

The training center was connected to the Brotherhood's big house by a subterranean tunnel hundreds of yards long, the concrete turnpike for pedestrians linking the Pit at one end, where Butch and V and their *shellans* stayed, and the hidden escape route off the mountain at the other. Syn strode through its confines with purpose, hands dug into the pockets of his leather jacket, boots booming over the bald floor. Manny had done a bang-up job with his needle and thread routine—not that the various slices on Syn's thigh and across his abdomen had mattered much to him—and by nightfall, the damage would be healed. As much as he hated to feed, he had taken one of the Chosen's veins a week ago, so he was at full strength.

Thank God. He couldn't have stood the idea of drawing the blood of another female now, no matter how professional and compassionate those sacred Chosen were. It might have been all but a medical procedure to them, but he didn't want to get that close to anyone but Jo.

As he resumed considering her future, his thoughts became so deep that the next time he noticed anything around him, he was stepping out from under the grand staircase in the mansion's foyer, his destination reached.

Things were fairly quiet, even though everyone was out of the field following the skirmish at the outlet mall. The Brothers had taken the *lessers* to the Tomb, wherever that was, but the rest of the Bastards and the other fighters were home—and you'd think there would be the normal commotion and conversation in various rooms. Nope. Things were somber as people played a little pool but mostly kept to themselves, and this made sense. There was a lot going on, and a lot at stake.

Trying to keep out of sight, Syn stayed behind the curve of the stairwell's base and got out his phone.

There was only one person he wanted to talk to.

Well, actually there were two, but he was starting here.

Composing a text, he hesitated before sending the missive. Except he could see no other way out of his situation. After he hit send, he crossed his arms and leaned back on the gold-leafed balustrade.

A moment later, the flap door the staff used to access the pantry and kitchen swung open, releasing a chuckle of low laughter as someone muttered, "—yeah, well, sixty percent of the time, it works every time."

"Ron Burgundy is a God," somebody else said.

Balthazar stepped through and made sure the door closed. "Hey."

Syn nodded and looked at his boots, noting that there was *lesser* blood on them. Then again, there was *lesser* blood down the front of his shirt. On the sleeves of his leather jacket. On his hands and under his nails.

"I should have taken a shower first," he heard himself say.

"That shit doesn't bother me."

"Not before seeing you." Before being with Jo, goddamn it.

"You okay, cousin?"

Syn focused on the floor in the center of the foyer, on the mosaic depiction of an apple tree in full bloom. When he tried to speak, he just ended up rubbing his nose. His brow. His jaw.

"Tell me," Balthazar said, "that you didn't kill her."

"Kill who?" When his cousin gave him a level look, Syn cursed. "Are you fucking kidding me. She's with Manny right now."

"All right. Good." Balthazar glanced around. "So do I need a shovel for another reason?"

Syn drew his palm down his face. "No."

In the silence that followed, his eyes surfed over the other luxurious details of the mansion's formal receiving area. Considering he had spent most of his life sleeping inside caves and tree trunks in the forests of the Old Country, he still could not fathom how he'd ended up in this royal castle of marble and malachite columns, and gold-leafed mirrors and sconces, and crystal chandeliers. It made him feel like an interloper.

Then again, he had often felt other-than, even among people he knew well.

"I love her," he blurted roughly.

There was a pause. As if Balthazar couldn't understand what had been spoken to him. "Jo? What are you—wait—"

"And for that reason, I am going to ask you to ... to service her during her transition. You're the only person I can trust with the female I love."

As much as she wanted to use Syn himself, he couldn't let that happen, especially not after he'd heard her talking about her conception. His violent nature was too close to that which she feared was true about her sire's—and though she did not know this parallel, he most certainly did. He had never done to a female what her father might well have done to her *mahmen*, but as if killing females—even if they deserved it—was much better? He had taken lives in a perversion of justice, as a vigilante who accepted money he did not need nor use for his deeds— and oddly, it wasn't until now that he felt the burdens of his crimes.

After everything he had done, Jo would not accept him if she knew his truths, and he could not bear to tell her them.

Therefore, he had to act as if she had full knowledge of him.

And get someone else for her.

It was only the decent thing to do for the one he loved.

CHAPTER FIFTY-THREE

Guess Syn wasn't coming back, Jo thought as she put her phone away and paced around the break room. She had returned to this caloric enclave about an hour ago, after she and Manny had talked for a long time about their childhoods. Their households growing up. What they had studied in school. And on the subject of higher education, he had made a point to tell her that their mother would be proud of her for having gone to Williams and been accepted into that Yale program. Those comments, coming from him, had made Jo tear up all over again—though she had hid the reaction as best she could. No more Kleenex for her. At least not in front of him.

Not in front of anybody.

They had also spoken a lot about what it meant to be a vampire. What the war with the Lessening Society was. What the Brotherhood and the Band of Bastards were. How the religion worked and the way the civilians and the aristocrats lived.

Also the importance of the species being separate and staying separate from humans.

That reality was what stuck with her the most, although everything he had shared with her had seemed important. If she did go through the change, she was going to have a lot to adjust to, and she wanted to get a head start on all of it, if she could.

Refocusing, she went back over to the vending machine. There was no need to put any coins or bills in. It was a dispenser only, not about any kind of revenue stream—and the free food, in addition to the state-of-the-art nature of this facility, made her wonder where all the money came from. The answer to that was way down the list of her priorities, though. And hey, like she was about to argue with chocolate on the gimme?

Pressing one of the buttons, she watched the corkscrew spin . . . and then a Hershey bar dropped down with a clunk. Groaning, she bent over, pushed open the flap, and retrieved the candy bar. The wrapper came off easily and she tossed that in the trash. Then she took a bite and kept pacing.

As she chewed and swallowed, she thought about Manny. The female doctor who had taken the sample. Those fighters at that site . . .

. . . and Syn.

More than anything, she thought about Syn. Especially about the way he had killed those things back at the outlet mall. Thanks to Manny, she now understood why he'd been so vicious about it all. He had been protecting her and avenging his own species against an enemy that had murdered innocents for centuries.

It certainly put the violence in perspective. And made it much easier to accept.

Then again, when she had asked if he would help her during her transition, she had voted with her feet already, hadn't she. But Syn had always made her safe. Always.

As she came up to the armchairs, she sat down with a total lack of grace, letting her butt land where it did. Looking up by the TV, she checked the time on a wall clock and frowned. It was past three thirty a.m. Five and a half hours had gone by? How was that even possible?

Then again, it also felt like five years since she had ridden here with that yellow-eyed man.

Male, rather—

The door swung open.

First, she merely looked up. But then, as she saw the hyper-composed faces of Manny and Doc Jane, she slowly rose to her feet. She didn't know either of them well enough to extrapolate much, and she wasn't sure whether that was bad or good.

"So what were the results?" she asked.

The female doctor—Jane—smiled, but it was in a professional way. "Why don't you sit back down?"

"I'm going to die, right?" It was the only thing she could think of that was worse than finding out she wasn't related to Manny. "I'm sick or I'm—"

"You're my sister," Manny said.

Jo sagged with relief and let her body take the advice of the doctor. As she landed back in the chair, she focused on her brother's—her brother's!—his face. "Is this bad, though?"

Stupid question. Really just was. The situation was complicated, and not in a fricking Facebook way.

"No, no." Manny came forward and sat down next to her. "Not at all. I'm thrilled."

"Then why don't you look like it."

Jane came over and sat on the sofa. "Let me explain a couple of things. So vampire blood is very different from that of humans. Much more complex. We can now, however, isolate specific properties of it—or maybe identifiers is a better word—and as I told you, we have a database of that kind of information. So when we compared your and Manny's blood, we were able to see clearly the commonalities, the kind that indicate you are siblings."

"Okay." Jo looked back and forth between the two of them. "I'm waiting for the other shoe to drop."

"We have the same father," Manny said. "But not the same mother."

Jo opened her mouth. Closed it.

Strange, how she could feel an instant grief for the loss of someone she had never known, and was actually not tied to. Still, it was a relief to think that poor woman hadn't suffered something no one had wanted to contemplate.

But then who was her birth mother?

Jo tried to hold on to what had been confirmed. "So Robert Bluff is my father."

"Yes." Jane nodded. "He is."

"Can you tell me anything about my birth mom?"

"No, I'm afraid we cannot. She was definitely a human, though. We know that for sure." Jane leaned in and put her hand on Jo's knee. "My *hellren* is going to look into it. From what you told Manny, about how you were adopted out of a diocese in Philadelphia from St. Francis Hospital here in Caldwell, it's possible that my mate can find something, anything, about you. It wasn't uncommon for there to be clandestine adoption programs running back then, for example. Anyway, we'll do our best. I can imagine how important it is for you to find answers."

Jo nodded and prayed there would be something, somewhere.

"I just want to know the real story." She looked at Manny. "But you're definitely half-vampire too?"

"Yes. The confirmation of this, I must confess, has taken me by surprise, even though it shouldn't be a shock. I've long guessed—and so have others—that this was the case, even though my mother's never said anything about it. But enough about me." Manny put his hand on her shoulder. "I'm really glad you're my sister. I can't wait for you to meet my wife—"

"But what if I don't go through the change." Jo shook her head and checked the screen of her phone. Still no reply from Syn. "Then I'm not in this world. Then we're enemies."

She'd been toying with a fantasy about the future, one where she and Syn ended up on the same side of the species divide and shared a long, much longer than she ever expected, life together. But considering he wasn't even responding to her texts, that all seemed highly ephemeral.

It had probably been a never-happen from the start.

"Let's cross that bridge when we come to it," Jane said. "We don't know what's going to happen with your transition."

Jo thought of Syn.

"I just don't want to lose my family," she whispered, "before I even know them."

The silence that followed was the kind of the thing that took a while to register. And when it did, she frowned.

"What else," she demanded. "There's something else, isn't there."

As things got quiet again, Jane and Manny locked eyes—like they were mentally playing rock, paper, scissors for who got to drop the next piece of news.

CHAPTER FIFTY-FOUR

As Butch was chauffeured into the training center's parking area, he decided that, on balance, he was doing good. Not wicked, frickin' good, of course. But certainly better than fairly good, and probably a little improved over pretty good.

At least this was his operating principle right up until he tried to get out of the passenger side of the fucking R8. Qhuinn, because he was a bossy little shit, and because he felt like he had a debt to repay after Butch had done what he had to protect the guy against the Omega, had refused to allow him to drive out of the forest to the training center on his own.

And okay, whatever, the brother had had to carry him out of the Tomb.

But come on. So he'd had a liiiiiiiiiiiiiiiittle trouble walking after he'd done his duty with all of those *lessers*. V had taken care of him, though, and he was going to be just. Frickin'. Fine.

As Qhuinn killed the engine, he looked over. "Do you need any help getting—"

"Oh, my God," Butch muttered, "I'm not an invalidate. Invalid. Whatever."

With that, he swung his door open like a boss, planted one of his shitkickers on the cement, and—

Fell out of the car like a drunk, landing on his face.

As he lay there in a sprawl, arms and legs kinked at strange angles, one boot still in the fucking R8, he thought of *The Wolf of Wall Street* scene with the Countach.

#nailedit

The sound of Qhuinn hustling around the front bumper was the sprinkles on the top of the shit sundae, and the sight of the steel tips of those shitkickers—right at eye level—was no value add either.

"I got this," Butch said as he lifted his cheek off that cold cement. "I needed a shave anyway."

Unfortunately, the pathetic way he dragged his body up to the vertical cured him of any ego he might have had left. He did, however, manage to stand on his own—and he was clapping his jacket to get the dust off when the van drove in.

The stench preceded its parking.

"Whoa," Butch muttered as he got a load of the smell. "We're going to have to hose that fucker out."

Qhuinn sneezed and rubbed his nose. "Either that or burn it."

The van pulled in a couple of spots down, not that the distance helped dull the stank. Hell, you could have left the thing across the river and Butch probably would have smelled it.

The good news was that as the back of the vehicle opened, V was not any better at the disembarking thing. The brother stumbled as if his knees were over-oiled, and was only able to catch his balance on a last-minute, all-points-of-the-compass spread that made him look like he was about to be strip-searched.

As all kinds of other brothers clown-car'd out of the stink-mobile, Butch and V headed into the training center together. Neither said a goddamn thing. The determination had been made, back in the ante-hall of the Tomb, that a medical check wasn't a bad idea. But fuck that. V had been starved, and all Butch could think of was how great a hot shower would be.

They didn't make it anywhere close to the locker rooms or the vending machines.

Doc Jane stepped out of a treatment room just as they came up to the clinic area, and something in the way she and V looked at each other made Butch realize that ending up here on account of a checkup had all been a pretense. This had been planned.

"What's going on?" Butch asked.

Jane took a deep breath. "I think you should come into the break room for a moment."

Glancing at V, Butch muttered, "So you needed M&Ms bad, huh."

"We'll go together." V nodded toward the door in question. "Let's do this."

Butch closed his eyes. "No offense, but after the last four hours and forty-three minutes—not that I was counting—I don't have a lot of energy for any bullshit."

"This is not bullshit."

"Okaaaaaaay."

Falling in with V and Jane, he had no idea what was waiting for him as he pushed opened the door. Except then he stopped and frowned.

Manny was sitting on a chair next to Jo, that human woman—and as soon as they saw him, Butch thought it was a little strange that they held on to each other's hands. But like he mattered in whatever their tie was?

Unless . . .

"So I guess you two are related?" he said slowly. "Congratulations—you know there are some physical similarities."

"Yeah," Manny murmured as he stared over with intense eyes. "There are."

Jane cleared her throat. "And it seems as though there are some other ties here."

"Who else—and please tell me it isn't Lassiter—"

"You."

As Jane spoke the word, Butch blanked for a moment—because, hello, after the night he'd had, he hadn't expected to be adding family members to his Christmas list on top of everything else. But then he thought back to a photograph Manny had shown him a while ago, one of a man who had looked shockingly like Butch himself.

"Sonofabitch," he murmured. "So the hunch was right."

✦   ✦   ✦

Talk about whiplash, Jo thought. So far this evening, she'd gone from thinking she had a mom, to learning she didn't have that mom, to discovering who her father was . . . and adding two brothers to her family tree.

Oh, yeah, and then there was the whole vampire thing, too.

Details, details.

But at least she wasn't the only one who was at the end of the bungee cord of life. Butch, the one with the Boston accent, the one she had seen that first night in the Red Sox baseball hat, the one who had seemed so nice earlier at the scene of all the carnage . . . was also looking a little poleaxed.

Join the club, she thought.

Doc Jane spoke up. "Yup. The bloodline database—which you'd previously given a sample to, but which Manny had not—confirms that you and Jo have a first-degree male ancestry in common with him. You all have the same father."

"Holy . . . shit." Butch looked over at the male with the goatee who he'd come in with. "So this means she's also related to—"

The male cut him off. "We're going to have to talk about the implications of it all later."

"Yeah, we're going to have to."

When Butch turned to Jo, she rose to her feet and tried to not look as if she were recording every nuance of his face. "So . . . um. Hi."

She stuck out her hand. And as it floated there on the breeze by its lonesome, she felt foolish and dropped her arm. Just because the male had accepted a guy he already knew so readily did not mean the courtesy had to be extended to a stranger who was more human than his kind. For the moment, at any rate.

"Sorry," she said as she rubbed her palm on the seat of her jeans.

"Well, I'm not," Butch said roughly. "It's really nice to meet you, sis."

The next thing she knew, she was being pulled into a hard hug—at the same time Manny was being yanked up off the sofa. Butch had the arm span to hold them both . . . and after a moment, Jo let herself fall into the embraces.

Her brothers.

For the first time in her life, she was among her own family, and part of her was overjoyed, her destination reached, the search over. The problem was, she knew better than to start making Sunday dinner plans for the next seven hundred years. If she didn't go through her transition, they were going to have to make it so she remembered absolutely nothing about this seminal moment in her life.

Manny had explained how it had to work.

With the war coming to an end, there could be no chances with the secrecy of the race. Especially not with a human . . . who happened to be a reporter.

CHAPTER FIFTY-FIVE

About an hour before dawn, Jo was taken back to the real world, and what a chariot she had to ride off into the sunrise with. The long, powerful black Mercedes was, like, Uber Titanium or something—and naturally, it came with a driver in uniform.

Who happened to look like something out of a P. G. Wodehouse novel.

If he hadn't been introduced to her as Fritz, she would have called him Jeeves.

Not that Jo spent all that much time talking to him. Before they pulled out of the underground parking garage, he apologized profusely and explained that the partition between the front and the back had to be raised for security purposes—and she'd told him she understood. But like there was any other response?

As a result, she knew nothing of where they were. The rear windows of the sedan were so deeply tinted, they might as well have been made of funeral draping, and then there were her eyelids. The subtle ride of the luxury suspension, coupled with the deep bucket seat, meant things felt like she was in a cradle, and after all the drama, it wasn't long before she—

"Madam?"

Jo woke up with a spastic slapping, her panic-palms hitting the leather acreage of the back seat like it was a horse's rump.

The butler, who had opened the rear door and was leaning in, looked apoplectic. "Madam, my sincerest apologies! Forgive me, I have been attempting to rouse you and—"

"It's okay, it's all right." Jo pushed her hair out of her face and blinked as she glanced past his shoulder. "That's where I live."

Stupid response. Like he'd thrown a dart at a map of Caldwell's suburbs and had no idea where they were?

"Yes, madam, I have returned you safely unto your abode."

In another panicked flare-up—this time, an internal one—Jo went into her brain and double-checked what she remembered of the night. Thank God, she had it all: The fighting scene at the abandoned mall, the training center's facilities, the blood tests . . . Manny and Butch . . . Syn.

Who she had not been able to say goodbye to. And who still hadn't texted her back.

The butler stepped to the side as she got out, and even though he stood by her, clearly waiting to be dismissed, she had to take a moment to look toward the light in the horizon. A new day had arrived.

In more ways than one.

"Thank you," she said to the—what were they called? *Doggen?*—butler.

"You are most welcome, madam." The old male bowed low. "I will see you to your door the now."

He closed the car up and locked it, and then they walked together to the entrance of her apartment building.

"How can you be out in the sunlight?" she asked.

The butler's snow-white brows went up. "I, ah, it is my kind. We are able to tolerate it quite well. It helps us serve our masters. We can perform tasks that they cannot when the sun is high. It is our pleasure to be of indispensable utility."

He reached forward to the heavy door, and Jo, concerned he would struggle, leaned in to help him with the weight. But that old man pulled things open like they didn't weigh a thing.

So much stronger than he looked.

"So, um . . . thank you," Jo said as she stepped inside.

She expected to say her goodbyes there. Instead, he followed her all the way to her apartment, a cheerful, sprightly figure in his formal uniform—who got some serious attention from her neighbors as they stepped out of their own door for their morning jog.

The couple from across the hall stopped dead in their Lululemons as they got a gander at him.

"Hi," Jo said to the pair. No reason to make an introduction.

"Greetings," the butler said as he bowed low.

Before he could offer to go in and scramble them up some eggs or maybe make their bed, Jo gave a wave that she hoped was the kind of hi-goodbye her fellow tenants would be efficient in returning.

And to think that a butler would be the least of the things she might have to explain.

After the couple hopped out of the building, Jo unlocked her door and turned to the *doggen*. "I'm going to say thank you again."

"Call us if you need us, madam." He presented her with a card and bowed low. "And I shall be pleased to collect you at any time."

He didn't leave until she had closed herself in, and she was willing to bet he waited until he heard the turn of the dead bolt before taking off.

Going over to the big window in the front, she pushed the venetian blinds aside and waited for him to emerge onto the sidewalk and get back in the car. As the Mercedes eased away from the curb and drove off, she looked at the business card. Only a number. No name or address.

What did she expect, though. Vampires-R-Us?

The shaking started as she sat down on her couch, knees together, ankles touching, hands resting on her thighs, just as she had been taught by her adoptive parents.

As her eyes traveled around her meager belongings—the framed photograph of a field of sunflowers on her wall, the notebook she'd left out before she'd gone to work, the sweater draped over the chair in the alcove—she didn't recognize anything at all. Not the things she owned or those she had recently touched. Not the towel she had used on her own body and hung on that rod there in the bath. Not the bed she could see through the open door, the one that she always slept in.

Jo didn't recognize even the clothes she had on. The boots seemed owned by another, the jeans something borrowed, the fleece and jacket the sort of thing she had taken from a kind soul who had wanted her to stay warm in the brisk spring night.

And the longer she sat here, in a quiet that was only interrupted when the couple above her started moving around to begin their day, she became even more estranged from herself.

Memory by memory, Jo sifted through her childhood, her school days, her college era, and then, more recently, her job at that real estate company, her unrequited crush on her playboy boss, and her meeting of Bill that had gotten her to the CCJ.

From time to time, in a relationship, perhaps with a lover or a friend, maybe even with a family member, information came to you, either firsthand, through something you witnessed, or secondhand, through something you heard from a credible source, that changed everything.

Like a bright light turned on in a dim room, suddenly, you saw things that you had been unaware of. And now that you did see them, even if that light was later extinguished, you could not return to your earlier opinion of, and connection to, the space. The furnishings. The wallpaper and the lamp.

Forever changed.

It was a relatively normal phenomenon, inevitable as you opened your life to others.

You just never expected it to happen with your own self. Or at least Jo didn't.

Fumbling into her pocket, she took out her phone. Syn still had not called or texted, and she told herself not to try him again.

A minute later, she was calling him, and when she got his voice mail, she meant to hang up. She told herself to hang up. She ordered her hand to drop the damn thing away from her ear—

"Syn," she heard herself say. "I, ah . . ."

Closing her eyes, she added her second palm to the hold, as if the cell was a precious object with a slippery surface, prone to a drop-and-shatter from which she would never recover.

"Can you please call me. I need to talk to you. I need to talk to . . . someone."

To you, she amended in her head.

Everybody she had met in that underground facility had been kind to her . . . solicitous, concerned, and beyond nonthreatening. But the one she wanted to connect to, the anchor for her, the voice she needed to hear, was Syn's.

There were all kinds of reasons this made no sense.

But it was the only thing she could choose in this situation that was, on all other levels, so completely, fricking unreal and out of her control.

Of course, she could only do the dialing part on her end.

Whether he answered her?

That was another thing she had no influence over.

◆   ◆   ◆

Butch was on his leather sofa in the Pit, legs stretched out laterally across the cushions, torso propped against the armrest, when V looked up from his Four Toys.

"According to the tunnel's security camera, we've got another visitor."

"Like Grand Central here this morning." But Butch didn't care. There was no sleep to be had. FFS, he couldn't even pretend to be dozing. "Who is it?"

When there was a subtle knock, they both called out, "Yup!"

The door up from the underground tunnel opened, and—

"Balz," V said as he refocused on his monitors. "How're ya."

The Bastard glanced down the hall where the bedrooms were. "You got a minute? Are your *shellans* asleep?"

"Nope." Butch pushed himself up a little higher. "Marissa's staying the day at Safe Place."

"And Jane's at the training center." V sat back in his ass palace. "What's up."

Balthazar was the kind of thief who, after he'd been in your crib, you'd probably want to perform an inventory of every single thing that was worth more than five bucks—even if the guy had been right in front of you the entire time. Fortunately, he was also the kind of thief who had an off-limits safe list, and all members of the Brotherhood and the Brotherhood's household, were on it.

"Have a seat," Butch said as he bent his knees to create room. "You look like I feel."

Balz came over and took a load off, groaning as he sat back. But instead of launching into whatever topic was clearly constipating his pie hole, he crossed his arms over his chest. Worked his jaw like he was trying to wear down the ridges of his back molars. Rolled his shoulder until it cracked.

"So your cousin was just here," Butch murmured. "Did you miss Syn on purpose? Or is it luck."

When the male didn't say anything, Butch got to his feet and went to the kitchen. "Scotch?"

"Yes. Please."

"Hand-rolled?" V offered from the computers.

"Yes. Please."

The poor Bastard didn't speak until he had drank half the Lag Butch poured him and smoked half the cigarette V gave him.

And when he decided to talk, he still had to clear his voice. "So, Butch . . . I understand that you're a direct relation of Jo Early, the half-breed—"

"Please don't call her that," Butch said.

Balz inclined his head in deference. "My apologies. The female."

"Thanks. And yeah, she's my sister."

"Indeed . . ." Balz tossed back the last of the scotch. "Look, there's no easy way to say this. Syn has asked me to be the one who attends to her. In the event the change comes."

Butch sat up. "Excuse me? No offense, but what the hell business of it is his—"

"He's bonded with her."

Easing back into his recline, Butch decided he was really done with life's little curveballs. Although . . ."You know, in a way, this is a good thing. I was getting ready to have a super-fun conversation with the guy—'cuz there's no way I want him alone with my sister."

Balz took a drag on his hand-rolled. "He's never done anything like this before."

"You mean fed a female in her transition?"

"No, watched out for one like this." Balz tapped his cigarette into his empty glass. "And I'm the closest one to him. Which is why he asked me."

"What'd you say?" V asked.

"I have a bad habit of cleaning up after my cousin. So of course, it was a yes. I figured you"—he glanced at Butch—"would be witnessing the transition if it comes for her. You and Manny, that is. No matter what Syn's saying, you two are in charge. She's an unmated female, and you're her closest male relations. It's ultimately your choice."

Butch stared at the guy with fresh eyes. Funny how you considered a male differently when he was going to get close to your sister.

The only opinion he'd ever had about Balz was that you wanted to chain your wallet when he was around—preferably inside your pants. Other than that? The fighter was brutal in the field, quick with the snark, and you had to respect the way he looked after that loose cannon cousin of his. So all the way around, he was a good addition to the roster.

Now, though, Butch thought the Bastard was a little too good-looking. Too well-built. Too well used—and by that, he was not talking about in-the-field hours.

More in-the-sheets was what he was thinking.

"You will witness it," Balz repeated. "Nothing will happen other than her at my wrist. I swear on my *grandmahmen*—who is the only female I have ever honored."

As the Bastard looked over, his eyes did not waver. And after a tense moment, Butch found himself nodding.

"All right," he said. "I'll consent. Have you talked with Manny about this?"

"I figured I'd start with you."

"Tell Manny it's okay with me—but he and I will both be there, so you need his permission, too."

"Of course. I'd expect nothing less. If it were my sister, I'd do the same."

"And Jo gets a vote. If for some reason—"

"Absolutely." Balz put his hand up. "If she doesn't like me, we'll get someone else."

"Assuming there's time," V interjected. "Personal choice is all well and good, but biology is going to win this argument."

"She can meet him at nightfall," Butch said.

"Anywhere, anytime. It's all about whatever makes her feel more comfortable."

This was going to work out, Butch thought when the Bastard eventually left.

If only because Syn was likely not to kill the very guy he'd asked to take care of Jo.

Or at least...there was a better than average chance that he wouldn't. Bonded males were a thing. And that was before you added on that Bastard's penchant for murder.

"Can you tell me if she is going to live?" Butch asked his roommate tightly.

V leaned out around the monitors again, and his diamond eyes answered the question before his voice did. "I'm sorry."

"Nah, it's cool. I know what we're up against. It's just...I lost one sister already. I don't want to lose another."

Although technically, he'd lost all of his family—even his mother, in spite of the fact that he could still see her. Odell O'Neal had Alzheimer's and was in a nursing home. Which was the only reason he could visit her on occasion.

"Can we keep Jo," he said, "even if she stays human. And I don't mean as in, in a closet somewhere. If she's related to me, she's related to Wrath—and he needs to know this."

"He already does. Jane told him everything."

"So he'll let Jo stay."

"I don't know. It's a big risk."

"Manny's here."

"Because Payne mated him. You think Syn's getting her name carved in his back anytime soon?"

"Jane's here."

"I let her go first, though." V got a distant look in his eyes. "Worst hot chocolate I ever made."

"Murhder has Sarah."

"Again. See also, mated male and *shellan*."

"Goddamn it. Doesn't it count if she's my sister? Manny's?"

"If she stays a human? I don't know, cop. I really don't. What I am sure about is that we're stretched thin as it is and the war is hitting a crucial point. Plus there's that little supernatural bait-and-switch shit with that 'old friend' of yours in the basement of that building we visited tonight. You want to tell where, in this panoply of crap, we have room for an unattended human to come join the party?"

Butch cursed and looked at the glass Balz had been drinking out of. If his stomach still wasn't iffy from what he'd done in the Tomb, he would have been sucking back the Lag like you read about.

But he was kind of done with the sucking for the foreseeable future.

Or . . . at least until nightfall.

CHAPTER FIFTY-SIX

Y ou're fired. Effective immediately."

As Jo sat across from Dick in his office at the paper, she was somehow not surprised. What was a shocker, if you considered the strong-arm tactics she had used just earlier in the week to keep her byline, was that she really didn't give a shit.

Having made his pronouncement from on high, Dick smiled with all the trademark satisfaction of a letch who had gotten what he wanted. Not sex, this time, no. But she was out, and that clearly made him a happy congestive heart failure patient.

"And before you ask, Miss Early, we're restructuring the newsroom and eliminating the online editorial position as part of a further round of cost savings." Dick sat back in his chair and put his hands on the flanks of his protruding stomach like he'd just eaten. "Going forward, we're outsourcing all our online support. It's the wave of the future. So there is no way you can frame this in any other fashion, and I've already cleared it with our lawyers. If you try any kind of retaliation against me personally, regardless of what you may think the grounds are, I'm afraid I won't be able to give you a reference—"

Jo got up. "Do I get severance or am I filing unemployment right away?"

Dick blinked like her pragmatism had stunned him. "Two weeks' severance, effective today, and you'll have health benefits through COBRA for eighteen months. But I want you out of the newsroom right now."

"Fine. Do you have anything for me to sign?"

"My lawyer is mailing everything to your home address with instructions. But you have the termination letter on your email as we speak. It is nonnegotiable, however."

"All right, then."

As she turned and walked away from him, she could sense his confusion. But it wasn't the kind of thing she was going to bother clearing up for him.

"I'm serious, Early," he belted out. "Don't try anything. You won't like what happens to you."

With her hand on the doorknob, she looked over her shoulder. "I'll sign everything and you won't hear from me again. And you won't last long at that desk. It's a race between the paper closing and your heart clogging from that diet of yours. Either way, I'll leave you to your fate."

She didn't wait for a response, and closed the door quietly behind herself. Heading over to her desk, she sat down and glanced at Bill.

Her friend was staring at the monitor in front of him, clearly not seeing the email displayed on it.

"So I'm going now," she said.

Bill jumped and glanced over. "Sorry, what was that?"

She swiveled her chair to face her friend. "I'm leaving."

"It's early for lunch—"

"They're eliminating my position."

"He just *fired* you?" Bill said with a recoil.

She put her hand out before he could entertain any thoughts of trying to be a hero. "No, it's okay. Really. I'll find something else. I'd rather you keep your job than have my own."

Bill glanced at all the empty desks around them and then pedaled his rolling chair over to her. As he kept his voice low, she was tempted to tell him not to worry about discretion. It wasn't like there was anybody else to hear.

"You should fight this," he whispered. "You've done tremendous reporting on the—"

"Like I said, I'll find something else. The economy's good, you know? And at least I have some bylines now." She put her hand on his shoulder. "Don't worry about me. I'll land on my feet. I always do."

"This isn't right."

"Actually, it's good timing." She looked at her uncluttered desk and realized she didn't need a box to put her personal things in. She had no "personal things" to box. "I feel the need to reinvent myself."

"Away from Caldwell?"

"Yes. And Pennsylvania. And . . . anywhere else I've ever been." Jo looked at her friend and knew she was covering her bases. Whether she went through the transition or not, she was not staying where she was. "But we'll still keep in touch, I promise. You and Lydia have been beyond good friends to me."

As her phone went off, she didn't bother checking to see who was calling. It was undoubtedly another scammer. Telemarketer. Survey about nothing she wanted to be surveyed about.

It sure as hell wasn't going to be Syn.

"Let me send you all my notes and drafts so you're up to speed on the articles." Jo signed into her computer. "I'll email them now before my login gets canceled."

After she was finished, she turned to Bill. Her friend was staring down at the floor.

"I'm going to be fine," she told him.

"It's not right." He shook his head. "Dick is . . ."

"Named appropriately." Jo leaned down under her desk and got her purse. "We can just leave it at that."

To make sure she hadn't forgotten anything, she quickly went through all the drawers. Nothing but stationery and office supplies that were owned by the paper anyway.

"I don't know how to cancel my pass card," she murmured.

"I can take care of it. I was the one who created it."

"Okay." She got up. "So . . . I guess I'll see you around, okay?"

"Promise?"

As the man stared up at her in a forlorn way, she had a feeling she wasn't going to see him again. Or maybe that was just her mood talking, rather than any kind of prescience. Either way, her chest hurt.

"Yes, I promise," Jo said.

Before there could be any kind of awkward hug thing happening, she took her swipe card out of her jacket pocket and handed it to Bill.

"That's that," she said with a smile.

Giving his shoulder a pat, she walked away, heading for the rear door into the parking lot. Before she stepped out for the last time, she glanced back. She had liked the job. She had loved Bill.

"Tell Tony I said bye?" she called out.

Bill nodded. "I will."

And then she was out in the morning sunlight which was surprisingly warm. Stopping, she looked up to the sky, squinting and covering her eyes with her hand. She had never before thought of the sun as something to avoid, outside of the skin cancer thing.

Being a redhead and all.

Now, as she tried to focus on the great glowing ball, she felt her heart skip beats—

The door burst open behind her and Bill jumped out. There was a pause, and then they were giving each other a hug.

"Anything I can do," he said as they pulled apart. "I'm there for you."

"Just take care of your Lydia, k?"

"We can still go hunting," he offered. "You know, for things that go bump in the night."

Jo thought of everything she'd witnessed firsthand. Everything she now knew. "I think I'm going to retire my paranormal researcher hat, too."

"You're giving up? I tell you, one of these days we're going to get our proof."

"I don't think there's anything out there . . . that shouldn't be there."

Jo gave his arm a squeeze, made another promise to call him, and then hustled off for her car. As she got in, she tossed her purse into the passenger seat and looked at all the wrappers in the wheel well. The fact that Syn had sat there just a matter of nights before. And gone back to her apartment. And made love to her . . .

"Stop it."

She was putting the car in reverse when her phone went off again and she almost let the thing go. The idea that it could possibly, maybe, okay-probably-not-but-still, be Syn was the only reason she went bag diving, and when she pulled out her cell, she cursed.

McCordle.

Well, she needed to talk to him anyway.

Accepting the call, she continued backing out of her parking spot. "Hey, I was going to c—"

"I need you to meet me ASAP."

"Listen," she said as she put the car in drive, "I'm not working at the CCJ anymore. Anything that has to do with—"

"Where are you?"

"I'm leaving the paper. Which is my point. You need to get in touch with Bill. He's back at work now—"

"Meet me at Market and Tenth. There's an alley one block in on the left."

"I told you. I'm not with the CCJ anymore. You need to take all this to Bill—"

"This is about you, not the articles you've been writing. Come *now*."

◆　◆　◆

"I'm not going out into the field tonight."

As Syn spoke the words, he did not look up from his position on the floor of his bedroom suite's closet. He did not sit up. He did not get up. He did not lift his eyes.

It wasn't because he wanted trouble with Tohrment, who was the organizer of the shifts, the pairer of fighters, the buck-stops-here for everything war related. No, he didn't look up because he did not *want* trouble.

"I know," Tohr said. "You texted that you're taking yourself off rotation to everybody. I guess what I'm interested in is why and what your plans are if you don't go out to fight."

Syn closed his lids against the glare of the overhead light—which the Brother had turned on as soon as he'd walked in, uninvited.

"I don't have any plans," Syn said.

"You sure about that?"

"Yup." He repositioned the wadded-up shirt he was using as a pillow. "No plans at all."

"You're just going to keep lying here after sundown?"

"I may go to the weight room. Might go downtown for a burger. You never know where the mood will take a person."

"Syn."

When the Brother didn't say anything further, Syn became aware that he was going to have play pupil tag or this looming thing Tohr was rocking, coupled with these awkward, unanswered inquiries, was going to continue till the end of time.

"What," he said as he glanced in Tohr's direction.

"What's going on with you?"

"I'm developing the skills necessary to be a throw rug. This requires a great degree of horizontal work and concentration."

"Listen, I know about Jo Early—"

"Yes, you do. She is a half-breed I was trying to protect, and she's related to Butch and Manny, and she's on the verge of her transition. No, I'm not going to be the male she uses. Her brothers are aware of this, and that's all there is to know about absolutely everything."

"When are you coming back on roster?"

Syn looked away to the vacant hanging rods that made a circle of the walk-in. "I don't know."

"So you're out permanently?" Before Syn could back off the Brother, Tohr spoke up. "And no, I'm not going to back off. I'm responsible for partnering up all of the fighters, including the Band of Bastards. I have to know your intentions so I can plan."

"I don't know."

"You don't . . ." Tohr lowered himself down onto his haunches, those navy-blue peepers sharp as blades. "You realized what is at stake, right? You've been knee-deep in the cesspool of this war for centuries, just like the rest of us. And you're quitting at the end? What the hell is wrong with you?"

Syn debated whether or not he could let the insult slide, given that, considering his reputation, what was wrong with him was kind of self-explanatory. But then he thought about Jo.

Meeting her had changed a lot for him. Had changed . . . pretty much everything. And he had the strangest sense that if he spoke of this, if he said it out loud, it would be real. It would be forever.

Sitting up slowly, he prayed he could get the words out.

"I don't want to kill anything anymore," he said in a voice that cracked. "Ever."

CHAPTER FIFTY-SEVEN

J o went where Officer McCordle told her to go, even though when
she got to Market and Tenth and found the alley, she wasn't sure
which side of it she was supposed to turn in to. She went left on
a whim, and when she saw the squad car, she pulled up grille-to-grille
with it. Getting out, she was totally numb.

McCordle motioned her over through his front windshield and
popped the passenger side door. As she got into the squad car, she felt a
stifling warmth and smelled spearmint gum, aftershave, and fresh coffee.

Shutting things up, she turned to the cop. "What's this about—"

"We have reason to believe there's a credible hit out on you." The
police radio squawked at a low volume and the laptop mounted on the
center console spooled all kinds of data on its matte screen. "I want to
show you some footage from the FBI feed."

It was a commentary on how her life was going that a police officer
telling her the mob wanted to kill her was an also-ran.

I'll see you and raise you I'm-a-vampire, she thought.

Instead of going into the computer, McCordle got out his cell
phone. "The FBI got warrants to surveil both Carmine Gigante's cement

business and the Hudson Hunt and Fish Club. The night after Johnny Pappalardo was found dead in that alley, a man met with Gigante at the latter. In that meeting, Gigante acknowledged that he asked the man to kill Pappalardo, and maintained that it had been done in too showy a way. He demanded that the man make things right by killing you."

"Okay." She watched the officer tap the screen of his phone. "And?"

"The man said he would take care of it. Your name was specifically used—hold on, I have to scroll through to get the right file."

"Are you supposed to have this video?" God, she just wanted to go home and sleep right now. "I mean, shouldn't I talk to the FBI." Not that she cared one way or the other. "I can call whoever I need to." And that was a problem, wasn't it—the no-caring thing. "I mean—"

"Here it is." He tilted his phone toward her and clicked the volume button up. "Let me know if you've ever seen this guy?"

The video was in black-and-white, shot from what appeared to be the upper corner of a windowless, grungy office. As she tried to orient herself, she had a mental image of someone drilling a hole in a ceiling's Sheetrock and feeding in something of a fiber-optic nature. Whatever.

Okay, so there was a man sitting at the desk, a fat, older man who she recognized as Gigante. And then someone came in—

Jo's heart stopped.

The man was tall and broad. Dressed in leather. And he had a Mohawk.

Swallowing hard, she tried to make her ears work. There was some kind of conversation happening on the little screen, but she couldn't seem to hear anything. Sure, the phone's speaker was tinny to begin with and the audio quality pretty poor. Then again, her brain was spinning with the implications—

"You know what, it's your lucky fucking night. I'm going to do you a favor. I'm going to give you a chance for redemption. As opposed to a grave."

All at once, Gigante's words came through loud and clear. And then she heard . . .

"You take care of this reporter problem for me," the mob boss said in the video, "and I'll forgive you for fucking up the Pappalardo hit."

Say no, she thought. *Tell him you won't do it. Tell him—*

"I'll take care of it," Syn said with absolutely no emotion at all. "What's the name?"

"Jo Early."

Jo sat back abruptly. "I've seen enough."

McCordle paused the video. "Do you know him?"

Looking out through the windshield, she traced the details of the alley: the trash that had gathered inside the sunken doorways, deposited by capricious wind gusts. The fire escapes that ran down the buildings' brick walls, cheap necklaces decorating the flat cleavage between rows of windows. The car on the opposite side that had a busted window, no hubcaps, and a string of curses scratched into its paint.

She thought of the night she had run from the police helicopter with Syn.

Had he planned to get her out of sight in that restaurant to do the hit? And then reconsidered when he'd found out she was like him? As in not human?

If she failed to turn into a vampire, was he going to kill her then? Gigante might be dead, but his organization continued, and from everything she'd learned about the mob, they had long memories. And how was a vampire doing hit jobs for humans? Didn't that violate the separation of species rule?

As she considered the implications and danger of it all, images filtered through her mind and she tried to mine her interactions with Syn for clues as to his intentions.

"The FBI is going to contact you later this afternoon," McCordle said. "I wanted to get to you first because I don't think they realize that just because Gigante is dead, it doesn't mean you're safe. I tried to get them to understand this, but they're short-staffed and focusing on Frank Pappalardo's retaliation. They're trying to nail him for Gigante, Senior's killing before the violence explodes. Meanwhile, you're here in

Caldwell, walking around, unaware of anything. This hit man is at large and Gigante's son, Junior, is still alive. Who knows what can happen."

"Thank you," she said dully.

"So?"

Jo looked over. "I'm sorry?"

McCordle pointed at the screen of his phone. "Have you ever seen this man before?"

Taking a deep breath, she made herself look at the image of her former lover.

"No," she said. "I haven't."

◆   ◆   ◆

When you worked a nine-to-five job, it was amazing how much you couldn't get done during the week. After Jo left McCordle, she filled her car up with gas. She went to the dry cleaners and picked up her single pair of dress slacks. She hit the grocery store, buying some basics and two bottles of Motrin. She retrieved a pair of shoes from the cobbler's—that had been waiting there for three months.

So it was basically a Saturday happening on a Thursday.

And all the while, she waited for the FBI to call her.

By the time she returned to her apartment, it was almost two in the afternoon. Still plenty of daylight left, and it wasn't like she had to worry about someone shooting at her. She already knew who her hit man was, and he couldn't go out in the sunshine.

No worries there.

After bringing in her grocery bags and her dry cleaning, she locked herself inside with the dead bolt and the chain, and put everything away. Then she went through her mail, looking for bills. She had about two months of cash on hand, and a credit card with seventeen hundred dollars of airspace on it. Impending transition and death threats aside, she was going to have to start her job search immediately.

And her financial imperative was almost a relief. If she hadn't had to worry about something, anything, she would have gone insane.

The FBI called at 4:34—not that she knew it was them from the number. It was only after she listened to the message left by the special agent that she learned who it had been. They wanted her to phone back right away. They wanted her to come to the field office—or the agent could come to her, whatever was easiest for her. They wanted her to know that this was a serious matter, requiring her urgent attention.

Jo put her cell facedown on the table and refocused on her laptop. She had updated her résumé a month ago—almost like she'd known what was coming, huh. So it was the work of a moment to upload it on Monster.com, and start searching receptionist jobs in Caldwell. Long-term goal of departure aside, she figured it would be important to stay put until . . . well, until her body decided what it was going to do. After that? Who knew.

"Damn it," she muttered as she sat back.

Instead of resuming the job search, she went over to the *CCJ* website and browsed through the articles that had been posted in the previous five hours. Was Bill doing that now? It had to be him. No one else was in the newsroom and God knew Dick wasn't good for anything other than being a dick.

Eventually, she ended up going into the archives and re-reading the articles and updates she had written. She also looked at the photographs of Gigante and his son together, and then Johnny Pappalardo dead in that alley. And mourned the dreams she'd enjoyed for such a short time.

She was still sitting at her kitchen table when the people upstairs came home from work at six.

And she was still sitting there when the sun went down and night came.

And still sitting there when the hairs on the back of her neck stood up at attention.

Without knowing what her instincts were picking up on, she rose to her feet and went over to the front window. She had closed the venetian blinds flat after the butler had left that morning, and she didn't want to tip off whoever it might be that she was on the alert. Angling herself awkwardly, she tried to see out the gap next to the window frame. Yeah, nope. Plus with the lights on in the apartment, she couldn't really see anything in the darkness outside.

Walking backward to her bedroom, she snagged her gun from her purse on the way. The lights were off in there, so she went right to her window and looked through the slats—

There was a figure.

Standing right there.

Jerking back against the wall, she fumbled with the gun, taking the safety off. Then she went for her phone, even though she wasn't sure who to call. The FBI? No, McCordle. Unless . . . 911? But what was she reporting exactly—

The cell went off in her hand and she jumped. When she saw who it was, her heart pounded.

She was still trying to make up her mind whether or not to answer when voice mail kicked in. But instead of leaving a message, the caller texted her.

I'm outside. Can we talk?

CHAPTER FIFTY-EIGHT

S yn had felt like it was important to approach Jo's window by himself. He didn't want to frighten her, and more than that . . . he
didn't want anyone seeing how emotional he might get. He'd listened to the voice mail she had left him earlier in the day about a hundred times, and each replay had carved another piece out of the inside
of his chest.

She had sounded so alone. So scared.

He had tried to call her every hour, on the hour, and failed to press
send each time. He had no clue what to say to her, and now that he was
standing outside her bedroom window like a stalker, he discovered that
physical proximity had not improved his vocabulary.

The scent of her registered first, that fresh meadow perfume entering his nose and running throughout his body. Then he heard the soft
footfalls.

The latter stopped. The former continued to ride the air currents to
his nose.

Syn turned and faced the female who had stolen his heart.
"Hello, Jo."

"What are you doing here?"

There had been no way of knowing what his reception was going to be, but he hadn't anticipated so much anger.

"I'm sorry I didn't call you—"

"What do you want."

Not a question.

Syn frowned. "Are you okay?"

She walked forward, coming down the side of the apartment building, closing in on him. Actually, she was outright marching.

"I'm *great*," she said as she halted in front of him. "And I'm also armed, in case you've come here to earn your money."

As she pegged him with hard, hostile eyes, he took a step back. "What?"

"I saw the videotape." Before he could ask for a better explanation, she snapped, "The one where you agree to kill me for Carmine Gigante Sr.? To make up for the fact that you didn't do what you said you would to Johnny Pappalardo? Tell me something, how does a vampire like you manage to become a mob hit man without getting into trouble with the Brotherhood? It strikes me as a risky side gig, given the whole keep-us-a-secret thing."

"I didn't hurt you," Syn said.

The laugh that came out of her was the very definition of sarcasm. "You didn't shoot me—for sure. But the night is young, isn't it. And you're here to check and see whether I'm a vampire or if I'm still a human, right? So tell me something, Syn, what are you going to do if I don't change. Are you the one who's going to put me in my grave? I mean, it's killing two birds with one stone, isn't it. You silence a problem for the species and collect cash from the mob. It's a smart move."

"You don't know what you're talking about."

"Don't I? I watched the videotape. It's on a cop's phone incidentally—so FYI, they're onto you. The CPD and the FBI. But hey, you can take care of that, can't you. Just a little erase job on their memories and you're scot-free. Or are you? What are you going to do about the videotape? The records. The reports. Things are going to be tricky if any of that falls into the media's hands."

Syn crossed his arms over his chest. "I saved your life last night against those *lessers*."

"No, you tore a bunch of your enemies up because that's your job, and obviously because you like to kill. It had nothing to do with me."

"Didn't it? Were you in my mind at the time?"

"No, I was on the sidelines, watching how much you get off hurting people."

Looking away, Syn shook his head. "Slayers are my enemy and soon to be yours."

"If I turn. And we both know that's not a done deal, is it. I could not go through the transition, in which case, I'm an issue for you. But again, and fortunately, you're really good at killing, aren't you."

As he tried to think of what he could say, without lying, that was, she lowered her voice. "I don't want to ever see you again. You lied to me about what I am. You lied to me about why you were around me. I . . . I made love to you, thinking that you were someone— *something*—you're not. And I have to live with all that. But I am not adding one more goddamn thing to that list of bad choices and stupid delusions."

Syn glanced over his shoulder. When he looked back at Jo, she had started moving away, all the while, keeping her eyes on him as if she expected him to hurt her.

I did the right thing, he thought. He'd made the right decision.

"Wait," he said.

"No." Jo shook her head, her red hair moving around her shoulders. "No more. I can't stand looking at you—"

"I came to introduce you to my cousin. He's willing to be available for you if you go through the change."

When she stopped dead, Syn motioned to the shadows.

As Balthazar stepped into view, Syn felt like he'd been shot through the chest. But in so many ways, his life had led up to this point.

Yup. The only way to care for the female he loved . . . was to let her go to another.

◆   ◆   ◆

Jo focused on the male vampire who emerged out of the shadows. He was built like Syn, powerful and dominating, and his coloring was the same. Dark hair—not-Mohawked though—and pale irises. But his features were different, and mostly in the eyes. His were more narrow.

Or maybe it was just that they'd narrowed the moment he regarded her properly.

To his credit, he didn't do a head-to-toe sweep on her body, and there was absolutely nothing sexual in anything about him.

"This is Balthazar," Syn said roughly. "He is a fine male of distinction—"

"Actually, I'm a thief." When they both looked at him, the vampire shrugged. "We need to start this out on a truthful note. I'm a thief, but I'm not ever going to steal from you, and I only want to help."

He put his hand out. And seemed prepared to wait until she felt comfortable touching him. No matter how long it took.

Jo approached slowly. It was hard to see anything other than Syn, and her emotions made that tunnel vision worse. But the idea that she might have to . . .

"Hi," she said, extending her own palm.

As they shook, the male stared at Syn, something passing between them. Like a vow. Or a promise.

Jo released her hold and lowered her arm. "Who do you steal from? And what do you take?"

Balthazar shrugged. "It depends. Sometimes it's because they have so much they need a haircut to make things fairer. That's my Robin Hood shtick. Sometimes it's because they have something I want. I'm less proud of that one, and I do try to even that score. You know, give them something of equal or greater value that they may need or like."

There was a pause. "And?" Jo prompted.

That pale stare narrowed again. Then the voice dropped low. "Annnnnnd sometimes people need to be taught a lesson. It's amazing how losing something you care about can reprioritize things. I do not apologize for that one. Ever."

Jo blinked. And then found herself nodding. "Okay."

She looked at Syn. He had taken a step back so that he was mostly hidden in the darkness outside the reach of the building's security lights. And when he took another, he was nearly invisible, nothing but an outline in black blending in with the night.

"Your brothers will be there," Balthazar said gently. "And Doc Jane will come so you have medical support. You will never be alone with me and there will be nothing sexual about it. I swear this on my honor—which, okay, fine, I don't have a lot of, but what I do have is yours. You can trust me. All right?"

Jo searched that lean, hard face. And for some stupid reason, she got teary.

No, wait. She knew why.

In spite of everything that had gone down, and everything she knew about Syn . . . she still wanted it to be him.

"All right," she said in a hoarse voice.

With that response, Syn took a final step away, the darkness enveloping him so completely that it was as if he disappeared—

"Syn?" she said.

Jo lurched forward and waved her hands around where he had been standing—well, waved one of her hands and then the gun she was still holding. There was nothing there. Not even the scent of him lingered. As her heart pounded, she turned to Balthazar.

"What happened to him?"

"Oh, hasn't anyone told you? We have tricks. Poof! Bye-bye. And you know the whole bats, garlic, and crosses stuff is for crap, right? That's only in the movies."

"Will I be able to . . ."

"Dematerialize? It depends. Not everyone who's a half-breed can." He made a face. "Do you find that term derogatory? I mean, I don't want to disrespect you."

Jo glanced at the male and felt as helpless as a heroine in a Bruce Willis movie. At least the ones from the late eighties.

"I don't know what to think or feel, about anything."

She went back to staring at where Syn had been—and felt like the sudden absence of him was a great metaphor for their relationship. *Poof!* And he was gone.

She should be grateful. Relieved. Liberated.

Instead, she hurt. All over.

"So you love him back, huh."

Wheeling around, Jo recoiled. "What did you say?"

CHAPTER FIFTY-NINE

The following night, the night when the war ended, there was no moon in the clear velvet sky over Caldwell, New York. No stars twinkling from their heavenly perch, either. The galaxy itself seemed to hunker down, taking cover to avoid shrapnel.

As Butch stepped out of the Pit's front door, he glanced up and felt a dread he had never known. Then he looked to the mansion's grand entrance. The heavy panels that locked tight to protect those inside swung open, and one by one, the Brotherhood emerged. Z was the first out, his skulled trimmed hair and brutal, scarred face the kind of thing Butch had gotten used to seeing. Phury was, of course, behind his twin. Then it was Tohrment. Murhder. And Rhage. Qhuinn and John Matthew. Blay was with them. After that, the Band of Bastards emerged, led by Xcor—

"I love you."

At the sound of his *shellan's* voice, Butch turned. Marissa stood behind him, terror in her eyes, as if she knew, without him saying, what he sensed was true. This was it.

Touching her soft cheek, all kinds of things went through his mind. But as before, as always, none of the promises he wished he could make to her were under his control, and he was not going to have the last thing he told her be a lie.

"I love you, too."

Leaning in, he was aware of his black daggers biting into the pads of his chest as he kissed her.

"I'm going to stay home tonight," she said.

The reason why went unspoken. She never missed work, but this was a "never" kind of night.

"Beth asked me to come over to the big house." Marissa's beautiful eyes searched his face like she was looking for which way the winds of fate were blowing. "You know, to watch a movie."

"Can I suggest a comedy?"

"We're going with Fockers. The whole series."

"Stiller and De Niro. Excellent choice."

They fell silent. Sometimes, between married people who had remained connected after the nuclear bright glow of sexual attraction dimmed, there were no words needed. No words that could be enough. The emotions went too deep.

"I'll call you," he said.

"Please."

They kissed again, and it was a long one—it reminded him of the way they had made love before he had gotten up to get showered, get dressed, get armed. And then she stepped away . . . and walked across the courtyard, her head down, her arms wrapped around herself.

A widow walking.

The brothers parted as she mounted the great stone steps and approached the open door, and as she passed through them, the huge males bowed to her in respect. Before she went inside, Marissa looked back at Butch and raised her palm.

He raised his own in return.

And then she was gone, the heavy door into the vestibule closing behind her, cutting off the sight of her slender form as well as the light that spilled out into the night.

"I dreamed of you," Vishous said from back inside the Pit.

Butch shut his eyes and cursed—although he couldn't say he was surprised. His roommate's visions of the future were only ever about death, and everyone's grave was close by this evening.

"Did you." Butch glanced over his shoulder. "You going to tell me?"

V was dressed for war, in his leathers and with all his weapons on his body, but he was staying back on the home front. He and Rhage, as well as Rehvenge, with all his *symphath* traits, plus Payne and Xhex, were going to guard the mansion. Meanwhile, Manny was in the field already, down at the garage with the mobile surgical unit on standby, and Doc Jane, who, thanks to her ghostly status, could get anywhere in the blink of an eye, was preparing for a mass casualty event in the training center.

As Vishous came forward to the Pit's open doorway, his lithe body moving like the predator he was, Butch was aware of bracing himself like he was about to be punched in the gut.

"The cross," V said gravely. "The cross will save you."

Butch fumbled into his muscle shirt in a panic. But like he would leave home without the damn thing? It was his fucking existential AmEx.

As he pulled the heavy gold weight out, he rubbed the cross with his thumb. "Right here."

V nodded. "Keep it on."

"Always."

There was a pause. And then the hug came. As they embraced, Butch wished his roommate was coming out with him. As much as he respected the rest of the brothers and fighters, there was nobody he'd rather have at his six.

"I can be to you in a heartbeat," V said roughly.

Butch nodded as they parted. And then he stepped off the stoop and crossed over to the R8. The plan was in place. The responsibilities defined. The territories assigned and the weapons and ammo apportioned.

There was nothing else to talk about.

Tohrment rode shotgun into town with Butch, and neither of them said a thing. When they got to the garage, they left the R8 in its parking space, checked in with Manny, and hit the streets.

And almost immediately . . .

. . . Butch knew which direction to go in.

◆   ◆   ◆

When Syn got back to the mansion from Jo's, he went around to the side wing and knocked on one of the French doors of the billiards room. He didn't use the front entrance because he had no interest in crossing paths with anyone. He'd said his piece to Xcor about removing himself from the fighting, and now he was going to pack up his shit and get out of the house. Out of the way. Out of this world of war he had been in all his life.

He had no idea where to go. But he'd spent centuries living off his wits, surviving night to night, nothing permanent to ground him or sustain him. So hey, this change in living situation was not going to be a news flash.

Out west, he was thinking. Or maybe to the south. Staying in Caldwell was a big, fat not-it.

And he had to leave right now. If he didn't, he was likely to go back to Jo and beg or something. For what, though, he didn't know. She'd found out about that shit with the mob, and it had validated everything he had not told her—

The French door was unlatched and opened, but the male who did the duty was not a servant. Vishous was more like a force of nature, and his mood, which was snarky on a good night, was sharper than those blades he made for everyone.

"Thank you," Syn muttered as he entered.

V shut things up, the cold getting cut off. "I was going to come find you."

Eyeing the archway on the far side of the pool tables, Syn crossed his arms over his jacket. "You're not talking me out of leaving."

"Like I would bother?" V cocked a brow. "Your business isn't mine, and you haven't been conscripted or anything. Everyone is free to go. You're not required to fight—"

Syn turned away. "I just wanted to be clear. That's all—"

"—but you're a pussy if you don't."

Pivoting back sharply, Syn felt his upper lip twitch. "What did you say?"

The Brother shrugged and walked around behind the bar where the bottles of top-shelf alcohol were lined up, soldiers ready to be called into service. He casually got one of the tall glasses from where the crystal was kept, but instead of pouring himself his usual strong dose of Goose, he hit the fruit juice. Six inches of fresh orange.

He tested the lip of his glass and swallowed. "Mmm, tasty. And you heard me. You're a pussy if you quit."

Syn stalked over to the bar, images of picking the Brother up and throwing him into all those glass bottle testing his impulse control. "What gives you the right to judge that?"

"The fact that I'm staying in the war and not expecting other people to do my work for me. The fact that my best friend is out facing the Omega right now. The fact that my brothers are with your cousins and comrades, in the field, trying to save the race. Meanwhile, you're standing here in front of me, worried about yourself, thinking about yourself, butt hurt over some female you met how many days ago? 'Scuse me if I'm not impressed with your special snowflake routine. I'm too busy living in the real world and worrying about who's going to die tonight."

"You have *no* idea what I've been through."

"I held my dead *shellan* in my arms. So I'm pretty sure that's Yahtzee. But whatever, you do you—"

"You don't understand what my sire was like."

V pointed to his own chest. "Bloodletter. You want to compare résumés with that shit?"

"I can't orgasm."

Vishous opened his mouth. Then shut it. "Okay, you win. And this is coming from a guy who's only got one nut."

"It's not a contest." But Syn felt his temper abate a little. Although what a triumph, right? "And I'm tired of the killing."

"So you're giving up." V shrugged and put out his palms. "Hey, don't glare at me, true? You need to stare at your decision in the bright light of conscience and own that shit. Hating my ass is not going to help you with that."

"I'm not quitting. I'm just done."

One black eyebrow lifted. "You're going to have to explain how those two are different to me."

Syn walked around, and then stopped at one of the pool tables. He considered flipping the thing to release some pent-up energy, but then he just trailed his fingertips in between the scattered, colorful balls, the green felt offering a soft resistance.

"I wasn't in the war for the species," he heard himself say. "I was in it because I liked to kill. For the sport. For the cruelty. For the outlet. And I don't have that drive anymore."

"What's changed?"

"I saw myself through another's eyes. And the reflection was too close to my father's for my liking. I was always determined not to be like him. I made rules and safeguards to guide that side of me. I had standards. In the end, though? The result was the same. I was killing him over and over again by proxy—but it wasn't helping me and I became him in the process."

"I heard that you were taking side jobs even here in Caldwell."

"I did."

Vishous poured himself more orange juice, the sound of the liquid filling his glass loud in the silence. "Past tense."

"I'm giving up a lot of things as of tonight." Syn picked up the cue ball and rolled the white weight around in his palm, wiping off a smudge of blue chalk. "No more of that."

And it wasn't just word service. Something was fundamentally different for him. Ever since his transition, his *talhman* had always been inside of him, a monster prowling the fence line of its enclosure, looking for signs of weakness, opportunities for escape, lapses in oversight.

No more. There was . . . a strange silence in the center of him.

But he wasn't numb. Oh, no, he was definitely not numb. He had a constant, weighted pain on his heart, to the point where he struggled to take a deep breath. It was the loss of Jo, of course—and he had a feeling the mourning was going to stick with him for the rest of his life. True love, after all, could be expressed in many different ways, but the one commonality to it was that it lasted. It was a permanence, in whatever form it took.

Especially when it was lost.

"You told Xcor, then?" V asked.

"Yes."

"What did he say?"

"Not much."

"How'd you feel when you were telling him?"

Syn stared at the perfectly smooth surface of the cue ball. "It is what it is."

"You're not bothered at all that he and your cousins are out there without you?"

"You're trying to lead me to a conclusion."

"No, I'm trying to make you see past yourself." V came around from the bar, glass of OJ in hand. "But yeah, I was going to come and find you. I have the answer to the question you asked me yesterday. About that female you knew from the Old Country."

Syn looked up with a jerk. "You found her? Is she here? In the New World?"

His words came out fast, like a tommy gun.

V's diamond eyes narrowed, his expression becoming remote. "She came over in the nineteen fifties. With her *hellren* and her young. A boy and a girl."

Syn closed his eyes and pictured the female running in that meadow around her parents' cottage with her pretrans brother. "So she mated. Who is her mate?"

"An aristocrat."

Popping his lids open, he frowned. "Tell me it is a love match."

"Yes."

Syn exhaled in relief. "This is good news. I've always wondered what happened to her. If I had believed in a benevolent creator, I would have prayed for just what she got. Where did she settle?"

"Here in Caldwell."

"Really. Well, that's good. She's safe here—"

"Sunnise was killed in the Raids." As Syn looked over in horror, V continued, "Along with her *hellren* and both her young. Murdered. By the *lessers*."

"You're lying. You're telling me this to—"

V looked bored. "You think I would waste a split second on making this shit up? They were slaughtered in their home about seven miles from here. In the death photograph I saw, which was taken by a blooded relation of hers, she was holding her daughter. She had tried to shield the young with her own body. The *hellren* and the son were decapitated."

When Syn heard something crack, he looked down. The cue ball in his hand had split in half, powdering under the pressure he had exerted upon it.

"You asked me to find her." V finished his OJ. "And I did. What you do with the information, like everything else in your life, is up to you."

With that, the Brother left the billiards room, the sound of his shitkickers drifting away until all Syn knew was the dense silence around him.

And the agony in his chest.

CHAPTER SIXTY

At the base of the alley downtown, Mr. F grabbed the back of the slayer's parka and yanked the other *lesser* around. Putting his face into his subordinate's, he spoke in a voice he had never heard come out of his mouth before.

"We stay together." He looked the other two dead in the eye. "The four of us stay the fuck together or I will kill you myself."

That was not an empty threat. Even though they were all technically immortal, he was done with the whole fucking thing. The Omega had meted out such a punishment with dawn's arrival that Mr. F could barely walk. He could also barely hear, the ringing in his ears the kind of background noise through which he couldn't decipher anything softer than a scream.

He had been tasked with finding recruits.

He had been told that it was his last chance.

And he had been aware that the Omega had changed. No more stains on the white robe. No more weakness. Nothing but a horrible power that seemed to gather further strength as the hours had passed.

Mr. F had been used as a piece of exercise equipment, and his misery had fueled the abuse further. When he had finally been cast out of *Dhunhd* and sent back to this world, he had known that he was being toyed with and lied to. As soon as he got the recruits in order, he was going to be demoted.

Or whatever was worse than demotion.

Tonight was his one shot at survival—on his own terms. If he didn't execute faultlessly?

"We stay the *fuck* together," he snapped.

The other two seemed too overwhelmed to argue about anything, and that was good for them. And as for this one with the AWOL ideas? Mr. F was going to break him like a horse if he had to.

"Now, we are going this way." He pointed in the direction the internal signal was coming from. "And you are going to go together."

When nobody moved, he yelled, "March!"

Mr. F took out one of the three guns he had. He'd given the knives and the ropes to the others.

"If you don't start moving, I will shoot you myself," he growled.

As he and his troops started off, he felt nothing like himself. He was another person, and not because of the initiation into the Lessening Society. The pressure he was under, the limited choices he had, the torture he had endured, had all hardened him into something else. Gone was the pacifist, druggie, fuckup. In its place . . . a military man.

And he meant exactly what he'd said.

He would stab them if he had to. Drag them if he must. Kick them and coerce them—anything to get them funneled down this fucking alley and into those goddamn motherfucking Brothers who he could sense, clear as day, just blocks away.

Mr. F knew he was right about where their enemy was. And he didn't have long to get the validation he didn't require.

One hundred yards later, two figures rounded the far corner and stopped.

Mr. F's troops stopped as well. And so help him God, he was prepared to jump-start them in the ass with his boot.

"You get in there, and you fucking fight," he snarled with menace. "Or what waits for you if you run will be so much worse than anything those vampires will do to you, I promise."

◆   ◆   ◆

As Butch and Tohr squared off with a quartet of slayers, Butch breathed in deep, though his sinuses were not what he used to measure the threat. He relied on his instincts. As he always did.

But he didn't believe the information that came to him.

"These can't be it," he whispered.

Tohr tilted his head to his communicator and gave their location in the too-well-lit alley. Immediately, one by one, fighters began appearing. Some on the roof. Some behind them. Some off to the side.

Those three *lessers* didn't stand a fucking chance.

But Butch was not allowed to fight. When he went to run forward and engage, Tohr held him back.

"No. You and I stay here."

As the brother pulled him back into a doorway for cover, it took everything in Butch to stay put. Everything. But the battle didn't last long. Qhuinn and Blay attacked from up above, jumping off the roof-lines of the buildings they'd materialized onto, and re-forming right on top of the enemy. And the two males used the low-tech weapons the slayers had been armed with to incapacitate them.

One. Strangled by his own rope by Blay, then hog-tied facedown on the pavement.

Two. Stabbed in the gut by Qhuinn, then dropped when both its hamstrings were sliced with its own knife.

. . . and three. All but decapitated by the mated pair as the two *hell-rens* went after it at once, a pair of daggers going deep into the throat. As the head went loose and hung backward on the spine, the chain-links in its hand were used to immobilize its arms.

All told, it took less than four minutes, and no one else had to get involved. Done and dusted. Okay, not dusted, not yet. That was Butch's job.

And yet he didn't walk forward. Looking around, he tried to define what he began to sense.

"You okay?" Tohr asked.

Butch reached into his jacket and gripped his cross. Then he shook his head and looked around the alley again. "No, this isn't . . . right. Something is . . ."

Somebody came up to them. Someone else. Then all kinds of brothers and fighters. They were all talking and looking at him, excited. Bubbling with aggression and triumph.

That was very premature.

All at once, Butch began to pant, his chest pumping up and down as an urgency, a warning, an alarm, vibrated through his body.

"Go . . ." he croaked.

"What?" Tohr said.

"You need to all go . . ." He threw out his hand and grabbed onto somebody's arm. "Go . . . you need to go . . . *goooooooooooooooooo!*"

None of them listened. Not one. The males he loved most in the world, his brothers, his friends, his family, clustered around him, trying to argue. Looking worried. Attempting to calm him by offering placation.

And that was when the hum started. Low, at first. Then growing in intensity. Why couldn't they hear the warning, Butch thought as he panicked. Why couldn't they feel the impending doom—

The first of the security lights exploded down at the far end of the alley, the fixture blowing up and showering sparks down the sweaty side of its building. And then another across the way. And another.

The flaring bursts of sparks were inexorable, closing in on the three fallen slayers who were writhing on the pavement as well as on those who Butch could not bear to lose.

"You have to leave or you're going to die!" he screamed as all the buildings on the whole block went dark, inside and out.

Ducking both hands into his jacket, he outted his forties—and began shooting at the asphalt in a circle. As the brothers and fighters jumped back and then scrambled for cover, he didn't look at where his bullets were ricocheting. He was only focused on what was coming through the darkness.

The evil was no longer one entity.

It was a tide of all the *lessers* that had ever been.

And they were about to break through into this world and take over everything.

"Get out of here!" he yelled at the top of his lungs. "Run!"

CHAPTER SIXTY-ONE

The power in Jo's apartment started to flicker around eight o'clock. First, her lights dimmed and then reluctantly came back on. Then there was some strobing. Finally? Total darkness in her apartment.

"Damn it," she said as she patted on the sofa cushion next to her and found her phone.

The building had no generator, and when she went to the power company's website, she discovered that all of Caldwell was out of juice. There was a total blackout, it seemed, and for kicks and giggles, she hit refresh a number of times, watching the reports come in on the map. It was like gophers popping out of holes in the grass.

Putting her phone down, she let her head fall back. What did it matter. Now that her résumé had been submitted everywhere it could be, it wasn't like she had any plans past staring off into space—and waiting to see if her body exploded.

Waiting to see if she needed to call that other male.

Waiting to feel better.

She could most certainly handle that to-do list in the pitch black.

Note that she wasn't preparing to feel normal again. Nah, she'd way given up on "normal." She was shooting for an improvement to "passable," which would certainly be better than where she was currently—

When her phone rang, she wondered whether it was the power company reaching out—which was nuts. Like they'd be calling two million people individually to give them an update on their outage?

Picking her cell up, she frowned when she saw who it was.

"McCordle?" she said as she answered. "And before you ask, yes, I've spoken with the FBI. I told them the same thing I told you, I don't know the guy—"

"I have another video to show you. I'm sending it to your phone."

Swallowing a curse, Jo switched her cell to her other ear. "Look, I've done what I can with you all. I appreciate you keeping me in the loop, but I'm not interested in—"

"We got it wrong."

"Got what wrong," she muttered.

"The man with Gigante on that videotape." There was a rustling, and then McCordle addressed someone somewhere around him. When he came back on, he spoke in a whisper. "We got cell phone footage shot by Gigante's bodyguard on the night they were all murdered. Turned out he was filming while it happened. The man in the first video at the Hudson Hunt and Fish Club killed all three of them."

"Well, he's a hit man." Jo tried to keep the boredom out of her voice. But come on, the last thing she needed right now was even more confirmation about how stupid she'd been with Syn. "That's his job, right?"

"He killed them to protect you."

Jo jerked up. "What?"

"Watch the video. Then call me back—and keep this between us. As usual."

When McCordle hung up on her, she held her cell phone like she might drop it even though she was sitting down over a rug. Then again, her hands were shaking like you couldn't believe.

The text came through a moment later. Just a video. Nothing else.

She started the thing up, her screen glowing in the darkness with a blue light. There was distortion at first and a fuzzy screen. And then the camera herky-jerk'd and steadied. The vantage point was an extreme angle upward, as if whoever was taking the footage was sprawled on the ground, and they were filming into an SUV's interior, through an open passenger door.

When the focus tightened, and the lighting recalibrated, she saw a man sitting behind the wheel. When he turned around to the back seat and leaned into the light from the door being ajar . . .

It was Syn.

Clear as day, she could see his face. As well as the gun in his hand.

And then he said, "I don't have a problem killing females—or anybody. But I'll be damned if you hurt Jo Early. Say good night, mother-fucker."

After that, he pulled the trigger, some kind of muffled *shhhhooo* going off.

Jo's heart beat so hard, she couldn't hear anything else. Not that there was much more to go on. The video cut off shortly after that.

She watched it two more times before calling McCordle back.

He answered on the first ring and she didn't bother with any "hellos." "Where did you get this?"

"The FBI raided the Hudson Hunt and Fish Club earlier today. It was on a cell phone in the pocket of a coat that also happened to have Gigante's son's ID in it."

"So you've arrested Junior?"

"No. We have his coat, for all the good that does us. Again, the cell phone belonged to Gigante's main bodyguard. We believe the guy took the footage during the shooting and then the phone was retrieved before anyone came on scene by Gigante's son. That's just conjecture, though. At any rate, it looks like that hit man had a change of heart when it came to you. The FBI's calling you about this soon, but I figured you'd want to take a deep breath."

"So he wasn't going to kill me after all."

"He killed to protect you, it looks like. You're sure you've never seen him before?"

"Ah, no. Never."

"Well, hopefully we'll find him—before Gigante's son does. That hit man better be a professional because what's out looking for him has one hell of a score to settle."

As Jo ended the call with McCordle, she eased back on her sofa, but she didn't stay that way for long. Seconds later, she was up on her feet and using the flashlight on her phone to find her coat and her bag.

She put her first call in to Syn on the way to her car.

The second as she headed downtown.

The third as she parked close to where she had first met him, in an alleyway behind Market Street. As she got out, she looked around. The whole city was draped in darkness, the usual ambient glow from the skyscrapers, street lights, and lower buildings extinguished as the result of a colossal blackout.

And that was when she heard the sound of the wind.

Except there was no gust rustling through her clothes or her hair.

An eerie sense of foreboding tightened Jo's neck muscles and made her look over her shoulder. Something was very wrong.

Or maybe it was just all the drama getting to her.

✦   ✦   ✦

As the shock wave went through the alley, the release of unholy energy blew everything out of its way, brothers tossed high in the air and slammed into the flanks of buildings, dumpsters sent rolling with their contents spilling out like blood, fire escapes peeling off their moorings and flying off like they were nothing but cobwebs.

Butch braced himself against the gale, lifting his forearms to cover his face, leaning in to the rush while desperately trying to stay on his feet. Against the hurricane-like force, his leather jacket was blown back, his hair streaked from his forehead, his lips pulled away and teeth exposed.

And then justlikethat it was over.

With the headwind ending so abruptly, Butch lurched forward and had to catch his balance, dropping his arms and swinging them wide.

So he was blinded by a light that was so intense, it was like he was pummeled by the illumination. Back up with the arms, this time so his retinas didn't get deep-fried. The glow quickly ebbed, however, and he was able to focus through blinking lids.

The Omega was standing in the center of the alley, his robing brilliant white and totally clean, his power refreshed—or resurrected was more like it. The new-and-improved evil was nothing like the faded version of late. Just as Butch had predicted, the Omega was stronger than ever before.

Shall we try this anew, the warping voice said inside Butch's head. *I believe you will find I am much rejuvenated.*

As Butch kept his eyes on the evil, he used his peripheral vision to check on his people. Not one of the brothers or the fighters was moving. They were all corpses, wiped out by the Omega's wrath.

I can feel your pain. The evil laughed in a low curl. *It is so satisfying.*

The Omega walked forward and stopped in front of the three *lessers* who'd been so easily subdued. The hood on the white robe dipped down as if it were regarding its creations. Then one of the sleeves lifted and a black, smoke-like appendage emerged.

In a series of pops, the corporeal forms of the slayers turned into dirty puffs of air, and the Omega pulled the exhaust into its sleeve, reabsorbing its own essence.

Just as Butch reached for one of his daggers, the Omega looked up. *Oh, no, no, we mustn't do that.*

The evil extended its handlike form and gathered in its palm a swirling of energy.

We tried this once before, remember? I wager it will be a different experience for you the now.

The Omega let it rip, pitching a fastball of concentrated nasty, and the impact was like getting hit with a bee's nest, a million stinging nettles biting into every inch of Butch's skin as he was blown off his feet into the wall behind him. The aftermath of the hit was worse. As the initial sensation faded, he felt as though he were bathed in the misery of humanity, all the suffering of all the ages boiling inside of him until he cried out in wretched pain.

Sliding down the bricks, he landed on his ass and looked up.

The Omega advanced further, floating over the asphalt. *Impressed with my effort? Surprised? It's not the result of a good day's sleep, but you already know that, do you not. Remember when my sister had her little chat with you in the church?*

Butch nodded because he wanted the evil to keep talking. "What about it?"

It was a violation of the rules of our game, and the rectification was getting my hearts back. The Creator awarded me the knowledge of that location—this after I have searched for them for centuries—and as you can see, I made the most of the reclamation of my property.

The evil took a little spin, as if it were showing off its pretty new robing.

Butch snuck one of his hands inside his jacket and locked a grip on the hilt of one of his daggers. If he could get close enough, if he could get a clear stab in the center of its chest? Maybe that would be enough—although he wasn't under any misconceptions of what would happen if he did manage to deep-stick the motherfucker. If a normal slayer popped and fizzed when the penetration occurred? The Omega was going to relight the whole fucking city.

My sister's miscalculation has cost her the entire war. I have won. And you will be my prize. The Omega's sleeve lifted toward Butch. *Our social acquaintance has lasted quite long enough. I believe I now wish for a more intimate association.*

The evil's energy entered Butch through the soles of his shitkickers, and the vibration traveled up his calves and his thighs, through his torso and into his head. Flexing against the onslaught, he strained and contorted, trying to fight the ownership that he could feel was coming.

But like a revving engine, the disrupting power only ramped up, getting higher and higher, until he was nearly bent backward and his flesh could no longer contain the shock waves within its corporal confines.

It was as he strained and kicked his head back that he saw the figure approaching.

A female. In a parka. With red hair.

Surely he was imagining this. What the hell was Jo Early doing—

Butch shook his head. She had to go—she was going to die!

Just as he was sure he was going to explode and be consumed like the slayers had been, the internal pressure eased up and he was able to breathe again.

A visitor . . . we have a visitor, do we? the Omega said in Butch's head. *And you know her, do you not. Your half-sister. What a marvelous surprise. Let us bring her into this, shall we?*

There was a high-pitched scream, and then Jo levitated off the ground and was swept forward, compelled to the Omega, the toes of her boots dragging over the asphalt. She fought the pull as best she could, flailing at the invisible spell that had taken her over, but there was nothing she could do. She was as helpless as the rest of them.

I'm afraid she is not my type, the Omega announced. *Or I might enjoy a further kind of torture of you, my dear friend. Still, she will be a nice addition to the family when this is all done.*

The Omega cast Jo aside like she was a rag doll, flipping her into the flank of a building, her body shattering the panes of a window, the glass raining down as she fell in a slump to the pavement.

"You fucking bastard!"

Butch leaped up and hit the ground running, catching the Omega by surprise. Raising his black dagger high, he plunged it into whatever he could, stabbing over and over again—

The Omega roared with fury. Grabbing Butch by the throat, it shoved its threat off, Butch's body going spinning off to the side, the dagger flying out of his palm.

And then there was no more posturing, no conversation, no half-ways.

The energy that came at Butch hit him and stayed put, penetrating into his very molecules, a cloud of agony that was going to blow him apart within seconds. As he screamed, he saw white and stopped breathing.

Just before he lost consciousness, he remembered what V had told him before he'd left the Pit. The cross. The cross would save him.

With his last quantum of strength, he pushed his hand under his muscle shirt and took out his gold cross. Holding the symptom of his faith forward, he focused his eyes on the Omega, as if he could will the evil back to *Dhunhd*.

Through slack lips, he began to pray. "Hail Mary, full of grace . . ."

The Omega's laughter rang out in Butch's brain. *And you think that will help?*

The suffering intensified even further.

CHAPTER SIXTY-TWO

At the moment of his death, Butch thought of Marissa, of course. Vishous, too. And also the others who had stayed back home. They were going to be mourners for the rest of their lives and he hated it.

And then there was Wrath. He was never going to get over this. Almost all of the Brotherhood lost and most of the fighters in the house gone, too? Thank God he had Beth and L.W. to keep him from spiraling. He had spent so many centuries after his parents had been murdered by the Lessening Society angry and disconnected.

He had to continue to lead. He had to rebuild.

The vampire race had to go on after this carnage.

As the suffocation get worse, Butch could feel his heart slow down. Slower. Slower . . .

"Marissa," he choked out.

His last thought was of the way they had kissed goodbye. That final moment would have to last until they met in the Fade. Assuming there even was a place to go after death now that the Omega had won. What kind of spoils would come with the evil's victory?

Butch drew his last breath picturing the aristocratic female who had saved him from his gray, alcoholic existence, rescuing him with her love and her—

The screeching noise was something between a jet airplane skidding out on a tarmac, an industrialized balloon being popped with a pin, and seven thousand air horns going off at the same time.

And then Butch was able to breathe a little. And a little more.

And finally, fully.

With air in his lungs, his sight came back—not that that helped much. Because he had no clue what the hell he was seeing.

The Omega was still sending out all his claiming power, but there was a deflection. A block. A . . .

Something standing between the source of the evil and Butch was taking it in the—

It couldn't be.

She couldn't be.

Butch staggered up to his feet, using the building behind him as a crutch because his balance was for shit. Wheezing, but breathing, he gave his eyes every opportunity to come clean with what was really going down.

Nothing changed.

The woman who had introduced herself as his sister's former friend, who had showed up with a busted face and a bad story, who had taken him back to a crib which twenty-four hours later didn't exist, had staked herself in front of him and was taking everything the Omega could throw at her.

With her stiletto heels planted, and her beautiful body straining, and her brunette locks flowing in an unholy wind, she had extended her own palm and was channeling the evil into herself.

And suddenly the balance of power seemed to change.

The Omega was no longer throwing the shit out. The woman—female—whatever the fuck she was—was sucking him in. Butch knew this because the Omega took a step back, and another—and then it seemed unable to go any further.

The woman moved forward. And got even closer.

A wind began to swirl around them, currents made of air that were strong as steel, and the woman yelled out a curse—

The Omega's white robe rotted away, the folds staining brown and gray and then going threadbare, revealing the dense, black hole of malevolence that they covered. A face emerged from within the stain, a tortured face, a face that was screaming—

Right before it blew apart.

The evil exploded, waves of energy released, breaking windows and blowing holes in the brick walls of buildings. But then came the sucking in, the ownership, the claiming of the power.

In the aftermath, there was only the woman left in the alley. The woman ... and the bodies of Butch's brothers and his fellow fighters. And his sister, Jo Early.

The woman looked at him over her shoulder. Then she turned around.

"Who are you?" Butch said hoarsely. "Really."

"I did a good job with your sister's friend, didn't I?" She smiled in an almost shy way. "I got into your mind and looked around. I figured it was my best shot."

"Tell me."

"I have been known by many names, but I have always been female so it would be rude of you to ask my age. I am the Omega's little sister. I am Devina."

Butch weaved on his feet as he tried to understand what she was saying. But then things came back. "That night of Throe's party. When the shadows attacked the guests ... something left the house from the upstairs window ..."

"And walked through the snow, leaving glowing tracks." Devina smiled. "That was me. Poor Throe. He was no match for me. I needed a soul to switch places with and he made himself available."

"Why did you save me?" Butch asked.

Devina smoothed her perfectly beautiful brunette hair. "I was lost until I saw you sucking back one of those *lessers*. I was just walking around this city, miserable and dejected, night after night. And then you talked to me about the nature of love and the female you fell for. You made me feel like that could happen to anyone. Including a demon like me. So I owe you."

She glanced around. "So these are your people, huh? Don't worry, they're not dead. Just stunned. They'll come to, and you should proba-bly clear out. There's a hush over this city, but it won't last. It never does."

The relief was so tremendous, Butch nearly fell over. "Thank you."

Devina shook her head in a regretful way. "We're even now. So after tonight? We're on different sides. You need to know this."

"So the war is going to restart with you?"

"In a manner of speaking. But I don't discriminate like my brother did. I'm an equal opportunity killer, humans, vampires, wolven. I don't give a shit as long as it's fun."

"Fair enough."

The demon stared at him for a long time. "That *shellan* of yours is a lucky female for sure."

With that, she turned away. And that was when Butch was able to properly focus on the cropped jacket she had paired with her micro-mini and her sheer black hose and her Louboutins with the red soles.

On the back of the black fabric, chunky crystals had been mounted and sewed in a pattern . . . that formed a perfect Georgian cross.

"Holy shit . . . Lacroix," Butch stammered.

She paused and twisted around. "My jacket?"

"That's Christian Lacroix, isn't it. Vintage. From the nineties."

The demon smiled so widely she became resplendent. "You know your fashion. And yes, I bought it new thirty years ago. Isn't it just stun-ning?"

"Absolutely beautiful. A real showstopper."

"You say the sweetest things."

"And Vishous is never wrong."

Devina seemed confused at that. But then she shrugged. "Whatever. I'll be seeing you around—oh, and there's one left. You better go take care of it. And somebody is coming, one of yours. Goodbye, Brian O'Neal."

"Goodbye . . . Devina."

The demon nodded once and then lingered a moment longer.

After that, she was gone.

But certainly not forgotten.

◆   ◆   ◆

Mr. F watched the entity dematerialize from the shadows he'd been hiding in since he'd sent those three *lessers* down to their immortal deaths. And for a split second, he toyed with the idea of trying to run. He had a bunch of fully loaded guns on him, and except for the *Dhestroyer*, all the other vampires were still in a stupor. So it wouldn't be hard to make a getaway.

But no. This was what he had engineered.

Taking all his weapons in hand, he stepped out from the doorway. The *Dhestroyer* noticed him instantly and went for his gun, but Mr. F called out to his enemy.

"I'm putting everything I have on me down."

Mr. F dropped the guns on the asphalt and kicked them away. Then he took his jacket off and let it fall to the ground. As he put his hands up and did a slow turn so that the *Dhestroyer* would know he presented no harm, the cold of the spring night bit into his unholy flesh and he shivered.

When he finished his full circle, he faced the Brother. "Please . . ." he said in a voice that cracked. "Take me now. You're the only way out. Please, I'm begging. End this for me. End this . . . for all of us."

Mr. F was the last *lesser*.

After centuries of warfare, he was the last of his breed, and he didn't want to go out in a blaze of glory. He just wanted to go out.

The Brother frowned and seemed to breathe in the air, his nostrils flaring. And then he limped forward.

"I only want this to end." Mr. F knew he'd already said that, but what did it matter. "I've wanted my life to be over for quite some time now. Please . . . let it be here. Let it be now."

The addiction. The Omega. The war he had been drafted into without his consent.

The Brother stopped and leaned down to the pavement, his narrowed eyes never leaving Mr. F. When he straightened, he'd picked up something, there was something in his hand.

Even in the darkness, Mr. F knew what it was.

A black dagger.

Mr. F closed his eyes and let his head fall back. As the Brother resumed his approach, and the heavy footfalls grew closer, Mr. F got calmer, especially as the scent of the vampire became loud in his nose and he could feel the heat coming off of the male's massive, deadly body.

"It ends here," the *Dhestroyer* said.

"Thank you," Mr. F whispered.

The strike did not come through the heart. Instead, the blade streaked across the front of Mr. F's throat. As black blood bubbled up, he started to choke, fluid entering his lungs.

Giving himself up to the death he had begged for, he let himself go loose, but he didn't fall to the ground. The vampire caught him before he hit the pavement, and Mr. F opened his eyes.

The *Dhestroyer* lowered his face down and the two of them looked at each other.

Then the vampire opened his mouth . . . and began to inhale.

CHAPTER SIXTY-THREE

Syn pounded down Market Street in the darkness, following the scent of *lesser*. The sheer amount of the stench made him throw some more power into his legs. It was as if an entire army of the enemy had shown up in the field from out of nowhere—and what the fuck was up with the lights? Caldwell's power had been cut for some reason, only the anemic glow from fixtures powered by emergency generators giving distant stars to some of the skyscrapers.

Not that he gave a fuck.

He re-formed downtown in the quadrant he was usually given, over by the meatpacking district, but as soon as his nose had caught a whiff of this? Cue the running—and he would have dematerialized, but he didn't know exactly where he was going.

Besides, it was only a matter of a couple of blocks—

The SUV came out of nowhere, rounding the corner from one way as Syn rounded the turn from the other. As the headlights blinded him, he slammed into the front grille, and was so pissed off by the inconvenience, he shoved back at the vehicle, pushing it out of his way.

Then he took off running again.

That slayer stench was a calling card not to be ignored.

One final corner later and Syn went stealth, slowing his speed so he could move in silence, nothing but the creak of his leather jacket to warn anyone of his arrival—

Syn slowed.

Syn stopped.

The carnage was the kind of thing that the brain could not process. Bodies, everywhere on the ground, and he knew them all. It was the Brotherhood. The Bastards. The fighters. Too many to count or to comprehend. And in the middle of the horrible scene . . .

Butch was holding a *lesser* in his arms, bending it backward as he inhaled, the black smoke passing from the slayer into the Brother. And as he continued to draw, the skin of the undead became a bag round the skeleton, all the muscle melting away under clothes that started to slip free of the body, the cheeks hollowing out, the eye sockets growing deep, the lax arms and hands becoming sticks.

Butch continued to take the essence of the Omega into himself until there was nothing left.

Not even the bones.

The last of the clothes fell to the ground at the Brother's feet, ribbons that had been pants and shirts, jacket and holsters.

Butch staggered, fumbling with something.

He was clearly injured as well.

Syn surged forward and caught the male, holding him up. "Butch . . ."

"It's over . . ." came the reedy reply to the question Syn couldn't voice. "It's all over. The last *lesser* is gone."

Gathering the fighter against him, Syn closed his eyes on a wave of self-hatred and guilt. The *Dhestroyer* Prophecy had been wrong— or at best, incomplete. The Omega had been destroyed. But so had the Brotherhood—

The sounds were so soft at first that, in his grief and regret that he had come too late, that he had failed to serve those he revered against a

common enemy, he did not notice them. But then the chorus of movement, the shifts of boots upon the ground and of leather upon leather,
registered. All around, the Brotherhood and the Bastards and the fighters were stirring, life animating limbs that had been terrifyingly still.

"They're okay," Butch said in a groggy way. "Coming . . . 'round."

Syn's only thought was that he was the last man standing. Literally.
His second was that he had to control the scene. He was relieved that
this alley wasn't one massive open grave, but there were hundreds of
thousands of humans, cops, and assholes out and about in the darkened
city. There was no backup to be had, either. The fighters on hand at the
mansion to protect Wrath had to stay put.

From the midst of his battlefield assessment, plans began to formu-
late instantly, and the first was to get Manny over here. The next was to
call V and get some *mhis* up. If the Omega was gone, the Brother should
be safe to—

Butch grabbed onto the front of Syn's jacket. Hazy hazel eyes
seemed to not want to focus as he struggled for words.

"Tell me," Syn said urgently. "What can I do for you?"

Butch's shaking hand lifted. "Take care of my sister."

Syn wheeled around, and that was when he saw her. There. Against
the alley's damp and dirty foot, Jo was lying in a heap, her red hair tangled, her limbs all at bad angles.

In a rush to get to her, Syn almost dropped the Brother like a piece
of trash—

The first gunshot caught Syn by surprise, sizzling past his left ear.
The second hit him in the meat of his shoulder. The third went into
his arm.

Years of training took over as his brain got jammed by adrenaline.
He ducked and covered, protecting Butch as he dragged the floppy bag
of Brother out of harm's way. Turned out he made a passable bullet-
proof vest: Another lead slug went into him somewhere in the chest and
something must have hit his calf. But Butch was spared. The bad news
was that there wasn't much to hide behind, the alley having been peeled

of the normal shit—like big trash containers and abandoned cars—that typically accumulated in Caldwell's colon. Plus there were the Brothers who were struggling to wake up and defenseless as newborns, and Jo, who he feared was dead.

An inset doorway was the best that he could do, and he propped Butch up as there was a pause in the shooting. The sonofabitch with the gun was exchanging clips.

This was Syn's only chance.

Diving a hand into his jacket, he—

Felt only slippery shit.

He couldn't seem to grip anything, and he pulled out his hand in confusion. Red, everywhere. He'd been shot in the palm.

Putting his body in the way to protect Butch, he went leftie—and at that moment, the lights came back on in Caldwell. Sure as if someone had cranked the dimmer switch back in the direction of wouldja-look-at-that, suddenly he could see his enemy. A dark-haired human dressed in black.

The mobster's son. Carmine Gigante Jr.

He had to have been driving that SUV Syn had bounced off of.

Syn's shoulder injury meant his second-choice hand was numb, some kind of nerve cut. So when he went for his gun, he had no strength in that hold, either.

Gigante's progeny didn't have that problem. Junior readily brought his weapon up again, and this time he had plenty of sight to go by. The muzzle pointed directly at Syn. A death shot, if there ever had been one—

The gun went off with a pop and Syn knee-jerked into his torso—but it wasn't like he could stop the bullet. Gasping, bracing, trying to stay conscious . . .

The mobster dropped to the pavement, his weapon skittering away from his palm, the back of his skull cracking as it fell back onto that filthy, hard asphalt.

Syn looked down at himself in confusion.

"T-t-torso."

He nearly tripped on himself as he wheeled to the voice of his female. "Jo?"

His beautiful, brave, extraordinary female was holding her double-gripped gun straight out with stiff arms. Everything was shaking on her, her legs, her shoulders, her head—even her teeth were chattering. But those arms and those hands were rock fucking solid.

"You t-t-told me . . ." she stuttered. "Aim for the torso. It's the b-b-biggest target."

Syn let out a strangled sound as he lunged for her. His body was full of lead and leaking like a sieve, though, so it was a messy reunion. Not that he gave a shit.

He disarmed her as he landed next to her on the ground and pulled her against him.

"It's okay, I've got you," he said as he held her to his heart.

"I c-c-can't stop shaking," she said into his throat.

"It's over. It's okay . . . it's over."

Closing his eyes, he allowed himself one brief moment of reunion. Then he got on his communicator and started barking out orders. When the responses came in, from Manny, from V—and especially from Doc Jane as she materialized out of thin air right next to Butch, he relaxed a little and pulled back.

Staring into Jo's wide, shell-shocked eyes, he brushed her hair out of her face. "Are you okay?"

She was trembling so badly, her molars were castanets, and speaking was hard. "You weren't going to kill me, were you."

"What?"

"You weren't. You were protecting me. You killed Gigante to keep me safe."

Syn shook his head. "None of it matters anymore. As long as you're all right—"

"You were trying to save my life." Jo grabbed the front of his leather jacket. "I'm so sorry. I was wrong about you. I was so wrong—"

"Shh. You have nothing to apologize for."

"I do. Syn, I—"

"Everything is forgiven," he said because he had the sense it was the only thing that would calm her, and he was worried about whether she'd been shot.

Plus, that was a true statement. He would always forgive her, even though, in this case, there was nothing to excuse. At all.

"I love you," she said. "You and only you. No matter what the future is, I need you to know that. I need to say the words to you."

As her miraculous statements registered, Syn lost his voice—or he would have spoken back to her what she had said to him. Lacking words, he touched her hair with awe, and as if she understood what he meant, she turned her face into his bloody palm and kissed it. Then she kissed it again. Then she—

The moan she let out was part relief, part starvation. And then her lips locked onto his bullet wound, the suction hesitant. At least for the first draw. For the second, however, she swallowed hard and moaned again, turning her whole body to the source of the blood flow, seeking sustenance.

Fuck. Her transition was here—

Rearing away from his palm, Jo let out a plaintive howl, her eyes confused and focused at the same time. "What's happening? What's . . . happening to me?"

"It's okay," he soothed her, "I'm going to give you a better draw."

Biting into his wrist, he made sure the punctures were nice and deep, and then he brought the wellspring to her lips.

"Latch on," he told her. "*Drink of me so that I may give you strength.*"

When he realized he had spoken in the Old Language, he nearly translated, but she didn't require the vocabulary. She formed a perfect seal over his vein and started to take from him in earnest, her eyes frightened as they held his own, her trembling getting worse instead of better.

"I will not leave you," he said. "Until it is done—"

"Syn, we need to get you looked at—"

At the sound of the male voice, he jerked Jo even closer to him, his body forming a cage around her own. As he let out a vicious warning growl, the circle of Brothers, who had formed around them without him realizing it, jumped back like they had seen a rattlesnake in the grass.

All at once, the alley was bathed in red.

Upper lip curled back, fangs fully extended, Syn was ready to attack—

He shook himself back to reality. Clearing his throat, he said, "Shit. Sorry."

Butch pushed his way through the crowd. In a fond tone, he murmured, "I gotta approve of how you follow directions, Syn. I asked you to take care of my sister and you are. It's a real example for others."

Feeling suddenly shy, Syn stared down at his female and tenderly brushed her cheek. "If she'll have me, I'd like to care of her for the rest of her life."

◆   ◆   ◆

It was all such a blur.

As Jo's hormones went wild and her body was taken over by an unstoppable force, she had trouble putting the events that led up to her transition in proper order. Then again, did any of that really matter? She was with Syn and she was . . . doing something that would have been repugnant and shocking at any other time in her life.

Instead, it was natural. It was . . . right.

With her lips to his wrist and the taste of dark wine down the back of her throat, she gave in to what her body seemed destined to do: take from him to survive.

And as she drank, the chill that had trembled through her very bones gradually abated, replaced by a warmth that flowed freely, filling her up from the inside out.

Closing her eyes, she kept taking what Syn provided her, aware that she was being moved, that there was some kind of relocation happening, not that she could track much of what was going on. And then there was movement, subtle and uneven. A soft, engine-like purr. Was she in some kind of vehicle?

Summoning her eyesight, she lifted her lids . . . and saw a whole lot of medical equipment in a cramped space. And was she on the floor?

"It's okay."

All it took was the sound of Syn's voice to make everything all right. Not that she had been worried, anyway. With him, she was safe.

"We're in the surgical unit," he said softly. "Manny's driving us back to the training center. We just left downtown."

She wanted to release his vein to speak, but her mouth refused to follow that order.

"Don't worry," he murmured, "the partition is shut. We're alone."

As if she were worried about privacy? The only thing she cared about was that he was with her.

Nursing from his life spring, she memorized his features. The deeply set eyes. The Mohawk. The hollow cheeks and strong jaw. His wide shoulders. His heavy pectorals and thick, powerful arms . . .

Another need began to rise inside of her.

And as if he read her mind, his lids lowered. "Yes," he purred. "I can give you that, too."

Somehow, he managed to reposition her flat on her back on the cold, hard metal floor—not that she cared—and she helped him with her jeans as best she could, kicking off her boots, dragging the lengths down with socked toes. All the while, she was aware of making mewling noises, begging him, pleading with him.

Her core needed him as much as her changed demanded his blood.

She felt his fingers slip and slide against her sex first, and then there was a pause.

"I love you, Jo," he said roughly.

Releasing his vein, she stared up into his harsh face. "I love you, too."

Jo cried out as he entered her, his thick erection filling her up. And then he started pumping, slowly at first, just a rocking—and she intended to follow his rhythm. She could not. She had to relatch with his wrist so all she could do was absorb his thrusts. Faster. Harder.

Jo closed her eyes again. In the back of her mind, she knew this was unfair to ask of him. Given that he could not find release, it would only hurt him in the end.

But the sex was something he seemed determined to give her.

No matter the cost to himself.

That was the man—male, rather—she loved, however. He would do anything, absolutely anything . . .

. . . for his female.

CHAPTER SIXTY-FOUR

S yn must have checked that that partition, separating the treatment space from the mobile surgical unit's cockpit, was locked in place a hundred times.

Okay, that was an exaggeration. But only a slight one.

He did not want anyone to see Jo undone as she was, being intimately serviced by her male—had she really told him she loved him?—and that especially included one of her brothers. Not that he was worried about defending his female, even against a member of her own bloodline.

He may have turned over a new leaf with his *talhman*, but he was still a killer. His reaction as he'd been approached while feeding his female proved it.

Looking down into the face of his *shellan*, he watched the way her head moved back and forth as he penetrated her and retreated, penetrated and retreated. The feel of her hot, wet core was going straight to his head, and then there was the sight of her at his vein. His hips jerked and began to pump on reflex, something taking over him.

As the rhythm of his pelvis increased, Syn began to pant, the pleasure ramping up inside of him even though it had nowhere to go. But what the fuck did he care. Beneath his surging body, Jo was in ecstasy, her arousal scent thick in the air, her body absorbing his thrusts, both her hands locked on his forearm to make sure his vein didn't go anywhere away from her mouth.

Giving himself up to the sex, his body rode the wave, closing in on the terminal moment that would not come, the lip of pleasure from which he would never fly, the culmination that was an ever-moving target he would never close—

Syn's eyes squeezed closed and his molars locked.

Sweat broke out across his face, down his neck . . . and over his chest under his clothes.

Slapping into the seat of Jo's pelvis, he groaned deep in his throat as the pleasure pinpointed into pain, the worst it had ever been because his female was the very best he had ever—

The orgasm crackled through Syn's body as his hips locked into place, all of the tension releasing in an explosion of sensations that brought a sacred easing, an indescribable floating peace, a soaring exhalation as he ejaculated over and over again, filling his female up.

Syn dropped his head down, his forehead against the corrugated floor of the surgical van. For a moment, he thought he was losing consciousness, everything spinning. But then he returned to his body.

And continued to pleasure his female.

It was a new landscape of experience, and he explored it with her, the pleasure rising up again, finding that potential, renewing the ascension. The second time it happened for him, as he approached the release, he wondered if it wasn't going to fail on him. After centuries of impotence, he expected more of the same even after his first data point to the contrary.

He was wrong.

He orgasmed again.

And again.

And again.

As did his female.

It turned out his body just knew what it wanted. And it had saved itself through entire eras of progress and innovation and revolution and evolution . . .

. . . for the one female it wanted to give itself to.

What a wise choice, Syn thought with a smile as he started to ride the waves once more.

◆   ◆   ◆

Butch needed to be driven back to the mansion in the R8.

Even after V materialized downtown and went to work on him, he didn't have the energy to do more than respirate. Fortunately, his best friend was on it. In fact, Vishous was straight-up empowered. In spite of doing his cleansing routine, and throwing up *mhis* around the scene in the alley, he was snappy as a spring motherfucker.

Then again, winning the war had a way of perking a brother up. Especially after Butch and his roomie had just conference-called their females and gotten to play the victorious warriors returning to the home front with the spoils.

Which, okay, fine, were nothing but some serious bragging rights. What the fuck did it matter, though! The happiness in Marissa's and Jane's voices was more than enough of a reward. Plus, hello, everyone was coming back with a heartbeat.

Although Syn was going to need some surgery. Assuming the Bastard didn't let Jo drain him dry in the back of that RV. At least Manny was watching over them like a hawk.

Letting his head lull in the direction of his bestie, Butch rolled his eyes. "I still can't believe it. It's over. It's done. The Omega is gone."

"But we got a replacement." V glanced over. "Your little friend."

"Balance, right?" Butch went back to looking out the front windshield. "It's all about balance. Did you know your mom had another sister?"

"No. But there's a lot I don't know about her."

"Well. There you go."

As V's phone went off with a text, he nodded at the unit in the console. "Check that will you. I'm feeling like I want to keep my eyes on the road tonight. Fuck only knows what happens next."

Butch snagged the Samsung and put in his roommate's passcode. As the thing came alive, he went into the text that had just come through. When he saw who it was from, he nearly put the screen back facedown.

Tossing the damn cell out the window also had an appeal.

Things were going so well. Couldn't they have a moment's peace—

"What is it?" V glanced over. "Something wrong?"

Butch sat up in the passenger seat a little higher. "Um . . . it's, ah . . . here lemme open it. It's a link."

"From who?"

Yeeeeeah, maybe we'll just wait on that, Butch thought. "Lassiter" was not a name he wanted to be tossing out all willy-nilly—

"What . . . the . . . fuck," he breathed.

V's foot came off the gas, that surgical RV they were trailing getting ahead of them. "What."

Butch shook his head and restarted the video. "It's Curt Schilling."

Vishous's recoil was so great, the other brother nearly snapped his neck. "*The* Curt Schilling?"

"TheCurtSchilling." As in the Boston Red Sox right-handed, bloody-sock'd pitcher who had led the team to its first World Series Championship in eighty-six years, finally breaking the Curse of the Bambino after an agonizing drought. "The fucking Curt Schilling!"

"What's he doing on my phone!"

"I don't know!"

Okay, fine. It was quite possible the two of them were sounding like ten-year-old little boys. But it was TheCurtSchilling.

"Play it! Play it! Play—"

"I am! I am! I am—"

V wrenched the R8's wheel to the right and slammed on the brakes, halting them on a shoulder of the road. Then the pair of them knocked heads as they leaned down to the screen.

Curt Schilling—TheCurtSchilling—looked into the camera that was videotaping and seemed a little confused as he spoke.

"Well, this is a new one. But hey, I'm game. Ah—Vishous?" Then on a mutter, "Helluva name you got there." More normally now, "This is from your good friend, Lassiter. He wanted you to know that he's really sorry for what he had to do. It was for your own good, and you know this, but he probably could have handled things better." Another mutter, "Hope this doesn't involve a woman." Normal again, "Anyway, he wants you to know that he respects the hell out of you, and he said to tell you congratulations on your historic win. You and your roommate have saved everyone who matters and he promises that he'll stand by both of you, forever." Mutter. "Seems like a nice guy." Normal. "Oh, and he tells me that not only are you and your roommate, Butch, watching this together, the two of you are diehard Red Sox fans. Go Sox!"

Schilling turned around and fiddled with something behind him. "One more thing. He paid extra to Cameo for this. He said it would mean the world to you both."

From out of a stereo speaker, the unmistakable strumming and horns started.

Then, Neil Diamond's famous voice: "Where it began, I can't begin to know . . ."

The anthem of the Sox. The song that every Sox fan knew by heart. The lyrics that took you back to your first game at Fenway, and the hot dogs, and the sunshine on your face as you cheered for your team, and prayed that maybe this year, after so many years, after so many struggles, after whole generations of fans had been denied the victory, now this year it would happen and the faith and the hope and the loyalty would be rewarded.

With the win everyone wanted.

"Fuck," Butch choked out.

"Goddamn it," V muttered.

"—was in the spring," Diamond continued, "Then spring. became the summer . . ."

As tears started to fall, messy, nasty, thank God-they-were-alone-in-the-dark tears, V grabbed for Butch's hand—or maybe it was the other way around.

And then, all three of them, TheCurtSchilling included, sang at the top of their lungs: "Sweeeeeeeeeeeeeeeeeeeeeeeeeeeeeeeeeeeeeeet Caroliiiiiiiiiiiiiiiiiiiiiiiiiiiiiiiiiiiiiiine . . ."

In the aftermath of unexpected, hard-fought, and hard-won victory, Butch held on to his very best friend, and sang the one song that could have broken through his manly shell to expose the child's heart that still beat within his fully grown chest.

That fucking angel was *so* hard to hate, he really was.

". . . reaaaaaching ouuuuuuuuuuuuuuuut, touuuuuuuuuuuuching me-eeeeeeeee, touuuuuuuuuuuching yoooooouuuuuu . . ."

CHAPTER SIXTY-FIVE

The night after the end of the war, Jo woke up in a bed with her male. They were both naked between soft sheets, and the silence in the luxurious room, in her body, was a relief.

"You okay?" Syn asked in a groggy way.

"I think so." As his eyes popped open and it looked like he was about to run for a crash cart, she smiled. "I mean, yes, I am. It's just a new me, you know?"

Stretching everything she had to stretch, she was relieved to find that the aches and pains that had racked her for the last twelve hours were abating. Her stomach was hungry, the chills were gone, and other than a pair of sharp-and-pointies where her canines had been—the pair she'd been born with had fallen out like baby teeth sometime during the day—not much was different.

She'd made it safely to the other side.

And she was with exactly who she wanted to be with.

On that note, they spent some time smiling at each other. She knew that there were big adjustments ahead. A new way of life, a new way of being, and she was nervous about it—but excited, too. In the intervening days since she'd learned of the transition, she'd had some time to preemptively consider the repercussions of being another species entirely, but that was nothing compared to the yup-it-actually-happened.

Two things calmed her, however. One, she had come through the change healthy. Thanks to Syn's blood, she was alive and well.

And secondly? She had him. With Syn by her side, she knew she could handle anything life threw at her.

As if he knew she was thinking about the future, he said, "We can take it slow, if you want."

"You mean . . . like, us?"

"Yes. I don't want you to feel like you have to come live here with me—"

"Where are we?"

"The First Family's mansion. With the Brotherhood and your brothers and my cousins and the other fighters . . . their families . . . and a lot of *doggen*, including Fritz, who you've met."

Jo glanced around the beautifully appointed bedroom. Antiques. Silk wallpaper. Drapery that was like a ball gown.

"How big is this place?" she asked, because it was a simple question she'd be wondering about for a while now.

"I don't know. Fifty rooms? Maybe more?"

Lifting her head, she blinked. "Wow. That makes the Early house seem like a cabin."

"Your parents?"

As she nodded, she found herself frowning. "What do I do about them? Do I keep in touch? Can I?" She thought of Bill and Lydia. "And what about my friends out in the human world, not that I have many?"

"You can see them as much or as a little as you want. We'll manage it. No one is going to isolate you."

"Good. I don't how much I'm going to want to . . . my parents are complicated. And I still don't know who my birth mother is."

"I'll be there to help you look for her. Whatever you need, it's yours."

"So . . . about this bonded male thing."

Syn stretched like a panther and then kissed her. "Nailed it."

"You sure did." Jo couldn't keep the smile off her face. "And I would like to live with you here. There's nowhere else I'd rather be. But there has to be something I can do for work, right?"

"Absolutely."

"Are you just going to say yes to me about everything?"

"Yes." Syn winked. "I am."

Jo kissed him and got serious. "Thank you," she whispered.

"For what? I've not really done anything."

Reaching up, she traced the features she loved so much with her fingertips. "For giving me a home. A proper home."

"Well, this mansion isn't mine—"

"I'm not talking about the building we're in." She thought of her lonely childhood, her sense of being lost in the world even as she lived around other people. "More than the answers to who I am, I've been searching for a home. You are my home. You, and only you, are my shelter and my comfort."

"I don't deserve that." His expression darkened. "Jo, there are still things you have to know about me. About things I've done. I mean, I'm not that person anymore, but—"

"I will listen to everything and anything you have to say. But you need to know that the male you are now, and the male you've always been with me, is the one I will love forever."

"You make me want to be a hero, not a sinner."

"Well, from my point of view, you're *very* good at the former. And after everything that's happened, I believe I am in the best position to judge that, don't you think."

They started kissing again, and that led to . . . all kinds of things. And as he climaxed inside of her once again, Jo held her male tightly. He was right. There were things to learn about him, and things he had to learn about her, stories to share and feelings to express—not all of them happy-go-lucky. But they had plenty of time for those sorts of things.

When you had a happily-ever-after, you had time.

When you had true love, you had everything you needed.

As Syn collapsed on top of her, breathing hard and sated once more, she stroked his back and smiled up at the ceiling. Except then he pulled back sharply.

"What is it?" she asked.

"I know the first thing we need to do together as a couple."

Jo breathed in as part of replying to him, and that was when she caught the scent of bacon. As her stomach let out a howl, she held up her forefinger.

"Eat breakfast."

Syn laughed. "Well, yes. And we call it First Meal in this house."

"Tomato, tomahto, as long as there's bacon involved and some eggs, and chocolate somehow, I'm good to go."

"You can have everything you want—but if you're moving in with me?" He kissed her as if he couldn't resist doing so. "We're going to go out and buy some furniture for my room."

"You don't like this antique look?"

"This isn't where I normally sleep—I have nothing in my room." Syn kissed her some more, his sex stirring yet again. In a low purr, he murmured, "And you and I are going to fill it up, together."

Jo chuckled as they began moving as one again, so happy—and kind of honored—that she was the only female his body had ever released into.

"Filling up is something you're quite good at."

"But I better keep practicing," he said against her mouth.

◆   ◆   ◆

It was another hour before Syn could quit it with the sex. And even then, when they got in the shower, he couldn't resist pressing his female up against the warm marble wall and finding his way inside of her again.

But finally they were heading out of the guest room they'd been given. He had a limp, and at least four bullets still inside his body, but it was nothing that couldn't wait for Manny's attention—

As they came out the far end of the Hall of Statues, Jo lost her stride and widened her eyes as she focused on the painted ceiling high above the grand staircase. And the gold-leafed balustrade. And the many doors that went off in both directions.

"Dear Lord . . . this place is incredible," she whispered with awe. "It's a palace."

"Actually, it truly is a home first and foremost, no matter how fancy it is." Syn took her hand and led her down the grand staircase, heading for the laughter and chatter which were bubbling out of the formal dining room. "And the people in it are a family."

When they bottomed out on the mosaic depiction of that apple tree in full bloom, he gave her a moment to look around, and then brace herself. As he'd explained in the shower, the whole crew was in there, Wrath having given everyone the night off—so First Meal was in full swing and then some.

"They're going to love you," he said as he urged her forward.

"Well, some nice female's already lent me their clothes," she said as she nodded down at her clean jeans and sweatshirt.

"That was Beth. The Queen."

"Oh. Wow."

As soon as they entered the archway into the dining room, all the people around that huge table stopped talking. And then came the screech of chairs being pushed back, and high-pitched, excited "hi"s from the females, and too many people coming over all at once, everyone eager to welcome the new member of the family.

Literally.

At the head of the table, Wrath got to his feet, and as soon as he spoke, everyone shut the hell up. "My cousin has arrived."

Jo's eyes popped wide as she got a gander at the last purebred vampire on the planet in all his glory: The sunglasses, the ass-length hair, the black leather, and the tattoos on the insides of his massive forearms.

Plus the golden retriever.

And the baby in his arms.

Syn took Jo's hand and led her down the formal room, whispering in her ear about how to handle the meet-and-greet of the male who was her blooded relation.

"Do I call you Your Majesty?" she asked with respect.

"Nah." Wrath put out his hand. "Just my name. I don't stand on all that bullshit cult of position stuff."

Jo took his palm in her own and, just as Syn had coached her, bent down to kiss the massive black diamond that every King had always worn, from Wrath's sire, all the way back to the first ruler.

"I know you've already met my *shellan* when she gave you the clothes, but this is my son, L.W.," the King explained. "And this is George."

"He's beautiful."

"And the kid's not bad, either, right?"

Jo laughed. Then she said, "Thank you for welcoming me into your home."

Wrath's nostrils flared. And then he smiled that fierce smile of his.

Putting his huge hand on her shoulder, he said in his commanding voice. "You're family. Where else would you live?"

Jo ducked her eyes and seemed to have to blink away the tears. As Syn slipped an arm around her waist, so she knew he was there for her, she said, "You have no idea how long I've waited for this moment."

"Blood is thicker than water," the King said gently. "And your blood, your place, is here with us."

As Wrath nodded, like everything was settled and that was that, Syn folded Jo up against his chest. Over the top of his beloved, he inclined his head once to the King.

It was a vow. Freely given, and forevermore.

He would ever fight to protect the King and the people in this house—not because of what Xcor had sworn to sometime ago, or because fighting served a perverted inner need, but because he would always protect those who were his family.

And all of them were in this room.

Wrath lifted the sacred ring of the ruler, and nodded back, accepting the pledge. After which . . . it was time to eat.

As Syn took Jo over to the two seats that had been saved for them, he said, "Bacon and chocolate, right?"

"Oh, my God." Jo took his hand and squeezed it urgently. "Yes. Please. How did you know?"

CHAPTER SIXTY-SIX

As Syn and his female, Jo, made their way to their places at the meal, Wrath stepped to the side and found himself still grappling with his new reality. The war was over. Finally.

Holding his son in his arms, he imagined the faces of the people sitting around his table. He could tell who was seated where by the sounds of the voices, and also the scents. But it wasn't the same as being able to see.

Still, he would take what he had and be grateful.

Whispering a command to George, he let his dog lead him where he wanted to go, the pair of them making steady progress to the base of the grand staircase. The ascension was an easy one, and at the top, Wrath continued straight ahead, entering his study.

With a deep breath, he pictured from memory what was across the space.

The chair.

The ancient, carved throne, that his father had sat upon.

As Wrath crossed over toward it, he went back into his past and recalled being in that crawl space in the Old Country's palace, watching as the *lessers* streamed in and slaughtered his parents. So helpless he had been, a weak pretrans, hidden by his *mahmen* and his sire, protected by those he should have protected.

When George signaled he'd arrived at his destination, Wrath reached out into thin air, moving his hand around until he found the throne's high back. It seemed apt that the King's ring made contact with the old wood with a clonk.

Holding L.W. extra close, he gripped the carvings that had been made so long ago.

"It's over, Father," he said in a voice that cracked. "It's done. We won."

As a wave of emotion overtook him, he sat down and arranged his blooded son in his lap, holding his precious one close.

That was when he heard the meow.

Angling his head to the sound, he frowned. And then . . . "Analisse?"

The Scribe Virgin's presence registered as a weight in the room. He wasn't sure he could describe it better than that.

"Yes," she said in that voice of hers. "'Tis I."

To cover his emotion, he chuckled. "I asked you a question, did I. Such a no-no."

"Those nights are past, my old friend."

Wrath sensed her moving closer to the desk. "We won. But you know that, don't you."

"Yes."

"I wish my father were here to see this. My *mahmen*, too."

"They can. They are always with you."

Wrath had to clear his throat. And then he tried—and failed—to keep the pride out of his voice. "This is my son. Another thing you already know, right?"

"Yes." The affection in her voice was a surprise. "I know many things."

"So you're not completely gone, then. The cat, though? Really."

"I have been with your Queen since day one."

He had to laugh. "That makes me happy."

"You are a fine King. You have done your father proud."

Behind his wraparounds, he started blinking hard. "Don't say shit like that. You'll melt me."

"And as for your son, he looks like you."

"Does he?" He ran a fingertip over L.W.'s soft hair. "You know, his eyes have changed. They were blue. But now they're green. Beth doesn't want me to know. She's kept it a secret—but I overheard her talking to Doc Jane about it. I don't care. He's perfect the way he is."

"Yes, he is." There was a pause. "Here. See for yourself, my old friend."

All at once, his vision opened up from a pair of pinpoints, the apertures widening in perfect concert, providing him with a crystal clear vision of Little Wrath . . .

. . . that carved him in half.

Gasping, he fumbled his wraparounds off and beheld his blessed born son, from the face that was a carbon copy of Wrath's own, to the jet-black hair that was growing in thick and healthy, to the limbs and torso that, even in this still nascent stage, promised to be powerful and strong.

And then there were the eyes.

Clear . . . and icy green just like Wrath's own. And they stared back at him with a gravity that made no sense. How could the young know how important this moment was?

"He knows," the Scribe Virgin said. "He is a very old soul, that one."

Wrath looked up. And there she was, a glow of light in the form of a female, levitating above the Aubusson rug just on the other side of the desk.

"He will be a fine ruler," she said. "He will live long and succeed your legacy with one of his own. And yes, he will find love. In all this, you may put your faith."

Wrath stared down at his son. The tears in his eyes were doing his fucking nut in. He knew this wasn't going to last and he didn't want to waste one second of it on blurriness.

"*You have given me such a gift this night,*" he said in the Old Language.

"*You have tallied long and hard. You deserve it. Now be well, Wrath, son of Wrath, sire of Wrath.*"

Wrath looked up. "I still owe you a favor. Remember?"

Even though the Scribe Virgin was just a light source, he could swear she was smiling at him. "Oh, I have not forgotten. And in time, you will give me my due, I promise you that—now, though, here comes your *shellan*. I shall give you a moment with her, and then—"

"I know. Be well, Analisse."

"And you, old friend."

Just as the Scribe Virgin disappeared, Beth appeared in the study's open doorway. "Wrath, are you . . ."

She stopped talking as he looked up at her with eyes that properly focused. Then she put her fingertips to her mouth.

"Wrath?" she said urgently.

"You are so beautiful."

As she rushed over to him, he made note of her flowing dark hair and her lovely skin, her eyes and her body, her . . . everything. His eyes were starved for what fed into them, and when she got in range, he took her hand and pulled her into his lap. Then he looked down at George.

"And hello there as well, you good boy."

He stroked the golden's perfectly boxy head. Then he stared at his son and his *shellan*.

"How did this happen?" Beth choked out as she touched his brows.

"It's a gift from an old friend." He stroked her hair. Her face. "And it's not going to be for long."

"The Scribe Virgin was here?" she said with shock.

"She's always with us, as it turns out."

Wrath kissed his *shellan*. Kissed his son. Kissed his dog.

Then with one last look at the three of them, he closed his eyes. It seemed important for him to have control over the re-loss of his sight.

If he'd had to watch his family fade from him, he would have panicked. But by doing it himself, it was less traumatic.

"L.W.'s eyes are green now," Beth admitted with contrition. "They changed a while ago. I didn't want you to be upset."

Wrath smiled. "He's perfect. Just the way the Scribe Virgin made him."

"I love you," his *shellan* said.

Taking a deep breath, Wrath slowly opened his lids . . . and saw nothing now. But his family was still with him. He could feel the weight, the warmth—and the fur—of all of them.

With peace and love in his heart, Wrath said, "And your voice in the darkness is my reason for living."

CHAPTER SIXTY-SEVEN

Downtown, as a rare blood moon shone its eerie light upon the twinkling city, a figure in white appeared on the top of one of Caldwell's two span bridges. Later, people would debate whether it actually existed. Paranormal enthusiasts would say yes, and that it was a ghost or a wraith. Skeptics, on the other hand, would maintain that the pictures taken of the mysterious apparition were doctored.

Oh, and the Area 51 aficionados were convinced it was an alien.

As with so much in life, what folks thought they saw depended more on who they were than what may or may not have been before them.

The stone-cold truth, however, was that a demon did in fact materialize to that arch, and she did look over the city as if it were hers for the taking.

And as for what she wore? It wasn't a robe like her big brother had sported.

No, when Devina decided to pick that seminal spot for her declaration of dominion, she was wearing a wedding gown.

It seemed apt. And the shit was not vintage.

The ball-gown-style dress with the tight bodice and the peeka-boo panels at the cleavage and on the ribs was a brand-new, never-before-worn Pnina Tornai. Devina had chosen it from all of the available stock at the most exclusive boutique in town, putting the satin and sparkles on and three-way-mirror'ing it before she came down here for her big reveal. The dress was all her, elegant but flamboyant, expensive and exclusive. Just what she would walk down the aisle with some night.

Brian O'Neal was correct. She only needed the right partner.

And until someone of male extraction volunteered for that role—and really, what were the chances of that—she was marrying Caldwell.

This city would be her spouse and she was going to enjoy expressing her special brand of love all over its streets and—

At first, Devina couldn't comprehend what obstructed her view of the highest skyscraper in the financial district.

But there was something on the other bridge.

Standing with feet planted and body braced.

Devina narrowed her eyes. It was a male. Dressed in . . . were those hot pink zebra tights? And what was that shirt? Was that . . . *Barney?*

"Jesus Christ," she spat.

All at once, from behind those broad shoulders, a set of gossamer wings extended outward as blond and black hair spooled loose from some kind of tie.

No, it wasn't J. C.

Lassiter, the Fallen Angel.

As Devina narrowed her eyes and her temper rose, he smiled at her. And lifted one of his hands. With an elaborate show, he blew her a kiss, turned that palm around . . . and extended his middle finger at her.

And thus the next generation of conflict was born.

ACKNOWLEDGMENTS

With so many thanks to the readers of the Black Dagger Brotherhood books! This has been a long, marvelous, exciting journey, and I can't wait to see what happens next in this world we all love. I'd also like to thank Meg Ruley, Rebecca Scherer and everyone at JRA, and Lauren McKenna, Jennifer Bergstrom, Abby Zidle, and the entire family at Gallery Books and Simon & Schuster.

To Team Waud, I love you all. Truly. And as always, everything I do is with love to, and adoration for, both my family of origin and of adoption.

Oh, and thank you to Naamah, my Writer Dog II, who works as hard as I do on my books! And for Arch, who has stepped up in a major way lately!